Easing the Pa

Easing the Passing
The Trial of Doctor John Bodkin Adams

Patrick Devlin

faber and faber
LONDON · BOSTON

To Twenty-one Grandchildren
and 'Remoter Issue'

First published in 1985 by
The Bodley Head Ltd

This edition with a new Postscript first published in 1986 by
Faber and Faber Limited
3 Queen Square London WC1N 3AU

Printed in Great Britain by
Redwood Burn Ltd
Trowbridge, Wiltshire
All rights reserved

British Library Cataloguing in Publication Data

Devlin, Patrick Devlin, *Baron*
Easing the passing : the trial of Dr. John
Bodkin Adams.
1. Adams, John Bodkin—Trials, litigation,
etc. 2. Trials (Murder)—England—
London
I. Title
344.105'2523'0924   KD373.A3

ISBN 0-571-13993-0

CONTENTS

LIST OF PLATES

1. Dr John Bodkin Adams.
2. Superintendent Hannam.
3. Melford Stevenson, QC, (left) with his junior, Malcolm Morris, at the Eastbourne hearing.
4. December 1956. Superintendent Hannam supervises the exhumation of one of Dr Adams's patients.
5. 24 January, 1957. Dr Adams, concealed on the floor of a police car, leaves Eastbourne for Brixton prison. The public was fascinated by the case.
6. Geoffrey Lawrence, QC, Leading Counsel for the Defence.
7. The Attorney-General, Sir Reginald Manningham-Buller.
8. The presiding judge.
9. Dr Douthwaite.

DRAMATIS PERSONAE

ACCUSED: John Bodkin Adams MD
VICTIM: Mrs Edith Alice Morrell

COUNSEL FOR THE CROWN:
  Attorney-General: Sir Reginald Manningham-Buller QC, MP
  (later Viscount Dilhorne)
  Melford Stevenson QC
  Malcolm Morris
COUNSEL FOR THE DEFENCE:
  Geoffrey Lawrence QC
  Edward Clarke

LORD CHIEF JUSTICE: Rayner Goddard, Lord Goddard
LORD CHANCELLOR: Sir David Maxwell Fyfe, Viscount Kilmuir
DIRECTOR OF PUBLIC PROSECUTIONS: Sir Theobald Mathew
RECORDER OF LONDON: Sir Anthony Hawke
PRIME MINISTER: Harold Macmillan MP

MRS MORRELL'S SOLICITOR: Mr Sogno of Lawson, Lewis & Co
DR ADAMS'S SOLICITORS: Hempsons

POLICE TEAM:
  Detective-Superintendent Hannam
  Sergeant Hewitt
  Inspector Pugh of Eastbourne Constabulary

NURSES:
  Nurse Randall
  Nurse Stronach
  Sister Bartlett (Mrs Hughes)
  Sister Mason-Ellis

EXPERT WITNESSES FOR THE CROWN:
  Dr Arthur Henry Douthwaite MD, FRCP, MRCS
  Dr Michael G. C. Ashby MA, MB, MRCP, BS, FRSM, MABN
EXPERT WITNESS FOR THE DEFENCE: Dr Harman MD, FRCP, FRCS

CLERK OF THE COURT: Leslie Balfour Boyd
JUDGE'S CLERK: William Sorrell

PRINCIPAL DATES

1899

21 January Birth of John Bodkin Adams

1921 He qualifies as a medical practitioner

1922 He joins a large practice in Eastbourne

1930 He prospers and buys Kent Lodge in Trinity Trees, Eastbourne

1948

25 June Mrs Morrell, aged 79, has a paralytic stroke while visiting her son in Cheshire

5 July Mrs Morrell moved by ambulance to a nursing home in Eastbourne where she is attended by Dr Adams

9 July First prescription by Dr Adams of morphia

21 July First prescription of heroin

1949

30 March Mrs Morrell settled at Marden Ash, Eastbourne

28 April Mr Sogno, solicitor, summoned by Dr Adams to make a new will for Mrs Morrell

9 June New will under which Dr Adams receives a canteen of silver (probate value £276)

21 June Nurses' notebooks begin

1950

8 March Dr Adams tells Mr Sogno that Mrs Morrell wishes to make a new will, redeeming her promise to leave him her Rolls-Royce

24 August Mrs Morrell makes a new will, adding to the bequest to Dr Adams the Rolls-Royce and an Elizabethan court cupboard, but these additions to take effect only if she is predeceased by her son

12 September Dr Adams goes on holiday: Mrs Morrell very angry

15 September Codicil cutting Dr Adams out of the will

16 September Dr Adams returns to attend Mrs Morrell

18 September Dr Adams resumes his holiday

24 September Dr Adams attending Mrs Morrell again

23 October Codicil torn up

1 November 'Murder period': beginning of lethal doses alleged

13 November Death of Mrs Morrell

1956

14 March Death of Mr Hullett, leaving an estate of £94,644 with a legacy of £500 to Dr Adams

14 July Mrs Hullett makes her will. Out of an estate of £137,302 she leaves her Rolls-Royce to Dr Adams

17 July Mrs Hullett draws a cheque for £1,000 in favour of Dr Adams

18 July Dr Adams presents the cheque and asks for it to be specially cleared

19 July	Mrs Hullett takes a massive dose of barbiturate and falls into a coma
23 July	Death of Mrs Hullett
	Inquest formally opened and adjourned
21 August	Inquest resumed: verdict of suicide
1 October	Dr Adams in conversation with Supt Hannam talks of the legacies he expected from Mr Hullett and Mrs Morrell
24 November	Police search of Kent Lodge for dangerous drugs. Dr Adams says that Mrs Morrell had been given all the drugs he prescribed for her
26 November	Dr Adams arrested on minor charges, viz. failure to keep a register under the Dangerous Drugs Act, false statements under the Cremation Act, forgery of NHS documents. He appears before the Eastbourne magistrates and is granted bail There is a conversation at the police station at which he refers to 'easing the passing' of Mrs Morrell who, he says, was dying anyway
27 November	Dr Adams committed for trial at Lewes Assizes on the minor charges and is granted bail
19 December	Dr Adams is charged with the murder of Mrs Morrell and remanded in custody
1957	
14 January	Commencement of committal proceedings at Eastbourne on the charge of the murder of Mrs Morrell. The Crown alleges that the accused murdered also Mr and Mrs Hullett
23 January	Dr Adams committed for trial at the Old Bailey for murder of Mrs Morrell
18 March	Trial at the Old Bailey begins
9 April	Dr Adams acquitted
15 April	In the House of Commons Mr Wigg asks the Attorney-General, Sir Reginald Manningham-Buller, to institute an inquiry into the conduct of the prosecution. He refuses
1 May	Mr Wigg raises the matter on the adjournment of the House and the Attorney-General replies
30 June	Dr Adams resigns from the National Health Service
26 July	Dr Adams pleads guilty at Lewes Assizes on all the minor charges and is fined £2,400
22 November	Dr Adams is struck off the medical register and remains off it for four years
1983	
5 July	Death of Dr Adams, leaving an estate of £402,970

THE LAST PRESCRIPTIONS

Extracted from Exhibit 4A

Nos.				
83	8 Nov.	Heroin	40 tablets:	6½grs.
84		A linctus with heroin		
85		Morphia	40 tablets	10grs.
86	9 Nov.	Heroin	25 tablets	6¼grs. *Repeat twice as required*
87		Morphia	25 tablets	12½grs. *Repeat twice as required*
88	10 Nov.	Heroin	25 tablets	6¼grs. *First repeat of 86*
89	11 Nov.	Hyperduric morphia		6grs.
90		Morphia	25 tablets	12½grs. *First repeat of 87*
91		Heroin	25 tablets	6¼grs. *Second repeat of 86*
92	12 Nov.	Paraldehyde	4 oz.	
93		Heroin	75 tablets	12½grs.

NOTE: These figures show that the quantity of opiates, i.e. heroin and morphia, prescribed during this period amount to 78¾grs. In his opening speech the Attorney-General gave this quantity as 79½grs., which quantity, the Crown inferred, had been injected into Mrs Morrell. In the course of the trial the Crown conceded that some deduction had to be made for an unknown quantity left over after the death of Mrs Morrell.

1

The Case for the Crown

On the morning of 18 March 1957 one John Bodkin Adams, a doctor from Eastbourne, was brought from Brixton prison to the Old Bailey, there to be arraigned on a charge of murder and to plead thereto.

Clerk of the Court: John Bodkin Adams, is that your name?
Prisoner: Yes, sir.
Clerk of the Court: You are charged that on the 13th day of November 1950 you murdered Edith Alice Morrell. Are you guilty or not guilty?
Prisoner: I am not guilty, my lord.
Clerk of the Court: Members of the jury, the Prisoner at the Bar, John Bodkin Adams, is charged with the murder of Edith Alice Morrell who died on 13th November 1950. To this indictment he has pleaded not guilty and it is your charge to say, having heard the evidence, whether he be guilty or not.
Attorney-General: May it please your lordship. Members of the jury, as you have heard, the accused is charged with the murder of Mrs Edith Alice Morrell who died on 13th November 1950. To that charge he has pleaded not guilty and it is now my duty to outline to you the case for the prosecution.

The jury, having now heard for the third time in less than three minutes that John Bodkin Adams was charged with the murder of Edith Alice Morrell, has thus been made acquainted with the most important fact of forensic life, which is that everything of any significance is said at least three times over. For this is a trial by word of mouth. It is true that every word of the evidence is taken down in shorthand and—exceptionally since this is going to be a long and difficult case—a daily transcript will be supplied, but only to judge and counsel. There will also be exhibits: most of

1

the exhibits will be documents and all the important ones will be put before the members of the jury, one copy for every two, not to be taken home and studied but so that they can follow when a passage is put to a witness. For the rest they must rely upon their memories aided by much repetition.

The Attorney-General continued. He was not an orator, but his manner was earnest and either, as some might say, impressive or, as others, ponderous.

> Before I say anything more, I want to say this. I expect that many of you, if not all of you, have read something about this case in the press. It will be surprising if you have not. You may have heard some rumours about it. Indeed, you may have heard a great deal about Dr Adams. It is your duty, members of the jury, to hearken to the evidence and to give a true verdict according to the evidence, and that means that you must put out of your minds anything you have heard or read about Dr Adams and about this case.

The warning was not superfluous. For eight months past the newspapers had been full of the accused and his supposed victims. Indeed, the public must now have been surprised at the sparseness of the indictment. Only one murder, and that—for it was now 18 March 1957—committed over six years before. What the audience was now to hear was a severely pruned version of what they had already read.

It was, the Attorney said, a very unusual case, a charge of murder against a doctor.

> The submission of the Crown is that Dr Adams by the administration of drugs to Mrs Morrell, drugs given by him and given upon his instructions, killed her, and our submission is that those drugs were given to her with the intention of killing her.

'A word about Dr Adams,' the Attorney went on. He was a Doctor of Medicine and a Bachelor of Surgery. For many years he had held a hospital appointment as an anaesthetist, which meant that he would know a lot about dangerous drugs.

Then there came a word about Mrs Morrell. She was the wealthy widow of a Liverpool businessman. On 25 June 1948 when she must have been seventy-nine years of age or very near to it, she had a stroke which left her paralysed on the left side. She was staying with her son in Cheshire and was taken to the Neston Cottage Hospital. On 5 July she was driven by ambulance to a nursing home in Eastbourne. There she became one of Dr Adams's patients. On 9 July there was the first prescription of morphia and on 21 July the first of heroin. She moved from one place to another in Eastbourne until on 30 March 1949 she settled at Marden Ash, a house in Beachy Head Road. There she lived a bedridden life attended by day and night nurses until she died.

Heroin and morphia are derivatives of opium, the Attorney said, very powerful drugs, heroin the stronger. During the ten-and-a-half months of 1950, that is, until she died on 13 November, Dr Adams prescribed for her 165grs. morphia and 139½ heroin. Very large quantities, the Attorney-General said. Some time later he told us that a maximum daily dose of morphia should be ½gr. and of heroin ¼gr. This enabled us to calculate roughly that the doctor had kept near to the maximum in morphia but exceeded it in heroin by about 75 per cent. But, as the Attorney told us, the tolerance of human beings to morphia and heroin varies considerably and can be acquired.

They are very valuable drugs to administer to a patient who is suffering from very severe and prolonged pain. And they are also dangerous drugs, one reason being that their administration over a short period induces a craving for them. The drugs themselves produce a feeling of wellbeing after they are given, also a craving to continue taking the drugs and a feeling of dependence upon the person who is kind enough to go on providing them.

Members of the jury, why did Dr Adams prescribe large quantities of morphia and heroin for this old lady suffering from the effects of a stroke but who was not suffering pain? Why did he do it? . . .

Why were they prescribed? Perhaps you may think that the answer lies in the changes made by Mrs Morrell in her will after she had been taking these drugs. I will call Mr Sogno, Mrs Morrell's solicitor, and he will tell you that on 28 April 1949 the accused telephoned to him and said that Mrs Morrell was extremely anxious about the contents of her will and wanted to see Mr Sogno urgently that day. Mr Sogno went to see her and she made another will. In that will she bequeathed to Dr Adams an oak chest containing silver.

A photograph of the chest was exhibited at the trial. It is in fact a very large canteen with an equipment of silver for the dining room.

Mr Sogno did not appear on the scene again for nearly a year. During that time Mrs Morrell continued to live uder the same regime of drugs; evidently there was nothing in particular for the prosecution to draw attention to.

Then on 8 March 1950 Dr Adams called on Mr Sogno without an appointment and a conversation took place, members of the jury, which you may perhaps think was a very curious one. He told Mr Sogno that Mrs Morrell had promised to give him her Rolls-Royce in her will, that she now remembered that she had forgotten this and that she desired to give him also the contents of a case which was in a locked box at the bank, a case which Dr Adams said contained jewellery. Dr Adams went on to say that, although Mrs Morrell was very ill, her mind was perfectly clear and she was in a fit condition to execute a codicil. Mr Sogno said that, as the proposed gifts were of considerable value, might they not stand over until Mrs Morrell's son came at the weekend. But Dr Adams then suggested that Mr Sogno should prepare the codicil and that that codicil should be executed and later destroyed if it did not meet with Mr Morrell's approval. Is not that rather an astonishing suggestion to come from a doctor? It shows, does it not, a certain keenness to have that done?

On 19 July 1950 Mrs Morrell executed a codicil to her will leaving to Dr Adams, if her son died before her, her house and all her personal chattels. On 5 August 1950 she executed a fresh will leaving to him the oak chest containing the silver and, if her son predeceased her, the Rolls-Royce and an Elizabethan cupboard . . .

In September 1950 you will hear that Dr Adams went on a holiday away from Eastbourne and during that time Dr Harris, his partner, visited Mrs Morrell. On 12 September you will hear that a codicil was executed, Dr Adams being away, by Mrs Morrell revoking the gifts to the accused and you may ask what happened about that. You may perhaps conclude that that was executed in consequence of Mrs Morrell's annoyance at being left at that time by Dr Adams.

The Attorney-General then produced various graphs construc- ted by Dr Ashby, the second of his expert witnesses, to show the increasing quantities of heroin and morphia given to Mrs Morrell in 1950 in the last ten-and-a-half months ending with her death on 13 November. In the last six days there was prescribed for her

40½grs. morphia and 39 heroin, a quantity so large as to make any acquired tolerance negligible. Why? Why were those amounts prescribed? She was not in acute pain. The nurses will say that for a few days before her death she was comatose or semi-conscious. Drs Douthwaite and Ashby will say that there was no medical justification for these doses, which she could not survive.

What was his object? Why did he prescribe these large quantities for which there was no medical justification? The submission of the Crown is, members of the jury, that he did so because he had decided that the time had come for Mrs Morrell to die. He knew, did he not, a lot about her will. He knew she had made a will not carrying out her promise to leave him the Rolls-Royce. You will hear he knew about the bequest to him in the will of August of the oak chest and cupboard. Whether he knew of the execution of the codicil while he was on holiday and what happened to it you may perhaps discover in the course of this trial. If he did, he may have felt it best Mrs Morrell should not have any further opportunity of altering her will to his disadvantage.

'I will now tell you,' the Attorney went on, 'about some other evidence.' The night nurse had once in the middle of the night found Mrs Morrell in a state of collapse. She told Dr Adams that she did not think that heroin suited the patient. The doctor stopped the heroin for a while and 'the collapsed condition ceased'. But then he started it up again. There was another occasion, a fortnight before her death, when after an injection Mrs Morrell could not be roused. These injections, like several others, were not made up by the nurses from the prescriptions but taken by the doctor from his own bag and he did not tell the nurse what they were, which was very unusual. A few days before her death, when she was unconscious and so not suffering, she had jerky spasms 'so severe that they nearly jerked Mrs Morrell out of bed'. Dr Douthwaite would say that this was the effect on the spinal cord of excessive doses of heroin. On the last night, when she was in this condition, Dr Adams filled three-quarters full an abnormally large syringe, 5cc instead of the usual 1 or 2, and told Nurse Randall

that she must inject it into this unconscious woman. She did so. The accused was in the dining-room. She came back to him and she gave him the empty syringe. He refilled it with a similar quantity—an unusually large amount on each occasion—and

5

he told her to give it to Mrs Morrell later if the patient, the unconscious patient, did not become quieter. Well, Mrs Morrell's spasms quietened down for about an hour and then gradually they became more severe. Nurse Randall did not like giving another large injection so soon and she telephoned to Dr Adams, but he was out. At 1.00 am, Dr Adams having given her those instructions—and, of course, it was her duty to obey them—she gave the second injection. Mrs Morrell gradually became quiet and about 2.00 am, she died.

Members of the jury, what possible medical reason can there be for these two injections into a patient who was in a coma and already suffering from excessive morphia and heroin causing convulsions? The prosecution cannot tell you what these injections were. They were given to Mrs Morrell in that condition. She may indeed have been a dying woman when they were given to her. But, if she was, we submit that it was murder by Dr Adams giving lethal prescriptions in the period 8th to 12th November. If on the other hand these two injections did accelerate her death, then that was murder by Dr Adams. The prosecution will submit that the only possible conclusion to which one can come is that he killed her deliberately and intentionally.

Members of the jury, the case for the prosecution does not stop there.

The first extra that fortified 'the only possible conclusion' was the form required for Mrs Morrell's cremation. On it the doctor, in answer to the question whether he had any pecuniary interest in the death, had written 'Not as far as I am aware'. But for that false answer, the Attorney said, there might have been a post-mortem and the amount of the drugs in the body might have been determined. That was on 13 November 1950.

'Now I come to 1 October 1956,' the Attorney said: Detective-Superintendent Hannam of New Scotland Yard was then making inquiries at Eastbourne and he met the accused casually. The passage of seven years from the murder to the police inquiry was not otherwise alluded to by the Attorney. If a juror had wanted to know how it came about that at the end of that time a detective was casually meeting the doctor in the course of his inquiries, he would have had to consult the rumour-mongers whom he had been told to ignore.

The Superintendent would say that in the course of general conversation there was a reference to the chest of silver; the doctor said that he knew that Mrs Morrell was going to leave it to him and also the Rolls-Royce. The Superintendent referred to the doctor's answer on the cremation form. It was not done wickedly, the doctor said, 'We always want cremations to go off smoothly.'

The next conversation was on 24 November 1956 when the Superintendent showed the doctor a list of the dangerous drugs which he had prescribed for Mrs Morrell in 1950. She had them all, the doctor said, 'poor soul, she was in terrible agony'.

'Terrible agony!' the Attorney commented. 'And the nurses say that she was in a coma for days before her death.'

The Attorney now switched to what the experts would say. Dr Douthwaite that 'if the drugs prescribed in November were used on the patient, the result would have been death; that a doctor with reasonable and ordinary experience in medicine would know that; that one with a diploma in anaesthetics would have special knowledge of drugs of that sort'. Dr Ashby that 'Mrs Morrell could not possibly have survived the whole of the drugs prescribed in the last five days or any major portion of them; that no doctor could have any doubt as to what the administration of morphia and heroin on that scale would mean'.

The Attorney wound up with the final conversations with the police. On 26 November when Hannam said that he was inquiring into the death of Mrs Morrell, the doctor said:

Easing the passing of a dying person is not all that wicked. She wanted to die. That cannot be murder. It is impossible to accuse a doctor.

That must refer, must it not, to the two injections which he had given Nurse Randall to give her the night she died. The prosecution submitted that they were given not to ease her passing but to accelerate her death.

On 19 December he was arrested at his house by Superintendent Hannam, charged with murder and cautioned.

Dr: Murder. Murder. Can you prove it was murder?
Supt: You are now charged with murdering her.
Dr: I did not think you could prove murder. She was dying in any event.

Is that what you would expect an innocent man to say, the Attorney asked, when he is charged with murder, or is it what a man might say if he had committed a murder but thought he had done it so cleverly that his guilt could not be proved? As they left the house Dr Adams grasped his receptionist's hand and said to her, 'I will see you in Heaven.'

Members of the jury, I submit to you that the evidence which I and my learned friends will call before you proves, and proves conclusively, that this old lady was murdered by Dr Adams.

A quarter of a century has now passed since the trial of Dr Adams, long enough to allow publication without indecorum and not too long to destroy recollection. What I am writing is not primarily a descriptive account but an analytical narrative of the progress of the trial. For the most part it was what was passing through my mind. It is the sort of talk that would have gone on in the evening if I had been explaining to an interested amateur the significance of what had happened during the day. There was much to explain. Most trials are no more than the acting out of the prosecution's opening speech diversified by the struggle of the defence to infect the mass of material with the reasonable doubt. This trial was quite outside the usual pattern and fascinating in its twists and turns.

Yet the whole story of Dr Adams was not told at the trial. The story emerges from his long years in practice at Eastbourne during which he acquired a curious reputation as a legacy hunter. It slips through the death of Mrs Morrell in 1950 which passed unnoticed at the time. It bursts into the news in August 1956 after an inquest has been held on the body of another wealthy patient, Mrs Hullett. After that the rumours spread to cover many other names, including that of Mrs Hullett's husband who had died six months before her.

So it came as no surprise to the public to hear in December 1956 that Dr Adams had been arrested and charged with murder. What was a surprise was that he was charged with the murder, not of Mrs Hullett, but of Mrs Morrell who had died so long before. Then, when the preliminary proceedings in the Morrell case were begun before the Eastbourne magistrates in January 1957, the public learnt that the Crown would be calling evidence to show that Dr Adams, although not formally charged with the murder of either Mrs or Mr Hullett, had in fact murdered both of them. But when the trial began at the Old Bailey nothing at all was said about the Hulletts. The name was not mentioned until the last day after Dr Adams had been acquitted. Many people believed that, if the doctor had been tried for the murder of Mrs Hullett instead of Mrs Morrell, he would have been convicted.

I shall try to explain how all this came about before I continue with the narrative of the trial.

2

Eastbourne

Eastbourne is well known as a very pleasant resort on the Sussex coast which has among its inhabitants an unusually high proportion of the elderly and affluent who can afford to live where they choose rather than where a business or a profession has fixed them. For the same reason, although there are many doctors in Eastbourne who, I am sure, have higher aims, the town has a special appeal for those whose medical ambitions are satisfied by a comfortable private practice such as was still to be enjoyed in the 1950s.

Dr Adams came to the town in 1922. He was born on 21 January 1899 in Randalstown, County Antrim, where his father was in business as a jeweller and was also a JP. It was a strict Protestant household. The son qualified as a medical practitioner in 1921. In the following year he answered an advertisement in an evangelical paper for 'a Christian young doctor-assistant with a view to partnership' in a large Eastbourne practice and was given the place. In 1926 he obtained his doctorate at Queen's University, Belfast and in 1941 his diploma in anaesthetics.

He prospered. In 1930 he bought a large villa called Kent Lodge in Trinity Trees which runs behind the Grand Parade and is convenient for the Esperance Nursing Home. By 1957 he was the senior of the four partners in a lucrative practice. In the 'antecedents' of the accused, which the police prepare for every trial, he was described as 'fairly well-to-do' with investments bringing in a gross income of about £2,000 and £25,623 18s. 1d. on deposit at the bank. He had a passion for motor cars; at the time of his arrest he had four in his garage. His hobbies were shooting and photography. He never married. He was a teetotaller.

He was not, I believe, a skilful physician. But the elderly and affluent are not especially prone to difficult diseases and can always afford a consultant. What they appreciate is sympathy, care and attention and these they got from Dr Adams in abundance. So, it is fair to say, did the National Health patients of whom Dr Adams had his quota. Indeed, Dr Adams at the time of trial and to the end retained the loyalty and devotion of many of his patients of all sorts.

But there were two things about his style that aroused comment, at first perhaps only among doctors and nurses but for some time before 1957 in wider circles. The first was his lavish use of what are called the drugs of addiction, heroin and morphia. The second was his interest in his patients' wills. With many of them he was on friendly, or at least sociable, terms; as a bachelor he had no family life. It is not unnatural that wealthy patients should think of a remembrance in their wills to a doctor who was not only a friend but who had looked after them with special care. Dr Adams did not leave such a thought unnourished. He was not content, metaphorically speaking, to have a box at the surgery into which legacies could be dropped; he carried round the plate. As an alternative to cash the deceased's Rolls-Royce was welcome.

His interest in wills first attracted attention with a court case in 1935. An elderly lady, who had been his patient for six years, made him her executor and left him £3,000. The family unsuccessfully contested the will. The flow of bequests was not stemmed. The police estimated that they were worth £3,000 a year in the decade preceding the trial. This seems to be rather high; it must have included gifts in kind as well as in cash. A detailed list of legacies between 1944 and 1955 shows fourteen bequests totalling £21,600, but this excludes, for example, Mrs Morrell's elderly Rolls-Royce (a 1929 model) and the chest of silver. There was an estate in 1954 of £7,000 out of which Adams got £5,200. But generally the legacies were in the hundreds of pounds and not sizeable proportions of the estate; the testators were usually around eighty when they died.

These two manifestations of his professional life as the dispenser of drugs and the persuasive legatee were not, it was said, disconnected activities. A supplier of heroin can acquire a dominating influence over those dependent on it. A sensible man would have thought of this. But an even more sensible man would have thought first of the impropriety and folly of a doctor's pestering his patients for a legacy. Dr Adams was not a sensible man; he was on the contrary a stupid, obstinate and self-righteous man. He was also an indiscreet and incessant talker. If he talked to his acquaintance as freely as he was later to talk to the police, he may well have extolled the advantages of the legacy (on which the duty was payable out of the estate) over the heavily taxed professional fee. There is no evidence, however, that he offered to take a reduced fee in consideration of a legacy. He seems to have thought of it more as a golden handshake from beyond the grave. A handshake is all very well on a retirement from the business world; it is not the same thing when it is payable on death to the man whose business it is to keep death at bay. Even the unsuspicious might wonder whether Dr Adams ever felt that the time had come to correct the tardiness of nature.

With so much combustible material piled up it seems in retrospect to have been inevitable that sooner or later it would go up in flames. But it was not the case of Mrs Morrell from which the spark flew. Her death in 1950 passed unnoticed. The kindling came in July 1956 with the death of a patient, Mrs Hullett. It was this death which started the police investigation into Adams's past. They completed a file for the Director of Public Prosecutions of a dozen or more deaths among the doctor's patients. The affair was considered to be of sufficient importance or difficulty for the Director to refer it to the Attorney-General at an early stage. To the surprise of some of his advisers the case selected by the Attorney for prosecution was not the Hullett case, but the six-year-old Morrell case. Mrs Hullett was kept in reserve and made the subject of a second indictment.

Notwithstanding the acquittal of Dr Adams in the Morrell case, there were many who believed him to be a murderer who had escaped the gallows and who were fortified by the thought that on the strongest case against him he had never been tried. Moreover, the Hullett case played an unusual part in the early stages of the Morrell prosecution. So I must tell the story.

Mrs Hullett became Dr Adams's patient after the death in 1950 of her first husband, a Mr Tomlinson. She was then in her forties and he had been the headmaster of a school in Eastbourne. She was terribly distressed by her husband's death, Dr Adams said, in poor health physically and in a nervous condition, talking of suicide. Dr Adams says that he got her much better and found new friends for her. One of these was Mr Hullett, a wealthy resident in Eastbourne then in his sixties, recently widowed, whom Dr Adams used to visit every Sunday morning. The acquaintance ripened into a marriage which was a great success. Mr Hullett suffered from what Dr Adams called 'various functional nervous illnesses' and the new Mrs Hullett still suffered from time to time from a nervous rash. Dr Adams looked after them both and continued to visit every Sunday morning.

In November 1955 Mr Hullett went into hospital for a serious internal operation. He was brought home by ambulance at Christmas and nursed there under the supervision of Dr Adams. He became well enough to move about. On 13 March he went out for a drive with Mrs Hullett and the nurse and they all had a drink at the Pilot Inn. After dinner at home, which they had down-stairs, he had what the nurse called one of his 'breathless attacks', which he had from time to time after exertion. The nurse sent for Dr Adams who arrived about 8.30 pm. Mr Hullett was then on a chair in the lounge, 'he had had a bad headache and I wasn't happy about him', Dr Adams said. They seemed to have talked until about 9.00 pm when Mr Hullett wanted to go to bed. The doctor helped him to walk slowly upstairs. When the night nurse came on duty she found him 'rather flopped in his chair', but she heard him tell Dr Adams that he felt all right. The doctor left to get an injection. He returned at 10.30 when Mr Hullett was in bed and gave him an injection of hyperduric morphia. Five minutes later he was asleep and his breathing became very heavy and stertorous. He woke up at 6.00 am, asked the time, said that there was nothing he wanted and went straight off to sleep again. Half an hour later he died in his sleep. Dr Adams was, of course, sent for and gave the cause of death as cerebral haemorrhage accompanied by coronary thrombosis.

Mr Hullett left £94,644. Subject to a number of small legacies, including one of £500 to Dr Adams, the whole went to his widow. In accordance with his policy of smoothing cremations, the doctor did not mention the £500 in the cremation form.

No one supposed that Dr Adams was to blame for Mr Hullett's death. He continued to attend Mrs Hullett, who was known to have implicit faith in him. She was in a very nervous and depressed state and talked of taking her life. She told Dr Adams that she had nothing left to live for and that she had gone up to Beachy Head. He wanted her, he said, to see a psychiatrist, but she refused. Letters found after her death show that in April she was seriously contemplating suicide, but she must have thought better of it. Ever since her husband's death Dr Adams had been giving her sodium barbiturate because she said that she could not sleep. His practice was to call every morning about 10.00 am and give her two tablets of $7\frac{1}{2}$grs. each—a normal dose, the experts said—later reduced to 6 and then to 5grs. He continued to visit regularly.

In the evening of 19 July Mrs Hullett went to bed early complaining of a headache. About 10.00 pm she took a massive dose of barbiturate; the post-mortem showed that she had 115grs. circulating in her body. She fell into a coma, never came out of it and died on 23 July.

The timing was perhaps impulsive. An old friend had just arrived on a visit and they had plans for the next day; as she went to bed she spoke to the parlourmaid about breakfast the next morning. But her depression had not gone and she had continued to tell Dr Adams that she could not go on without Jack, her husband. There were found with the April letters two more of the same sort dated 2 and 4 July and after writing them she had completed her preparations. Her will was drawn up on 12 July and she went to the bank to execute it on the 14th. She had asked Dr Adams to be an executor, but he declined. She left her estate (net value £137,302) to her family, apart from half a dozen specific bequests to friends. One of these was £4,000 to Mr Handscomb who had agreed to be an executor; another was her Rolls-Royce to Dr Adams. So the doctor knew that a will was being made, but not, Mr Handscomb said, that he was a legatee.

She had dealt also with one other piece of unfinished business. Her husband had promised to buy Dr Adams a car. There seems to have been no doubt about that. Both Mrs Hullett and Mr Handscomb knew of it. But it was not in the will. Mrs Hullett had resolved to compound the promise for £1,000. On 17 July she drew a cheque in the doctor's favour for this sum.

She must have given it to him—he was seeing her every day—on the 17th or the 18th because at lunch time on the 18th he took it to his bank. There, after signing the paying-in slip which the cashier made out, he asked when it would be cleared. The cashier said that it would be presented on the 20th and the doctor asked if it could be cleared sooner. The cashier said that it could be specially presented and the doctor requested that this should be done. Asked if he wanted to be specially advised when it was cleared, he said that he did not. The cheque was cleared on 19 July. In the ordinary way it would have been cleared on the 21st; and, of course, if after taking the fatal dose Mrs Hullett had not lived until the 21st, it would not have been cleared at all.

It was not unusual for Mrs Hullett to sleep late. On the morning of 20 July the maid found her asleep when she brought in her orange juice at 8.00 am and still asleep when she took up her breakfast tray at 9.00 am. It seemed to the maid to be a normal sleep. Dr Adams called as usual. He opened the door of her bedroom and listened to her breathing. It was normal and he did not go to the bed, saying that he would let her sleep. At 12.15 the maid went to the bedroom and drew the curtains, but Mrs Hullett slept on. Lunch was held back. At 3.00 pm the maid rang up Dr Adams's receptionist and said that she was worried. Dr Adams got the message while he was at a meeting at Lewes. He told the receptionist to send Dr Harris at once and said that he would go as soon as he got back.

Dr Harris got to the house about 3.30. He found Mrs Hullett comatose. Hearing of the headache and of some giddiness, he diagnosed a cerebral vascular accident such as haemorrhage. He was told that Dr Adams had been giving her sleeping pills every night. He looked for an empty bottle but did not find one. He gave an injection of coramine and left a message for Dr Adams.

Adams arrived about an hour later and called for Harris to come. They discussed the diagnosis. Harris asked about an overdose of drugs and Adams said that it was not possible. He agreed with Harris's diagnosis. He arranged for a night nurse and decided himself to spend the night in the house.

At the inquest Adams said of this conversation that barbiturate poisoning did not enter his mind: 'I thought I had the tablets tightly cleared up.' Suicide, he said, he did not consider at all.

Harris thought that the patient ought to be moved to hospital. But Adams said that she had an intense dislike of nursing homes and hospitals and that he had promised her that he would never allow it. Harris felt that she was Adams's patient and that 'one had to feel that he was doing the right thing'.

Harris advised taking a second opinion, but Adams thought that this was unnecessary. Adams did, however, on the next morning, which was Saturday, 21 July, ring up Dr Shera, a consultant pathologist, and ask him to make various tests and take samples for analysis. Shera asked if the patient was 'on barbiturates'. Adams said that she was and signed a request for an analysis of the urine for 'an excess of barbiturates'. But before the report of the analysis was ready the patient was dead.

Meanwhile on the Saturday afternoon Adams decided—'in case', he was to say at the inquest, 'there was any question of barbiturate'—to get some megimide, a preparation he had heard of as the latest form of antidote for barbiturate. He went round to the hospital where they opened a new box for him. The instructions with it were to give 3 to 5cc every five minutes until recovery; the average dose would be between 100 and 200cc. Dr Adams did not read the instructions. Instead he asked the house surgeon what the usual dose was. The surgeon told him—so Dr Adams was to tell the coroner who was not favourably impressed—to give 10cc and not to repeat if it did no good. This was what he did.

Thereafter he spent each night in the house, getting up in the middle of the night to give Mrs Hullett various injections. She died on Monday at 7.23 am.

Harris said that he had told Adams that, if the patient died, there would have to be a post-mortem. Adams thought of having a private post-mortem which apparently sometimes happens at the instance of the relatives when the medical attendant is not sure of the cause of death. Early on the Sunday morning he had rung up the coroner to inquire about this. The coroner was naturally surprised to hear that the patient had not yet died. He told Adams curtly that after the death the ordinary notification should be given. It certainly was an unusual conversation and could be taken as an indication that Dr Adams wanted to hush things up.

On the Monday morning, 23 July, Adams drafted a letter for himself and Harris to sign. It was not in the formal language of a report but in the discursive style of who said what to whom, which Adams favoured, beginning with the deceased's marriage 'to an adoring and rich husband'. He wrote that he had strictly doled out to her sodium barbiturate: 'she could not possibly have secreted any of this'. He concluded:

> In my opinion and Dr Harris's, death was due to a cerebral lesion, probably involving the Pons with secondary complications in the lungs. Because of Pathologist's findings being inconclusive, and cremation requested, we are reporting the facts fully to you

to which Dr Harris added in his own writing,

> as we do not feel in a position to issue a death certificate.

Adams's handling of the situation was at best inept.

On 23 July the coroner, having contacted the Chief Constable, formally opened an inquest. A post-mortem was ordered and the inquest adjourned to await the result. A statement to this effect was on the same day issued by the Chief Constable and com-

municated to the local press. On the next day the newspapermen
descended upon Eastbourne and the headlines began.

The inquest was resumed on 21 August. The coroner in his
examination of Dr Adams probed a number of criticisms. 50grs.
sodium barbiturate taken all at once could be a fatal dose; this was
3½ days' supply of what was being prescribed. Knowing of Mrs
Hullett's suicidal tendencies, he asked, what precautions did Dr
Adams take? Adams replied that he personally doled them out at
two tablets a day. But he agreed that Mr Hullett had barbiturates
and that after his death no steps had been taken to retrieve any
that might have been left over. He agreed also that when he was
on holiday in June, he gave Mrs Hullett in advance 36 tablets to
cover the period. When he got the call on 20 July and sent his
partner, barbiturate poisoning never entered his mind.

Why was there no day nurse, he was asked, in a case in which
he thought it necessary himself, as well as a night nurse, to spend
the night in the house. Because during the day there would be
people about, he answered; besides the staff, there was a guest
staying who had been a qualified maternity nurse. Dr Shera, he
was reminded, was a pathologist and not a physician: why in a
case in which the best advice could be afforded did he not call in a
consulting physician? The answer was because he did not think it
necessary.

Fourteen other witnesses were called, the last of them being
Detective-Superintendent Hannam.

> *Coroner:* The Chief Constable has invoked the help of Scotland
> Yard and I understand that you are in charge. Do you wish me
> to adjourn this inquest?
> *Supt:* I have no application to make to you.

In his summing up the coroner offered the jury a choice of four
verdicts: an accidental overdose, suicide with or without the
qualification of a disturbed mind, and an open verdict. As to the
fourth, he said that there was no evidence that anybody gave her
the dose, but that if the jury did not think that she took the tablets
herself, they should return an open verdict. As to the first, he said
nothing to encourage it, leaving the jury in effect to choose
between the second and the third. If they thought that she had
made up her mind to take her life, they should return the second;
if they thought the letters insufficient evidence of that, they
should return the third. He discoursed on negligence but without
telling the jury how, if they found that there was negligence, they

were to express their finding, whether in the verdict or otherwise. He told them firmly that they were concerned only with criminal negligence which was 'of so gross a nature that it falls just short of murder . . . a reckless disregard for human life and public safety'. Lack of medical skill did not fall into that category. They might think it extraordinary that the doctor, knowing the past history of the patient, did not at once suspect barbiturate poisoning, but an error of judgement or careless treatment was not criminal negligence.

The jury's verdict was that the deceased committed suicide and the court found that she died after swallowing barbiturate tablets 'of her own free will'.

The inquest had attracted the crime reporters of the whole national press and they had gorged themselves not only on the evidence but also on the rumours with which the town was buzzing. All of them, save one, were swiftly convinced that Dr Adams had despatched countless of his elderly patients so as to lay hands on the money he had persuaded them to leave him. On 22 August the *Daily Mail* printed a sensational report of the inquest and in another column on the same page a report of an investigation by Scotland Yard into the mass poisoning of wealthy women in Eastbourne during the past twenty years. An estimate of 400 victims was given. Other newspapers followed at a distance but not so far behind as to preserve them from libel damages after the trial was over. On 31 August Michael Foot, then the editor of *Tribune*, called it 'one of the most appalling examples of newspaper sensationalism and persecution in the history of British journalism'.

The inquest, ending with the sinister appearance of Scotland Yard, and the blaze of hostile publicity would have shattered the ordinary GP. But Dr Adams was unperturbed. On the day after the inquest Percy Hoskins, the chief crime reporter of the *Daily Express* and the one journalist who had kept his head, travelled up to London with the doctor on the 8.30 am train from Eastbourne. He found him quite unconcerned and his warning to Adams that he was in serious danger made little impression.

3

The Police Inquiry

The police team was constituted in accordance with the pattern approved by the best detective stories. It consisted of the superintendent and his sergeant from New Scotland Yard, Hannam and Hewitt, and of the local man, Inspector Pugh of the Eastbourne Borough Constabulary. All three were present at most of the interviews with Adams.

The police, as well as everyone else active in the prosecution* from the Attorney-General downwards, believed firmly (many of them still do) that Adams was a mass murderer of the nastiest type, a poisoner of those in his care. He certainly was a legacy hunter of not a nice type (the police files are convincing on that), but not the nastiest because he was not secretive about it. It may have been his talk which originated the rumours which the nurses and the relatives of dead patients were ready to confirm.

These composed the combustible material which the inquest had set alight and the press fanned into a bonfire. The *Express* and the *Mail*, rivals as always, were on different sides. Percy Hoskins of the *Express* was not only horrified by the witch-hunt but believed Adams to be innocent of murder. Rodney Hallworth of the *Mail* was and is sure that he was guilty. The latter's book† shows the author to have been in close contact with Hannam and Hewitt; it is the main published source of information about their activities.

He describes Hannam as a man whom you either liked or disliked. 'Sartorially elegant', with expensive tastes especially in cigars, he was nicknamed 'The Count'. He came into fame in 1953

* Sir Theobald Mathew, Director of Public Prosecutions since 1944 and before that for twenty years a practising solicitor in the illustrious firm of Charles Russell & Co, does not seem himself to have been among the very active.

† Hallworth, Rodney, and Williams, Mark, *Where There's a Will*, Capstan Press, 1983.

in the Teddington Towpath Murder when he was created by the press 'Hannam of the Yard', the title that corresponds to the *de* and *von* of Continental nobility. He had a good opinion of himself. In the witness-box he was not content, as most police witnesses are, to keep on the defensive, stonewalling if necessary. He liked to take charge. 'If you will help me to help you, sir,' was one of his lines that did not go down well with Mr Lawrence. There was to be a moment at the trial when they came near to what the newspapers like to report as a 'duel', but it was averted.

In the usual police inquiry the detective is presented with a crime and starts looking for a suspect. Hannam was presented with a suspect and his search was for a crime. A painstaking inquiry at Somerset House found 132 wills in which Dr Adams was a legatee. In this large field Hannam had to select what was provable as murder. There was very little hard evidence obtainable. Most of the deceased were cremated, but that after all is the end of many who are not murdered; it had been Mrs Morrell's expressed wish before she met Dr Adams. The doctor's death certificates favoured cerebral thrombosis as a cause of death, but by now everyone was beginning to suspect that the doctor was not a first-class diagnostician.

In these circumstances a policeman's thoughts turn easily to the expedient of getting the suspect to crack and much talk of cracking passed between Hannam and Hewitt. The Morrell and Hullett cases were among the dozen or so put on a short list. The first police interview with Adams in which Mrs Morrell was mentioned was on 1 October 1956; before then statements had been taken from the nurses. There may have been earlier interviews concerning other cases. Certainly there was a long statement taken by Inspector Pugh for the Hullett inquest. Of course only the parts of the police notes which referred to Mrs Morrell were admitted at the trial. But that other cases were brought up appears from the occasional entry in the depositions: 'The conversation then turned to other matters.'

The series of interviews was contrived to create alarm, worry and suspense. It is under such conditions that a guilty man finds it difficult to keep quiet; he worries whether a word on this or that may not divert suspicion or strengthen his hand at a trial. Above all, until he is driven to the point of standing on his rights, he must be as forthcoming as innocence would suggest, and an innocent doctor does not refuse information to the police about the death of his patients. So he has to talk, while watching every word.

A murderer must have a cool head to keep still. In crime stories the criminal sometimes gives himself away by second and third murders of those whom he thinks may have a clue to the first. In real life he is (there being no need to keep the story going) less drastic, but the nature of the over-reaction to danger is the same.

Hannam and Hewitt were among those who could see no explanation except that of murder for legacies followed by deaths. It was as if upon enrolment in the investigating team they had taken an oath of loyalty to that idea. Their job was not to question it but to find in as many cases as possible the sort of proof that would satisfy the law. They were both sound policemen who would keep ardour within bounds. They knew the formal rules and would obey them.

Hannam's approach was gentle and skilful. He might be looking for breakdown and confession but he was ready to snap up any contributions to the proof he needed. He knew the quantity of drugs prescribed, but he had no direct proof of the quantity injected; but the doctor could hardly refuse all information about what had been done with his prescriptions. Most of all the detective needed proof of the motive which only the doctor could supply. He knew that the doctor had not in strict law got anything under Mrs Morrell's will. But did the doctor know that? Here he must be careful. If his questions seemed to be setting a trap for the doctor, a jury would not like it.

Cracking Dr Adams turned out to be like cracking a soft-boiled egg—one tap and the yolk was over the brim and away. Dr Adams, apparently oblivious of the fact that he was being subjected to skilled interrogation, talked on and on. The Hannam-Hewitt note-taking must have been superb.

At the end of the inquest the hunter and his quarry had been properly introduced to each other by the coroner. If the doctor had known the part he was expected to play, the ceremony would have been like the referee presiding over the shaking of hands before the fight. As it was, the doctor gave the policeman a polite welcome and an assurance of help.

The introduction justified the superintendent, on 1 October 1956, in pausing outside the garage of Kent Lodge just as the doctor was putting his car away.

Good evening, doctor, did you have a good holiday in Scotland?

This civil inquiry led to an account of the shooting party and of the extent of the bag and to a description of various scenes of sporting activity. This topic exhausted, the doctor passed on to a general account of his life. After describing the death of his father and brother, he focused on the early highlights, how he had worked too hard, how he had qualified and taken a position at Bristol, how he had seen a position advertised at Eastbourne and failed to get that position but been offered another one and how he had gone to Eastbourne for an interview and sent photographs of himself and taken the job. He had had a Christian upbringing, he said, and it was all God's guidance and leading that had brought him to Eastbourne.

Then he referred to the rumours and said that all who knew him knew they were untrue; as for those who believed them, there was nothing he could do; 'I think it is all God's plan to teach me a new lesson.' He passed on to the death of his mother and the successful transportation of her body to Ireland where he had her laid with his father. From this death he passed naturally to the death of a cousin, 'a sweet Christian soul', whose memory was an inspiration to him even now. Then:

Dr: You are finding all these rumours untrue, aren't you?
Supt: I am sorry to say that is not my experience . . .
Dr: It is strange, I live for my work, I gave a vow to God that I would look after my national poor patients, day and night I will turn out for them, I never ask anybody else to do it for me, I think this makes people jealous of me.

This led on to a description of his day, starting with the seven o'clock news. On this particular afternoon he had been to Brighton for the general meeting of the YMCA.

Dr: If only others worked as hard as I do. What have you been told about me? [*There followed a conversation about other matters.*] You haven't found anything else?
Supt: Doctor, I have been anxious about some of the gifts you have received under wills from your patients.
Dr: A lot of those were instead of fees, I don't want money, what use is it, I paid £1,100 supertax last year. [*The Superintendent mentioned the chest of silver.*] Mrs Morrell was a very dear patient. She insisted a long time before she died that I should have that in her memory and I didn't want it, I am a bachelor, I have never used it. I knew she was going to leave it to me and her Rolls-Royce car, she told me she had put them in her will, oh yes, and another cabinet.

Supt: Mr Hullett left you £500.

Dr: Now, now, he was a lifelong friend. He was a very ostentatious man about his wealth; he liked to talk about it. There is no mystery about him; he told me long before his death that he had left me money in his will; I even thought that it would have been more than it was. [*Conversation about other matters*.] Every one of these dear patients I have done my best for. I have one thing in life and God knows I have vowed to him I would—that is, to relieve pain and try to let these dear people live as long as possible.

Supt: Doctor, I have examined the cremation certificate forms you filled in in your own handwriting for Jack Hullett and Mrs Morrell and you have said on them that you were not aware that you were a beneficiary under their wills. That is quite a serious offence.

Dr: Oh, that wasn't done wickedly. God knows it wasn't. We always want cremations to go off smoothly for the dear relatives. If I said I knew I was getting money under the will, they might get suspicious and I like cremations and burials to go smoothly. There was nothing suspicious really. It wasn't deceitful.

Supt: I hope I shall finish all these inquiries soon and we will probably have another talk.

Dr: Don't hurry. Please be thorough. It is in my interests. Good night and thank you very much for your kindness.

The next move in the cracking process was the search of the doctor's house on 24 November for dangerous drugs, combined with the presentation to him of the list, Exhibit 4A (see page *x*), which he had prescribed for Mrs Morrell seven years earlier. The combination was astute. If the doctor was hoarding dangerous drugs, the most likely source of supply would be the surplus from unused prescriptions. The search which accompanied the presentation of Exhibit 4A would remind the doctor of the perils he would encounter if he were to say that not all the drugs on Exhibit 4A had been given to the patient: he would be asked what he had done with them.

Hannam believed in keeping the press well informed: perhaps it was part of the cracking process. When the team arrived at Kent Lodge, the newspapermen were on the doorstep and at the windows. They included foreign journalists; interest had now been aroused in the USA as well as in Europe. Hannam, who liked to take charge of any situation in which he found himself, directed that all the blinds should be drawn. Doubtless this encouraged the reporters to draw on their imaginations.

The time was 8.30 pm and the police found Dr Adams, as perhaps they had expected, in a dinner jacket and just leaving to take the chair at a dinner of the YMCA. He met them as they were coming in and said, 'There is no question of a statement, for I have been told not to make one.' Mr Hannam said that he had a warrant issued under the Dangerous Drugs Act to Inspector Pugh to search the premises. The team then went into the surgery where they waited—with some confidence, I dare say—for the statements which Adams had been told not to make.

Adams began by asking what was meant by dangerous drugs and was told morphine, heroin, etc. He said, 'Oh, that group. You will find none here. I haven't any. I very, very seldom ever use them.' Hannam then asked to see the doctor's register: a doctor who obtains a supply of dangerous drugs for use in his practice must keep a register showing how they are acquired and how disposed of. Dr Adams had not, however, allowed himself to be encumbered by a register. 'I don't know what you mean,' he said. 'I keep no register.'

Hannam then produced Exhibit 4A.

Supt: Doctor, look at this list of your prescriptions for Mrs Morrell. There are a lot of dangerous drugs here.
Dr: Now all these I left prescriptions for, either at the chemists or at the house.
Supt: Who administered the drugs?
Dr: I did, nearly all, perhaps the nurses gave some, but mostly me.
Supt: Were any left over when she died?
Dr: No, none, all was given to the patient.
Supt: Doctor, you prescribed for her 75 heroin tablets the day before she died.
Dr: Poor soul, she was in terrible agony. It was all used. I used them myself.

Adams asked to see the list and Hannam gave it to him, running his finger over prescriptions No. 87 to No. 91.

Dr: There might have been a couple of those final tablets left over, but I cannot remember. If there were, I would take them and destroy them. I am not dishonest with drugs. Mrs Morrell had all those because I gave the injections. Do you think it was too much?

Supt: That is not a matter for me, doctor. I simply want to get at the truth. Were those drugs taken to the house by you?
Dr: No. The chauffeur collected them and I got them from the nurses.

Then the search of the surgery began. Hannam's evidence is that 'the accused flopped into his chair beside his desk and held his head in both hands and appeared to be crying'. There were two cupboards, one on each side of the fireplace. While one was being searched Adams went to the other and with a key on his chain unlocked the centre compartment and took out two objects which he put into his jacket pocket.

Hannam, who had no doubt been waiting for this, at once began to interrogate.

Supt: What did you take from that cupboard, doctor?
Dr: Nothing. I only opened it for you.
Supt: You put something into your pocket.
Dr: No, I've got nothing.
Supt: What was it, doctor?

Adams then produced two bottles of hyperduric morphine.

Supt: Doctor, please don't do silly things like that. It is against your own interests.
Dr: I know it was silly. I didn't want you to find it in there.
Supt: What is it and where did it come from?
Dr: One of those I got for Mr Soden who died at the Grand Hotel and the other was for Mrs Sharp who died before I used it.

All this happened in the evening of Saturday 24 November. On the Monday morning the doctor was arrested and brought before the magistrates on thirteen minor charges, four of them being of false representations under the Cremation Act 1902. He was granted bail on condition that he surrendered his passport; this was doubtless the object of the exercise. More than 120 people crowded into the small court to see the respected doctor conducted to the dock by a detective and stand there with a uniformed sergeant beside him.

Mr Hannam had now completed not only his dossier in the case of Mrs Morrell but also his inquiries in about a dozen other cases which constituted his short list for the Attorney-General's consideration. The list included the two Hullett cases and the case of

Downs.* These are the only three in which evidence has been put on oath. Mr Hallworth of the *Daily Mail* gives some particulars of some of the others; they are not sufficiently detailed to show their strengths and weaknesses. Certainly none of them looks as strong as Morrell, even after allowing for the fact that that case was six years old.

Mr Hallworth gives also an account, which he must have got from Hannam and Hewitt, of the meeting in the Attorney-General's room in the House of Commons at which the Attorney selected Morrell and instructed Mr Hannam to charge Dr Adams with her murder.

The arrest for murder was at Kent Lodge in the morning of 19 December. The press of course was in attendance. The French, less sedate than the British who were ready to wait for what they were about to receive, had a reporter and a photographer in the surgery. Hannam ordered them out. The rest of the scene is as described by the Attorney in his opening speech: 'Murder. Can you prove it?'

Two days later the press was able to report the exhumation during the hours of darkness of two more supposed victims. But the subsequent post-mortems yielded nothing beyond another crop of rumours.

The public was fascinated. The affair was so convincing dramatically, the casting so good. Had the doctor been black-a-vised and of sinister aspect, it would have been one of those crime stories which make good enough theatre for an audience which cannot see it happening to them. But Dr Adams was a family doctor. True, he was a bachelor. But he was one of those bachelors with amplitudes which seemed to strain his waistcoat and with features so comforting as to make him the equal of any family man. He had practised in Eastbourne for thirty-four years. He was in partnership with three other doctors with the reassuring names of Snowball, Harris and Barkworth. The fear that such a man with access to so many bedsides was a poisoner sent shivers down the spine. No one now supposed that the two or three patients whose cases were being exhibited by the police were the only victims. For most of the public the gap of six-and-a-half years presented no difficulty. It was easily filled with any or all of the patients who during that time had died.

Yet he was not a lone and deserted figure. There was in Eastbourne still a band of loyal patients who would not believe

* See page 192 below.

anything against him. Twenty-seven years later, when the time came for the great legacy hunter to distribute his accumulations, they were divided between the forty-seven surviving friends who had stood by him in his time of trial.

For the others who were still ready to believe anything that they heard against the doctor rumour was now, at least in Britain, driven underground. Any newspaper tale that would influence a jury would be contempt of court. When Adams said 'Can you prove it?' he had unwittingly defined the channel through which the story had now to flow. Before the magistrates the stream, despite the efforts of the defence to confine it, would still be wide. But after that the law of evidence would narrow it. Twelve men and women, chosen at random, their minds purged by the trial process of irrelevance and prejudice, would answer not the many tongues of rumour nor even the quiet questioning of those who sought the truth. Their thought concentrated on the single issue, they would only say in one word or two whether or not they were satisfied beyond reasonable doubt that Dr Adams murdered Mrs Morrell. Urging them to answer that they were not, there were no longer only the few voices that could be heard above the hubbub but champions picked from the law's army of mercenaries, trained to defend the abandoned and to work for pay.

4

The Committal for Trial

It is at this point that the criticism of the Crown's conduct of the prosecution begins. To understand the criticism it is necessary first to understand the nature of the preliminary proceedings in crime.

In civil proceedings any plaintiff can as a rule sue any defendant. It has never been so in England in the case of serious crime. It would be a grievous thing for an innocent man if anybody who wished to make a charge against him could put him at once to the stress and cost of a public trial.* In this respect the English procedure is not exceptional. What differentiated it from most other European countries, Scotland being included in the majority, was that by an accident of history from the middle of the nineteenth century until 1967, when as a result of the Adams case the procedure was changed, the preliminary inquiry was almost invariably held in public and open to the press. Secret trials are abhorrent. But the investigation of a supposed crime and the inquiry whether there is a case against any particular suspect is not a trial. It may come to nothing. Then the airing of unfounded suspicions may prove very damaging to an accused, as they did to Dr Adams.

What I have described as an accident of history arose out of the absence in England until 1879 of an official prosecuting system. In France, for example, the preliminary inquiry was conducted by the *juge d'instruction* who worked in private on the compilation of his dossier. In Scotland the work was done administratively by the procurator-fiscal. But in England it was discharged among

* This sentence is quoted from *The Criminal Prosecution in England*, OUP (1960) p. 89. This book consists of lectures which I gave at Yale University in 1957, the year of the Adams trial. It can therefore safely be consulted by anyone who wants a contemporary account of the nature of the preliminary proceedings at this time.

many other duties by the justices of the peace whom a great legal historian has called the 'men of all work' of the legal administration. In this capacity the justices were described as 'examining magistrates' in the statute of 1848 which regulated their proceedings. But the bulk of their judicial work was the trial of petty crime for which naturally they sat in public. For a long time after 1848 it was erroneously assumed that as examining magistrates they must likewise sit in public. Although the error was corrected by the Magistrates Courts Act 1952, it takes longer than five years for men of law to change their habits.

The proceedings which began at Eastbourne on 14 January 1957 were before the examining magistrates, laymen advised on legal points by their clerk who was an experienced solicitor. As a matter of course they would sit in public and they would know that the public in this case would include the press of the world. If an application was made to them to hear any particular witness in private, they would know it to be most unusual but would be advised by their clerk that they had power to grant it. The accused and his representatives were entitled to be present throughout but could not be required to take part.

Whether in public or in private, the magistrates would hear the evidence of all the witnesses for the prosecution. In practice this meant that the statement which the witness had already given to the police and from which he was being examined would by a process of question and answer be turned into a sworn deposition for use at the trial. The defence is entitled to cross-examine, but usually, if they do so, they are only skirmishing. If they wanted, the defence could give battle by putting the accused and any other witness in the box to disprove the Crown's case. But they would be fighting against the odds, for the Crown has at this stage to show only that there is a case to be tried; if the defence were defeated on this issue, they would have disclosed their case prematurely. So almost invariably the defence is reserved and, unless the Crown's case can be punctured without disclosure, it goes for trial. The defence is then in the advantageous position of knowing the whole of the Crown's case—for the rule is that, if the Crown wants at the trial to produce any additional evidence, they must give written notice of it—without having disclosed any of their own.

Before I recount what happened at Eastbourne I must explain the problem that confronted the Crown in presenting their case. They believed that the doctor was systematically killing off his patients to get the money they had left him in their wills. The usual way of handling this situation is to select half a dozen of the clearest cases, file an indictment with six counts and put all the others on a list of offences which the accused is invited to admit and have taken into consideration when sentence is being passed. The accused usually accepts this method of trial by sample. But it would hardly be seemly—taking the rumoured 400 as the doctor's tally—to ask for 394 other murders to be taken into consideration. Anyway, by an ancient rule of practice which still applied in 1957, there should not be more than one count in an indictment for murder.

Nevertheless, it was recognized that, while murders had to be tried only one at a time, there might be cases of 'system', as it was termed, in which evidence might be given of murders which were not being tried—so as to aid in the proof of the one that was.

But murder cannot be proved simply by alleging other murders and hoping to convince by force of numbers. Two conditions have to be fulfilled before evidence of another murder is admitted. The first is that each murder, whether it be the one charged or one of those relied on in support, must on its own facts give rise to at least a strong suspicion of guilt. The standard of proof in the criminal law is proof beyond reasonable doubt. Suspicion, however strong, is not enough. Suspicion means that the facts are capable of either a guilty or an innocent explanation. But an innocent explanation, which is credible in a single case, may cease to be credible when it has to be applied to a number of similar cases: by this means the reasonable doubt, which defeats proof in a single case, may be removed. The second condition, which is really implicit in the first, is that all the other murders shall be 'strikingly similar' to the murder charged and to each other.

The classic example of cases of system is the celebrated case of the Brides in the Bath in 1915. The accused in that case was Joseph Smith who married bigamously a lady of some means. He got her to make a will in his favour. He bought a bath and placed it in a room which had no lock. He took her to see a doctor, suggesting that she suffered from epileptic fits. Then she drowned in the bath, leaving the widower to lament that she must have been seized by a fit.

These were circumstances to set the neighbours talking. But there was no sign of violence. No one could explain just how Mrs Smith had drowned. There was nothing to implicate her husband: suspicion but no proof. Mr Smith was not charged.

But then after an interval and in another neighbourhood the process was exactly repeated—the moneyed wife, the will, the purchase of a suitable bath, the unlocked door, the suggestion of epilepsy, followed by the unexpected death by drowning of the new Mrs Smith. Again Mr Smith was not charged.

For the third time the series was enacted. But this time the police had evidence of the two earlier cases. They were never able to produce a convincing explanation of just how the murder was done. But the two earlier cases offered convincing proof that somehow or other Joseph Smith had done it. He was convicted and hanged.

It was on the strength of this principle of law that the Crown, while charging Dr Adams with the murder of Mrs Morrell only, alleged that he had murdered also in similar circumstances Mr and Mrs Hullett.

The parties at committal proceedings are not usually represented by counsel, but these proceedings were not usual. The Attorney-General did not himself appear: that would have been unheard of. But the other counsel who were to take part in the trial were all there; Mr Melford Stevenson QC and Mr Malcolm Morris for the Crown, instructed by the Director of Public Prosecutions; Mr Geoffrey Lawrence QC and Mr Edward Clarke for the defence.

Mr Stevenson began by outlining the Crown case on the death of Mrs Morrell. When he approached the Hullett evidence Mr Lawrence rose to object to it as inadmissible. If it was admitted, he asked that it should be heard in private. If it was given in public and at the trial the judge excluded it, it was not humanly possible, he said, that a jury would not have been influenced by it. Mr Stevenson replied that, while he could not consent to a hearing in private, he would not oppose it.

This reply (which, as it later appeared, had been decided by the Attorney in consultation with Mr Stevenson) has been criticized, I think with justice. Counsel was using a formula which a judge would understand as meaning that, while counsel himself had nothing to say against the application, he (or more probably his clients) might be embarrassed if he were to give a formal consent to it. The result would be that a judge, taking the application as unopposed, would grant it unless he had some strong objection of his own.

But lay magistrates cannot be expected to have a mastery of the nuances that judge and counsel employ. The Crown should have given them a clear lead. They had no idea what to do. They decided first to hear the evidence in private: having heard it, they decided that it should be given in public.

Mr Stevenson took first the case of Mr Hullett. He described the heart attack, the summoning of Dr Adams, the injection of hyperduric morphia followed immediately by the deep sleep and stertorous breathing, the awakening at 6.00 am, the conversation with the nurse and the death half an hour later. The Crown's case was that this injection was lethal. Dr Douthwaite was called as the chief expert. A small injection of morphia would, he said, be quite the right treatment, but anything more than $\frac{1}{4}$gr. would be risky. He inferred from the deep sleep and the stertorous breathing that the injection was $\frac{1}{2}$ to $1\frac{1}{2}$grs.

But the Crown had more deadly evidence of the size of the dose. Dr Adams had taken the morphia from his own stock and so was entitled to replace it. On the day after Mr Hullett's death he went to the chemist with a prescription for 5grs. hyperduric morphia which he asked to be delivered to Kent Lodge, his home, and charged to Mr Hullett. So either the doctor had injected 5grs. or he was being dishonest.

Mr Lawrence did not waste time in argument about which. With two questions in cross-examination he killed the allegation of murder stone dead. In answer to his first question Dr Douthwaite said that, having regard to the awakening at 6.00 am and the conversation, it was quite impossible that the injection could have been as much as 5grs. In answer to the second, he agreed that the conversation made it unlikely that the dose was lethal; subsequently he agreed with Dr Adams's certificate of coronary thrombosis.

The facts in the case of Mrs Hullett seemed to make it an obvious case of suicide, as the inquest had found. The process by which Mr Stevenson proposed to transform it into a case of murder by the doctor is not easy to follow. He recited the long list of barbiturate prescriptions between 1 May 1956 and the fatal dose on 19 July. But he did not meet the point that until 14 July Adams had nothing to gain and something to lose by Mrs Hullett's death. The will that gave him the Rolls-Royce was not made until 14 July; until he got the cheque for £1,000 his hope of a car or its cash equivalent was dependent on Mrs Hullett remaining alive. So a decision to kill must presumably have been taken some time between the morning of the 17th, the earliest time at which Adams could have got the cheque, and the late evening of the 19th when Mrs Hullett took or was given the fatal dose. I say 'took or was given' because the case as put by Mr Stevenson was that Dr Adams murdered Mrs Hullett 'whether she herself administered the fatal dose or whether she did not'.

It is wildly improbable that, after Mrs Hullett had retired to bed, pleading a headache, in the evening of the 19th, Dr Adams paid her a secret visit and dosed her against her will. It is not, however, inconceivable that Dr Adams, having seen at close quarters the misery of his friend, was willing to assist her in a decision to end her own life. This would be murder, both legally and morally. Not the warmest advocate of euthanasia would condone its performance under the superintendence of a doctor whose fee was a legacy of a Rolls-Royce and a cheque for £1,000.

How did Mrs Hullett obtain the 115grs. of barbiturates which the pathologist found in her body? This is the crucial question. The simplest explanation is that from time to time she kept back one, or perhaps both, of the tablets that had been doled out to her every day since her husband's death on 14 March. The amount found in her body came to about ten days' supply.

But there were circumstances to support a sinister suggestion. Why, unless he anticipated a speedy death, did Adams have the cheque specially cleared? Why did he conceal from Dr Harris and Dr Shera that he had been prescribing barbiturates? Is it credible that, as he said at the inquest, he had no suspicion of suicide?

I pass from the facts of each death as they were related to the magistrates to the supposed similarities that linked them with each other and with the death of Mrs Morrell six years before and which were relied upon as justifying the Crown in tendering the Hullett evidence. Since the allegation of the murder of Mr Hullett collapsed, I need not detail the points at which Mr Stevenson assimilated it to the others. It is sufficient to say that they closely resembled the points he advanced in the case of Mrs Hullett, which I give below.

On the face of it Mrs Hullett's death bears a distinct resemblance to the death of the first Bride in the Bath. There is, of course, the difference that Mrs Hullett was a willing victim and the Bride was not, that is, the difference between being the actual murderer and the abetter. Apart from that, in each case the accused's relationship with the victim gave him the same sort of opportunity and in each he profited by the crime. So in each case there was suspicion but no proof. The Bride might have died by an accidental drowning; Mrs Hullett might have committed suicide unaided.

If the police had found among Adams's patients two other cases, not too long before Mrs Hullett's death, in which the patient died by an overdose of pills prescribed by Adams and left him a legacy, suspicion might, as in the Brides in the Bath, have been converted into proof. But though the investigation, as it later appeared, went back for ten years, the best that could be found was the case of Mrs Morrell. The manner of her death bore not the least resemblance to the death of Mrs Hullett and, if the doctor was guilty of that, it was as an abetter and not as a principal.

The alleged similarities were:

1 That both patients were rich.
2 That both left legacies to the doctor.
3 That for both the treatment was heavy drugging.
4 That both were under the influence of the doctor.
5 That in both cases there was an anxiety to secure the prize, as evidenced in Mrs Hullett's case by the clearance of the cheque.

But to aid in the proof the similarities must consist of oddities or abnormalities. It is, for example, odd to have a bathroom without a lock; it is abnormal for a newly married wife to be thought to have epilepsy. Features that are not uncommon are for this purpose of no significance. There was nothing uncommon about two rich patients in Eastbourne. Nor is it significant that with an interval of six years between them they left their doctor a legacy which was quite small in relation to the size of the estate. This disposes of the first two items.

As to the third and the fourth, the experts in the Hullett case did not criticize the drugging as too heavy and they were not drugs of addiction; there was no evidence in either case of undue influence. As to the fifth, the anxiety in each case was dissimilar. In Hullett it stemmed from the fear that the patient might die before the cheque was cashed; in Morrell from the fear that she might linger on.

I should have been very surprised if the Crown had in the Morrell case persuaded any judge that the Hullett evidence was admissible. But without it there was enough in the Morrell case to commit Dr Adams for trial. After a hearing that lasted for nine days he was duly committed.

5

How I Became Concerned

The Lord Chief Justice at this time was Rayner Goddard. He was a judge of the old school which by 1957 was going out of fashion. He stood for law and order, firmly buttressed by capital and corporal punishment. He respected tradition but not the pomposity which is so often confused with it. He was, he would admit, a little impatient. He did not sit silently behind the scales of justice watching for a grain to be added to one scale and a scruple to the other. The scales inside his mind were jerking all the time and the movements were fully signalled. At the end of the first day you might think that all was lost; at the end of the second that all was won; at the end of the third the balanced judgment would be pronounced.

The mind that was a little too lively for the judicial process was a joy in social intercourse. He delighted in that, in talk of all sorts, in good food and wine. He read a lot and was full of information on the byways of the law. But he liked talk, quiet or convivial, not particularly with the good and the great, and would accept an invitation from anyone he thought might be interesting. Thus he first dined at our house while I was a member of the junior Bar who had occasionally appeared before him. I do not suppose that he expected very much besides conversation. 'What is this?' he exclaimed with totally unconcealed astonishment after the first sip of the first wine. After that our acquaintance progressed. As time passed, we were divided in outlook, though not in friendship, by some deep differences of opinion: but for me he was always a truly lovable man, an exciting mixture of youth and age. He was then just coming to the end of his eightieth year.

It was in talk with Rayner that I first heard of a doctor who was allegedly murdering his patients in Sussex after first getting them to leave him all their money and whom the Attorney-General was

34

hoping to lay by the heels. Sir Reginald Manningham-Buller, the Attorney-General, was a friend of Rayner and they saw a good deal of each other in term time at the Inner Temple. They had a lot in common and not only in their ardent belief in capital and corporal punishment; but the Attorney, though a generation younger, had none of Rayner's breadth of view nor of his flexibility.

Brief and casual talk on maybe two occasions was the only acquaintance I had with the case. I do not remember reading anything in the newspapers. So readers who wish from now on to put themselves in my position must 'dismiss from their minds' (a favourite judicial injunction) all that I have written in the preceding chapters.

I remember—this must have been during the committal proceedings—some discussion about where the trial should take place. In the ordinary way it would be committed to the assizes at Lewes, which is the county town of Sussex, and the judge going that circuit would preside at the trial. But assizes are fixed in advance for a definite period and a case that might last two or three weeks would not be easy to fit into the calendar. To send a second judge to Lewes would strain the resources—the court buildings, the judge's lodgings and the hotel accommodation—of an historic town living much on its past. There were two alternative expedients. One was to order a special assize which could be held at Eastbourne, a place that would be much more convenient for the medical and other witnesses concerned, not to mention the public attracted to the spectacle. The other expedient was committal to the Old Bailey, the Central Criminal Court to give it its modern name, which ordinarily draws its cases from the London area. It is more commodious than any assize court and would probably be just as convenient as Eastbourne.

Rayner thought of taking the case himself. It was then still the custom for the Chief Justice to take important trials. Quite apart from the dramatic interest, the case was a very important one for the medical profession, which was naturally worried by the thought that the prescription of drugs might lead to a charge of murder. While Rayner was turning this over in his mind, he came into contact with probably the one resident of Eastbourne who was equipped with the preliminary ignorance so desirable for the impartial juror. He was a man who had been a contemporary of Rayner at Marlborough, and who about this time came across Leonard Schuster, Rayner's favourite nephew, and told him how much he would like to meet Rayner again. To this Rayner would always respond. He wrote to the old boy a chatty letter about the old days and mentioned the possibility of a meeting. He was getting rather old, he said, and near his retirement, but he might possibly come to Eastbourne to try Dr Adams though that would probably be his swansong. The old boy wrote back commiserating with Rayner on his advanced age and on what he supposed to be his poor health. 'But why try Dr Adams?' he wrote. 'Surely there are better people in Harley Street.'

Rayner could certainly have undertaken the trial—he lived for another fifteen years—but he might have found it rather wearing. Moreover, his usual duty was to preside in the Court of Criminal Appeal. There might well be an important judgment to be delivered on appeal in the Adams case and he felt, he told me, that he ought to reserve himself for that.

By this time it had been decided that the case would go to the Old Bailey. A judge of the High Court, nominated by the Chief Justice from among those who are at the time sitting in London, goes to the Old Bailey each session to try the most serious cases. By the end of January the Chief knew that I was more or less, as it is so delicately phrased in the Diplomatic Service, *en disponibilité*. Officially I was sitting in the Commercial Court, but it was then at its nadir. Today it flourishes and keeps five judges fully occupied, but then it was not providing me with work for more than a fraction of my time; for the remainder I had to be found odd jobs. The Chief, who had a finger for every pulse, was wondering whether the Commercial List, as it was then more strictly called, justified its separate existence. On 27 January I sent him a long letter with some proposals for reform which he said we should both discuss with the Lord Chancellor. My letter revealed that in the current term the commercial work was likely to take about three days in the month. The Chief decided that I should be better occupied trying Dr Adams. So he assigned me to the March session at the Old Bailey, saying characteristically that, if I could not manage all the other cases besides Adams in the Judge's List, he would come down and help.

I remember that we had some general discussion about the trial. The enormous interest which the case had aroused and the prejudice which might have been created against Dr Adams made it, I thought, very desirable that the jury should be guarded from all external influences. No one knows who will be on a jury until after the trial has begun. After that during any adjournment a juror is exposed to outside contacts. Without imagining any wicked attempt to suborn, it is obvious that, where in preliminary proceedings the prosecution's case has been published in full and generally discussed as well as garnished with rumour, any outside contact may be dangerous. A juror might be casually reminded of a rumour that he had not noticed or had forgotten or he might be offered well-intentioned medical advice.

It was not until the middle of the nineteenth century that any difficulty arose since before then there were no adjournments. Trials were short and judges sat until late at night, if necessary, to get a verdict. Then judges began to allow juries to separate after warning them not to discuss the case. But this relaxation was never allowed in capital offences. In them the jury was held incommunicado from beginning to end. They were housed in a separate part of a hotel under the watchful eye of the jury bailiff and newspapers were censored. The difficulty of finding hotel accommodation in wartime had caused this practice to be abandoned after 1940. I did not know whether or not at the Old Bailey it had been resumed. But, if not, I saw no reason why it should not be revived for a case where every precaution ought to be taken. I must have mentioned this to Rayner—so much is clear from a letter that I wrote to him—but I have no recollection of any discussion: neither, it became obvious, had he.

Rayner, who knew more about the case than I did, was more concerned with the Hullett evidence of 'system'. He said that its admissibility would be an important point for me to decide. He thought that it would have been better if the evidence had been heard in camera. I felt that any application by the defence for evidence of doubtful admissibility to be heard in camera ought to be granted. Rayner suggested that at the trial I should say something to that effect. I did not feel that I had the seniority to speak *ex cathedra* and asked if I might add the weight of his own authority. He agreed. I made the pronouncement in the course of my summing up. It led directly to the statute that now restricts the reporting of committal proceedings and indirectly to their present moribund state. Today the defence usually accepts the witness statements which the police have taken as telling them what they want to know and much time is saved.

All this must have happened before 19 February. On that day I wrote to the under-sheriff at the Old Bailey and asked him to come to see me to discuss what arrangements could be made for segregating the jury.

6

Counsel in the Case

I had another preliminary duty to discharge. This was to fix the date for the hearing. This is a good time for me to say what I knew about the three leading barristers, the Attorney-General and Melford Stevenson QC for the Crown and Geoffrey Lawrence QC for the defence. The Attorney and I were the same age, fifty-two. Stevenson and Lawrence (though the latter in a wig looked the most youthful of the four) were fifty-five.

Melford, who had played so large a part at Eastbourne, had now little to do. If the Attorney-General had been called away, Melford would have taken over the prosecution, but the Attorney missed hardly a minute. Nevertheless, I expect that Melford was a strong influence in counsel. He must have been chosen by the Attorney-General as his No. 2 and he shared his outlook on life. Without knowing what bodies, political or other, Melford belonged to, it would be safe to say that he was on the right wing of all of them. He became better known, even famous, as a judge (he went on the Bench at the end of 1957) and the last of the grand eccentrics. He had a biting wit, much enjoyed by most of the Bar and not so much by litigants.

At the Bar, as well as at the Garrick, his conversation was always a delight. I remember once joining a group to whom he was telling a story about a female client who had outwitted him and whom I joyfully recognized as an unfavourite aunt of mine. She was suing an estate developer from whom she had bought a house. Melford told her firmly that she had no case. The developer had turned out to be a bit of a rogue, but unfortunately in ways that were irrelevant to any of the issues. Melford said that he would try to get a settlement. He got a very good offer which she turned down flat. A week before the case came on the defendant's counsel nearly doubled the previous offer and Melford told her she would be mad to refuse: she did refuse. In court, while they were waiting for the judge to come in, the defence said that they would pay the claim in full. 'Your aunt, my dear Pat,' Melford said, 'is, as I should have expected, a very remarkable woman: but with only a dim perception of the borderline between litigation and blackmail.'

The Attorney-General was called Reggie by friend and foe alike because he was the sort of person who obviously ought to be called Reggie, the son of a Northamptonshire baronet, Eton and Magdalen, a Tory MP since 1943 and embedded in the right of his party. I had had a casual acquaintance with him for some time. He had, I am sure, chosen the Bar as a profession not out of any interest in justice or the law but because it was generally thought to be good ground for a career to grow in, especially if fertilized by politics.

It was in 1923 that Lord Chancellor Birkenhead had spurred the hearts of the young (Reggie and I were then sixteen or seventeen) with his rectorial address to the students of Glasgow University: 'The world continues to offer glittering prizes to those who have stout hearts and sharp swords.' Reggie never learnt swordsmanship but he was effective with a blunt instrument and certainly had a stout heart. What was almost unique about him and makes his career so fascinating is that what the ordinary careerist achieves by making himself agreeable, falsely or otherwise, Reggie achieved by making himself disagreeable. Sections of the press, which he permanently antagonized, liked to parody his name by calling him Sir Bullying Manner. This was wrong. He was a bully without a bullying manner. His bludgeoning was quiet. He could be downright rude but he did not shout or bluster. Yet his disagreeableness was so pervasive, his persistence so interminable, the obstructions he manned so far flung, his objectives apparently so insignificant, that sooner or later you would be tempted to ask yourself whether the game was worth the candle: if you asked yourself that, you were finished.

The outer man was large and imposing; the inner of strong convictions which he deemed it to be his stern duty to implant not only within his own autocracy but throughout any area where he thought or hoped that he could overcome resistance. His zeal for the conversion of souls was equal to that of any of the great mediaeval bulldozers of religious orthodoxy. He was neither a saint nor a villain. But since most of his convictions were wrong-headed, he was ineluctably a do-badder, by which I mean a person whose activities bear the same relation to villainy as those of a do-gooder to sanctity.

His dislikes, however strong, seemed to me impersonal. They did not exclude many small kindnesses and courtesies. There was no malice in him. At least I do not think there was. Clumsiness? Almost invariably. Stupidity? Yes, from time to time. Amounting to perversity? I think that it must be conceded that sometimes it did. And might there have been on occasions only a dim perception, as Melford might have put it, of the borderline between perversity and malice? Possibly.

From the first he cast over me the spell that Widmerpool casts on the readers of *A Dance to the Music of Time*. I thought this before I had heard it said on good authority that the character of Widmerpool in fiction owes something to Reggie in real life. A serious student of Bullerism should re-read Anthony Powell's chronicle, a pleasant occupation anyway. The reappearances of Widmerpool, each time surprisingly on a higher rung of the ladder, are glimpses of how Reggie's climb in real life appeared to his contemporaries.

Barristers in Parliament used to have their own private ladder to the temple of fame. Junior office for the ordinary politician is a testing time; he may or may not make good. But once the barrister MP had become a law officer—Solicitor-General first and then Attorney—all he had to do in the old days was to wait for empty shoes to step into. Until the Socialist government of 1945 set a different example, the successful lawyer-politician was a powerful candidate for the top places in the judiciary.

The advice that was given in my time to those awaiting their chance of mounting the politico-legal ladder was to acquire a substantial practice at the Bar before entering the House. If Reggie was given this advice, the one unorthodox thing he ever did was to disregard it. His neglect of it was a great success. He did not bother much about a practice and went into Parliament in 1943. He held minor office in the brief caretaker government of 1945; this gave him a toehold on the promotion ladder. In 1946 he took the silk gown of the KC that is given to MPs for the asking but he still did not trouble to get more than the random brief. Again his neglect turned out well. His toehold could, for he was unremittingly industrious, be improved if he made himself useful in opposition in the House. When the time came, the toehold triumphed over the substantial practice which had been acquired by his Eton and Magdalen contemporary, Hylton-Foster.

When the Tories came back into office in 1951, they carried with them into the House two former law officers. The senior, David Maxwell Fyfe, was a distinguished barrister, but much more interested in politics than in the law; he was offered the Home Office and accepted it. Walter Monckton, the former Solicitor-General, was uninterested in politics and only doubtfully Conservative. He was already a public figure, having been King Edward VIII's counsel in the abdication crisis of 1935, and had a large practice at the Bar. He hoped to be the new Attorney-General. But Mr Churchill, who wanted industrial peace and was ready to pay for it, rightly thought that Walter, who had charm and persuasiveness as well as ability, was the best man to buy it for him at the lowest reasonable price. Reluctantly Walter went to the Ministry of Labour.

Thus both law offices were thrown open to competition. Had there been strong competition, Reggie's lack of forensic experience might have been fatal. But the increasing professionalism of politics had thinned the supply to the House of first-class barristers and 1951 was a year of famine. There was only one possible choice for Attorney-General, Lionel Heald. He was an able lawyer with a large practice of the right weight. He provided the necessary substance, making it possible (and maybe as a party matter desirable, for Lionel had been in the House for only a year) that Reggie's eight years of political service should be recognized. Thus Reggie became Solicitor-General. Many thought that Hylton-Foster would have been much the better choice, but he too had been only a year in the House. Then there began what the Socialists later dubbed the thirteen years of Tory misrule. Reggie's progress was not to be disturbed by a period in opposition; he never had to acquire a practice.

The Bar was not enthusiastic and some thought that Reggie would not make the grade. I was one of the few to know otherwise. One of his rare appearances was in the Commercial Court with a brief that the leader in his chambers had returned at the last moment. He performed with complete competence and, as was always to prove the case, he had mastered his brief.

In 1954 Lionel Heald, never hungry for the sweets of office, went back to the Bar and Reggie succeeded him as Attorney-General. In April 1957 Rayner would be eighty and it was being said that in the autumn he would retire. Here was a glittering prize indeed. Reggie had now for a number of years discharged the normally unglamorous duties of the law officer fighting the battles of the Revenue and the other great government departments. The fortune-tellers at the Bar were eager to see how he would perform in a spectacular criminal trial.

Doctors subscribe to the Medical Defence Union. The name of Hempsons, their solicitors, is well known in the Temple. They were to defend Dr Adams. Since the case affected the profession (not only would it be disagreeable to have a doctor convicted of murder, but it was most alarming to feel that what might be only too lavish a prescription of drugs for a dying woman could provoke such a charge), it was certain that they would spare no expense. But for their leader they did not go to one of the Old Bailey regulars. They engaged a quiet and conscientious barrister who had acquired a high reputation in what was called 'local government work', principally rating cases, but embracing also every sort of dreary dispute in which local authorities and their natural opponents engage. Geoffrey Lawrence QC was a man who would certainly master the medical technicalities in the Adams case but not, one might have supposed wrongly, a man equipped with the arts of the jury advocate.

The junior counsel on each side was a sound and experienced criminal practitioner. Malcolm Morris for the Crown was the son of a distinguished QC and was himself to end his life on the Circuit Bench. He was nominated for the case by the Attorney-General who perhaps did not overlook the fact that he too was Eton and Magdalen. Edward Clarke for the defence is the grandson of the celebrated Victorian advocate of the same name and in the third generation of his family to practise at the criminal Bar. He, like Lawrence, would have been picked by the solicitors. In 1964 he became a judge at the Old Bailey.

I have interposed this account of the dramatis personae at the point in the narrative where I was passing to my duty to fix a date. A date for a long trial must be fixed sufficiently in advance to enable counsel and solicitors to make their arrangements. Ordinarily this would be done by communication between the judge's clerk and the clerks to counsel and without much regard to counsels' convenience; they were paid to be available. The Attorney-General was not quite in that position. He had parliamentary and other public duties to perform and so was entitled to special consideration. A quarter of a century had passed since I devilled for the Attorney-General of the day, but I remembered it to have been the custom in a long case for the trial judge to send for him to discuss the date. So on 19 February I wrote a note inviting him to come to see me.

I thought that I would also get his reaction to the idea of segregating the jury. It would mean sitting on Saturdays since the jury could not be left for a long weekend with nothing to do; this might conflict with the Attorney's political engagements. Strictly, since Lawrence would have an equal voice in this, it was a matter for a joint invitation. But I took it for granted that it would be acceptable to the defence.

The Attorney came on 21 February and began at once by telling me that he had decided not to use the Hullett evidence in the trial of the Morrell indictment. Exeunt the Brides in the Bath. He said that he would tell Lawrence later in the week.

He told me also that he intended to apply to the Chief Justice for leave to file an indictment for the murder of Mrs Hullett. If there was an acquittal on Morrell, he intended to ask that this second indictment should be proceeded with at once. If there was a conviction on Morrell, he said that he had not made up his mind whether or not to go on with the Hullett indictment.

This stirring news made the original agenda for the meeting very humdrum. We discussed the probable length of the trial and a suitable date for it. (Eventually I fixed it for 18 March.) I told him my thought about the segregation of the jury and said that I was getting his and Lawrence's views while taking steps to see if it was practicable. He approved the idea; in particular, he was concerned that the jury should not have access to newspapers. That evening I sent a note round to Lawrence to tell him that I had seen the Attorney-General and wished to pass on to him what had been said.

Next morning there was a letter from Reggie to say that on reflection he felt considerable doubt about reverting to the pre-war practice of jury segregation. Rumours, he said, would be circulating during the trial. But since almost every juror in the country would already have heard the rumours, this made, he thought, a thin ground for action that would cause very great inconvenience. He ended with the suggestion that I should consult the Lord Chancellor because of the possibility of questions being asked in the House.

This, I thought, showed a lack of *savoir-faire*. Judges do not, when taking judicial decisions, consult the Lord Chancellor, nor are they to be influenced by the possibility of questions being asked in the House. Nor indeed do judges consult the Attorney-General as such; it was as counsel in the case and not in his

political capacity that I was talking to Reggie. When eventually
(for he took his time about replying to my invitation) I heard what
Lawrence had to say, I realized that I had been treading on
slippery ground.

Fortunately the appointment with the Lord Chancellor to
discuss the stagnation in the Commercial Court had been made
for the 25th. Fortunately also his Permanent Secretary, George
Coldstream, was one of the best and most discreet of government
servants. I told George privately the position on jury segregation,
said that I regarded it as a matter for my judicial discretion and
did not propose to involve the Lord Chancellor, but that I should
like the Chancellor to know, in case he heard of it from another
source, that I intended no disrespect. Later I got a message back
from George saying that the Chancellor was definitely of the
opinion that he should not be approached. The Chancellor,
incidentally, was the David Maxwell Fyfe, now Lord Kilmuir,
who had gone to the Home Office in 1951; he was a man I knew
well and admired.

The next morning, 26 February, Lawrence surfaced. Since on 4
March I gave Rayner the gist of our talk, I shall insert here what I
wrote.

> When I saw Lawrence, he was extremely reserved. It is clear
> that he feels very bitterly about the conduct of the prosecution
> to date; of course I did not ask him why and he may have no
> justification for it, but he is, as you know, a quiet and well-
> balanced person. He said that he thought a fair trial was now
> impossible anyway. He said he did not wish to say or even
> listen to anything that might fetter him in taking whatever
> action he thought right in the interests of his client. He
> criticized my having seen the AG without his being present; I
> told him I saw nothing objectionable in that, since we had
> discussed only the machinery for the trial and he was being
> kept fully informed. (So that you get no false impression of him
> personally, his manner of saying all this was quite perfect.) On
> the question of the jury he said he would like to consult his
> junior; and that is how the matter stands.

I was taken aback by Lawrence's vigour which in any other man I
should have thought to be slightly paranoiac. What he would say
when he heard that the Crown was abandoning the evidence to
which he had unsuccessfully objected I hardly cared to imagine.
As it was—and of course I did not then know all the facts—he
was obviously and deeply disturbed. What he said to me was

COUNSEL IN THE CASE

emphatic. He was not really interested in jury segregation: the harm was done: he listened only sufficiently to avoid impoliteness. At the end he repeated that there was no possibility of a fair trial. I said that, if I took that view, I should not be going to the Old Bailey to try the case. On this discord he left.

It could hardly matter to the case for the prosecution whether it was presented to jurors who had slept at their own expense in their own beds or at the City's expense in hotel beds. So one might have supposed that Reggie, having expressed his view, would have been content to leave the decision to the man whose job it was to take it. But this was not Reggie's way. Whatever the subject, as soon as he had been vouchsafed a vision of what was right and proper, he could not stand idly by while rightness and propriety were in jeopardy. By the end of February he doubtless had intelligence that the Lord Chancellor was not girding his loins for the fray. So he carried his fears to the Lord Chief Justice.

All judges are and must be independent, but every judge recognizes the head of his division, the Lord Chief Justice being the head of the Queen's Bench, as *primus inter pares*. Nevertheless, the *pares* usually prefer to decide for themselves when the moment has come to bring in the *primus*.

On 1 March the Chief wrote:

My dear Pat,

The Attorney was speaking to me yesterday about the arrangements for the Adams case. It is not of course for me to dictate, but do you think it necessary to have the jury locked up? It is a good many years now since a jury was locked up in a murder case. It certainly has not been done since 1939 and considering that the case may, for reasons which you know, last a fortnight or three weeks, it would be a very great hardship and probably be strongly resented by the jurymen. At any rate, I would be grateful if you would have a word with me before you finally decide on locking them up and of course if this is to be done ample notice will have to be given to the Sheriffs.

Yours ever
Rayner

I had acknowledged the Attorney's note and told him that I should write again after I had seen Lawrence; by this time I was quite determined that I would talk to no one until after I had heard what Lawrence had to say. And I was pretty well determined that, if he wanted segregation, I would tell him to make a formal application in open court. Too much was being done behind the scenes. Meanwhile I thought it would be a good thing if Reggie was told to shut up. But on this I had to write diplomatically to the Chief. I have quoted the account I gave of my conversation with Lawrence. My letter to Rayner continued:

> Meanwhile, I think it would be much better if the AG kept quiet. He has put his points and it is no use pressing them further until I have heard Lawrence's. Already he has spoken to the Chancellor; and in his note to me suggested that questions might be asked in the House and suggested that I should go and see the Chancellor. Put like that, I did not think I could: it might be twisted to mean that in a matter, which under the Act is clearly one for judicial discretion, government discussions took place behind the back of the other side. I explained my view to Coldstream. Now the AG has spoken to you in a way that might be twisted to mean that he wanted pressure brought to bear. Of course I know that would be all nonsense and that his only anxiety is to avoid what he thinks may be a false move. But there may be a lot of nonsense talked after the verdict.

> If Lawrence answers that he is against a lock-up, that settles it. If he is for it, I think the prosecution would be wise to join with him in asking for it, whatever the inconvenience. If it can be said of the prosecution hereafter that they led before the magistrates prejudicial evidence, failed to press for it to be heard in camera, dropped it at the trial and opposed a measure that might have minimized its effect, it would be a very damaging criticism: but that is not my affair.

> . . .

> But now my strong feeling (do tell me if it is wrong) is that, in view of Lawrence's attitude and the AG's interventions, it might be better if I took my own decision. There are times when it is better to reach the wrong decision for lack of good advice than the right one in a way that might be criticized.

Six days had now gone by and I had heard nothing more from Lawrence. So my clerk telephoned to say that I assumed there was nothing more that he wished to say. The reply was that he would like to see me before court on the following morning. In the afternoon the Recorder of London, Tony Hawke, an old friend, telephoned a tale of woe from the City Sheriffs. There was no longer any regular hotel accommodation, they said, and no one who was familiar with the practice: it would cost £300 a week. (It is salutary now to recall that, after allowing for the jury bailiff and other incidental expenses, the cost of board and lodging per head would have been about £3 per day.) I was not much impressed by this. I felt that if the prosecution had been eager to guard the jurors against intimidation, difficulties would have been overcome and £300 a week considered to have been well spent. Certainly the practice of segregation was later resumed for some cases though the abolition of capital punishment in 1965 meant that murder was no longer distinguishable from other grave crime.

Nor did I think it likely that jurors would be resentful. What they resent is not the work nor the sacrifice of time but the tedium of hanging about with nothing to do. It is very different when the citizen is called upon to take part in an historic institution and for a brief period to be one of those who make the vital decisions instead of having to submit to them. For most a sensational trial has all the excitement of an unexpected break in routine. There is the stir caused by the policeman who calls at the juror's home to collect the overnight bag. There is the odd experience of spending several evenings with eleven strangers. There is the Sunday excursion to some place of interest. I doubt if there are many anxious to avoid the experience.

The next morning—it was now 5 March—Lawrence called, but only to say that he did not wish to depart from the position he had taken up. The Attorney-General had told him of his intention not to use the Hullett evidence at the Morrell trial but on a separate indictment. This, he said, only strengthened his view that a fair trial was quite impossible.

If he really believed this, and he had now said it three times, he was no doubt tactically right to abstain on the question of segregation. If he could not get a fair trial, he could at least get a fair appeal. He must have felt that his client's best hope was to get the conviction quashed on the ground that the jury had inevitably been prejudiced. The argument would not be assisted by measures to diminish the likelihood of further prejudice. Certainly much damage had already been done. I did not feel strongly enough about the efficacy in these circumstances of segregation as a prophylactic to enforce it against an inert establishment, a hostile prosecution and an indifferent defence. So I went to see the Chief in the afternoon and told him the proposal was dead.

*

47

I found him unhappy about the Attorney's application for leave to file a second indictment. But since all the Hullett evidence was already on the depositions, he felt, he told me, that a committal could only be a formality; he doubted the wisdom of the course, but that was a matter for the Attorney-General. Like most judges who are said to be prosecution-minded Rayner had a deep respect for the traditional safeguards, whether they were logical or not, that favour an accused. One of these, an emanation perhaps from the maxim that no one should be put in jeopardy twice, is the feeling that the prosecution is entitled to one bite only. Presumably it had picked its best murder and it went against the grain to allow it another shot with the second-best.

The Chief's assumption was that the Attorney intended to proceed further only if there was an acquittal. But to me he had said that he had not made up his mind what he would do on the second indictment after a conviction on the first. On the surface this seems strange. We were still in the days of capital punishment and a man cannot be hanged twice. Protection against a successful appeal on the first indictment could be achieved by asking for the second to stand over until after the appeal on the first had been heard.

But there was more to it than this. A conviction on the first would have created a delicate situation, adding another curiosity to the case of *R*. v. *Adams*. The 1950s was the decade of the great debate on capital punishment. Such debates divide the electorate into the enlightened who are believed ready to receive a new gospel; and the unenlightened believed to be controlled by instinct or prejudice or tradition. At this time the enlightened who wished to see capital punishment abolished would have been outvoted in the country by the unenlightened. This made life difficult for any government which wished to appear enlightened but did not wish to be outvoted. It is in this situation that the individual Member of Parliament comes into his or her own. A private member's bill, for which the government allows time for debate, commits it to nothing. By this means it had been ascertained that there was a majority in Parliament, composed mostly of Socialists but with a sizeable content of Conservatives, in favour of abolition.

The Tory Government in power in 1957 found a solution in a dividing line between capital and non-capital murder, the latter being punishable only by life imprisonment. The result was the Homicide Act 1957 which Reggie as Attorney-General piloted through the House of Commons. The dividing line has been much criticized and in fact it survived for only eight years. It had been framed not so much to distinguish between degrees of murder as to placate the various sections in the community who were most vociferous for the retention of the death penalty. The police officer, for example, naturally expected protection against the gunman: this was one of the five categories of capital murder. The most criticized omission from the categories was the cold-blooded murderer, notably the poisoner. There was also a general feeling that two murders, especially a repeated poisoning, would be one too many. So a separate section provided that

> a person convicted of murder shall be liable to the same punishment as heretofore if before conviction of that murder he has, whether before or after the commencement of this Act, been convicted of another murder done on a different occasion.

In simpler words a second murder would still carry the death penalty.

The bill received the Royal Assent and so passed into law on 21 March, which happened to be the fourth day of the Adams trial. But this was not the crucial date, for under the Act the change in the law was not to affect indictments signed before the date of commencement. Both the Adams indictments had been so signed. So the old law still applied to the Morrell indictment and had Dr Adams been convicted I should have passed sentence of death. No doubt it would have been commuted; the Home Secretary could not have allowed death to turn on a date of commencement. But if then Dr Adams had been convicted on the second indictment, would there have been a second commutation? Commutation then would have looked like a guarantee of immunity for double poisoners under the new law. We shall never know the answer to that. Nor shall we know whether one of Reggie's objects in pressing the second indictment was the death of Dr Adams.

7
The First Day

It was at the end of the first chapter many pages ago that the Attorney-General concluded his opening speech. It lasted only for two hours, brief when compared with the witnesses for the Crown who were to take two-and-a-half weeks. It had been an advocate's speech, more aggressive than had by 1957 become usual for counsel for the prosecution. The tone suggested a higher degree of villainy than the facts seemed to warrant. Court Number One had heard of many worse crimes than that of a doctor hastening the death of an old lady, even if he did get a chest of silver by way of acknowledgment.

The tone was appropriate to what was not said. It was matched to the great unuttered about which everybody in court knew at least a little, myself perhaps least of all. I knew as a fact that there were rumours, but I had not heard or read any myself; I had not read any press reports; I felt that Lawrence was exaggerating. Testimony given after the trial was over shows that he was not. Mr Chuter Ede, for example, a former Home Secretary, said in Parliament that anyone reading the newspapers, and not merely the sensational newspapers, would have been bound to form a most unfavourable view of Dr Adams. Mr Reginald Paget, QC, MP described the state of affairs as being one in which it was impossible to empanel jurors who had not heard a mass of rumour. The Attorney-General himself said much the same thing when, after changing his mind about segregating the jury, he wrote to me that almost every juror in the country would have heard the rumours.

A court of law cannot dispel rumour: it can only exclude it. Because it is excluded, the defence cannot fight it. The doors of evidence are locked against it and the windows shuttered, yet the cracks are never effectively sealed. It is there in the atmosphere, the impalpable enemy with whom the defence cannot get to grips. Mr Lawrence could not be heard to demonstrate that talk of the murder of Mr Hullett was nonsense and of the murder of Mrs Hullett feeble stuff. All the same, I think that he was under-estimating the virtue of the jury. When people talk of a jury being prejudiced, they always seem to be visualizing a group of men and women gossiping in a pub; they do not allow for the effect of the legal process on the common mind. I never for a moment contemplated the possibility that the trial of Dr Adams would not be fair.

Lawrence may have been too apprehensive. But undoubtedly the prosecution erred grievously over the Hullett evidence. First, they introduced it without proper consideration of its admissibility. Second, by withdrawing it as perforce they had to do, they prevented its weakness from being exposed.

As to the first, in all the cases I have known or read about there has not been one in which evidence of 'system' has been tendered to the magistrates and then dropped. Before they presented the evidence in public the Crown ought to have made quite certain that they were going to tender it at the trial. All the factors that should have governed their decision on that point were as well known to them before the committal proceedings as after.

As to the second, persons with a low opinion of criminal lawyers would find a simple explanation of the prosecution's manoeuvres. Were they not skilfully providing the inlet through which prejudicial but inadmissible evidence might flow into the trial? It is inconceivable that any idea of this sort would occur to Reggie or Melford or to any other member of the Bar with whom I have ever had any dealings. Lawrence would not imagine it. But he might well be appalled by the recklessness with which the prosecution had behaved and shocked by their apparent indifference to its effect upon the defence.

The opening speech was, as is customary, immediately followed by the short, more or less, formal witnesses. These were the chemists who supplied the drugs for Mrs Morrell. They were formal in the sense that their evidence was not likely to be challenged. But they were very important.

The doctor was accused of murdering by the administration of a dangerous drug. For proof of the act of murder the Crown offered two alternatives. The second and, as it seemed from the opening speech, the subsidiary alternative was by one or other of the last two injections. I call it subsidiary because the Crown's main case seemed to be that by then Mrs Morrell was dying, already murdered by the other method. But I take the subsidiary first because it was the simpler and serves as an introduction. Nurse Randall had seen the doctor preparing the dose and had received his instructions to inject it. An hour later the patient was dead. The doctor must therefore say what it was. If in the circumstances it was lethal, it concluded the case: if it was not, the Crown proceeded to the alternative.

The alternative was a more complex type of murder. It was murder by overdose, but not by means of a single dose. The task of the prosecution would be to prove that the quantity of the opiate drugs* administered over a certain period was such as to build up in the body a fatal accumulation. Unfortunately it had no precise record of what was injected over any period. The only record it had was of what was prescribed. It had to convert this into a record of what was injected. For this purpose it intended to rely, first, upon an admission by the accused, and, second, upon inference and calculation.

The prescriptions for the last six days, the Attorney-General had said, totalled 79½grs. It seemed from the evidence that Superintendent Hannam was going to give that Dr Adams had been eager to admit that he himself had injected it all. I had the feeling—I do not suppose that I was alone in having it—that this admission was not going to count for very much in the end. I had not from the opening speech received the impression that the doctor was a man who weighed his words. An admission of this sort is strong evidence against a defendant, but it does not preclude him from saying that he was mistaken or muddled or even lying. The management of an elegant withdrawal in the witness-box would not be beyond Mr Lawrence's powers.

So it would probably come down to inference and calculation, a method which could be used to cover the whole period and not just the last six days. Each prescription was dated. It was, the Crown would say, to be inferred that one succeeded another when the latter was about to be exhausted. So it could be calculated that the period between the two dates was the period of the injection of the latter quantity.

* The dangerous drugs with which this case is concerned are all derivatives of opium, i.e. heroin, morphia or morphine, and omnopon which is 50 per cent morphia. They were all at some time being given to Mrs Morrell; usually it was heroin at the same time as one of the others. When considering the permissible size of a daily dose, it is the total of all three (reckoning omnopon at 50 per cent) that is to be taken into account.

So the proof would rest mainly on the inference that what was prescribed was injected. The chemists would lay the foundation by proving what was prescribed and that it was delivered either to the doctor or to the sickroom. After that other witnesses would have to take up the tale and, as it seemed to me, negate the possibility of any leakage between the point of delivery and the injecting syringe. There was after all a flourishing black market, in heroin especially.

The drugs were all dispensed by H. R. Browne, Chemists of 44 Cornfield Road, Eastbourne, and three of their employees were called to prove it. None of the original prescriptions could be produced; the law requires them to be kept for two years only. But when a prescription is brought to the dispensary by the patient or, as here, a servant, it is copied into the prescription book under the date on which it was presented and with the name of the doctor who signed it. If it is a 'repeat' prescription, a similar entry is made on each date on which it is repeated. The witnesses were not asked exactly how the repeat is activated, but it seemed clear that the customer could obtain the second and third deliveries without recourse to the doctor. A prescription is as a rule made up on the day it is presented, so that the date in the book is also as a rule the date of delivery to the customer.

There are certain drugs, commonly called dangerous drugs, perhaps more accurately described as 'restricted drugs', which statute forbids a chemist to deliver without a prescription signed by a doctor authorized under the statute. They include all the opiate drugs. A witness had prepared a list of these drugs delivered from 1 January 1950 onwards and charged to Mrs Morrell's account. This list, marked Ex[hibit] 4A, became a key document. It was nearly the same as the list (one suspected that this latter list had been marked Ex. 4) that had been shown to Adams by Hannam on 24 November. All the prescriptions in Ex. 4A were signed by Dr Adams except for two signed by Dr Harris when Adams was on holiday.

The next witness was Mr Reid. He was an independent chemist who had been brought in to examine the records and to calculate, for example, the quantity of each drug supplied over a period. Among other interesting bits of information he told us that a 5cc syringe would hold not less than 10grs. heroin in solution.

Lawrence cross-examined these four witnesses in a perambulatory way. The opening speech had been a brief extraction of vivid sequences from a medical treatment that lasted for nearly two-and-a-half years. Lawrence was out to demonstrate that these were only the occasional narrows in a broad and sluggish stream. Ex. 4A listed only the dangerous drugs. Lawrence wanted to know about all the other sedatives that had been prescribed. And of course there were many other medicines prescribed, were there not? Tonics, eye-drops, ointments, lotions—Lawrence examined lists of them and inquired about their various purposes. At the end of the day he startled Mr Reid.

> *Mr L:* Well now, Mr Reid, I ask you this question because you are the chemist who has been called in to put the matter in order, so to speak. What I am anxious to get at the earliest possible stage is a complete list of prescriptions of whatever kind of the medical treatment that was prescribed by Dr Adams for this lady. In order to get that it is quite clear we have to go through the books to before January 1950?
> *Mr Reid:* I would have thought eleven months would give one a reasonably clear picture of the character and nature of the thing.
> *Mr L:* I was not asking you to express an opinion about that. I was suggesting we might have the whole picture. It is to be found in those prescription registers?
> *Mr Reid:* Undoubtedly.
> *Mr L:* Would you be good enough to find it for me and get out a list?
> *Mr Reid:* If the court so orders, sir.
> *Mr L:* My lord, it is, if I may say so, in the view of the defence of the utmost importance that this complete list should be available . . .
> *A-G:* My learned friend represented Dr Adams at the police court and this is the first indication we have had of this nature. . . . My lord, I hope we will not be blamed if it takes a little time. . . . I am told that doing it for 1950 the investigation took $2\frac{1}{2}$ days. . . . I am making no complaint, but it is unfortunate that we were not given any indication . . . we will do our best now.

The Attorney's reference to the police court was like the occasional archaism in the foreigner's excellent English, one of the little things that showed him as not quite up to date in the practitioner's world. 'Police court' was an expression that had fallen into disuse about twenty years previously; it had been condemned as suggesting to the public that in courts of summary jurisdiction it was the police and not the magistrates who dispensed justice. But his point was a good one. He accepted it as the duty of the Crown in a criminal case to place before the court all the relevant facts and within reason to include what the defence claims to be relevant. But it is at the committal proceedings that the prosecution evidence is displayed; if the defence wants more detail, it should be requested then.

I was beginning to wonder about a gap in the chemists' evidence which I thought more important than the harmless medicines and the pre-1950 treatment. In his opening the Attorney had referred several times to the doctor making up injections in Mrs Morrell's bedroom from drugs which he took from his bag. If these had been opiates, which was what he was suggesting, they would have been, he said, additional to the quantities in Ex. 4A. No doubt a doctor must have restricted drugs among those ready for action in his bag. Does he obtain them on his own account and does the chemist record it? If so, there would have been a record of opiates supplied to Dr Adams at the crucial times.

The Crown was now ready to embark upon the nurses' evidence. There were four to be called. There was Nurse Randall who had featured in the opening as the innocent injector of the last fatal doses; she had been the night nurse for the whole of the time. She and Nurse Stronach, who did a few weeks of night duty in June 1950 and of day duty in the second half of October, looked like each other and like the popular idea of a hospital nurse. The two married nurses were a contrast. Sister Mason-Ellis was fairly tall; she looked more delicate than she can have been but she tired rather easily in the box. She was the relief nurse. Sister Bartlett was girlish and zestful. She had married after 1950 and became Mrs Hughes. But for everyone except the shorthand-writer who had to be correct, she retained what was, as it were, her stage name. She came as day nurse on 20 August and stayed to the end.

So in what might be called the murder period in November the night nurse was Randall; the day nurse was Bartlett from 9.00 am till 9.00 pm, but relieved by Mason-Ellis from 2.30 to 6.30. Sister Bartlett, though not on duty at night, was sleeping at Marden Ash. Of these four the most important as a witness was Nurse Randall. It would be natural to call her first. It is customary in a long case for the prosecution to give the defence a list of witnesses in the order in which they will be called; Randall was first on that as she had been first on the depositions.

But it was Nurse Stronach's name that was now called. This

seemed to disconcert Mr Lawrence and there was a subdued colloquy on counsels' bench from which it surfaced that the Crown had not expected to reach the nurses' evidence that day and Stronach was the only one available. The prudent judge, however, hears only what is addressed to him, to the jury or to a witness. Anyway, it was nearly time to adjourn.

It is the duty of the judge when the jury first separates (this jury had lunched by themselves, as they did throughout the trial) to warn them against discussing the case with outsiders or to allow their minds to be influenced by anything they might already have heard. The jury in the box looked intelligent and responsible. What I should have liked to have said to them would have run on these lines.

At the beginning of his opening speech the Attorney-General asked you to try to dismiss from your minds all that you might have read or heard of this case before. This, I do not doubt, would be sufficient warning, if one is needed, to caution you against attention to the sort of gossip and rumour that may have come casually to your ears.

But in this case there has been more than that. Only two months ago, when the prosecution presented to the magistrates the evidence which they intended to submit to you as proof that Dr Adams murdered Mrs Morrell, they included evidence to support allegations that Dr Adams had murdered two other patients under whose wills he likewise benefited. This evidence has been widely reported in the newspapers. You are not going to hear it in this court. It is highly probable that some of you have read and will now remember what was in the newspapers two months ago. I am not going to ask you to dismiss it from your minds as gossip or rumour because that would be an idle request. It is not gossip but evidence given on oath by responsible witnesses, some of whom you will be listening to in the next few days. It is not rumour but evidence put forward by the Director of Public Prosecutions. Nevertheless, I must tell you to dismiss it from your minds.

That is much more easily said than done. I think that it may help you to do what at first may seem impossible if I tell you now at the outset of the case rather more of your function than has been conveyed to you in the words of the formal charge that 'it is for you to say whether he be guilty or not guilty'.

The top men and women in government, in business, in the

services, the army, the navy, the police or what you will, all those who have to take the difficult and important decisions that affect the lives of their fellow men, are not left to do so unaided. They do not themselves go out to ask questions and to get answers. The material which is put on their desks has been collected and sifted by subordinates and stripped down to the issues which have to be decided. The decision-makers rely upon their subordinates to do their work thoroughly and skilfully. They must not be troubled with anything that is not essential for them to know. The skill lies in the exclusion of the irrelevant.

The trial process is designed to put you, the jury, in the position of the big decision-makers, which is what for this case you are. You are where you are because a man is entitled to have his innocence or guilt decided not by professionals but by his fellows. It is the business of the lawyers—judge, counsel and solicitors and all those who have made painstaking inquiries into the facts of this case—to give you as laymen the professional help that you need. All that glitters is not gold. One of my most important tasks is with the help of counsel to make sure that the case for the prosecution is sterling, that it has the minimum strength which a professional would say is necessary for conviction. It is for you alone to say whether it is strong enough to carry conviction. But it is for us professionals to give you the assurance that you are not being offered a sham; that might be difficult for the amateur to detect. It is our duty to see that only relevant material properly proved is put before you. Irrelevance can be misleading as well as a waste of time. If it is never admitted into your mind, you don't have to bother about dismissing it. This is why it is excluded as evidence in this court.

Unfortunately in this case it got by a mistake into the preliminary process. The Attorney-General, who is ultimately responsible for all prosecutions in this country and who is here in person to exercise his responsibility, has obviously decided not to put before you certain suggestions which were put to the magistrates.

We may take it that, having considered the appropriate principles of law, he has decided that there is nothing in the material to demand your attention. You are not, as it were, being asked to deny a hearing to a man who has something useful to say to you, but to a man who thought that he had but who now realizes that he has not.

If I had said this and in particular alluded to the other alleged murders and if then Dr Adams had been convicted, the conviction would certainly have been quashed in the Court of Criminal Appeal. Moreover, if I had said it, I think that probably I should have been indulging a personal preference for clearing the air. Many experienced lawyers would find a flaw in what I have just said. They would suggest that to equate the jury and top decision-makers in government and industry is to equate the general public and the élite. The only safe course, it is felt, is to keep a jury in the sort of ignorance which guarded the virtue of Victorian maidens. Modern education challenges these assumptions. I am not at all sure that we have got the right technique for the modern jury. Until we have found that, it may be better to stick to the rules. After all, most of what we read in a newspaper lies lightly on the memory until recalled. The rules keep out recall and a judge should not run the risk of stimulating it.

Anyway, what I did say went as far, I think, as in 1957 it was prudent to go. I explained the danger of discussion.

Once you start discussing a case, it leads to an exchange of views; and once it leads to an exchange of views, you might hear people's views about the case which would be outside the evidence you are going to listen to in this court, and that might easily therefore influence you. So please be quite resolute that you will not tolerate any discussion of this case by anybody in your presence at all, and that is not merely acquaintances and strangers, but that is families and friends.

I mentioned specifically the danger of looking back at the committal proceedings.

You have heard them referred to in the course of the case so far and to some extent they may be brought into the evidence here. You may think, if I did not give you this warning, that there would be no harm in reminding yourselves of what took place at those proceedings. But, there again, members of the jury, there might be harm. It does not follow that the case will be presented in exactly the same way here as it was before the magistrates. It does not follow that witnesses who gave evidence before the magistrates will give exactly the same evidence here.

So ended the first day. To be followed, I supposed, by a week or so of tranquillity. There would be a procession of nurses deposing to the injections given every night by the doctor. There would be estimates, to be derived from the prescriptions, of the amount injected. The defence was unlikely to show its hand until the Crown doctors went into the box.

8

Counterattack

Nurse Stronach's examination-in-chief was short, divided between the last few minutes of the Monday and the first few of the Tuesday. Mr Stevenson got her to describe the usual routine. Each evening she gave Mrs Morrell ½gr. of morphia. Later, about 11.00, Dr Adams called and she saw him prepare another injection, she knew not what, in a 1cc syringe. She did not see this injection actually given because by Mrs Morrell's wish the nurse was not in the room; she did not like the nurse to be in the room unless there was something she had to do.

Mr Lawrence began his cross-examination by taking the witness once again through the routine as if to fix it on the record and adding one or two details, such as that she never gave heroin or omnopon. Then he appeared to recollect something that Mrs Mason-Ellis had said before the magistrates about injections being recorded in a book. Yes, indeed, the witness said. Everything was recorded, injections, medicines, doctor's visits; this was usual nursing practice. 'So that if only we had got those reports now, we could see the truth of exactly what happened night by night and day by day.' Mr Lawrence spoke as if yearning for some unattainable black box after the crash.

'Yes,' Nurse Stronach said, and added stoutly, 'but you have our word for it.'

'I want you to look at that book, please.' There had been indications that something was afoot. A large suitcase had been brought in and carried to counsel's bench, its bearer stooping respectfully as he crossed the line between the judge's chair and the dock. I have never found out the reason for the stoop. Some say that the judge's view of the prisoner must never be obscured, even for a moment; others say the like about the prisoner's view of the judge; there is another school which says that no one must pass the dock on the level lest he be thought to be trying to communicate with the prisoner.

There was no time for such musings. I was as astounded as was everyone else to hear that what the defence were producing was the daily record of the treatment from 21 June 1949 until death a year and a half later. From then on the whole case was to revolve around the books. I have never heard of such a thing happening. There are rare cases of special defences where the facts are first revealed by the defence. But these books contained the direct evidence for the administration of the poison which the prosecution had to prove. Normally while the prosecution's proof is being unfolded the defence tactic is to harry it by sniping. Sometimes a raid may be mounted into prosecution territory so as to reduce the opposing forces to the point where the reasonable doubt can enter. But here was the defence marching into the heartland of the prosecution and taking command of it.

How had this happened? Where had the books been all this time? These questions were not answered at the trial. There is no doubt that, as Nurse Stronach said, it is the regular practice for nurses to keep notes of this sort. Each nurse, when she comes on duty, sees what has been done since her last spell. The doctor likewise can be kept informed; Adams occasionally looked at a book. But they are not, it seems, meant to be kept after the illness is ended whether by recovery or death. Nurse Randall maintained in evidence that they belonged to the nurses and should have been torn up when they had no more use for them.

There is certainly no evidence that Dr Adams was interested in the fate of what might have been the chronicle of his efforts at murder. It seems that, had he been asked at the trial how he came to preserve them, he would have said that some time after Mrs Morrell's death they were parcelled up at Marden Ash and sent round to Kent Lodge. He had there a filing cabinet of the usual sort in which papers are stacked in expansible folders alphabetically. He filed the notebooks under M (standing, as a wag later observed, for Morrell and not for Murder). In 1954 his secretary, culling the files, removed the notebooks. But if she intended to destroy them, she had second thoughts and dumped them at the back of the shelf. Dr Adams told his solicitors that he had looked under M and found nothing. But they, making a more thorough search than the police had done, discovered the hidden treasure.

To be beaten by the defence in this way does not reflect well on Scotland Yard. They start with the advantage of the search warrant and the first opportunity. The case illustrates both the

qualities and the defects of the English pre-trial inquiry. The time
taken compares marvellously well with the proceedings of the
juge d'instruction. Scotland Yard had inquired into numerous
deaths and assembled evidence in at least three of them. The
inquiry may be said to have begun with the questioning of Mrs
Morrell's nurses in August 1956 and to have resulted in the arrest
of Dr Adams on 19 December 1956 and his acquittal on 8 April
1957. From one angle it is a good example of speedy justice; from
another a bad example of hasty justice. The prosecution's poor
performance gave an immediate and tremendous boost to the
defence in the eyes of the public. If the doctor had not destroyed
and the defence was anxious to produce the medical records, was
it likely that the doctor was guilty?

Lawrence's deft handling of the operation had proved most
effective. But Reggie also must be mentioned in despatches for
coolness in the face of the enemy. 'While engaged in the customary parade-ground manoeuvres,' the citation might have run, 'he
was suddenly assailed by a foe whose mobilization was thought
to be still incomplete. Forced out of his prepared positions, he
conducted his retreat in good order, making proper use of the
terrain.'

The terrain over which Lawrence was advancing was composed of the rules of evidence. The proof of a document as
authentic has to cover ground pitted with technicalities which is
normally avoided by prior agreement between the parties. But an
invitation to agree must naturally be accompanied by an offer of
prior inspection: this would have lost Mr Lawrence the element
of surprise.

This is not as important as it would be on the battlefield. In a
trial at law surprise cannot be allowed to defeat justice. But it had
secured for Mr Lawrence the legitimate advantage of demonstrating dramatically and conclusively that the evidence which the
prosecution had assembled from the sickbed was without the
written record worth little or nothing. Hence the elaborate
secrecy which now had to be paid for. The price was the
shouldering of the burden of proof of each entry, i.e. the admission by each nurse that each entry attributed to her was in truth
hers. Until the proof was given the entry could not be put in
evidence and—until put in—it could not be shown to the jury.
The Attorney-General was naturally unwilling to dispense with
the formality until after he had seen the book himself. Lawrence
was unwilling to show the book until after he had proved it
beyond the possibility of objection. He was manoeuvring with a

caution which seemed to fear that a false step might rob him of his prize. Two-and-a-half pages of transcript separate the appearance of the first unidentified notebook from his statement that the defence had all the nurses' notebooks from June 1949. Another two pages pass before the Attorney is given a copy of the book actually in use. This followed a ruling by me that Lawrence must conduct his cross-examination without the jury having copies of the book in front of them. This cut a path through the thicket of technicalities. I am not sure that it was strictly the correct path, but it served the purpose of hastening an agreed solution since cross-examination under these conditions, while possible, was very inconvenient. So copies of all the books—there were eight of them in the series—found their way on or below the surface to the Attorney-General. He and his team worked with the maximum of speed and the minimum of lunch and after the midday adjournment he agreed that the jury should have copies, provided that they confined themselves to the entries that were being put to the witness. I gave a direction accordingly.

Before then Mr Lawrence had in cross-examination exploited his advantage to the full. He began with the night of 4 June 1950 on which Nurse Stronach first came on duty and went on to read each detailed entry. Occasionally the witness fought back.

> *Mr L:* Look at 8th June: '12.30 midnight. Milk and brandy 2 drs and 1 Sedormid tablet. 6.0 am. Milk and brandy 3 drs. 7.45. Warm milk, 1 yellow tablet. Taken well of breakfast. Mrs Morrell has had a very good night. B.N.O.P.U. Again no record of an injection and again no record of a doctor's visit, is there?
> *Nurse S:* It is no proof that he did not call that night because I did not put it down here.
> *Mr L:* You realize this is a serious case, don't you?
> *Nurse S:* Indeed I do.
> *Mr L:* You realize that before you saw this book you told me that everything of importance, including doctor's visit if there was one, would have been put down by you, as a trained nurse, in your contemporary record made at the time, didn't you?
> *Nurse S:* Yes.
> *Mr L:* And that was the truth, wasn't it?
> *Nurse S:* Yes, as far as I knew it. I believe it to be so.

So it goes on. Nurse Stronach with the book in front of her does not always resist a natural tendency to read on to see what is coming next. This is checked. 'Do try to listen to what I am trying to put to you,' says Mr Lawrence.

Mr L: Please keep your eye on what I am asking you about, Miss Stronach.
Nurse S: I am.
Mr L: Do not turn your head. 'Milk and brandy and 1 yellow tablet in the morning.' Look at the 18th. Exactly the same.

And then at the end of each day's entry:

Mr L: No injections whatever given by you yet?
Nurse S: No.

This is the rough edge of the legal process. In ordinary life would not Miss Stronach be allowed to say: 'Well, now, it is six years since I wrote all this; give me twenty minutes to read through all my entries and then I shall answer your questions'? I have often heard counsel ask that a witness should be given time to read a whole letter before he is questioned on part of it. But Reggie was not the man to ask for indulgence for himself or for anyone else. Lawrence, sensitive by nature and courteous, was a different man when he was fighting for the life of a client against whom he believed the odds to have been stacked.

So we come to the end of June without injections and without visits by the doctor.

Mr L: As a trained nurse you would not have omitted to record the visit by the doctor and an injection given by him if in fact it had taken place while you were on duty, would you?
Nurse S: No, I do not think I would have done.
Mr L: Now then, let us go on to the next period . . . begins on 12th October . . . please do not go on turning the pages in advance . . . 'Hypo injection omnopon 2/3rd given at 4.30 pm.' Now, Miss Stronach, do not think that I am blaming you in any way or criticizing you for this—
Nurse S: No.
Mr L:—but do you remember telling me earlier this morning, before you saw these contemporary records, that you had never given Mrs Morrell any injection except morphia?
Nurse S: Well, I believed that to be true.
Mr L: Well, this entry shows that your memory was playing you a trick, doesn't it?
Nurse S: Apparently so.
Mr L: Well, it is obviously so, isn't it?
Nurse S: Yes.

Mr Lawrence moves on to 6.30 pm and past a little tomato soup and orange jelly and cascara 2 drs.

> *Mr L:* Now will you pay close attention to what follows in your writing on 12 October: '7.30 pm. Visited by Dr Adams. Hypodermic injection morphia gr. ¼, heroin gr. 1/3, omnopon gr. 1/3.' Is it here in your writing?
> *Nurse S:* It is.
> *Mr L:* You have there recorded the exact nature and the exact quantities of the injection which was given to Mrs Morrell when the doctor visited, have you not?
> *Nurse S:* Yes, I have.
> *Mr L:* So it is quite clear that on that occasion at any rate you knew what the injection was, isn't it?
> *Nurse S:* Yes, it certainly is.

At last Mr Lawrence came to 2 November, the day on which Nurse Stronach left and on which she had said, in what now seemed to be a different age before the advent of the books, that Mrs Morrell was in an 'almost semi-conscious condition and rambling'. The entry read:

> 6.45. Seems very bright this a.m. and not confused. Breakfast. Boiled egg, bread and butter, bramble jelly, 2 cups of tea.
> 11.00. Hot milk with soda water and brandy.
> 1.00. Lunch. Partridge, celery, pudding and brandy and soda . . .
> *Mr L:* Consumed by this semi-conscious woman?
> *Nurse S:* Yes.
> *Mr L:* Miss Stronach, let us face this: it is another complete trick of your memory to say that on the last day when you left Mrs Morrell was either semi-conscious or rambling, isn't it, now you see what you wrote at the time? [*A pause.*] Isn't it?
> *Nurse S:* I have nothing to say.
> *Mr L:* What?
> *Nurse S:* I have nothing to say.
> *Mr L:* You have nothing to say?
> *Nurse S:* No.

Rarely does a witness run into such an ambush where her own words leap from their concealment to assail her. It was a devastating cross-examination. When the news of it reached Nurse Randall, she must have felt like the passenger who failed to catch the aeroplane that crashed. We could understand now why Mr Lawrence had been put about by the substitution. He could have got Nurse Randall's recollection of ten-and-a-half months to compare with the notebooks while from Nurse Stronach he got less than two. But the Stronach period was quite enough for the demonstration. The case for the prosecution had been razed; they must begin to build anew on the books.

Poor Nurse Stronach! 'You have our word for it.' The gods had punished the touch of hubris.

9
Pause

Full speed and a minimum of lunch are not unusual experiences for a barrister. For him or her a day in court means not infrequently a gobbled sandwich. True, there are not often cataclysms of the magnitude produced by the nurses' notebooks. But often enough in the morning there arises some unexpected point of fact or law to which the answer has been promised in the afternoon. Usually the barrister's clerk is ready with a couple of queries from solicitor clients in other cases, for the barrister in court is incommunicado for three-quarters of the day.

A judge, however, can count on the hour diminished only by the time taken to disrobe and robe again and to walk to his Inn and back. Since for me this was Gray's Inn, the furthest from the courts, I reckoned the hour reduced to 35 minutes, provided I kept a blind eye out for buttonholers. There had been a common room for King's Bench judges at the Law Courts in the Strand. There the Treasury had proffered a meagre dish for judges too infirm to walk to their Inns. But not long before I was appointed in 1948 the number of seats on the King's Bench had been increased by two to seventeen (about a third of the present number), and the common room had been requisitioned for the two additions to double up in.

Things have always been different at the Old Bailey where the iron economy of the Treasury does not prevail. For the Old Bailey belongs to the City. The bench, which runs the full width of Court Number One, has to be long enough to accommodate theoretically the Lord Mayor and the aldermen who sit at sessions. The judge's chair is not quite in the centre, since the Lord Mayor, who attends ceremonially on the first day, presides. Thereafter there are usually one or two robed aldermen on the bench, their chairs not drawn up to it but set back to denote judicial inactivity.

At the short adjournment—an expression to be preferred to the vulgar 'lunch hour'—one of the two City Sheriffs comes to the Judge's room, which is just behind the court and separated by a corridor from the door that opens on to the bench. He leads the judge, still robed but unwigged, along the corridor through doors opened and shut by uniformed attendants to what one can only call, so strong is the impression of a palace, the private apartments. The Sheriffs entertain the four judges, the King's Bench Judge, the Recorder, the Common Serjeant and the Commissioner, as they were then, (whether the loaves and fishes have been miraculously extended for the judicial multitude which now throngs the building I do not know), and other selected guests, some from the Bar and some from the great world, to luncheon: dinner it used to be called in the old days when the customary fare was beefsteak and marrow pudding, and then there might be two dinners in the day, for the judge always sat to finish. The judge makes himself agreeable to the guests over a glass of sherry and then eats an excellent lunch, the hour uncurtailed by the walk to his Inn and back.

I remember that on this Tuesday I sat next to the Recorder, Tony Hawke. He asked about Reggie's opening speech which he had read in *The Times* that morning. Good, I said. Tony, who also read the evidence before the magistrates as reported in *The Times*, thought that the Attorney had 'opened high'. Tony had spent all his life at the criminal Bar, he was a shrewd man and he had the sensitivity which long experience gives. To open high was a mistake. Prosecution oratory had begun to go out at the turn of the century. Exaggeration and emphasis began to be bad form. The prosecutor behaved no longer as an advocate but as a minister presenting almost reluctantly the inescapable demands of justice. Quiet beginnings would be shown to lead quietly to regrettable but inevitable conclusions.

We did not discuss it further. But thinking about it later I began to feel that Tony was right. What after all had the prosecution got? The evidence of the nurses; the prescription list; some bits and pieces in the will. With these they had to struggle across a gap of six years. When the Court of Appeal is considering whether or not to order a new trial, a power which it has had since 1964, it commonly regards a delay of three or four years as so hampering to an accused that it prefers to acquit forthwith: this although the first trial will have fixed the facts in the witnesses' memory soon after the event. Here the nurses had left a routine case with nothing in it to invite remembrance, not the slightest suspicion of foul play. If there had been no notebooks, one could imagine the powerful attack that Lawrence would have launched. One could even begin to wonder whether the notebooks were not for the prosecution a blessing in disguise, giving the nurses' evidence the framework which it needed in order to stand up. But Lawrence would hardly have led them into court with such panache if that was all that they were destined to do.

The revelation of the notebooks, as soon as their impact began to be felt, which was not until the Tuesday afternoon, seemed to make the opening speech obsolete. It was not until some time later that, considering the speech then as an item of historical interest, I realized what had been wrong with it.

The opening speech in a murder case must present a convincing portrait of a murderer. He can be one of many types ranging from the sadist to the mercy-killer. Usually the facts of the case are themselves sufficient to portray him. Here they were not. Many of the public thought that the doctor's offence lay in the gift of death to the dying. Clearly Reggie was not prosecuting just for that. There lay in the facts of the case a character somewhere between the mercy-killer and the coldblooded villain who poisoned for paltry sums. A picture could have been painted of a doctor who used heroin to keep his patient happy, who in return expected baksheesh, a chest of silver or the like, who found himself having to drug more and more until it was too late to wean, and who saw at the end that he had to increase to kill. Could such a death be proved as murder? Very difficult: increasing the dosage has not the suddenness of the bullet nor the sharpness of a knife wound.

Presenting such a character would have been far beyond the range of Reggie's imagination. He had to settle for the storybook simplicity of the poisoner who was driven to the act when he saw his legacy slipping away. As he had put it in his opening, the doctor murdered 'because he had decided that the time had come for Mrs Morrell to die . . . should not have any further opportunity of altering her will to his disadvantage'.

This is a picture of a cool, calculating, utterly amoral man, more than a murderer, the traitorous healer who for a few pieces of silver spat on the sanctity of his profession. For six years his treachery was hidden. How was it brought to light? Not by clever detection; the passage of time had made that impossible. Nor by confession as an act of repentance. In conversation with the police, after he had been warned against making a statement, he answered the question, 'Who administered the drugs?', not by

69

saying that he could not now possibly remember who had actually administered what, but by saying 'I did, nearly all'. Not only his coolness but his memory had deserted him. For in fact, as it afterwards appeared, he had administered very few. No portrait painter in the world, seeking to put on canvas a credible face, could combine the features of a coldblooded murderer with those of a babbler who did not even need to be squeezed to blurt.

These are all thoughts provoked by the Recorder's luncheon comments. When I returned to court on this Tuesday afternoon, I found Reggie after what must have been a prodigious effort ready to complete the re-examination of Nurse Stronach and to conduct the examination-in-chief of Sister Mason-Ellis, putting to each the relevant entries in the books. Then Mr Lawrence started to cross-examine. After a few general questions and after pinning the witness to her contribution to the books,

> *Mr L:* And what you wrote and signed was everything of significance that happened on any tour of duty when you were there?
> *Sister M-E:* Exactly.
> *Mr A:* You wouldn't have left anything out any more than you would have put anything that was wrong?
> *Sister M-E:* No.

Lawrence announced that

> I have made a list myself of the appearances of this nurse in the books, which I think is complete and exhaustive. I shall be going through it and if I am detected in any omissions it will be my fault, but I shall be glad to be reminded of any.

He was not detected in any omissions.

This set the pace. Nothing was to be hurried. How did the total of injections recorded in the books compare with the total prescribed? What did the books say about the two murderous injections on the last night? This was what we wanted to know, but we must wait. There would be no pulling out of plums.

So apart from a flurry on the following morning which I shall describe when we get there, there was little movement for the rest of the week. Let me explain what we were all doing. What is the advocate's objective when he is questioning and why do judges question at all?

In an English criminal trial oral evidence is the rule and written evidence the exception. Oral evidence comes from the witnesses who are called by each side, so that a witness is either for the prosecution or for the defence. The judge has an inherent power to call a witness but it is virtually never exercised. All oral evidence is given by means of interrogation in public: the witness may sometimes be encouraged to 'tell my lord and the jury in your own words', but any attempt at a speech is at once curbed. Since 1925 formal evidence for the prosecution which the defence is not going to challenge has been given by the reading of the deposition taken before the magistrates.

At the trial the questioning is begun by the counsel calling the witness and is known as examination-in-chief. Then there is cross-examination by the opposing counsel; then re-examination by the examining counsel. The interrogation of all the witnesses can be completed without the judge asking a single question.

This is the adversarial process as distinct from the inquisitorial. In the former the judge presides at the trial by jury, directs the proceedings and rules on the law; he is not there to hold an inquiry. It is quite different from the Continental process where witnesses are summoned by the court and examined by the judges, the role of counsel being to tender a witness and ask supplementary questions. In this process a question, whether by judge or counsel, is in a form introducing the topic on which the witness is expected to dilate; the answer can be very long. The form is one which in English courts is used only for expert witnesses. There is not the distinction, which I am now going to elaborate, between questions in chief and cross-examination.

The object of the examination-in-chief, whose achievement is said by some connoisseurs to demand far more skill than the average cross-examination, is the final production of the story which has been hewn rather than refined by the proof-taker. The relationship between examiner and witness is in abstract something like the relationship between the actor and the director. I stress the abstract because the concrete is entirely different; the director functions at rehearsal and disappears from the performance; for the trial rehearsal is strictly banned and it is in the performance alone that the barrister participates. The barrister has to shape the story almost as it is flowing from the lips of the witness. The metaphor of shepherding is perhaps the more appropriate one. Like the good sheepdog the good counsel rarely barks.

Counsel's first object is, of course, to get the material which sustains his opening speech or is needed for the structure of his

final argument. His second object—this is what demands skill—
is to present his witness as convincing. It is not simply that he
does not want him to look a liar; the really dishonest witness is
quite a rare bird. But if he is a good character, counsel wants it to
come across. If, for example, his client is charged with careless
driving, counsel wants him to show himself as much a careful as a
truthful man.

One can see from this the serious disadvantage under which
the Attorney-General was labouring as a result of the defence's
coup de main with the notebooks. He could not present his case
effectively through his examination-in-chief of the nurses
because he, no more than anybody else, knew what his case now
was. He could not tell which little bits to stress and which to
gloss. He knew what was in the books of course; his industry was
prodigious and he would by now have read them from cover to
cover. But until he knew what his experts were going to say about
the books, he was paralysed. Until then the defence continued to
hold the initiative.

One may ask, though the answer will require a digression, why
the prosecution was not given time off to study the books. I may
say at once that if they had asked for an adjournment, I should
have granted it. It would have been brief, forcing their experts to
work at top speed because trial by jury cannot be held up for long;
and, as far as I know, it would have been unprecedented. At this
time the adjournment for any purpose whatever was as a practice
rather less than a century old. Before that a trial began in the
morning and ended that day, if necessary late at night. Neither
side made any prior disclosure of its case. Some still hold that the
best way of getting at the truth is for the witness to be caught
unprepared and denied the time to concoct. The criminal trial
proceeded on that principle until the beginning of the nineteenth
century. It was not until the statute of 1848 that the accused was
clearly given the right to see in advance the depositions of the
prosecution's witnesses and only by degrees after that was the
prosecution required to give notice of any additional evidence.

The prosecution itself was given no similar relief until 1967 and
then it was limited to cases of alibi. Before that if by chance a
weekend intervened between the accused's examination-in-chief
and the conclusion of his cross-examination, the police would
have time to check his alibi; an overnight interval would give
them time to do something; otherwise falsehood might prevail.
The prosecution always seems to have accepted this as the luck of
the game and made it a matter of machismo to seek no relief. I do

not think that justice should depend on the day of the week. If the prosecution of Dr Adams had been in the hands of inexperienced counsel, I should have offered an adjournment. But the Attorney-General could be expected to look after himself. Anyway I am sure that Reggie would have rejected any implication that he lacked machismo.

To return to the practice. Counsel examining in chief is not free to put what questions he likes. He must not lead and he must accept the witness's answer; to challenge it would be to cross-examine. In this respect defence counsel may be given a limited indulgence but the prosecution is held strictly to the rules. So from time to time one sees in the transcript Mr Lawrence saying, 'I must ask the Attorney-General not to lead', or 'I hope my friend will not try to cross-examine.'

In ordinary talk a leading question is often taken to mean an awkward or a penetrating one. This is not the meaning in law where it is a question which leads to the answer, i.e. is put in a form which suggests the answer that the questioner wants, in terms of the Latin grammar, a *nonne* or a *num* question. A skilful examiner-in-chief would not anyway want to use the blunt leading question: he would want only to tilt the answer: nothing is less convincing than a Yes or No to a set of words framed by the questioner.

The object of the cross-examiner is likewise twofold: to obtain the material he wants and to discredit the adverse witness. He is under no restrictions; he can challenge every answer and lead as much as he likes. He has only one obligation and that is to 'put his case'. If he wants to rely upon a fact which the witness is in a position to qualify or deny, he must give the opportunity.

The rules for examination-in-chief and for re-examination are designed for the favourable witness while cross-examination is for the unfavourable. What about the neutral or independent witness? Or the witness who may be favourable on some points and unfavourable on others? The system is not sufficiently refined to adjust itself to categories. The other side's witness can be cross-examined and your own cannot, except in extreme cases where the judge may give leave for the cross-examination of a hostile witness. Otherwise you must take what your witness gives you, be it good or bad. His deviations from whole-hearted support can only with great difficulty be minimized.

So it may sometimes be a delicate question whether you should call a doubtful witness or leave him in the hope that he will be called by the other side and that you will have the ease of cross-examination where you can suck from him by suggestive questions all that is sweet and, while you can only rarely succeed in having the bitter thrown away, you can nearly always water it down. Likewise, it may be a delicate matter whether to put to an independent witness a crucial question which he may answer one way or the other, or to play safe and leave the answer in doubt.

In these respects in the criminal trial the defendant is given a great advantage. Consistently with his stance as a minister of justice rather than an advocate, counsel for the prosecution must call all the independent witnesses. This meant in the present case all the nurses and all the doctors, even Dr Harris, the partner of the accused. The defence had the advantage of the uninhibited questioning of them all.

The judge is an arbiter, not an inquisitor. He must not run a line of his own. He has no battle to fight. He must not, as the appeal court has several times said, descend into the arena. He is a referee and not a player, but not a mere referee. In relation to the facts of the case as distinct from the law, his power resembles that of a constitutional monarch of the Victorian age. He can ask any question he likes when he likes or he can keep silent until he has to sum up. Complete silence is, however, no more the mark of a good judge than is loquacity. By the discreet use of his power he softens the rigidities of the adversarial process. He can, and often does, ask the question which neither side dares to ask; or the question which one side is not allowed to ask and the other does not want answered.

The judge is never concerned with the presentation of the witness but only with the obtaining of relevant material. The material which counsel wants is that which he would like to use, time permitting, in his final argument. The material which the judge is looking for is what he thinks the jury will need so as to decide the points which he will be putting to them in his summing up. These will be mainly, but not entirely, the points put by counsel. It is their responsibility to produce the evidence and a judge can always tell a jury to do their best with the evidence which counsel has provided. But the helpful judge questions so as to fill the interstices.

If there is an undeveloped subject, I prefer to give it to counsel to explore first. Many witnesses have a subconscious urge to give the judge the answer which they think he wants. For the same reason, although a judge is not bound by the rules, I try never to lead. This can be rather laborious. The witness is inclined to hedge until he thinks he knows what the judge is getting at. The spectator is inclined to say, 'Why not ask him straight out whether . . .'

Because the judge is not a player, he should never, except as first aid, take the ball from counsel. He can break in with a supplementary question which can be briefly answered without interfering with the line that counsel is following. Apart from this, I think that judicial questioning should be left to the end or when counsel is leaving a topic.

Judicial interventions take up proportionately much more space in any summary account than they do in the transcript. This is because a judge is or ought to be questioning only on the most significant points. Rather more than 95 per cent of the questioning as shown on the transcript of this case was by counsel. I should say that this is about normal.

10

The Defence Strikes Again

Wednesday morning. Mr Lawrence opens with a salvo of guns. Miss Randall's luck has not deserted her, for Mrs Mason-Ellis is still in the box and has to take the shock. The target is the custody of the drugs in the dining-room, a topic which I had originated. I had expected the Crown to get from the nurses very precise evidence about the delivery of the drugs prescribed and about how they were kept thereafter. Mr Stevenson had early on the second day got from Nurse Stronach that either they were fetched by Price the chauffeur or delivered by Browne the chemists. He was stopping there, but I wanted to know more.

Judge: Mr Stevenson, I should like to know from some witness sometime—this may not be the right one—what happened to the drugs when they came, where they were put, whether they were kept under lock and key and who had access to them.
Mr S: My lord, I will ask this witness if she knows. When the drugs had either been delivered by Browne's or fetched by Price, do you know what was done with them or where they were kept? Do not tell us if you do not, but if you do know, tell us now.
Nurse S: They were kept in a drawer to the best of my knowledge in the dining-room.
Mr S: Do you know whether it was locked or not?
Nurse S: I think so.

Obviously the prosecution in their preparations had not concerned themselves with the point. Soon after this the books were produced and Lawrence did not pursue the matter in cross-examination. He got it from the nurses that all the injections were recorded in the books; in his view, no doubt, the record superseded any inference to be drawn from the amounts prescribed. I had not in my thinking got as far as that and before she left the box I questioned Nurse Stronach further. Since before the case ended the topic was revived, I shall summarize here the evidence I got.

I asked first about how the prescriptions were written out and dealt with. Nurse Stronach said that the nurses would tell the doctor how the drugs were going and, when he thought it necessary, he would give the nurse a new prescription which she would hand to Price. When the medicine came, usually the same day, Price would bring it to the nurse on duty and she would put it in the cupboard.

Judge: And it was a locked cupboard?
Nurse S: Yes.
Judge: And the nurse had the key?
Nurse S: Oh yes. If we hadn't actually got it, we knew where we had put it. It was perfectly safe.
Judge: Where was it put, then, when the nurse had not got it?
Nurse S: Well, I always kept it in my pocket. I can't answer for other people.
Judge: But then you passed it on to the next nurse?
Nurse S: Yes.
Judge: So that when you wanted to make up a dose of your own, you would go and get the necessary material from the cupboard?
Nurse S: Yes, my lord.
Judge: And then lock it up again?
Nurse S: Yes.
Judge: When Dr Adams came, you told us that he went into the dining-room and you did not go with him. Did you give him the key?
Nurse S: No. If he wanted drugs from the cupboard he would ask for them, but he usually used his own drugs.

She went on to say that during her first spell of duty in June the doctor was using drugs from the cupboard which the nurse got for him. But in October he was using drugs from his own bag.

This was the setting for Mr Lawrence's *coup de théâtre*. We had adjourned on the day before on reaching the end of 1949 in the notes and were ready to embark on 1950. 'Before I ask you to resume looking at your notes,' Mr Lawrence said in a tone pregnant with drama, 'I want just to ask you this.'

A rapid series of questions elicited that the witness together with Nurses Stronach and Randall had last night travelled from Victoria to Eastbourne on the 6.45 train in the same compartment. They had the evening newspapers in front of them and were discussing the reports of the case. Furthermore, all three had that morning travelled back from Eastbourne on the 8.04 train with the morning papers in front of them discussing what was in them. Furthermore, before leaving the Old Bailey, the three of them had been seen by Superintendent Hannam talking together and been reminded of the judge's direction that they were not to discuss the case. Neither of the other two had heard Nurse Stronach's evidence; the rule in a criminal case is that a witness may not come into court until after he or she has given evidence.

How on earth did Mr Lawrence know? Surely the defence could not have had the witnesses trailed! The question was never answered at the trial. I was told the answer some years later. Not long after the 8.04 from Eastbourne arrived at Victoria an anonymous civil servant (other versions say that he was a city stockbroker) with a high sense of public duty rang up the Central Criminal Court and demanded to be put through to the barrister defending Dr Adams. The call was put through to the robing-room and just caught Mr Clarke in time. He got the facts in succinct detail and by 10.30 when the court sat Mr Lawrence was fully armed.

The informant told Mr Clarke that he had been in the same compartment as the nurses when they travelled down to Eastbourne the evening before. He had been so shocked by their discussion of the case that when he saw them the next morning waiting on the platform for the 8.04 he had joined them again. Then he had heard one of them say, 'Don't you say that or you'll get me into trouble.'

Mrs Mason-Ellis agreed that this had been said to her by one of the other nurses. What was it, she was asked, that she was told not to say. The witness's genteel attempt to avert the blow,

Really I cannot remember because I was not terribly interested, if I may say so,

was crushed by

I am not asking you to remember something that happened six years ago as the Attorney-General did yesterday,

and she confessed that there had been a little confusion about the drugs. They were not kept in a locked cupboard but in an unlocked drawer. The key in Nurse Stronach's pocket which she passed on to the next nurse was imaginary.

After this Mr Lawrence resumed 'where I left off yesterday' and made no further capital out of the incident. He put it briefly to Nurse Randall when she was in the box. She agreed about the unlocked drawer and said that it was not her who had said 'Don't you say that'. Certainly it is more probable that this was said by Nurse Stronach who was not summoned back to the box to be confronted with it. It was she who had committed herself to the locked cupboard which the other two were going to repudiate.

The incident left its mark. It displayed the defence as still holding the initiative with the prosecution on the run. It underscored the lesson from the notebooks, showing that even without the written record the fallibility of the nurses could be demonstrated.

Its permanent effect was to establish that the drugs were not securely kept. Whether this was going to matter depended upon whether the prosecution were going to stick to their case that all the drugs prescribed must have been administered. Since they made no effort to repair the damage and had probably by now added up the injections in the notebooks, it looked as if they were going to shift their case from the prescriptions to the recorded treatment.

The incident allowed a glimpse of the prosecution's 'downstairs', including the kitchen. Is it then true that the cases that come into court are cooked by the lawyers? Of course they are, or most of them. It is the nature faddists who have forced a sinister meaning on the verb 'to cook'. There are indeed delicious fruits and vegetables that are best eaten in their natural state and the good cook does not try to improve them. But in general uncooked food is indigestible as well as unpalatable. This is as true of unprocessed evidence. On the Continent the processing is judicial work performed by the *juge d'instruction*: in theory at least this is certainly the best way. In England it is called 'taking the proof of the witness': in Scotland it has the grander name of 'precognoscing'. The task of the proof-taker or precognoscer is like that of the responsible journalist. He is the first person to get the story. He wants it in the speaker's own words but wants it also to be intelligible. The journalist wants it to cover what the public wants to know rather than what the witness wants to say. The lawyer has a similar wish, but his coverage is much more limited: he wants only what is relevant to precise issues.

There is a popular notion that the way to get at the truth is to catch the witness unprepared so that he answers before he has time to think. This may be the right technique for the habitual liar but it flusters the truthful witness. For him or her truth does not arise from the untroubled waters of the mind like Botticelli's Venus naked from the waves. Its successful delivery often needs a midwife. This is not quite the right metaphor. Midwives have to take what comes, while the proof-taker has the temptation to shape the story.

In English litigation generally the person who takes the proof of a potential witness is the solicitor of the party who is going to call the witness. Solicitors are officers of the Court with a high professional standard to maintain; they are also highly trained. But in crime the spadework of investigation is done by the police, that is, the CID of the police force engaged, personified in this case by Superintendent Hannam. The first fruits of its work are the statements which the detective takes from those he interviews. The complete file of statements and exhibits is sent to the Department of Public Prosecutions where a qualified member of the staff prepares the brief to counsel.

Taking the proofs of witnesses six years after the event is not easy. Without some pooling of memories the proof-taker cannot expect to get a complete and accurate account of buried details. To pool memories and at the same time to ensure that the distinct and individual memory is not drowned is a very delicate task. It is probably beyond the powers of the detective, even one as experienced as Superintendent Hannam. The skills required for catching the hare are not the same as those required for cooking it.

Nor can the detective be expected to know exactly what details are necessary to the structure of the proof that has to be built up. In ordinary litigation the papers are sent to counsel for his advice on evidence. One of the Director's officers, a barrister or solicitor, should be responsible for ensuring that the police statements are comprehensive. In this case it is clear that Mr Hannam's attention was never directed to the custody of the drugs, notwithstanding that the Crown case at the outset depended upon proof of strict custody. Thus inadequate preparation led to unnecessary embarrassment.

I do not suppose that the incident took more than a quarter of an hour on the Wednesday morning and after it Sister Mason-Ellis lasted for most of the rest of the day. Then we had Nurse Randall for a day and a half. When the court adjourned for the weekend, we had got more than half of Sister Bartlett's evidence and become very familiar with the notebooks. Before she started her evidence, each nurse had 'refreshed her memory', as the Attorney put it in the customary jargon, from the books. A witness is supposed to speak from memory, not from notes, but may 'refresh the memory' by looking at a note made at the time. In fact by now, with one or two significant exceptions, the nurses were far too circumspect to have any memory left to refresh. 'I pledge my recollection to nothing outside the books,' Sister Mason-Ellis said feelingly on the Wednesday, 'because I couldn't speak truthfully.'

The Attorney examined and re-examined briefly and briskly, referring to particular entries only when he had a point to make. He did not allow himself to be embarrassed by the parts in his opening speech with which the entries did not conform. Mr Lawrence likewise ignored them; there was no longer any point in labouring discrepancies. So the Attorney read out stoically and without comment the entries which marked the collapse of the alternative theory of murder by the two injections on the last night in the large syringe. 'The prosecution cannot tell you,' he had said, 'what these injections were.' But the notebooks could. They were not of heroin or morphia but of paraldehyde, a safe soporific, and only one of them was recorded as administered.

The Attorney had also relied in his speech upon the injections which the doctor gave the patient out of his bag without telling the nurses what they were. The implication was that he was adding secretly to the opiates which the nurses were giving. The books confirmed that 'special injections' were given by the doctor but did nothing much to support the implication. A special injection, Sister Bartlett said, is what the nurse writes down when she knows that an injection has been given but not what it is. Nurse Randall understood that they were vitamin injections. Sister Bartlett once asked and was told that it was a pick-me-up. No one said that Dr Adams ever tried to conceal it. Dr Harris was also noted as giving special injections and, when he came to give evidence, he said that they were vitamin injections. So the point fell flat.

In contrast with the Attorney-General Lawrence read everything out. With each nurse he began with the first of her entries and went right through to the last. He was dealing now with witnesses subdued by the fear of treacherous memory. He needed no longer the *debellare superbos* he had used on Nurse Stronach. Now it was all *parcere subjectis*. He sought the help of the conquered.

Now, you see, I do not understand these things because I am
not a State Registered Nurse, but just tell me . . . am I right in
thinking, as a layman . . .

or

From what we have already heard I should imagine—and I
want you to tell me if I am right or wrong . . .

Of course, if they had told him he was wrong, he would not have
been so agreeable. But the method worked well with Nurse
Randall up to a point and he was talking to her for most of
Thursday. She was supposedly under cross-examination but
really playing the part of the Greek chorus to Lawrence's render-
ing of the notebooks. She was the most important of the nurses
since she had been the night nurse from the beginning and
almost continuously thereafter. What Lawrence was doing was
presenting to the jury the complete picture of the medical treatment for a year and a quarter before death to show how perfectly
normal it was and also how drearily dull. The phantom of the
murderous doctor waiting his chance to come on stage was
retreating further and further from reality. Lawrence could have
done it all solo had the ritual permitted it, like Dickens giving one
of his celebrated renderings. But the punctuating assents of the
nurse enhanced the effect and her occasional demurrings, calling
for some skilful shepherding back to the text, did not diminish it.
On only two points (which I shall mention later) did she do more
than demur.

   We had now the picture of the old lady's decline as it appeared
in the books. She had lived for a surprisingly long time after her
stroke, having her ups and downs, but in general getting neither
better nor worse. For many months she was on what was called
the routine sedation of $\frac{1}{2}$gr. heroin and $\frac{1}{2}$gr. morphia. This was the
hypodermic injection given every evening. She suffered no pain;
the books never mentioned any. This was the point that the
Attorney laboured, his case being, as he had opened it, that
severe pain was the only justification for using opiates. The
defence laboured restlessness and irritability as the justification.
The books recorded occasional 'brainstorms' when Mrs Morrell
became emotional, complained of everything and abused the
nurses. The defence said that this cerebral irritation resulted from
the stroke: the Crown said that the drugging was at least a
contributory factor.

   All were agreed that about the middle of August 1950 the long period on the plateau of routine sedation was coming to an end. The deterioration was accelerated in early September when Dr Adams went on holiday. Mrs Morrell was very angry and told Nurse Randall that she was going to cut him out of her will.

The charts which the Attorney-General had produced during his opening showed the steep increase in the prescriptions of opiates from then on. The notebooks recorded a corresponding increase in injections, though how far they kept pace with the prescriptions was yet to be calculated. In the last six or seven days, 6 to 13 November, during which, as the Attorney had said, the prescriptions of opiates totalled 79½grs., the nurses were given by Dr Adams discretion to administer heroin, at first ½gr. at a time and later 1gr., whenever necessary, which meant whenever she was restless. But the picture which the Attorney had drawn of drugs being pumped into a woman in a coma was not represented in the books.

The two points on which Nurse Randall would not yield, kindness and harshness being equally ineffective, came just before death. First, she would not abate her descriptions of the jerkings and spasms notwithstanding that they went beyond the paucity of language in the books. They were first noted in the night of Friday 10 November. She described them in chief as

> involuntary jerks, just sort of hit out at you with her arms and her legs would come up. . . . They were so bad that I was afraid to leave her. They almost jerked her out of bed.

But in the notebooks, perhaps because with most people words of description flow more freely from the tongue than from the pen, she wrote only of 'shakiness' and 'twitchings'.

Mr Lawrence had eventually to throw in all his reserves and the thunder of them was like the charge of the Imperial Guard at Waterloo.

> *Mr L:* Miss Randall, let us face this. You realize you are giving evidence in a very, very serious matter affecting Dr Adams, don't you?
> *Nurse R:* Yes, sir.
> *Mr L:* Are you standing there in face of this record made on the last night by you, are you standing there and saying, as a trained nurse with 25 or more years' experience, that when you wrote those words 'very shaky' and underlined them on the last night report, that they were intended to mean something

quite different from what they had meant when you used those very words in your earlier reports?

Nurse R: Yes, I do. They were more intense.

Mr L: What was more intense?

Nurse R: The shakiness, or the jerkiness.

Mr L: Ah! but you just told me that the shakiness recorded in your earlier notes had nothing whatever to do with twitchings or jerkiness, didn't you?

Nurse R: No, because they are quite different.

Mr L: What?

Nurse R: Shakiness and jerkiness.

Mr L: Are quite different?

Nurse R: Yes, sir.

Mr L: Well, that is what I thought. Then why, why, if you were recording something quite different on the last night, in the peace and quiet of what was then the room in which Mrs Morrell had died, why did you use the same words?

Nurse R: I just don't know. I suppose I wrote it down quickly.

Mr L: You suppose you just wrote it! Let me suggest the reason why you used the same words and underlined them. The reason was that you then, six years ago, were describing the same condition of shakiness that you had described months before, but that it was greater in degree but still the same kind of thing. That is the reason, isn't it?

Nurse R: I can only remember how very dreadful they were, the jerks.

Mr L: That is what you say now, but at the time you only put down 'very shaky', didn't you?

Nurse R: Yes. Well, I probably wrote it just as I was going off or something.

Mr L: But do you remember whether you did or not?

Nurse R: Well, I must have written it, yes.

Mr L: Well, of course. You don't remember whether you wrote it just as you were going off, do you?

Nurse R: I don't remember, no. I know I didn't write it at the time, because my time was occupied with the patient.

Mr L: You wrote it before you left the house that morning, didn't you?

Nurse R: I must have done.

Judge: Have you got now, apart from what is written down in the book, a clear recollection in your mind of her being jerky an hour and a half before she died?

Nurse R: I have. I never want to see anything like it again.

She was describing then the jerks on the last night. The recollection of them was coupled with the recollection of the two injections which she had given just before death. It was because of the continued jerkiness, she said, that she gave the second injection. Although she had not recorded it in the book, she was adamant that she gave it. Mr Lawrence fought this too. But since she had recorded the first as paraldehyde (though apart from the record she said that she had no recollection of what it was), and since by that time the patient was on the verge of death, it did not seem to matter whether she gave it or not. Except perhaps to her. She said impromptu (it was not admissible in evidence and the Attorney said sharply that he had not asked her 'that last bit'): 'Mrs Morrell told me that Dr Adams had promised her he wouldn't let her suffer at the end.'

Miss Randall finished her evidence at midday on Friday 22 March and she was followed after the adjournment by Sister Bartlett. She was the young and pretty girl who had joined the older nurses for the last three months. Someone, I think, must have told her that she ought to wear a hat in court and she had done the best she could with a skiing cap. It came down over her ears and interfered with reception, while her soft voice made her difficult to hear. This combination of circumstances led during her cross-examination to a tactful interchange

> *Mr L:* . . . and she was not so drowsy apparently?
> *Sister B:* Can I take my hat off, sir, because I can't hear properly. Is it permissible to take my hat off?
> *Mr L:* That is a question that should be addressed to my lord. My lord, the witness is asking if she may remove her hat because she does not hear very well with it on.
> *Judge:* Oh yes, certainly; and if at any time you find yourself getting tired and want to sit down, do so. But as long as you can stand, I think your voice carries better.
> *Sister B:* Thank you very much.
> *Mr L:* And will you realize that not only I over this side of the court want to hear what you say, but the ladies and gentlemen to your right want to hear it even more, so will you keep your voice up?
> *Sister B:* Yes, I will.

During the day, uncertain about whether it was going to be of any importance, I pressed on with my inquiries about the custody of the drugs. More information came from Sister Mason-Ellis. They came in phials or tubes. 'Little tiny thin tubes, very, very thin like a straw that one drinks from, and they are very, very small tablets and you dissolve them in a spoon with a very small amount of water over heat, or boiling water if you can get it.' Mr Lawrence had already ascertained that there was what the nurses called a 'hypodermic tray'. The different phials, heroin, morphia and omnopon, and also the other drugs that were used such as sedormid and atropine, were kept on the tray with the syringe. When not in action, the tray was kept in the unlocked drawer.

Nurses are required, Sister Mason-Ellis said, to keep a record of the drugs that come under the Dangerous Drugs Act. 'We are most scrupulous about this, because it is a very important matter for the nursing profession.' The record was kept on what she called 'a special paper'; as one sheet was filled, another was pasted on; one got the impression of a mediaeval roll. When a tablet was taken, the number left was written down. When a phial was nearing the end, the nurse would tell the doctor and he would give a new prescription. Normally this would be sent down to the kitchen (but the doctor 'might take it himself if he were passing') for collection and return through the usual channels. Specimen phials were exhibited and shown to the jury.

After the death the nurse on duty (who, as Sister Mason-Ellis prudently pointed out, was not herself) would hand the record to the doctor together with the drugs left over so that they could be checked up. Later, in evidence, Nurse Randall described the documentation more summarily as 'a little something' which told how much was left in the phial.

The nurse who did the handing over was Sister Bartlett. She was on day duty at the time of the death but was spending the night at Marden Ash. So she was present at the deathbed and took over the next morning and, after Nurse Randall left, was there when Dr Adams came.

There should by this time, if both the list of prescriptions, Ex. 4A, and the notebooks were correct, have been accumulated at Marden Ash substantial quantities of uninjected heroin and morphia, a valuable prize in the black market for anyone who could make away with them as perks. While none of the nurses looked as if she could be capable of that, it was fortunate that the most incapable-looking undoubtedly was Sister Bartlett. Early in the cross-examination she had exhibited a delightful ingenuousness. It had become Lawrence's custom to obtain from each nurse a declaration of her pleasure and relief at the survival of the notebooks. Hitherto it had been promptly rendered. But it took him fourteen questions, ending with a fervent 'I quite agree', to get it from Sister Bartlett. She simply could not understand what he was driving at. The extract is worth giving, for it illustrates that Mr Lawrence could be rather tedious as well as thorough in pursuit of minor objectives.

Mr L: Are you, like Sister Mason-Ellis, glad to know that they have survived?

Sister B: Well, I don't know that I have really thought about it. I don't think I quite . . .

Mr L: Perhaps you do not understand the question. Let me make it more plain. You realize that Dr Adams is standing his trial on a charge of murdering Mrs Morrell, don't you?

Sister B: Yes.

Mr L: And you realize that it is alleged that he killed her deliberately by means of drugs?

Sister B: Yes.

Mr L: And you always have known that before you gave evidence at Eastbourne, haven't you?

Sister B: I don't know, sir.

Mr L: What did you think he was at Eastbourne for?

Sister B: Oh, I see what you mean. Yes, sir.

Mr L: At Eastbourne you had to depend upon your memory, didn't you, as to what had happened six years before?

Sister B: Yes.

Mr L: For the purpose of giving evidence on oath for the prosecution against Dr Adams. That is so, isn't it?

Sister B: Yes.

Mr L: Now you know that the records that you personally as a nurse made day after day at the time in 1950 have survived?

Sister B: Yes.

Mr L: So that we can all look at them?

Sister B: Yes.

Mr L: So that therefore we can find out from day to day what you put down when everything was fresh in your mind?

Sister B: Yes.

Mr L: So we probably can get from those reports, cannot we, the truth as to what happened?

Sister B: Yes.

Mr L: My reason for suggesting that, like the other nurses, you may be glad to know they have survived is that you might be glad to know that, in such a serious matter affecting Dr Adams, people have not got to rely on their memories after six years

and are glad to have the records that were made at the time?
Sister B: Yes, I quite agree.
Mr L: Do you see what I mean now?
Sister B: Yes.
Mr L: And you quite agree, don't you?
Sister B: Yes, I quite agree.

The extract shows that during the intervening six years Sister Bartlett had, very naturally, given little or no thought to the case. Nurse Randall, she said, handed to her some drugs which were left over, but beyond that her memory was very hazy. A phial of morphia and one of heroin or omnopon, she thought; whether full or empty, she could not say. There was a record of drugs kept on a slip of paper, but she did not know what happened to it; quite possibly she tore it up. Nurse Randall had been even vaguer; she handed over what was left, but that was all she could say.

Atropine, 20 tablets, had been prescribed and delivered on 6 November, that is, a week before death. It was intended apparently for a mucus in the patient's throat. But it was also an antidote—a very weak one, Douthwaite said—to morphia. Lawrence called attention to it with the suggestion that a murderer would be unlikely to prescribe any sort of antidote to his chosen poison. Atropine is a restricted drug; so the 20 tablets should have been carefully dispensed. But it was not a marketable drug that anyone would have been interested in purloining. Lawrence took it as a useful example of the natural fate of drugs in the Marden Ash sickroom. With Sister Bartlett's aid he traced in the notebook that 10 only had been given to the patient. What had happened to the rest?

They must have been on the tray, the witness thought. If they were still there at the end, they would have been handed to the doctor; but that was all she could say.

But was any of this going to matter? Not much if the Crown was going to accept as complete the record of the injections in the books. But then what *was* going to matter? We were still waiting for a revised account of how the murder was committed. I was beginning to lose interest in all the pre-November details that had filled the week.

Public interest, however, did not diminish and the Sheriffs' seats behind counsel in the well of the court were all occupied. These seats are the equivalent of the Royal Box at Wimbledon and, as the Sheriffs are always very kind about finding places for the judge's friends, my wife and my clerk were kept busy with applications. On the last two rested also the responsibility for supplying the press with irrelevant and harmless information and refusing interviews and photographs. I was myself unwilling to alter my habit of walking morning and evening from and to our flat in Gray's Inn. For the first few days this was quite safe since the main flow of dramatis personae approached the Old Bailey from the Temple, but later I was caught once or twice. I find that, when cornered, it is better to submit than to make a fuss. So there is, or was, in the files of Fleet Street a picture of a 'human' judge signing an autograph for a small boy.

11

A Meditative Weekend

The court is adjourned till Monday morning. For me that means a weekend in the country. On Friday, the usual evening chore, the reading and marking of the transcript, can be postponed until Saturday. During the hearing I write down only the heads of the evidence, i.e. the topic that is being examined, and perhaps a phrase used. Then after dinner the transcript arrives and with a small glass of brandy and a large cigar I go through it, turning my note into an index to the transcript by giving each item its page number.

Now I did this on the Saturday, notwithstanding a strong feeling that it would never be wanted. The odds were, I thought, that on Monday morning the Attorney-General would throw in his hand. Everything now depended on his medical experts. They were, we knew, ready to say that $78\frac{3}{4}$ grs. of opiates, i.e. the quantity prescribed for the last six days less what was left over after death, meant *and could only mean* murder; or, as the doctors usually preferred to say (quite rightly, since murder was not a question for them) accelerated death. No one had as yet openly totted up the quantity shown in the notebooks to have been injected during the last six days, but I think it must have been the general guess—it certainly was mine—that it would be something substantially less. Would the experts be prepared to say the same about the lesser quantity? It is the words italicized that are so difficult. High probability is not enough: the stern demand of the law is for practical certainty. Nor is it enough for the expert to say: 'Myself I am quite certain, but I concede that another view might reasonably be held.' For, if another view might reasonably be held and the accused swears that he held it, how can he be said beyond reasonable doubt to have intended to kill?

Suppose that it could be so said. The affirmative answer would not make certain victory for the Crown. Even if Dr Adams was forced to admit that he knew that the doses were large enough to kill, the Crown would still have to tackle his plea that all that he was doing was 'easing the passing' in a case of inevitable death.

I had in my early days at the Bar, before I succumbed to the monetary attractions of commercial litigation, seen some work in the criminal field. In 1930 I had devilled for the Attorney-General of the day when he prosecuted at Lewes Assizes Sidney Fox for the murder of his mother by asphyxiation. There Sir Bernard Spilsbury, the leading Home Office pathologist, who never admitted to a doubt, had spoken with the voice of doom. In the following year I was junior counsel for the Crown at the trial of Mrs Hearn who was acquitted at Bodmin Assizes of murder by arsenic poisoning. Dr Roche Lynch was then the Home Office analyst; he was a little less inflexible than Spilsbury, but not much. These two were professional witnesses, nearly always for the prosecution, and they knew how to put it to a jury that theirs was the only possible view. So far as I knew, neither Doctors Douthwaite nor Ashby had given evidence in a murder trial before. It could not, I thought, have been easy in the first place to get them to commit themselves to the 78¾ grains of opiates as being necessarily murderous. Now they were to be suddenly confronted with a reduced figure. They would be like contractors who had quoted a price and then been given a weekend in which to say whether they would lower it by, say, a third.* I thought that they would be bound to refuse.

For the Attorney-General this would not be palatable. He was not the man for hauling down any sort of flag at any time and certainly not this one at this time. It was known that he intended to assert vigorously his claim to be the next Lord Chief Justice of England. As a claim it was not at all concerned with his merits which in relation to so great a judicial post could fairly be said to be negligible: what he was claiming was the time-honoured reward for political services.

Until 1880 there were two chief justices heading respectively the Courts of Queen's Bench and of Common Pleas. The former was the superior; its precedence was recognized in 1859 when its head was given the title of Lord Chief Justice of England. An attorney-general could hope for the Queen's Bench and

---

* This was just my guess at the time. In fact they were required to say that 30 out of the 78¾ grains would do.

frequently obtain it. But his incontestable claim, classified as 'from time immemorial', was to the 'cushion' (the word was coined in the conversation of the legal fraternity to express the comfort the place afforded to superannuated attorneys-general) of the Common Pleas. When that court was abolished in 1880, the Attorney-General's claim was transferred to and fixed upon the higher office that remained. Thereafter the demand had been honoured on five occasions and denied on none.

On two of these occasions the successful applicant had had to rely wholly or mainly upon the strength of his claim. The first of these was in 1913 when Sir Rufus Isaacs was appointed. He was well fitted for the place but, had he not had a claim, his indiscretion in the Marconi scandal in the same year would probably have prevented his being considered. The other appointment was when Lord Reading, as Sir Rufus had become, retired in 1921. The incumbent Attorney-General, Sir Gordon Hewart, insisted on his claim to the point of having the place kept warm for him for some months until it was politically convenient for him to take it. The senior puisne judge, Lawrence (with whom our Geoffrey was not connected), was appointed to fill the gap and sat until he saw his own resignation in *The Times*.

Hewart, who had towards the end of his term the misfortunes of ill health to contend with as well as those of his temperament, clung to office until 1940. While his appointment afforded the best technical support for Reggie's claim, his conduct in office was the worst advertisement for it. He has been called the worst chief justice since Scroggs and Jeffreys in the seventeenth century. I do not think that this is quite fair. When one considers the enormous improvement in judicial standards between the seventeenth and twentieth centuries, I should say that, comparatively speaking, he was the worst chief justice ever. When it first became known that Reggie would press his claim, many who would have tolerated the continuance of a custom that produced unobjectionable men, were stimulated into firm opposition by the thought of Hewart. This may have been hard on Reggie, but the fact is that, whether at their best or worst, neither man had a grain of judicial sense.

When Hewart went in 1940, he was succeeded by Lord Caldecote, a former attorney-general. When he went in 1946, the new Socialist government headed by Mr Attlee had been in office for only a few months. The Attorney-General was Sir Hartley Shawcross, a stripling of forty-three. He made no claim to the succession: with his prospects the office could not at that excessively youthful age have attracted him and he entirely disapproved of a political claim to it. It was in these circumstances that a successor was sought from the judiciary and the choice fell upon Lord Goddard, then a Lord of Appeal in Ordinary. While the speculation about the new appointment was going on, I had wondered whether Rayner, active though he was, would at the age of sixty-nine want to forsake for the highway the meadows of the House of Lords and had asked him if he would take the job. He did not say that, if asked, he would regard it as his duty to serve: he said: 'Who wouldn't?'

Rayner's appointment was not then generally seen as a new development; it was taken more as an exceptional measure to meet a rare situation. So when in 1951 Walter Monckton was denied the office of Attorney-General because he was wanted as Minister of Labour, he did not have to suppress his ambition to be Lord Chief Justice. Mr Churchill promised him the reversion —worth having when the man in possession was seventy-four—and the promise was renewed by the two succeeding prime ministers in their turns.

So when Reggie became Attorney-General in 1954, the succession was already pledged and there was no immediate cause for alarm and despondency. But neither was there any vacancy: Rayner in action remained at least ten years younger than his official age. In February 1957 Walter, now sixty-six, joined the Board of the Midland Bank and soon after became its chairman. It was thus and then, just as the Adams trial was about to begin, that the trumpet sounded for Reggie to make his claim.

It did not get a good press. Even if it had been well received, it would not have been allowed to end speculation. The succession to high legal office has been a matter for newspaper gossip and rumour since the time of Lord Mansfield. The press, which had for two or three years been waiting for Goddard to go, could not now permit a walkover. Other competitors must be found, the qualification obviously being newsworthiness rather than legal learning. In the former just at that moment I excelled. With a *cause célèbre* coming on, what could be a better diversion during the doldrums than to watch two of the favourites exercising on the same gallops? The columnists got to work and were often nasty about Reggie, while I enjoyed the immunity proper to one venturing out of the zenana of the judiciary. I have a letter from Reggie about this time answering what seems to have been a PS of condolence from me. He was hardened to them by now, he wrote, but they did disturb his family. He bore all the snides and sneers with great fortitude, the more creditable in that he is not likely to have allowed himself to be strengthened by the thought that he had brought many of them upon himself.

The columnists had, though I do not suppose they knew it, some solid ground for their fanciwork in that I was at this time the man whom Rayner wanted to succeed him. If only they had known it, a scenario of 170 years before was being deliciously reconstructed. In 1787 the long reign of Chief Justice Mansfield was drawing to an end in a cloud of newspaper speculation. He was known to favour as his successor Mr Justice Buller. Francis Buller had been made a judge ten years before at the early age of thirty-two. He was the prop of the old Chief's declining years and a great friend as well, to whom Lord Mansfield left a legacy of £2,000 'to be laid out in some small token'.

But Sir Lloyd Kenyon, who had become Attorney-General in 1782, claimed the place. In 1784 he had taken the Mastership of the Rolls, while continuing, it was said, to give political support to the Prime Minister, the younger Pitt, who, it was also said, when appointing him to the Rolls, had offered him the reversion, very valuable at Mansfield's age of seventy-nine, of the higher place. Buller was the better man. Kenyon is described as an industrious and able lawyer, but 'mean and boorish, and wholly lacking in refinement'. Mansfield held out for as long as he could. Then on 5 June 1788, 'under pressure of bodily infirmities which made it my duty to retire', he signed a deed of resignation. The political claimant got the place.

Exoriare aliquis nostris ex ossibus ultor. So Mr Justice Buller, who was said to have been severely disappointed, might have thundered. For I am sure that an eighteenth-century judge would have had the Aeneid, book 4, line 625 at his fingertips. What subtler form of avenger could there be arising from the Buller bones than a great-great-great-great-grandson who would become Attorney-General, assert his claim with the brutality of Kenyon and crush the Chief Justice's nominee?

Alas, history repeats itself only up to a point. As so often, Rayner changed his mind and his last judgment was wiser than his first. He was most scrupulous to tell me how he had come to change it. This, however, was nearly a year later. In the spring of 1957 and for a little time thereafter I was in the public eye as the challenger to Reggie.

12

Motive:
The Lawyer and the Police

Back to court on Monday morning. The half-expected announcement from Reggie that he could proceed no further was not
forthcoming. The examination of Sister Bartlett continued pla-
cidly. Her evidence was finished a little before midday. Then a
sign was vouchsafed.

When the first police witness was called, Mr Lawrence rose to
say that he had expected to hear first the medical evidence of
which he had received notice of additional evidence. The knowledgeable would rightly interpret the notice to mean that the
doctors had adapted their evidence to the new situation. The
Lawrence's preparation for questioning witnesses must have
been meticulous; he was put out by any variation in the expected
order of calling. He accepted the suggestion that he should put
off his cross-examination of Inspector Pugh until the next day.

I had found the notice on my desk when I got to the Old Bailey
that morning. I had looked at once at a new Exhibit 55 which
contrasted for the last five days the quantities shown in the
notebook as injected with those prescribed. Of 41grs. morphia
prescribed only 10½ had been administered; of 37¾ of heroin only
16. The quantities in the notebook, Dr Douthwaite said in his new
statement, were enough to make death certain: those prescribed
would have made it 'even more certain'. Dr Ashby, who in his
deposition had said that there was not 'the faintest possible doubt
that, if the patient had received even a large part of the total drugs
prescribed in the last five days, she would have died', did not in
his new statement deal specifically with this period. His statement was that the medication shown in the books after 4 November could only result in death.

So now we knew that the case would go on. It would be murder by successive overdoses as shown in the books, beginning on or about 5 November. The evidence of the Crown experts, when it came, would show *how* by this means Dr Adams murdered Mrs Morrell. But the Crown had also undertaken to show *why*. On this the chief witness, the man who proved the legacies in the will, was Mrs Morrell's solicitor, Mr Sogno, the senior partner in Lawson, Lewis & Co. of Eastbourne and evidently a busy man. He was not available on the Monday morning. The Crown had to start the police evidence and interpose him when he arrived after the midday adjournment.

I awaited his evidence with interest. The Attorney-General had left the Crown's case on motive in some confusion. He had told us that in August 1950 Mrs Morrell made a will leaving to the doctor the chest of silver, the Rolls-Royce and the Elizabethan cupboard. But under the will the last two of these three items were to come to the doctor only if her son, Mr Claude Morrell, predeceased her; the possibility of this was so remote that the bequests could not be regarded as more than a complimentary mention. Then on 15 September she revoked by codicil all her gifts to the doctor. Two months later the doctor murdered Mrs Morrell because, the Attorney had said, he had decided that the time had come for her to die. According to the Attorney, Dr Adams knew that she was not carrying out her promise to leave him the Rolls-Royce and 'may have felt it best' that she should not make any further alterations to her will. Did this mean that Dr Adams did not know of the codicil striking him out of it? The answer to that, the Attorney had told the jury, 'you may perhaps discover in the course of this trial'. Was Mr Sogno now going to tell us?

Mr Sogno said that he was first instructed in 1947. Mrs Morrell, it appeared, was a compulsive will-maker. She made one on 25 February 1947, another on 25 October of the same year, and another on 8 October 1948 which was altered by codicil on 19 March 1949. The last two dispositions did not mention Dr Adams whose treatment of her had begun in July 1948; evidently he was still on probation. But by April 1949 she was discussing her will with him at those tête-à-têtes when no nurse was present and when he was giving the vitamin injection and which lasted, Sister Bartlett said, for about a quarter of an hour. On 28 April 1949 the doctor conveyed to Mr Sogno a summons to the bedside to make a new will. Eventually on 9 June 1949 the new will was executed, the one in which the doctor was first rewarded with the chest of silver.

This must have been Mrs Morrell's notion, rather than his, of what was a suitable memento for him. What he wanted, and what he was getting around this time in legacies often in four figures, was tax-free cash. The chest turned out to have a probate value of £276 5s. At the time of the trial the doctor had it in his house, much of it still wrapped in tissue paper. As the fruit of a year's work and out of an estate of £157,000 it was disappointing. Lawrence contrasted it effectively with

> a whole series of personal legacies . . . four of £1,000 and one of £500 before we reach Dr Adams at all . . . Then Miss Randall £300 . . . the chauffeur £1,000 . . . The gardener £500 and all the dahlia plants.

Then there were six legacies to various charities, ranging from £100 to £1,000.

It was another nine months before the doctor was able to make any further progress. On 8 March 1950 there occurred the conversation between Dr Adams and Mr Sogno which the latter described as 'in several respects, in my experience unique'. Mrs Morrell, the doctor said, had forgotten about the Rolls-Royce she had promised him. She wanted him to have it; also a box of jewellery at the bank; he had been to the bank to make sure the box was there. She was, he said, in a fit condition to make a codicil or a new will. Mr Sogno suggested that, as the gifts were of great value, the matter should wait until her son came at the weekend. Adams replied that Mrs Morrell was very uneasy and wanted to get the matter off her mind. He suggested that the codicil should be executed and then destroyed if Mr Claude Morrell did not approve. Quite impossible, the lawyer said.

This led to a further bout of will-making, first a codicil of 19 July 1950, then a will of 5 August 1950 and finally the will of 24 August 1950 which was the one admitted to probate. But the only firm bequest which Dr Adams got under that will was the chest of silver which he had already been given in 1949. The Rolls-Royce was contingent on the son dying first. Nothing more was heard of the box of jewellery.

This evidence did two things. First, it created a very unpleasant impression of Dr Adams as a legacy hunter, not the less unpleasant because the hunt was so unsuccessful. Mr Lawrence could do nothing about that: Mr Sogno had recorded the conversations at the time in the usual solicitor's fashion and they were unchallengeable. Second, the evidence dissipated the Crown's theory of the doctor who bartered for legacies prescriptions of heroin. So abject a failure after two years of prescribing was too much to swallow. The picture that emerged of Mrs Morrell was not that of the helpless addict but of the tough old lady accustomed to the skilful use of her wealth to get what she wanted. The picture was illuminated by her drastic reprisal to the doctor's audacity in taking a holiday without her permission. This was not the revenge of an addict whose supply was cut off; she got from Dr Harris, who took Adams's place, as much as, if not more than, she had been getting from Adams. On 12 September she summoned Mr Sogno by telephone. His evidence was that she was very angry, but Mr Lawrence wisely declined his offer to repeat what she said. Rejecting the lawyer's advice, she instructed him to prepare a codicil cutting the doctor out of her will. He did so and she executed it the next day. The solicitor sent it to Mr Morrell who was the executor and who kept his mother's will.

So what now was the motive for the murder and how did the Crown prove it? The reader must follow me into a legal labyrinth from the end of which the motive emerges in an attenuated form.

Some time in October Dr Adams must have been restored to favour. The codicil was torn up and on 23 October Mr Sogno received the pieces from Mr Claude Morrell. Mrs Morrell doubtless thought, as anybody but a lawyer would, that the destruction of the codicil put back into the will the legacy which the codicil had revoked. Not so. The law cannot be treated so brusquely. The codicil had taken effect and had expelled Dr Adams from the will. Its validity did not depend upon the paper on which it was written. The pieces could be put together again; or what the law calls 'secondary evidence' could be given of its contents. The proper way of getting rid of the codicil, so Mr Sogno advised, was by the execution of a new codicil with all the solemnity of full attestation, that is, with new signatures by the testator and the witnesses, which would make the bequest all over again. I do not suppose that in late October Mrs Morrell was in a condition to be bothered with this. So Mr Sogno devised an ingenious alternative.

No one can claim under a will that has not been admitted to probate, that is to say, is not proved to be a valid will. The will of 24 August 1950 would be submitted to the probate registry by Mr Claude Morrell as the executor. He would normally also submit the codicil of 13 September since it varied the contents of the will: that it was presented in pieces would not affect its validity. If Mr

Morrell as executor had failed to prove the codicil, any residuary legatee could have required him to do so because, by cutting out Dr Adams, the residue was increased by £276 5s. But, as it happened, Mr Morrell was the sole residuary legatee as well as the sole executor; consequently the probate registrar ruled that there was no need for him to prove the codicil if he did not want to do so. Thus the only document admitted to probate was the will containing the legacy of the chest of silver.

Did then Dr Adams get the chest under the will or did he get it, as the defence contended, by the grace and favour of Mr Morrell? A nice legal point, but not one that matters. For this was all in proof of motive and motive can exist only in the mind. If a man holds the mistaken belief that he will inherit a million pounds, it is as good a motive for murdering the supposed testator as if his belief was correct. It is quite clear that, if Adams thought that the death of Mrs Morrell would give him the Rolls-Royce, he thought wrong. But what has to be ascertained is not what the will said but what Adams thought it said. It was the police who had interviewed him who had the evidence about that.

Thus the case for the prosecution had now taken shape as one of the oddest in the history of celebrated murder trials. Both method and motive were to be proved by statements by the accused made in friendly conversation with the police. What he said about method was contradicted by the other facts proved by the prosecution. What he said about the will was what he thought it gave him when in fact the whole legal testament, the will being only the major part of it, gave him nothing.

Even when unencumbered by the codicil, the will did not give Dr Adams the Rolls-Royce. That bequest was contingent on Mr Claude Morrell's pre-decease, which did not occur. Mr Morrell solved that problem with tact and without the knowledge of Mr Sogno. He simply instructed the chauffeur to take the car round to the doctor, who doubtless believed, as he was to tell the police six years later, that he had got it under the will.

When the police evidence was tendered at the trial, Lawrence rose almost at once to make his objections. He prefaced them with an exordium which showed that he was still on behalf of his client labouring under a sense of persecution. He hoped that he might say without impropriety

> that in this particular case above all others, it is essential in the interests of justice that nothing except that which is directly

relevant to the issue should be allowed in, and anything which is of a prejudicial nature and not relevant or only faintly relevant, should be excluded. I hope it is not necessary for me to rehearse before your lordship the reason why I single out this case for a submission of that kind. But it may very well be a matter within your lordship's own knowledge that this is a case where, naturally, for the defence I desire to keep the issue closely confined to the indictment which I have to meet, not for my own selfish purposes alone, but in order to secure that there should be a fair trial on this indictment without extraneous matters of a prejudicial nature being introduced into it. There has been enough and more than enough, if I may say so, in the past.

This, of course, was not in the presence of the jury. I dare say that Lawrence needed to say it in order to relieve his feelings, but it was not as a matter of advocacy a wise introduction. When a deployment of more precise arguments shows that an issue is hanging in the balance, considerations like these may be used to tilt it. But, thrown into the battle at the outset, they suggest a shortage of sharper weapons. As it turned out, there was no shortage and Lawrence succeeded on almost the whole of his submission. As for me, whatever I might do about countering prejudice would not take the form of incorrect rulings on the admission of evidence.

I was by now an admirer of Lawrence's forensic skill. The skill is exhibited not only in the effective use of word and manner, whether in speech or in questioning, but also in the strategy and tactics of presentation. Lawrence had already shown himself to be a master of questioning and was to show himself as a good forensic orator and a master of strategy. Only in one respect was he inferior to Reggie and that was in tactical sense. Reggie always seemed to know just how and when to intervene and to do it briefly and 75 per cent effectively. I say 75 per cent because success depended entirely on his first statement. He had no flexibility. He put a point crisply, but it was no use asking him any question about it because he could then only repeat himself. He reminded me of the sergeant-major at my school OTC who, when the response to the word of command was not to his satisfaction, could only repeat the passage from the drill book. This was not always incomprehensible, but the text sometimes suggested alternative possibilities which were distracting. A piece about 'carrying the body forward with the feet' with its evocation of a trunk left behind in the air lingers in my memory. Reggie was not quite anchored to the drill book. But he could not devise variations to an argument once he had, as it were, tabled it.

I have suggested that it was perhaps a mistake on Lawrence's part to press so heavily on the ill-treatment of his client in an argument on a point of law. I do not suggest that the sense of ill-usage was unjustified. The inadmissible evidence which the Crown introduced in the magistrates' court was not confined to the major importation of the two Hullett cases which Reggie had abandoned; there were other minor importations. The police had been pursuing two lines of inquiry. One led to the drug charges on which Adams was arrested on 26 November and the other to the murder charge on which he was arrested on 19 December. There was a junction of the two lines at the occasion on 24 November when Hannam and Pugh searched the doctor's house. They got then the evidence that supported the drug charges. They got also the admission, vital for the murder charge, that Adams had himself administered all that he had prescribed.

To evidence of the admission Lawrence could not and did not object. But he objected to all the other evidence as irrelevant to the murder charge. Clearly it was. To show that the doctor was careless or even fraudulent about drugs does not help to prove that he was a murderer. No principle is more important in the criminal law of evidence than the general rule that at the trial nothing discreditable shall be said of the accused unless it is offered in proof of the offence for which he is being tried. To discredit without proof is to smear.

Nevertheless, the whole of the evidence on the search, as I have recounted it in an earlier chapter, was admitted and published at Eastbourne. It was of course all one incident. The argument, I suppose, would have been that it could not without distortion have been split up. I do not think that that argument would have succeeded. Neither apparently did the Attorney-General. For when Lawrence had concluded his submission, Reggie pointed out that he had not in his opening address referred to the evidence objected to and said that in fact he was not going to use it. So it was all excluded and there went with it sundry references to other patients' wills, etc., which were irrelevant to the murder of Mrs Morrell. All that was left of the objection was one small point which Reggie did not concede, namely, the remark by the accused that he seldom used opiates.

So there was a short argument about that, which led incidentally to an interesting sidelight. The case for the prosecution was that the quantity used by Dr Adams was excessive and unnecessary. If in the box he disagreed with that, he could be asked whether he had used such quantities before. True, he might have changed his views since 1950, but the answer was one that he could be asked to explain. I could not, I said to Mr Lawrence, exclude the question in cross-examination of Dr Adams and I could not therefore stop the Attorney-General from laying a foundation for it.

This implied that the defence would be putting the accused in the box. Lawrence said that he could not commit himself 'with regard to the future course that this case may take'; it was too early for him to give any indication about that. I did not treat this as more than the non-committal answer which it is usually prudent for defence counsel to give about his plans.

I admitted the evidence, ruling that it was relevant as going to show 'whether it was or was not the usual practice of Dr Adams to use drugs of this character'.

It is easier now than it was then to understand Lawrence's distress. Here we have a repetition on a minor scale of the introduction and withdrawal of the Hullett allegations. There was no reason why the prosecution should not have made up their minds before the committal proceedings instead of after them that they were not going to tender the evidence about the search. At the trial Reggie did not even attempt to bring it in. He said simply: 'I respectfully agree with my learned friend that that part of this deposition has no bearing on this case.' The publication of this inadmissible evidence merited another black mark for the Crown.

But I doubt if the addition of a drug offence to the couple of Hullett murders did the defence any serious harm. Indeed, with hindsight I wondered whether the evidence would not have been more useful to the defence than harmful. Was it good tactics for Lawrence to keep it out? Might it not have helped to explain the 'admission' that all the drugs prescribed had been used? When Adams volunteered this, he knew that he had in the cupboard which the police would be searching left-overs from two cases. If what he then feared was a charge not of murder but of a drug offence, the so-called admission could be seen more truly as a false exculpation from the minor charge.

The police evidence sounded convincing and what they reported Adams as saying would have to be explained somehow.

The best way of explaining it would be to show that Adams was flustered and frightened when he said it. The incident would show what was frightening him. Possibly it was known to the jury anyway since it had been reported in all the papers. Moreover, a drug offence of some sort was to be inferred from what had come out at the trial. The fact that his house had been searched for drugs on 24 November and that on 26 November he had been arrested on 'certain charges' told the jury that he was in trouble. If they had been told that the particular trouble was that he had been hanging on to left-overs and failing to keep a proper register, they would hardly have treated it as evidence of murder; they might even have had some sympathy for the doctor in his humiliation.

But Lawrence may well have asked himself whether the 'admission' any longer mattered now that the notebooks had replaced the prescriptions as the evidence of what was injected. Moreover, in 1957 the tradition was strong that the accused should be supposed immaculate; it would have been thought rash for counsel to disdain the protection of the statute that forbade any aspersions upon his character.

There were two further conversations between Hannam and Adams which the Attorney-General had mentioned and which were now put in evidence — 'easing the passing' on 26 November and the remarks at the time of the arrest on 19 December. In cross-examination Lawrence handled all the interviews in a gingerly fashion. He suggested that Hannam had himself done all the talking and that Adams had said little or nothing. This sounded wildly improbable. 'He was most loquacious, and always has been since I have known him,' Hannam replied.

The most interesting feature was the 'Murder, can you prove it?' on the day of the arrest. When he mentioned this in opening, the Attorney had asked the jury whether it was what they would expect an innocent man to say or was it 'what a man might say if he had committed a murder but thought he had done it so cleverly that his guilt could not be proved'. In cross-examination both Hannam and Pugh put a different colour on it.

> *Mr L:* The inflexion of the voice on that word 'murder' was interrogative, wasn't it?
> *Supt:* Now, sir, I think it is only fair to say this: Dr Adams was a very, very shaken man indeed, and I am not going to suggest that there was any inflexion of any kind. I think he was very distressed.

Mr L: I think we can leave it in that way. It was quite obvious that your announcement of your arrest for murder was a shock?

Supt: It certainly was. He was very shaken.

This was Hannam. It encouraged Lawrence to probe a little further into Pugh's evidence.

Mr L: I thought I caught from the way you mentioned it yesterday that after he had been charged with murder and cautioned, he said 'murder' interrogatively?

Pugh: Yes, that is correct.

Mr L: Then there was a pause, we have been told by the Superintendent, of a few seconds?

Pugh: Yes, there was a pause.

Mr L: And he was looking at the Superintendent all the time, wasn't he?

Pugh: Well, when he said on the first occasion 'Murder?', he was looking at the Superintendent. The Superintendent was standing just in front of him. Then there was a pause and he appeared to look more intently at the Superintendent before he said on the second occasion 'Murder?'.

Mr L: And that was also interrogatively the second time? You know what I mean, do you, by 'soliloquizing'?

Pugh: Yes.

Mr L: He said 'Murder'? Like that?

Pugh: Yes, it was.

Mr L: We have been told by the Superintendent that he was shocked, shaken, by this announcement of murder?

Pugh: I would say that he was in a way stunned, or he appeared stunned.

By midday on Tuesday, the seventh day of the trial, we had finished with the lawyer and the police and were ready for the doctors. On balance I thought that the evidence we had heard had speeded the deterioration of the Crown's case. The evidence on motive was bizarre. It read like the chapter which gives an ingenious twist to the end of the detective story by revealing a quirk in the law which deprives the murderer of the fruits of his crime.

I have said that a false belief makes as good a motive as a true one. But murder is a serious business in which one would expect a serious murderer to have some solid ground for his belief. Here all the murderer had was a 'promise' by an old lady whom he must have known was continually changing her mind; Mr Sogno described her as very forgetful. May not Dr Adams's belief in legacies to come have been so lightly founded because they did not really matter to him very much? It is clear that he did not care about the chest of silver. He did care about the Rolls, but it was not a very splendid gift. It was nineteen years old, Price the chauffeur said in evidence, a black seven-seater limousine; it sounds like the sort that undertakers buy up cheap for use at funerals. He was vague about what was in the will. 'Oh, yes, and another cabinet,' he told Hannam: presumably a reference to the Elizabethan court cupboard which in fact he did not get either under the will or as a gift.

I had still to ponder the evidence that the doctor was shocked and stunned by the charge of murder. Was he putting on an act? If so, it was good enough to deceive two experienced detectives. Also it chimed with his volunteering three weeks before that he had himself given the patient 12½grs. heroin on the last day. If, when he said that, he had a charge of murder in his mind, he was running his head into the noose.

13

Doctor Douthwaite

Dr Douthwaite, the chief medical witness for the Crown, was in the box for most of Wednesday, Thursday and Friday of the second week, and was recalled to say more on the following Monday. There was a curtain-raiser in the shape of Dr Harris, whose brief evidence ended the Tuesday's hearing and began the Wednesday's. He was not an expert witness but he was, or could have been, a key witness. He had been Adams's partner for twenty years and took charge of Mrs Morrell when Adams was on holiday in May and September 1950. The latter period was a critical one, the start of a decline, when he found the patient 'extremely annoyed and angry' with Adams.

Dr Harris was a good and careful witness and, if he had had any view to express, would have been heard with great attention. But he was by nature a non-committal man placed in a situation which called for a non-commitment that would be amply justified by the lapse of time. As a locum he would naturally carry on with the Adams treatment. But I wondered whether he would have done so if he had definitely disagreed with it. I was no more successful than counsel in getting a positive answer to that.

Judge: Supposing you come to the conclusion that the treatment is harmful and likely to shorten her life, would you just carry on without saying anything to Dr Adams?
Dr H: It is a very difficult question to answer, my lord, because Dr Adams had definite ideas of treatment which were not necessarily my own, and I do not think I would have felt I was in a position to have said anything to him.
Judge: Do you recollect at this distance of time, looking back at the treatment that Mrs Morrell was having, having any seriously doubtful feelings about it from the point of view I have been suggesting to you?

Dr H: It is very difficult for me to recollect after all these years.
Judge: Do you recollect ever discussing with Dr Adams whether
it was the right or the wise treatment or not?
Dr H: I cannot remember discussing it with him, my lord, no.

I left it there. Obviously Dr Harris was not enthusiastic about the
treatment. But he could not testify at all about the murder period
in November, which was beginning now to be the starting-point
of my interest.

Enter now Arthur Henry Douthwaite of 49 Harley Street, MD,
FRCP, MRCS, Senior Physician to Guy's Hospital, the
recognized authority on opiates and, it is not irrelevant in this
case to add, a GP at Worthing for over four years from 1924. He
was just over sixty, very tall, very handsome, very commanding
but very courteous, always frank, never evasive. Also very
decisive: things either were or they were not.

Mrs Morrell's stroke in June 1948, which paralysed her left
side, was caused, he said, by a cerebral thrombosis, that is, a clot
in an artery of the brain. The right treatment is to mobilize the
patient as soon as possible. If she is not kept on the move, there is
a danger that another clot will form. Except for a single injection
of morphia if there is severe pain, the use of heroin or morphia is
quite wrong; it is even worse to use them in combination; the
sedation that is needed for sleep can be given by unharmful
drugs. Opiates discourage the process of rehabilitation, taking
away the desire to move; they cause constipation; they slow
down the respiration and may lead to the collapse of the lung and
pneumonia.

Worst of all, they are addictive. Heroin especially creates a
feeling of intense pleasure and excitement; a craving for more and
a dependence on the source who can thus acquire a complete
ascendancy. After two or three weeks of routine administration
the patient becomes an addict. She will also have acquired a
tolerance to the routine quantity and a larger dose will have to be
given to obtain the initial effect. The choice then lies between
increasing the dose and 'weaning'. Weaning means decreasing
the dose gradually to the point of stoppage. But increasing the
dose starts a 'spiral'. The process of overcoming added tolerance
has to be continuously repeated with ever increasing doses.

This was a clear theoretical statement of the consequence of
prescribing opiates. Of course to all such statements there can be
exceptions: in particular, as we were later to learn, the degree of

tolerance to opiates can vary enormously. So the next thing was to apply the general rule to the facts of Mrs Morrell's treatment when it soon became apparent that unorthodoxy had not met with the fate which it doubtless deserved.

For more than two years beginning in July 1948 the patient was being given regular daily injections of morphia and heroin. There was no evidence of craving or of weaning. As for complete subjection to the doctor as the source of the drug, we knew that after two years the patient was whistling him to heel. As to the effect of this regime upon her general health, the prognosis after her stroke was a six-months' expectation of life and she had done much better than that.

The period between the stroke and the death was divided into two roughly equal parts of a year each by the commencement of the notebooks in June 1949. In the first part the prescriptions kept fairly steady at 12 to 13grs. per month. In the second part they were also fairly steady but the monthly average increased to about 20grs. But for this second part there was also the clear evidence of the books. From 23 June 1949 until the end of October 1950 the daily routine of $\frac{1}{2}$gr. morphia and $\frac{1}{3}$gr. heroin was hardly ever varied.

The witness then summarized his conclusions. The treatment with opiates was unjustified; the certain consequence was addiction and Mrs Morrell was, he said, by 20 June 1949 a fully addicted patient. It seems to have been the lack of justification rather than the lack of success that was troubling him. He was not led to explain why events did not follow the course he predicted. As to the dosage in the last days the only conclusion could be that the intention was to terminate her life. The spasms at the end when she was semi-conscious were caused by the excess of heroin in the body, but were painless.

Neither the Attorney-General nor his witness had an adaptable mind. They clung to their formulations. This was shown most strikingly in the evidence that Dr Douthwaite was led to give about the two injections, administered on the last night, which the Attorney in his opening speech had alleged to be murderous.

The prosecution always disclaims any interest in securing a conviction and labours to show that its only duty is to present the facts fairly. Indeed, Reggie was to begin his closing speech by expressing this sentiment. Once the injections were shown to be of paraldehyde, he should have taken the earliest opportunity of conceding their irrelevance to a charge of murder. What was to emerge as the sum of the prosecution's medical evidence on this point—Douthwaite softened by Ashby—and what should have been volunteered at the beginning of it, was that the notebooks cleared the last two injections of any sinister implication. It had become clear that during the day the heroin injections were giving only short periods of rest and sleep. Moreover, they were causing the spasms which, painless or not, were very distressing to the nurses. It was sensible to make a change and to try paraldehyde, 'one of the safest of hypnotics' Douthwaite called it. It was in the end the judgment of the prosecution doctors, though disputed by the defence, that the paraldehyde, coming on top of the heavy dosage of heroin, would cause a loss of consciousness and probably accelerate death by an hour or two. But long before then hope had gone.

Nevertheless, both advocate and witness fought hard to retain some remnant of the point that the Attorney had opened about the last injections. At the end of his evidence in chief, after Douthwaite had stated his conclusion that the dosage in the last five days was intended to terminate life, counsel asked:

A-G: Bearing in mind the injections of heroin, what would be the effect on the brain centres of paraldehyde on top of that heroin?
Dr D: It would make the heroin more lethal . . . it would make death more certain than it already was.

Maybe this was literally correct. But the question and answer, set in the context of a murder to secure a legacy, conveyed, especially the word 'lethal', the idea that the paraldehyde was part of the villainy and the murderer's last throw. It left the impression that whatever Dr Adams had done, whether harmful or harmless or even beneficent, was going to be presented, not only by the prosecutor himself but also by his medical witness, as murderous. This impression was never removed. The last question put in re-examination was:

A-G: To what do you attribute her death?
Dr D: To drugs, morphia and heroin, possibly assisted by paraldehyde . . .

Later, when I pressed him on the point of the paraldehyde, he said that he was 'forced to draw the conclusion that Dr Adams gave the paraldehyde, perhaps because he was tired of waiting for the heroin to take effect, to bring about a quick and immediate result'. He said that the first dose of 2cc was in no way sinister or significant; it could have been given for a quite innocent purpose.

Judge: But you find yourself forced to exclude the possibility that the 5cc might have been given for an innocent purpose?
Dr D: I do, my lord.

I tried him out with 3cc.

Judge: And 3cc could have been done for an innocent purpose?
Dr D: Conceivably, yes.
Judge: But 60 per cent more means murder?
Dr D: Yes.

This answer left me bewildered: perhaps the jury as well. It seemed to me to be degrading orthodoxy to pedantry and to be carrying even pedantry too far. While it seemed absurd to make even a purely medical criticism of the use of a hypnotic (the standard dose was given in the British Pharmacopoeia as 5 to 10cc) intended to give relief in the last hours, I thought it unbelievable to bring such a criticism into a scheme for speeding a legacy.

In his presentation of his principal witness Reggie did nothing to soften the angularity. That Dr Douthwaite was a man of rigid integrity no one could doubt. That he was horrified at Dr Adams's reckless use of opiates was not surprising; it did not matter to him that in this case they had apparently done no harm. His creed was that opiates might be used for pain, subject to the earliest possible weaning, but never for distress. Reggie let him display himself as the Cardinal Inquisitor from the Holy Office of Harley Street, an image which thereafter Lawrence lost no opportunity of spotlighting.

But I must return to the end of the examination in chief. It was finished with about half an hour left of the day. Lawrence, who was as extravagant with time as the Attorney was sparing, had expected it to last until the next day and had not taken time to study the notice of additional evidence on which it was based and which had been served only on the day before. He asked for the indulgence of postponing his cross-examination until the next day. Reggie did not oppose the application. But it was a little triumph for him that, although it was the defence and not the prosecution who had dropped the bomb that devastated the case, it was the defence and not the prosecution who had to ask for relief. He rubbed this in in a very gentlemanly way.

My lord, I would only like to say this, that it was the introduction of the daily reports which necessitated a great deal of work being done examining them. The Crown had not seen them before, and it was not possible to serve notice of additional evidence until yesterday. My lord, I am sure my learned friends are not seeking to blame me, but I want to make it quite clear that notice was served at the earliest possible moment. I appreciate my learned friends have not had much time to consider that notice and indeed to consider Dr Douthwaite's evidence. Indeed, we did not have much time to consider the reports.

On the next morning, Thursday 28 March, counsel, as usually happens overnight, found 'one or two points which I ought to have put to the doctor'. Then Lawrence began.

> *Mr L:* Dr Douthwaite, my client, Dr Adams, in this case, as you know, is charged with the murder of Mrs Morrell?
> *Dr D:* Yes.
> *Mr L:* Before I embark upon my cross-examination of what you have said, I want to be quite clear what your proposition to my lord and the jury is in relation to the charge of murder. Have I understood it correctly in this way: that as a doctor and a specialist yourself you are saying that he formed the intention, as you say, 'to terminate her life' on 8 November, and carried that intention into effect over the next five days?
> *Dr D:* Yes.

Strategically in planning his cross-examination Lawrence had to choose between two courses. The crucial events were all in November 1950. One course was to concentrate on them, dismissing as irrelevant to murder all the previous history. By all means let the Crown show that Dr Adams's treatment of his patient was inexpert and incorrect. An unskilful doctor would mean an unskilful murderer; but the prosecution, when eventually they got to the crucial period, were going to have to show a very skilful murder indeed. It was not now a murder in which the doctor loaded a syringe and injected a killing dose. It was a murder by direction. It had to be committed by nurses who must be left without any suspicion of what they were doing.

Concentration on the crucial period is the course that would have tempted me. It would mean a short cross-examination, always an advantage with a jury. But it would leave with the jury (and with the public, for counsel had to look beyond the trial to his client's professional future) a picture of Adams as a bungling doctor who misused opiates. Would the jury be sympathetic to the argument that if there was a murder in the case, the murderer was not a bungler? Lawrence, who was a better and more experienced jury advocate than I had ever attempted to be, evidently thought not. His strategy from the beginning had been to present his client as a skilful, caring doctor who looked after a difficult patient for two years: could it be believed of him that, when she was at death's door, he had turned himself into a murderer? Boldly he presented this picture of his client to Dr Douthwaite. To a considerable extent he got the witness to accept it and at the same time to depict himself, on points which he would not accept, as doctrinaire.

It was not a ding-dong cross-examination of the traditional Old Bailey type. Mr Lawrence's local government practice must have given him a long experience of expert witnesses. He knew the maxims. Avoid petty and unnecessary conflict (if in general this is sound advice, before a jury, who will be bored and puzzled by it, it is imperative) and seek out avenues along which you can go hand in hand with the witness to the ends you want to reach. This as a general policy is not inconsistent with short and sharp encounters at any points at which the witness has incautiously exposed himself.

One of these occurred at the very beginning, though it was here the incompetence of the prosecution rather than any error of his own that had made Dr Douthwaite vulnerable. Lawrence attacked at once. The witness had attributed to Dr Adams the intention to terminate life, a murderous intent. He had said the same before the magistrates. Before he expressed that view on his oath, had he satisfied himself that he had every relevant piece of evidence before him? The witness said that he had.

But, he had to agree, all he had before the magistrates was a list of prescriptions going back only to January 1950. He had heard Mr Lawrence on the first day of the trial ask for a list from the beginning of the treatment. It had arrived three days ago and he had studied it, had he not? In fact a large part of his evidence yesterday was founded on it, was it not? Yes.

This earlier list began on 7 July 1948. Before that and immediately after the stroke on 25 June Mrs Morrell had been treated at a hospital in Cheshire. Did the witness, Mr Lawrence asked, seek information about that treatment? He did, he replied, and was told that it was not available; anyway it would not have materially altered the answers he gave about addiction.

My lord, I want the witness to look at a document which I shall be proving in due course . . . the nurses' notes taken on the case in the Neston Cottage Hospital in Cheshire from the outset of Mrs Morrell's illness.

So it was happening again. This time it was not going to matter so much. But once again it was the defence demonstrating that they had nothing to conceal; it was they and not the prosecution who were searching out the relevant documents.

And for those still interested in addiction there were points to be made. The patient had had one night only of severe pain on 27 June, after which morphia injections were given and continued for eight days. Was the witness criticizing Dr Turner who was then looking after Mrs Morrell? Yes: except for the one night of severe pain, he was. The Harley Street standard, one thought, versus the general practitioner's. Maybe Harley Street was right, at least theoretically. But can it be said that to be wrong is evidence of murder?

Mr Lawrence turned to the nine daily injections of morphia which were shown in the Cheshire notes.

Mr L: Would it have produced any appreciable degree of addiction?
Dr D: It depends very largely on the mentality of the patient. I cannot answer with regard to this particular person, but it is highly improbable.
Mr L: Do you remember what you said yesterday about addiction?
Dr D: Yes.
Mr L: The question of addiction is always a question depending on the individual, isn't it?
Dr D: Yes. I would qualify that. All individuals will become addicted if given drugs of addiction regularly, but at a variable length of time.
Mr L: That is exactly what I thought. There is no regular fixed standard of time within which everyone will become addicted to these drugs?
Dr D: No, there is no fixed time. That is quite true.

Counsel had completed his punitive expedition. He turned now to the main object of his cross-examination, which was to communicate through the witness to the jury the image of the caring doctor. He had an uncanny perception of the point to which he could get a witness to go. Here was a woman, stricken as she was moving into her eighties and brought, as it seemed at the beginning, to within six or twelve months of death.

Mr L: And short of a miracle, no doctor in his senses could think that he could restore a woman of seventy-nine or eighty to her pre-stroke health after there had been a brain lesion, as indicated in this case?

Dr D: Oh no. I agree with that.

Mr L: So what he has got to do is his reasonable best, isn't it?

Dr D: Certainly.

Mr L: For what is left of her life?

Dr D: Yes.

Mr L: And that would be, as I said, to make life as bearable as it could be to the patient?

Dr D: Yes.

Mr L: And in this practicable world, and in 1950, to make life as bearable as it could be to those who had got to look after her?

Dr D: Yes, that is a side consideration.

Mr L: Well, you say it is a side consideration, but let us face it, Dr Douthwaite, not from the consulting room in Harley Street, but let us face it from the angle of the general practitioner in the provincial town?

Dr D: Yes, I am quite aware of that.

Mr L: Where nurses in 1950 after the war were pretty scarce, weren't they?

Dr D: Yes.

Mr L: At a time when nurses are not going to put up with an infinity of trouble and difficulty?

Dr D: True.

Mr L: If the patient's life is made as bearable as possible for her, she is in a condition which enables her to be bearably nursed by them, then that latter factor redounds in favour of the patient, doesn't it?

Dr D: Yes. . . .

Mr L: And what he (the doctor) would have in front of him in this case would be, amongst other objects, two objects certainly: to keep her up and about as much as possible in the daytime?

Dr D: Yes.

Mr L: And to see that she had sleep at night?

Dr D: Yes.

Mr L: If she was not up and about in the daytime, she would get bedridden too soon?

Dr D: Yes.

Mr L: And if she did not get sleep at night, she would wear herself out with exhaustion?

Dr D: Yes.

Mr L: Exhaustion would lead to collapse, and with an aged woman like that collapse might very well contain the risk of a premature death?

Dr D: Yes.

Mr L: Now, whatever you might say about the use of these drugs, morphia and heroin, the fact is this, isn't it, recorded in these notebooks: that, broadly speaking, until September of 1950 this woman was being got up and about during the daytime?

Dr D: Yes, I can't remember up to what month that was, but I naturally accept your word.

Mr L: So far as sleep was concerned at night, she was having a regular routine injection at 8.30 of ½gr. morphia and ⅓gr. heroin, and during that period she was being assisted further to sleep by slight additional doses of barbiturates when necessary?

Dr D: Yes.

Mr L: That is the broad picture?

Dr D: Yes, I agree.

There followed vignettes of Dr Adams interviewing the boot-maker about special boots, of Mrs Morrell walking round the bed with her crutch and in her new boots, in the garden for one and a half hours, taking an interest in pre-stroke activities, once going out in the Rolls with the doctor to the launching of a new lifeboat, walking the length of the tennis court twice. There were manifestations of cerebral irritation, bad temper and abuse of the nurses. But they served only to season the dish which the witness had accepted.

To all this as it was put to him, Dr Douthwaite answered by giving almost unqualified assents. He was clear and candid, the model of what the ordinary witness should be, simple and trustworthy. But an expert witness must be something more. He is not dealing only with facts whose presentation in argument can be left to counsel. He has theories to advance which he must under the constraints of the witness-box to some extent argue himself. There is an art in this. In the cross-examination of the expert the art of the examinee must match the art of the examiner. It is of course the examiner who is in control. Lawrence was artful in giving the witness no opportunity to argue; Douthwaite was artless in not trying to make one.

What during this process was happening to the Crown's theory that Dr Adams was using drugs to bring the patient under his influence so as to get her money? It was not being demolished: it was not being mentioned: it was disappearing. Whether Dr Douthwaite himself really believed in it I do not know. What he did profoundly believe in was the wickedness of doctors who, if morphia and heroin had to be used, did not take the earliest opportunity of weaning their patients and so created a craving. Lawrence did not challenge this as a general proposition. He offered no provocation. He just let the facts demonstrate that what theory required to occur had not in this case come to pass. The question, 'If indeed she was addicted, what harm did it do?' hangs in the air. Nine out of ten counsel would have sent the cavalry clattering in to underscore the victory: 'In the face of all this, doctor, do you still maintain that . . . ?' Lawrence knew when to leave well alone. Whether or not the doctor still maintained his theory of addiction, craving and dependence no longer mattered a damn.

This took us to the end of August 1950, eleven weeks before the death. The dosage was increased. Lawrence's object from now on was to show that the increase followed the decline of an old lady moving to the close of life and was no sign of an evil intervention. The decline started with the cerebral irritation and restlessness caused by Dr Adams's holiday. It was indeed Dr Harris who first increased the dose. When Adams returned, both doctors experimented unsuccessfully with reductions. Later Dr Adams tried variations. And then when she was in the terminal stages, when it was plain that addiction could no longer matter, he gave the instruction that she was to be 'kept under'.

Apart from an occasional reminder that Dr Adams was arraigned on a charge of murder, the cross-examination until just before the end was conducted as if Mr Lawrence was appearing in a civil case in which his client was being charged with lack of skill. It was as if, before the Crown could begin to lay siege to the citadel of the reasonable doubt which to win it must penetrate, the defenders had moved out to defeat their opponents in the open field. It was when we were beginning to wonder whether the doctor had done anything wrong at all that Mr Lawrence asked the witness what made him postulate murder. It came down to one thing, the large quantity of morphia and heroin given in the last five days.

Lawrence then asked the crucial question.

Mr L: Before I leave this part of the case, you say that you formed that view, and were forced to it, about the intent to murder: you would conceive it quite possible, would you not, that another doctor reviewing the matter in the same way might not find himself forced to the same conclusion?

Dr D: I think that is clear, is it not? There could always be a difference of opinion.

This answer was very damaging to the Crown. Where there can be a reasonable difference of opinion there can also be a reasonable doubt. It was a surprisingly soft answer to come from Dr Douthwaite. It would never have been obtained by bellicosity. It was the reward for two days of quiet, patient, even tedious, cross-examination. It was an answer to be protected from casual damage and Lawrence prudently concluded his questioning almost at once. The Attorney re-examined at what for him was considerable length, but it was an answer beyond the power of the re-examiner to alter.

Then I began to ask some questions and the precious answer came apart in my hands.

14

Doctor Douthwaite's New Idea

It was the housemaid, now an extinct species, who was supposed to account for an unexpected breakage by saying that the object had come apart in her hands. The comparison with the trial judge is not inept. One of his lowlier jobs is to housemaid the case. It is his function before he sums up to the jury to get the evidence as clean and tidy as he can.

The state of the evidence was worrying me in one respect. The criminal law requires the guilty act and the guilty mind to coincide in time. The intent to murder must be in the mind at the moment when the hand is killing; or when, as in this case, another's hand is being instructed, then at the moment of instruction. This moment must be identified for every act of murder that is alleged and the jury directed that it is at this moment that the accused must intend death to result.

So at the end of the re-examination I said:

Dr Douthwaite, I want your help and it may be to quite a considerable extent. In due course I shall direct the jury that, before they can convict the accused, they must be satisfied that he committed an act of murder. That means, in the circumstances of this case, that he either administered the drugs himself, intending them to kill her, or he gave directions or instructions to the nurses which he hoped and intended, if carried out, would kill the patient . . .

If the case for the Crown is right, then one or more of those acts amounted to murder. I should like to be able, when the time comes, to assist the jury by pointing out to them precisely what in relation to each act it is that forces you, as you put it in your own words, to postulate that murder was being committed or attempted. . . . May I begin with the night of 7 Novem-

1. *Dr John Bodkin Adams (courtesy of The Photo Source)*

2. *Superintendent Hannam (courtesy of Popperfoto)*

3. *Melford Stevenson, QC, (left) with his junior, Malcolm Morris at the Eastbourne hearing (courtesy of Popperfoto)*

4. *December 1956. Superintendent Hannam supervises the exhumation of one of Dr Adams's patients (courtesy of Popperfoto)*

5. *24 January, 1957. Dr Adams, concealed on the floor of a police car, leaves Eastbourne for Brixton prison. The public was fascinated by the case (courtesy of Popperfoto)*

6. *Geoffrey Lawrence, QC, Leading Counsel for the Defence (courtesy of the BBC Hulton Picture Library)*

7. The Attorney-General, Sir Reginald Manningham-Buller (courtesy
of the BBC Hulton Picture Library)

8. The presiding judge (courtesy of The Press Association)

9. *Dr Douthwaite (courtesy of the BBC Hulton Picture Library)*

ber. . . . Are you forced to postulate murder in relation to that
dose?

Dr D: Not that single dose, my lord.

Judge: Do you mean by that that you might be forced to
postulate it in relation to the doses that come after?

Dr D: In the first place the dosage which had gone before, and
to be exact the doses which were not given of morphia, from
the 1st to the 5th, when only heroin was given.

This was the mysterious opening sentence of the longest answer
the doctor ever gave; it continued for more than half a page of
the transcript. Because of its length and because it was start-
lingly new, it was difficult to follow. It means going back to
1 November.

Mr Lawrence had been putting to Dr Douthwaite that Dr
Adams had in these last days been experimenting with variations
in the drugging. One variation that he had put was the dropping
of the morphia on 1 November, leaving only the heroin. Then in
the evening of 5 November the morphia was brought back to
deal, counsel suggested and the witness agreed, with increasing
restlessness. Lawrence then said:

> *Mr L:* Those entries are at least consistent with the views that I
> have just put forward, aren't they?
>
> *Dr D:* That the variation of drugs was being tried?
>
> *Mr L:* Yes.
>
> *Dr D:* Yes.

But now the witness saw it all in a different light in which the
planning and execution of the murder began on 1 November, a
week before the Crown's official date. The dropping of the
morphia on 1 November was the first act in the murder. The plan
was to drop it so that the tolerance to it could be reduced and so
that it could be brought back later and thereafter rapidly
increased in combination with large doses of heroin to take
deadly effect.

Like the housemaid whose first look is to see if the object is
mendable, I tried to find out if the witness would tolerate for the
new theory the same degree of dissent as he had for the old. But
no: an impossible view, he said.

> *Judge:* When you are dealing with another doctor, the very last
> thing you think of normally is murder?
>
> *Dr D:* Yes.

Judge: You explore every other possible hypothesis and reject it before you come to the conclusion that it is murder?
Dr D: Yes.
Judge: Is it your view that in dropping the morphine Dr Adams was merely changing the drugging, or is that an impossible view?
Dr D: I think that is an impossible view.

Then I took the doctor through all the remaining injections and concluded thus:

Judge: I am very much obliged to you, doctor. I think I have the picture now quite clearly in my mind. Your view, if I may summarize it, is really this: that the first time the design for murder emerges from the medical pattern is when he drops the morphia and concentrates on the heroin?
Dr D: Yes, my lord.
Judge: The only possible medical explanation of that being that he intends to re-introduce morphia with lethal effect?
Dr D: Yes, my lord.
Judge: And then and thereafter all the subsequent injections are given and any one of them could have been lethal?
Dr D: Could have been lethal, yes.
Judge: And can only be explained on the basis that they were intended to be lethal?
Dr D: Yes, my lord.
Judge: And that goes on until the morphia and heroin is dropped, and then he takes to paraldehyde, first, in the small quantity for an innocent purpose, and, secondly, in the larger quantity so as to bring about her death more quickly than the accumulation of morphia and heroin would have done?
Dr D: Yes, my lord.

I expected Mr Lawrence to ask leave to cross-examine Dr Douthwaite on his change of front, but he did not. Perhaps he thought that cross-examination would be superfluous. But I thought it fair that, if he wished for passivity, he should be made to embrace it. So when the time for adjournment came, I said:

Mr Lawrence, you heard me this afternoon ask a number of questions of Dr Douthwaite to which he gave certain answers. I did that primarily because I wished to elicit information for my own purposes. I do not regard it as any part of my duty to cross-examine witnesses either for the Crown or for the defence, but I was struck at the time, and I am still more struck on looking at the transcript, by certain divergences, particularly in the answers which Dr Douthwaite gave to me on the topic of variation of drugs and the answers that he gave to you in cross-examination. . . . If in view of those answers, you were to make an application that you should cross-examine further, I should consider it. But you are entitled to leave it where it is, of course, if you wish.

The court was now about to adjourn for the weekend and Mr Lawrence asked for time to consider the position.

There was now quite a lot on the agenda for the weekend's reflection. The first item was, of course, the eccentricity of Dr Douthwaite. The switch was disconcerting for the defence, but for the prosecution a change of direction in the middle of the case could be disastrous.

But, it may be asked, if it suddenly occurred to Dr Douthwaite that his previous evidence was mistaken, was he not right to say so? Was he not sworn to tell the truth and the whole truth? Certainly. But the criticism is not that the witness told what he saw as the truth when it suddenly occurred to him; it is that the possibility of the sudden occurrence ought to have been eliminated before the case began. Dr Douthwaite had taken himself back to a stage which should have been long since past, the stage at which one can say: 'Look here, you fellows, I think we are getting it all wrong.'

The trial has for many years ceased to be the place for the discovery of what happened. Before it begins counsel for the prosecution must satisfy himself that in essentials he knows what happened and how it happened and that his account of it proves the guilt of the accused. The sole issue at the trial is whether he can satisfy the jury that beyond reasonable doubt he is right.

The Attorney-General in his opening speech had given an account which the notebooks made obsolete. Before he could reconstruct his case he had to have the skilled interpretation of the contents of the books which only his medical experts could provide. They had the books by the evening of Tuesday 19 March and the result of their study was in the form of notices of additional evidence available by the morning of Monday 25 March. The four or five days available to them gave little time for discussion and none for the testing of experimental theories. What was demanded of them was a settled joint opinion, that is, the opinion of two independent minds going as far as they could in unison, on which the Attorney-General could base a revised case for the prosecution. Each must be ready to support all that they both said. The regular Home Office experts know this and commit themselves to nothing that is not their last word. To imagine the great Sir Bernard Spilsbury making a substantial concession is extremely difficult: to imagine him voluntarily changing his mind in the course of his evidence is an exercise to bring the word 'boggle' briefly into its own.

But then Spilsbury and his like were specialists in forensic medicine. The prosecution, when they seek expert assistance from those who are unused to the framework of a trial, must prepare them for the witness-box. Douthwaite and Ashby should have been cross-questioned until their opinions were stripped down to the practical certainties on which they could agree. They should have been warned that speculations, appropriate at the stage when doctors are still putting their heads together, would be out of place at the trial. Perhaps they were. But when one looks back at the little care given to the evidence of the nurses or to information about the supply and custody of drugs, one doubts it. Douthwaite did not look like a maverick. Maybe it was not even made clear to him that what was wanted was a joint opinion and not a pair of solos. If it was, he erred grievously in launching a new theory without consultation.

Professionalism usually marks the prosecution, often making the defence look amateur. In the Adams trial it was the reverse. The defence was a professional exercise from beginning to end, the fine preparation by experienced solicitors being topped by the high skill of Mr Lawrence. The prosecution lacked co-ordination. The Attorney-General with his ministerial duties had not, I suppose, the time to impose it. Melford, a dashing commander in the field, was not a chief of staff. From the beginning a weak case was bungled.

When Dr Douthwaite left the witness-box no knowledgeable onlooker can have been putting much money on a conviction. His switch from 8 November to 1 November as the day on which the murder plan was put into effect was really the last straw. Here was a case in which guilt depended on an expert reading of the medical history recorded in the notebooks. What jury is going to convict after the chief expert has changed his mind about the true meaning of the evidence? If the No. 2 expert changes his, he is taken to be following suit and loses his independent value. If, as happened here, he refuses to change, there is the rift at the centre which any opponent rejoices to find.

In murder cases that are not of primitive simplicity the proof offered by the prosecution should satisfactorily combine evidence of a motive powerful enough to drive the killer to the deed with evidence of the means to carry it out. It is often and correctly said that the prosecution does not have to prove motive. This is true in the sense that motive is not in law an essential ingredient of the offence: a motiveless murder is still murder: lack of motive is no defence. But when motive is lacking, the burden of the proof, normally shared between motive and means, has to be borne entirely by the means.

The Adams prosecution never had a massive case on motive. Rumour had not imputed to the doctor any attempt to make a fortune by a single stroke. Rumour had made it a 'Brides in the Bath' case where the murderer systematically collected tidy little sums by means which should be beyond detection. 'It is imposs-ible to accuse a doctor.' The reduction of the case to a single murder for an insignificant reward had gravely weakened the contribution which motive was making to proof.

And now the trial was sapping the proof of the deed itself. The case had begun as one in which the method of murder was temptingly simple—a huge increase in dosage which seemed to be beyond explanation. Then the notebooks appeared and re-duced the dosage to what might be manageable proportions where success would depend on the authority with which the prosecution experts could invest their opinions. Undoubtedly that authority had been shaken by Dr Douthwaite's vacillation.

There was, however, an alternative case to that presented. The Crown could jettison as insignificant the motive of financial gain. They could rest the case almost entirely on an allegation that the size of the November dosage, whether or not preceded by the device which Douthwaite had suggested, was so great as to prove an intent to terminate life for no good medical reason before its natural end. Euthanasia with a taint of legacy hunting! The fear that this was the sort of case that might be made was what had aroused the quite widespread apprehensions of the medical profession. The profession was not concerned about a doctor who murdered his patients for money; such a man, if indeed he existed, could be left to his deserts. What agitated the profession was the possibility of a verdict which would put a doctor who failed to prolong life in peril of a murder charge.

The crime of murder covers many ways of causing death, and within its enormous range the Home Secretary exercises uncon-trolled jurisdiction. Judges as well as juries are powerless.

Degrees of murder are unknown to English law. The taking of life is all that matters; the manner of taking is not considered. The law draws no distinction between fighters, robbers, sadists and mercy-killers. In 1922 the continent of murder was diminished by the detachment of infanticide, a statutory crime created in that year. Some day perhaps euthanasia will be treated likewise. But in 1957 euthanasia was, as it still is, murder.

The Crown's case as the Attorney-General had opened it was not explicit on motive. But the implication was plain that the accused killed Mrs Morrell either to get legacies which he knew or thought he knew were coming to him or to prevent her from altering her will to his disadvantage. Unless the Attorney made some new formulation, I proposed to address the jury on the footing that it was a murder for money. So much for the prosecution. The defence had not shown any sign of disputing the point that the deliberate acceleration of death for whatever reason was murder. Mr Lawrence had not expanded on 'easing the passing'. But the accused had talked about it. I felt that, whether or not it was in issue, the jury would want to know how far the law allowed the orthodox doctor to go in easing the passing. To ignore a natural curiosity may be to leave a puzzled jury and a puzzled jury may not be a good jury. I decided that, even if the issue was not raised, I would tell the jury how far the doctor could go before I told them that it did not matter.

Over the weekend the Attorney-General was doubtless taking stock of his remaining assets. He would have, it seemed to me, to choose between widening his formulation to include euthanasia and deflating his case to the point where he could gracefully abandon it. Not long before, I had seen the latter course pursued most skilfully by Sir Harry Hylton-Foster, the Solicitor-General. It was at the assizes at Devizes where I was presiding. A couple who lived in a village nearby were accused of the murder of a neighbour by administering rat poison. Much of the evidence against them was supplied by their own injudicious remarks. It created the sort of stir locally which the Adams case created internationally, but it did not rate more than a paragraph or two in the national press.

The Solicitor-General sensed at once the nature of the case and opened it piano. He answered a submission of no case by the defence by saying that, though he submitted that there was a case to answer (as to which technically he was right), he did not feel, now that all the facts had been explored, that it was a case in which it would be right for him to ask the jury to convict. The accused had behaved very foolishly, he submitted, bringing the case upon themselves and making it necessary that rumour should be investigated and dispelled in open court. This having been done, he was content that the jury should return a verdict of not guilty.

This was not Reggie's style. He was the fighter who never gave in. It was natural that at this turning point in his career he would not wish a prosecution on which the eyes of the nation were centred to end in a fiasco. But, if only he could have seen it, some public proof of judicial quality was just what he needed for the furtherance of his ambition.

But if he was determined to win or to go down fighting, would he see a mercy murder as worth winning? I thought it very unlikely. He had opened too strongly the theme of the wicked doctor. It was, however, conceivable that, rather than lose altogether, he might introduce mercy killing as an alternative to support a conviction if the jury rejected the sordid motive.

But the so-called malice that is the chief legal ingredient of murder is as much at home with benevolence as with malevolence. My direction to the jury would have to be that, if they were satisfied that there was an intent to kill, it was immaterial whether the intent was merciful or diabolic. This, if they convicted, would leave the Home Secretary with a pretty problem. He would have to make up his mind in secret on evidence which he had not heard and, since he could not himself possibly find time to study intensively seventeen days of transcript plus a pile of exhibits, largely on advice given him by anonymous officials without any close acquaintance with the processes of justice, whether the accused had killed in mercy or for money.

I worried a lot about ways in which I could help. A special verdict perhaps. Or an invitation to the jury to recommend mercy if they thought it deserved. Indeed, I was provoked by the inadequacy of the law of murder into too much thought. But if I shelved the problem, I might not have the amplitude of another weekend in which to consider it. I was not to know that the Attorney-General would take neither the course of abandoning the prosecution nor of shifting his ground, but a third course beyond the reach of my imagining.

On the morning of Monday 1 April, when the usual exercise of correcting minor errors (there were never any major ones) in the previous day's transcript was completed, Mr Lawrence rose to say that he had come to the conclusion that 'in the execution of my duty to my client, I should ask your lordship's leave further to cross-examine Dr Douthwaite'. This was cordially seconded by the Attorney.

The doctor stood by his new theory based on the dropping of the morphia. He was vigorously cross-examined about when he first thought of it. He agreed that he could not have thought of it when he was answering Lawrence's questions about the variation on 1 November. He almost, but not quite, agreed that the answers which he gave to Lawrence and to me respectively were irreconcilable. Mr Lawrence asked:

Mr L: On those two irreconcilable views, doctor, and I am not going to debate whether you said them both or not, what I want to know now is which of those two views is the one you finally adopt?
Dr D: The view that the morphine was re-introduced with a lethal purpose.
Mr L: And that involves the view that it was also withdrawn for the same purpose, doesn't it?
Dr D: Yes. . . .
Mr L: The truth of all this matter is this, Dr Douthwaite, that you first of all gave evidence on one basis to support a charge of murder and then thought of something else after you had started?
Dr D: That is quite likely. In fact, I think it is probable. I had been turning it over in my mind, but at what point it crystallized and became clear I do not know.

The witness had also said that each of the doses given after the re-introduction of morphia on 5 November was intended to be lethal. This meant that every dose between 5 and 12 November was an attempted murder. He had not meant, the witness said, that each dose was intended to produce death immediately or within two or three hours. 'The whole thing was based,' he said, 'on the mounting up of drugs in an individual who was dying and therefore excreting or destroying the drugs in her body slowly.' Was he then inferring, I asked, that Dr Adams refrained from giving a dose large enough of itself to kill? Yes, he was, the witness said, and agreed that that might have been because Dr Adams thought that too large a dose would arouse suspicion.

Judge: And what he did was to give a series of doses over a period, the combined effect of which he knew would kill?
Dr D: That is exactly what I meant, my lord.

This was the theory of accumulation. Mr Lawrence in unwonted heat characterized it as 'absolute rubbish', substituting after reflection, 'not founded upon sound premises'. There ensued a dialogue on the elimination of drugs from the body. It soon became nebulous, but out of the cloud as a stroke of irrelevant lightning there came one answer:

Judge: Do you mean that she was dying before 1 November?
Dr D: Yes, my lord.

As was not unnatural, Lawrence used the opportunity of further questioning to press another point. The dosage over the last few days, if it had been a case of inoperable cancer, would, he put it to the witness, have been well within the experience of the medical profession. Dr Douthwaite replied that it would have been a dosage suggesting a decision to terminate life. It was not he, he said, but counsel who had introduced the word 'murder'. His opinion was given in the case of an old woman who was not in agonizing pain. There was a profound difference between that and inoperable cancer.

Mr L: That means in your view these beneficial drugs may be used to this extent, to relieve the final pains of inoperable cancer, but they are to be withheld from a patient who is suffering the misery and distress and restlessness consequent upon senile disintegration and the damaged brain lesion?
Dr D: It is certainly my opinion that morphia and heroin should not be given for that condition even in the terminal stages. . . .
Mr L: Is the sole difference between the two this, in your opinion, that in the cancer case the use of drugs would be justified because of the presence of pain and in the other case they are not justified because there was only distress, which falls short of severe pain?
Dr D: Yes.

The accumulation theory gave the evidence on the design for murder a new twist. Was it a theory that was generally accepted? Would Dr Adams have known of it? Was there room here for error, ignorance or incompetence? I wanted to be sure both that Dr Adams had known just what he was doing and that Dr

Douthwaite knew just what he was saying. I pressed the witness on this for two pages of transcript. My last three questions were:

Judge: It is very important to see how far you go, because it would be very easy for a medical man in your position to say this: 'I am saying no more about this treatment by Dr Adams than this, that I think it was wrong, that I think it was dangerous, that I think it caused death, but whether it was administered through error, incompetence or an intent to kill, it is not for me to say and I am not saying it.' That is evidence you could give, or could have given, but you are going further. That is quite clear, isn't it?
Dr D: Yes.
Judge: You are saying it couldn't have been due to error, ignorance or incompetence, it must have been due only to an intent to kill?
Dr D: Yes.
Judge: It must follow that anyone who expresses a contrary view to yours on this point is expressing a view that he cannot honestly hold?
Dr D: Yes, my lord.

This was finality. Dr Douthwaite struck me as the sort of man who, having, as it were, enrolled under the banner of the prosecution and pledged his opinion (which must have been very influential in the launching of it), would be determined to stand fast. He was too staunch.

There was one other point I wanted to know more about. When the witness said that on 1 November Mrs Morrell was a dying woman, how much life was left to her? 'If I had seen her in October,' he replied, 'I would have expected her to live only for a matter of a few weeks, probably not more than two months.' That was the medical picture. And if, I asked, on 1 November Dr Adams embarked on his plan to kill, would he have expected it to take the thirteen days which in fact it did take? He might well have, the witness replied.

15

The Crown's Second String

Michael George Corbett Ashby MA, MB, MRCP, BS, FRSM, MABN was the No. 2 expert for the Crown. His visible contribution so far had been in the production of the graphs which the Attorney had exhibited in his opening speech. These of course had been constructed on the basis of the quantity prescribed, this being all that was then known. After Dr Douthwaite had left the box on Friday afternoon Dr Ashby appeared with some more graphs. I thought that they would be bringing the old graphs up to date by substituting injections for prescriptions. But the Attorney started him off with the old graphs and Ex. 4A. The following dialogue ensued.

Judge: Mr Attorney, I am not sure that I quite follow now what the prescriptions have to do with the case.
A-G: I think I can answer that straight away, my lord. I am not accepting for one moment that all the visits Dr Adams paid are recorded in the nurses' register and, my lord, I am putting my case as I opened it; I am putting it, first of all, on the quantities prescribed, and I am putting my case in this way, that on the nurses' register and the reports as well there is only one conclusion that can be drawn.
Judge: Yes, but are you suggesting, then, that all the quantities prescribed were given to Mrs Morrell?
A-G: Yes, my lord, I am relying on the police evidence that they were all used apart from the final few tablets, and I am relying on the prescriptions showing the quantities prescribed by the doctor, and I am saying that the inference to be drawn from those two—from the statements made to Superintendent Hannam plus the prescriptions—the inference to be drawn is that this lady had those quantities administered before her death.

Judge: All that I had in mind was that the evidence of the nurses appears to be that, generally speaking, when Dr Adams administered injections himself he did not draw it from what had been the quantity prescribed on the tray. So that if more than is shown in the books is given out of the quantity prescribed, it must be presumably because the books do not record accurately the quantities the nurses injected.

A-G: No, my lord, there is a fallacy there, my lord. The fallacy, in my submission, is this, and I shall hope to be able to satisfy your lordship of what happened, that some of the prescriptions did not go straight to Marden Ash, Mrs Morrell's home.

Judge: Did not what?

A-G: Did not go straight through to Marden Ash where Mrs Morrell was.

Judge: Oh, I see.

A-G: Some of the prescriptions went either to Kent Lodge or were collected by Dr Adams himself.

Judge: That is not the evidence so far.

A-G: My lord, that is not the evidence so far, because no evidence has been given on that, but when one compares certain entries in the nurses' register with the prescription chart—

Judge: So really you put your case as to the quantity that Mrs Morrell had, that it is shown at its highest, as it were, in the list of prescriptions—

A-G: Yes, my lord.

Judge:—and at its lowest in the nurses' books?

A-G: Yes, my lord.

Judge: I am much obliged. I did not follow that.

It was a pity that I interrupted him. Evidently my mind was not on his answer but was formulating the consequence of the (to me) surprising return to the prescriptions. I should have encouraged him to put his case on this point then and there. As it was, we had to wait until his final speech.

I do not think that I then attached full significance to his words: 'I am putting my case as I opened it.' What he had opened was inference only, the best he could do with the scanty material he had got; and he had failed to fortify it with any firm proof that administration to Mrs Morrell was the only way by which the quantity prescribed could have been diminished. But he had now got from the books direct evidence of injection coupled with the firm commitment by Dr Douthwaite, which he expected

Dr Ashby to confirm, that the quantity injected was deadly.

I could understand his keeping the prescriptions in reserve until after he had cross-examined Dr Adams. Indeed, this seemed good sense. But why put them in the front line? Why undertake the formidable task of proving that Dr Adams had succeeded without the knowledge of the nurses in injecting an unnecessary surplus?

Of course Reggie was an obstinate man who would fight hard against events that pushed him off the path he had decided to take. Was it just a repugnance to the comfortable cruise along the motorway which the notebooks offered him and a hankering to grind the gears on the old road on which he had intended to march to victory? Time would tell.

Now that the prescriptions were back in the case—I should say more truly back in my mind, for I now recollected stray questions that the Attorney had asked about them from time to time—the immediate point of interest lay in a comparison between the quantity prescribed and the quantity recorded as injected. The Crown had in Exhibit 35A prepared a list of the quantities prescribed for each month in 1950 and in Exhibit 54 a list of daily totals as recorded in the notebooks. The comparison was not revealing because in Ex. 35A the whole quantity prescribed was credited to the month in which the prescription was written notwithstanding that it was expected to last for some time ahead, maybe several weeks. Thus in July 1950, when the patient was receiving an almost regular dose of $\frac{1}{2}$gr. morphia, the amount prescribed is shown as nil.

So a more sophisticated method was adopted. There was produced for comparison with the daily total actually injected a notional daily prescription. This was calculated by dividing the quantity prescribed by the number of days for which the prescription lasted, it being presumed to last until the next one arrived to take its place. The result was presented in the form of a graph on which at first the two lines moved in uninteresting conformity. Then on or about 9 September the long period of the routine dose came to an end. Thereafter the line of actual daily injections fluctuates wildly while the prescription line is tamed to a notional average. Then in the last five days both lines shoot up like factory chimney-stacks towering above the squat line below, the prescriptions rising to 21grs. on the highest day while the injections get no higher than 8.

It soon became apparent from the questioning that neither side was interested in establishing an excess of prescriptions before November. The defence would be nervous of an excess at any time because it would be something for Dr Adams to explain away. If the Crown's case was to be that Dr Adams over-prescribed so as to obtain the surplus he needed for murdering Mrs Morrell, it would not help to show that the doctor was over-prescribing before he formed the intent to murder.

It would have been as easy to present detailed figures for the whole of 1950 as it was for the single week in November. Neither side did so. My own rough totting up for 1950 did not show a large discrepancy.

For the crucial period Dr Ashby had prepared another set of graphs. For this period he had perceived the danger in the assumption that each prescription would last until the next was delivered, since, when death intervened, there would be no next prescription. The new graphs showed each prescription as a vertical column rising on its appropriate square to a height determined by the quantity actually prescribed. We were invited to lay each column over on its side so as to get the correct visual impression. For a very amateur photographer like myself who was used to viewing horizontally in a projector a slide which he had mistakenly put in vertically, this was child's play. But then there came a point, as Dr Ashby lamented, when the column, as it was being toppled, was abruptly halted by the death and left in the air at a visually unimpressive angle.

What was to be done? It was not just the last column that was in difficulties. A glance at Exhibit 36A shows that there is no column on or after 8 November which can be made to lie flat; and the later and taller columns cannot be asked to do more than make a courteous inclination of the head.

I am myself unresponsive to 'visual impressions'—juries are supposed to like them—and find a table of figures much easier to follow. So I have extracted from Exhibit 4A the prescriptions signed on and after 8 November.* Omitting the small heroin content of No. 84 (which was a linctus for a cough) they totalled $78\frac{3}{4}$grs. of opiates. By orthodox standards they were shockingly lavish. Dr Adams had promised Mrs Morrell that he would not let her suffer at the end. After his visit at 6.30 pm on 9 November Sister Mason-Ellis made a note in the book:

(Dr Adams has left 1 tube of $\frac{1}{2}$gr. Sulph. Morph. Tabs. and 1 tube of $\frac{1}{4}$gr. Heroin Tabs. for future use only and wishes Mrs

* The table is set out on p. *x*.

132

Morrell to continue with ½gr. of Heroin when necessary, using the ⅛gr. Heroin Tabs.)

These tubes, which made up No. 86 and No. 87 in the table and came on top of the 16½ grains of opiates prescribed the day before (No. 83 and No. 85), were to be repeated twice if required. In fact the morphia was repeated only once, presumably because with Prescription 89 Dr Adams changed to the hyperduric morphia. The heroin was twice repeated on successive days.

Dr Adams's instruction, given on 9 November, was that Mrs Morrell should be given 1gr. heroin whenever she was restless or irritable—'an astonishing instruction' Dr Douthwaite called it—and on 10 November there was a further note 'hourly if necessary'. That could mean, though the maximum was never approached, 24grs. a day. So that the prescriptions, enormous though they seemed, were not out of line with the instructions. 'Heroin', Dr Ashby was to say, 'continues to give a pleasurable experience right up to the end unless used in inadequate quantities.' There was to be no danger of inadequacy with Dr Adams at the prescribing end.

Dr Ashby's columns were designed to accompany the submission that all, or almost all, the drugs prescribed were injected. Just as Mr Lawrence had as his signature tune a melody about the nurse's delight in the discovery of the notebooks, so the Attorney-General had as his first theme, given out by the brass to every medical witness, a demand to know whether he or she was aware of any reason why a doctor should prescribe drugs which he did not intend to be used. It always appeared that nobody was, though Dr Ashby, habitually cautious, qualified his answer by saying that he was aware of no legitimate reason. Since witnesses are not expected to start a dialogue, no one observed that, whatever a doctor might intend, he could not answer for the result. The doctor proposes but God disposes and few patients expire just after taking the last tablet.

Mrs Morrell died at 2.00 am on Monday 13 November. The last tablet would be the last of the 75 in Prescription 93 which had presumably been delivered on the Sunday morning, say, 15 hours before death. During this period the nurses record the injection of 3 tablets only. 75 tablets would have filled to the brim Dr Adams's 5cc syringe, provided that it had not been needed for the paraldehyde.

This on the one hand. On the other hand the Crown had it from the horse's mouth that Mrs Morrell had had at least 73 out of the 75 tablets. When Mr Hannam showed Dr Adams the list and pointed out the last entries, the doctor said at first that he had used them all himself: 'she was in terrible agony', he said. A little later, having 'looked at it for a second or two', he conceded that 'there might have been a couple of those final tablets left over'. To match the final couple Ashby had taken $\frac{1}{2}$gr. off his columns.

Evidence was now mounting which put Dr Adams's recollection under considerable strain. Apart from the dubious agony, it was difficult to see how an injection of 12$\frac{1}{2}$grs. heroin could be made to fit in with the events on the Sunday as recorded in the notebook. Then there was Sister Bartlett's evidence about the two phials. Undoubtedly the probability was that something was left over. Was it feasible six years later to start an investigation into how much?

The Attorney-General, however, gave no sign of weakening. From now on he was constantly referring to Dr Adams's admission as if it had some scriptural authority which it would be impious to question. Dr Ashby on the other hand was evidently a little worried by Sister Bartlett's phials. It would be very wrong, he said, to insert conjectures into the graphs. But he did modify the 'visual impression' by offering an alternative which lopped the final column of heroin by a third and removed altogether the final column of morphia and a bit of the preceding one. Put into figures, this meant that out of 41grs. of morphia prescribed 10$\frac{1}{2}$ were recorded as injected, 12$\frac{1}{2}$ were left over or lost, and 18 unaccounted for; of 37$\frac{3}{4}$grs. of heroin prescribed, 16 were recorded, 12$\frac{1}{2}$ left over and 9$\frac{1}{4}$ unaccounted for. Thus the quantity of opiates, which Dr Adams was to be presumed to have prescribed for use by himself to top up the doses injected by the nurses, was now reduced from 51$\frac{1}{2}$ grains to 26$\frac{1}{2}$, i.e. it was nearly halved. Mr Lawrence received this indulgence without visible emotion and asked no questions on it.

In my analysis here of the last prescriptions I have jumped far ahead of my thought at the time. As the stream of evidence flows gently past one does not attempt more than a pencil mark on the mind. I foresaw that Dr Adams would have some awkward questions to answer when he went into the witness-box. Until then analysis would be premature.*

Dr Ashby, having followed Dr Douthwaite into the box on the

---

* From now on I shall refer to this 27$\frac{1}{2}$grs. as the quantity over-prescribed.

Friday afternoon, very conveniently came to the end of his graphs at the end of the day which was also the end of the second week. This was a good stopping place. When on Monday 1 April he again followed Dr Douthwaite into the box (for Mr Lawrence, as we have seen, had taken up his option to cross-examine further), he changed his role from that of the expounder of graphs to that of the expert with the second opinion.

Dr Ashby was a neurologist, a consultant to six London hospitals. I suppose that neurologists know a lot about opiates and their proper use: anyway the defence did not question his authority to speak. He had had consultant status since 1949 and was, I should say, in his forties. He had not the carriage of an emissary from the Holy Office, which is not to say that he was not firm and clear, though cautious, in his views.

He was in the witness-box for Monday afternoon and the whole of Tuesday. Unlike the other witnesses with whom the Crown was brief and the defence lengthy, his time was almost equally divided between the two, each advocate trying ever so slightly to tilt the balance of his moderating answers. During the whole of his evidence the word 'murder' was mentioned only once, to be put aside by the witness with 'I do not think it is for me to say that.' He was ready to talk only about accelerating death.

A fortnight had gone by since the Attorney-General had made his submission on the Crown's case and he had not modified it.

> Why did he prescribe these large quantities for which there was no medical justification? The submission of the Crown is, members of the jury, that he did so because he had decided that the time had come for Mrs Morrell to die.

In this submission Adams was not represented, even in part, as a mercy-killing doctor who had strayed from orthodoxy: he was labelled as a villain out to enrich himself. But Dr Ashby would not concern himself with the second part of the statement, not with villainy nor with the chest of silver nor with the Rolls-Royce. He kept his words tightly to the first part of it, the issue of medical justification. Opiates for severe pain, yes: for distress, no. That was how Douthwaite had put it. Save that he softened it a little by adding to 'severe pain' 'the most dreadful discomfort', Dr Ashby agreed.

He was taken on a progress through the medical history during which most of the pre-November dross was brushed off the case. He did not endorse Dr Douthwaite's criticism of the Cheshire doctors. He thought that the severe pain then was arthritis (an old person immobilized, he said, can quite quickly develop pain in a joint) and that for the first few critical days the expectation of life would be too short to bother about addiction. By the tenth day, when she went to Eastbourne, the expectation would have been six months to three years and the morphia should have been stopped. He revealed himself as an enthusiast for weaning as strong as Dr Douthwaite, notwithstanding that in the case of Mrs Morrell the deleterious effect of the drugs was, he said, 'relatively slight' and that 'her health was not then obviously being much undermined'. There was no sign of craving; he pointed out that there was no report of her ever asking for an injection. But when in August 1950 her condition began to worsen and her require- ment of drugs to mount, weaning, he said, became the only alternative to disaster.

We were now reaching the murder period. Evidently the Crown was not going to adopt Dr Douthwaite's new idea, for they put the period to Ashby as beginning on 8 November. He did not demur and later he said that he did not regard the withdrawal of the morphia on 1 November as sinister or strange or as 'an act calculated to cause the death of the patient'. But, he said, she could not have survived the dosage of 6 to 12 November because of her age, her weak state of health and the suddenness of the increase over what had gone before.

When would it have been too late, he was asked, to begin weaning? On this his thought fluctuated. He disagreed with Douthwaite about all being lost by 1 November. But he thought that weaning begun then would have had only a slim chance of success, would have required a skilled team and involved some distress and suffering for the patient. But the patient could have stood it.

> My recollection of these books is that within two weeks of death she was bright and talkative; I think I am quoting correctly from memory. Well, I cannot believe the patient could not stand an attempt at weaning, on the basis we read out this afternoon, even at that stage. What was there to be lost?

A layman might ask: 'What was there to be gained? 'At the very best and at the expense of some suffering a brief incursion into the eighties of a distressful life. We have for eighteen months a minute account of her daily life in which there is no mention of any talk with her family, except occasionally her son, nor of a visit from any friend except Dr Adams, nor of any strong interest that she had in life except in the making of her will. Apart from the few domestic legacies which Mr Lawrence had read out, her money went to her son or, if he predeceased her, to charities of the sort that appear in the list which solicitors have ready for testators without ideas.

But Dr Ashby could no more ask himself what was to be gained by prolonging life than Mr Lawrence could ask himself what was to be gained by restoring Dr Adams to his practice. For each his profession cut off the longer view. The juror's view is not so circumcised. Certainly, it would be presumptuous for anyone to question the value of another's life and even in extremity life may be precious to the living. The thought is admissible only in the context of a criminal trial. Would any juror be willing to convict the doctor of any crime, let alone murder, because he, whether on 1 November or at any time in the autumn, accelerated death by rejecting an attempt to wean? All this part of Dr Ashby's evidence was appropriate, both in tone and in subject-matter, to a discussion between doctors at a sickbed trying to decide on the better course: to wean or not to wean. It was as if we were taking a breather from the murder trial and refreshing our minds with interesting medical talk.

Dr Ashby's evidence ended with the twelfth day of the trial on Tuesday 2 April. With it there ended also in substance the case for the Crown. It seemed to me that, barring accidents, all that remained was for the defence to canter to an acquittal. The medical evidence was split between Douthwaite and Ashby. The former had overcalled his hand and sown confusion with a new theory of the murder which neither the Attorney-General nor Dr Ashby was ready to support. Dr Ashby's evidence was really only to the effect that Adams, apart from behaving in a thoroughly unorthodox way, which fortunately did no harm, had not striven to his utmost to keep Mrs Morrell alive.

But where was the proof of intent to murder? It had to be found as an inference from the size of the dosage in the last five days. On this point all the stress that the Crown had laid on the misuse of opiates from the very beginning could now be turned against them. If during that period, when there was no allegation of murder, the doctor was in defiance of the rules prescribing excessive quantities, was it to be expected that towards the end he would do anything other than increase the flow?

On this point the effect of Dr Ashby's evidence was all for the defence. By the end of August, he said, weaning had become obligatory. The long period of cruising had at last come to an end and the doctor must either wean or increase. This was the dilemma. Could the jury be asked to say that to increase was murder?

If the medical evidence was disastrously split—Douthwaite going too far and Ashby not far enough—the evidence on motive was smashed. Both prosecution doctors were agreed that by 8 November at the latest Mrs Morrell was dying. If as a motive for murder a chest of silver, with or without an old Rolls-Royce, seems to be inadequate, the acceleration of its delivery by a few weeks is as a motive absurd.

So to my mind the defence was home, barring accidents. There might be a failure to produce adequate expert evidence in opposition, but with Hempsons as the solicitors this was unlikely. Moreover, the medical evidence for the Crown was now so weakened that the absence of professional opposition to it might not be fatal. The other accident would be, of course, that Dr Adams would say something silly in the witness-box.

But the next morning there was a turning point. Mr Lawrence rose to say that he had a submission which he conceived it his duty to make. His submission was 'that on a review of the whole of the evidence produced by the Crown in this case no sufficient evidence to support the indictment had been disclosed that would be a justification for allowing this case to proceed any further and calling upon the defence to deal with any matters that have emerged in real support of the charge'.

16

The Defence
Changes the Game

At the end of the last chapter I quoted the exact words which Lawrence used because they straddle the divide between 'no case to answer' and 'no evidence to support': with the foot perhaps more firmly planted on the latter than on the former. 'No case to answer' means that the proof offered is defective, perhaps because on one small though essential point there is no evidence at all or perhaps because a conclusion on the whole of the evidence would have to rest on conjecture instead of probability. It may be that there is no logical distinction between this and insufficient evidence. It may be also that in the civil case, where the burden of proof is discharged on the balance of probability, there is no practical distinction either. But the jury is now rarely used in a civil case and in a criminal case the burden is of proof beyond reasonable doubt. There is certainly a distinction between no case to answer and insufficient evidence to dispel reasonable doubt and one that I think should be maintained. The accused's right to silence depends upon it. If there is no case to answer, the right can be justified. But it cannot be just that an accused should not be expected to speak until enough evidence has been given to show that he was not only probably but almost certainly guilty.

Mr Lawrence developed his submission. After a time—quite a long time, for he did not like to be hurried—it became clear that what he was asking me to do was to withdraw the case from the jury as not proved beyond reasonable doubt on the medical evidence. He was giving me the argument which he might have addressed to the jury, though flavouring it with more copious extracts from the transcript than they would have been likely to enjoy. As an argument for the judge to stop the case this was hopeless. Plainly there was a case to answer. Two eminent doctors for the Crown were agreed that Mrs Morrell died from an overdose of drugs. Both asserted that the dosage was medically unjustified and that a doctor with Adams's qualifications must have known that it was large enough to terminate life prematurely. My feeling that, 'barring accidents', the Crown case was likely to fail was neither here nor there. I was the judge and not the jury and I was under no temptation to usurp the jury's functions. I thought that a case which had attracted so much publicity was best settled by the verdict of the jury subject to appeal. I felt also that to throw it out would be seen as a snub to the Attorney-General who had identified himself so personally with the prosecution. I mean the snub to the office rather than to the person. The office has become much more than that of the leading advocate for the Crown; it is now an office which plays a significant part in the administration of justice. These were my feelings. They could not have prevailed against the rights and liberties of Dr Adams. But once these had been assessed according to law (I was never in any doubt about the assessment), I was glad to see the law leaving the Attorney-General with his dignity unimpaired.

I let Lawrence take his time. It was not wasted since the jury as well as myself were listening to the argument. It began on the note that was now familiar.

> If ever there was a case in which the principle which I am invoking in my aid now should be strictly applied, it is this case for reasons which I need not and do not propose to develop before your lordship.

I supposed that it was his continuing disbelief in an unprejudiced jury that drove him away from seeking a verdict which to my mind he was so favourably placed to obtain. But he was a man of good judgment whose fears should not be dismissed as fanciful and I let him have his head. I allowed him two hours for a point that was worth two minutes. It was only when we were approaching the midday adjournment and Lawrence had said that he had finished with the medical evidence (though 'there are plenty of other passages that I could refer to') and would now pass to the evidence of the police that I stated my conclusion that the medical evidence 'does give rise to questions that can only properly be determined by the verdict of the jury'. The court then adjourned.

Of course when a good counsel makes a dubious submission of no case, the obvious explanation is that he is nervous about calling his client. Then any manoeuvre that will avoid the crux is worth trying. I cannot say how it was that I overlooked the obvious, but I did.

After the adjournment Mr Lawrence rose to say that his first witness would be Dr Harman: 'The defence have decided in the circumstances of this case not to call Dr Adams.' Sybille Bedford has described the scene, comparable with that which followed the production of the notebooks, 'a dozen and a half reporters stumbling over benches and each other to run the news to a telephone'. I really was surprised. The way ahead to an acquittal seemed to me so straightforward. Why had Lawrence decided to take refuge in an old-fashioned silence? Once again the structure of the case was transformed.

It remained until the nineteenth century a principle of English law that the evidence of persons interested in the result of the suit was inadmissible. It was supposed that the infection of an interest utterly destroyed the value of the evidence. A judge could discount the evidence for interest and give it a reduced value, which might be anything between nil and, say, 90 per cent. But discounting was thought to be (and probably was) beyond the mental capabilities of a nineteenth-century jury. Everybody knows that neither Mrs Bardell nor Mr Pickwick gave evidence in the famous suit for breach of promise.

The ban lasted longer in the criminal than in the civil procedure. The exculpatory evidence of an accused was deemed to be worthless, as indeed it frequently is, and, as a thought from holier times, it was considered that he should not be encouraged to add perjury to his other crimes. It was not until 1898 that an accused was permitted to give evidence on oath. His compulsory silence was not altogether a one-sided arrangement since it meant that he could not be questioned. The statute of 1898 allowed but did not compel the accused to go into the witness-box: the principle that a man could not be made to incriminate himself held good.

This statute revolutionized the trial. It brought the accused's own story out of oblivion into the heart of the proceedings. In nine cases out of ten he knew more about the facts than any other witness. The conduct of a trial in which he was silent had to be quite different from that of a trial in which the truth or falsity of his evidence in the box was the dominating question.

I have headed this chapter 'The Defence Changes the Game' because that is the metaphor which best illustrates what happened. The course of the trial was changed in the same sort of way as a game of chess is changed when a piece is sacrificed. Or the comparison might be between whist and contract bridge. In the latter the bidding tells the players quite a lot about each others' hands before the play begins: in whist they have only what they can infer from the course of play. Each of these parallels suggests its own comparison. One can compare whist, as the less sophisticated game, with the pre-1898 trial. But before 1898 there was only one form of trial and the parties knew in advance what it would be, just as the players know whether they are sitting down to whist or to bridge. After 1898 the pressures, which I shall describe below, in favour of calling the accused were so great as to make it by far the most likely form of trial. The decision to sacrifice his evidence was as disconcerting to an opponent as the unexpected sacrifice of the queen.

Let us measure first of all the extent of the sacrifice that Lawrence was making.

In all serious crime the prosecution has to prove the intention as well as the deed—the intent to kill, to wound, to defraud, whatever it may be. Without reasonably strong proof of the deed the prosecution is likely to founder in the early stages. So at the trial, more often than not, the real fight is about the intent. It is always the stronghold of the defence. It is the ground on which the accused has the advantage. The prosecution can only invite the jury to draw inferences from his acts. But he, if he can put enough conviction into it, can assure them of what was truly in his mind. 'I struck, but I did not intend to kill,' he can say: 'I levelled the gun but I intended only to frighten': 'I took the money, but I was muddled and thought it was mine.'

Before 1898 the prosecution and the defence were on more nearly equal terms. Unless the accused had given his mind away by utterance of it at the time of the act or by admission thereafter,* the prosecution had to prove intent by inference or presumption and the defence to cast doubt on it by the like means. The rule was, and still is, that a man is presumed to intend the natural and

---

* In the Adams case the admission on which the Crown was relying did not go to intent. The doctor admitted that he had given all the drugs, but not that he intended them to kill; he said that he intended to relieve 'terrible agony'. On that the Crown could argue that he must have intended the natural consequences of the act which he admitted, but they could not argue that he admitted that he intended to kill.

probable consequences of his acts. The defence that the accused might have intended only to frighten or might have been aiming at the arm and not the heart or might have been in a muddle could never have sounded very convincing when advanced by proxy. It is a defence that needs the personal testimony of the accused. Over and over again at the Old Bailey since 1898 the verdict has depended on the impression of innocence created by the accused in the witness-box. Has it, surviving hostile cross-examination, proved strong enough to make a jury doubt that he really intended to do what he did?

In the Adams case the defence was not, as it so often is, dependent upon the accused's own testimony. The first line of defence was that there was nothing medically unjustifiable about the doctor's treatment of his patient, which is the same as to say that he did not kill her. Could he not fight as he would have had to have fought before 1898 and win? If the defence could put a strong medical witness in the box, there was certainly a very good chance of an acquittal. But why was Lawrence, who was nothing of a gambler, staking all on the first line holding firm?

Moreover, it was not just a question of opting for the old pre-1898 game. The pre-1898 conditions could not be exactly repeated in 1957. There were new elements to be taken into account.

One of them, the least important, favoured the defence. This was the element of surprise. Before 1898 the prosecutor knew that he could not cross-examine the accused. After 1898 he thought it likely that he could; he would be disconcerted if he found that he could not. He might well be counting on making part of his case in cross-examination and would not want to alert the accused by indicating too clearly what sort of questions were likely to be put. His reticence would rebound upon himself if he found that he had no one to cross-examine. It looked as if Reggie had been saving a good deal, particularly about the prescriptions, for Dr Adams in the box.

But what profoundly changed the situation was that after 1898 the accused was no longer *obliged* to be silent. The pre-1898 advocate always made much of the dumbness forced upon his client: 'If only he could tell it to you himself upon his oath,' he would cry. The situation was reversed by the statute, which could have given it to the prosecutor to ask why, unless he had something to conceal, the accused did not speak. Indeed, there were many who feared that, so far from being liberated, the accused was being exposed to a new peril. The fear was so strong that the statute forbade the prosecutor to comment on the silence of the accused. But, spoken or unspoken, the comment was obvious. There was inevitably a grave risk that the jury would take silence as part proof of guilt.

The general English sentiment on this point in 1957 was, I believe, that

(a) it would be quite wrong to force anyone to speak, *but*
(b) it is difficult to see why anyone should be unwilling to speak unless he has something to hide, *but*
(c) it may be different if he is going to be questioned by a lawyer or a policeman since it is their trade to twist answers and make white look black.

There is the added complication of the judge whose attitude is likely to be influential with the jury and who can say what he wishes. Judicial sentiment in general accepted (a) as a factor and was more strongly impressed by (b) than by (c), not having the juryman's distrust of policemen and lawyers. Judges used to be freer with their comment than they would be today. 'Do you know what I would have said?' my colleague Toby Pilcher said to me over the port on our next circuit together. 'I would have said "And what do *you* think, members of the jury, of a doctor who attends a patient for two years and then will not go into the witness-box to explain how and why she died?"' Judges when on the bench have to sublimate many of their natural instincts: what better place to relax than in the Judge's Lodgings over the port? When Dr Adams made a second appearance in court, Mr Justice Pilcher, who presided, behaved, as will be seen, with high correctitude.

Counsel for the defence, who between them made the decision for silence (Dr Adams said afterwards that he took their advice), cannot have doubted that it would be a prejudicial factor; Toby Pilcher's reaction was, after all, the natural one. They must have had some very compelling reason for adding so substantially to the pile of prejudice which they believed to have been heaped up against their client.

They cannot have supposed that Dr Adams would be a good witness. What Mr Hannam called his loquacity seems to have been unquenchable. His statements to the police show how wide would be the spread of every answer. When, for example, Inspector Pugh in August 1956 was asking him about Mrs Hullett's death, they came to the point when it was relevant for him to say that Mr Hullett had a serious operation. The last four words that I have just written were all that were necessary to say it in. Dr Adams used one hundred and fifty.

He sent for me in the evening an SOS that he had a bad pain in his abdomen. I rushed up and he said: 'I have a terrible pain in my stomach.' I said: 'Have you had it before?' He said: 'Yes, I had an attack on the boat, but the ship's doctor paid no attention to it and thought it was the colic.' I examined him and to my horror I found he had a sub-acute obstruction of the lower bowel and I thought it might be cancer. I then had X-ray investigations which proved my diagnosis. I took him into the nursing home. I had Sir Arthur Porritt to operate on him. I told Sir Arthur: 'I have a patient with a ring carcinoma of the lower colon. I want you to come down and operate. He is one of my important patients and I want the best done for him.' I didn't ask Snowball to do it because I knew it was going to be fatal* and I thought if I had a local surgeon to operate, his relations might say: 'Why didn't you get a London man?' So I had Porritt. He brought his assistant and operated in the nursing home.

There would be little hope of keeping Dr Adams to the point. Counsel would have no idea of what he was going to say next. It was to be feared that he would continue from the box to assist the prosecution as lavishly as he had in his conversations with the police. Moreover, whatever he said could be studied and used in the trial of Hullett that was hanging over his head. Technically he would be a very bad witness, garrulous and unwary. It would be a gamble whether he would be technically so bad as to appeal to an amateur tribunal as genuine.

It was said after the trial that Reggie had been counting on a smashing cross-examination and that the decision not to call the accused was the masterstroke that confounded him. I do not think that it would have made all that difference. Reggie was an efficient cross-examiner and the witness had to mind his p's and q's which Adams was of course incapable of doing. Reggie would have had no difficulty in exposing him as a muddleheaded doctor with only an elementary knowledge of drugs. He might have broken him down into tears as had happened on 25 November when he was caught concealing drugs. He might have reduced him into a pulp. Then Lawrence re-examining would have reshaped him into a man to be pitied rather than condemned. But

* This does not sound very polite to Snowball, but one sees what he means.

considering the doctor's capacity to diffuse any issue by verbosity and considering the latitude to be accorded to a man on trial for his life, I doubt if Reggie would have come off best.

Counsel and witness would have been fighting with weapons as different as those of the gladiator with his sword and the retiarius with his net in the Roman amphitheatre. Reggie with a sabre, for he would be a slasher rather than a fencer, would score many hits. But an advocate does not get a verdict for murder by winning on points. To win he must capture, hold and convince the mind of the jury. For that the net is the more potent weapon. Of the few qualities that are known for certain about Dr Adams the one that stands out is the attraction he had for his patients. They felt him to be a doctor who took care of them and in return a large proportion stuck to him through thick and thin. A man who could have that effect on the ordinary men and women who come to a surgery or consulting room would not be helpless before a jury.

Reggie was not an artist like Lawrence. He would not even remotely have understood the mental processes of Dr Adams. If Adams was a murderer, he was not the crude sort that Reggie believed him to be. The truth was more complex. If it was not innocence, it was something which, if Adams had not been an Ulster Protestant, he might have revealed to a priest in the confessional. Or a psychiatrist in the half-light might have got the gist of it. But not a cross-examiner in open court. Not even, I would say, Mr Lawrence. Certainly not Reggie.

17

The Witness
for the Defence

Dr Harman was not just the sort of man, often the best the defence can get hold of, who is willing to go some distance out on a limb so as to inject into the expert evidence the reasonable doubt. His qualifications on paper were as good as those of the prosecution's experts. He was MD Cantab., FRCP, FRCS, Physician to St Thomas's Hospital. He had a large experience of cerebral thrombosis in elderly people.

From this respectable foundation he challenged quite a lot of the Douthwaite-Ashby dogma. The use of opiates was not to be restricted to severe pain; he had used it not only for helpless misery but also for restlessness and control of a disturbed patient. The use of heroin was unusual but not sinister. The combination with morphia was not dangerous.

Where there was a difference between Ashby and Douthwaite Dr Harman reinforced the Ashby view. Thus in a telling passage Dr Harman completed the destruction of the craving and dependence theory which Ashby had already undermined.

I have no great experience of treating addicts. It is true, of course, that addicts develop an attitude and a strong emotional relationship to people or places from which they get their drugs, but that is an anti-fact, that is, manufactured by the circumstances in which morphine can or cannot be obtained in western civilization. It doesn't occur in China where opium is easily obtained. If it can only be obtained through criminal circles at high prices, subject to blackmail etc. etc., then quite clearly this sort of dependence arises. But I don't see how that applies in this case. I don't know, we don't have any evidence that Mrs Morrell even knew she was dependent on morphine. She would only know if it had been withdrawn and if she had craving. In that case she would know what she wanted. Whether she knew it was morphine or not or merely whether she wanted the injection, she would know when she got the effect and when she had not, and I don't see any reason myself to suppose she did not think she could go on getting this from Dr Adams or from his locum, Dr Harris, who I believe treated her on two or three occasions; or a woman like that in a town like that could call on any doctor, and I cannot imagine any reasonable doctor refusing to give the necessary dose to an old lady who had become addicted. The only experience I have of long administration of morphine is in hospital, and, of course, one does not there notice any dependence on the person who comes around with the dose. It is the same as having a glass of water. That is necessary for life. One only develops emotional attitudes to the person who has water if you are dying of thirst.

Likewise, Dr Harman disagreed with the Douthwaite theory of accumulation; and more strongly with the Douthwaite theory on the withdrawal and re-introduction of morphia (from which Ashby had already dissented), pronouncing it to be 'inconceivable'. He firmly dismissed the paraldehyde as having had no effect on her life.

On other topics his attitude was that it was impossible to say one way or the other. He considered that most of the symptoms recorded in the books were symptoms of the illness and not of medication or drugging. The controversy on this point centred on an incident on 9 October 1950 when there is a record of a morning visit from the doctor and a special injection. The defence were clearly going to say that these injections were of vitamins or some other stimulant. The Crown wanted to say that they were injections of opiates taken from the quantity over-prescribed and concealed from the nurses. To make this sound convincing the Crown needed to show that the injection was followed by the symptoms of a heavy opiate dose. Their best exhibit for this purpose was the entry of 9 October. After the injection the patient became very drowsy and then semi-comatose; the lower lip was very blue. At 1.15 pm Sister Bartlett telephoned Dr Adams and he thought it was a stroke. Brandy was given without effect and the patient did not wake until 4.30 when she had slight difficulty with her speech. The incident did not frighten Dr Adams off special injections. He continued to give them daily though for some days Mrs Morrell continued to show signs of muddle and confusion.

Douthwaite and Ashby interpreted these symptoms as caused

by excessive drugging, but they both agreed that they were compatible with the stroke, which was what Adams had diagnosed. Their recognition of an alternative explanation made the incident of little use as evidence that Adams was surreptitiously adding to the drugging programme. Moreover, the Attorney never said whether or not it was an injection that was intended to kill. Presumably not, since it was outside 'the murder period', which—the Attorney interrupted Lawrence's final speech to clarify the point—did not begin till 8 November.

Dr Harman's opinion was that the incident was 'very characteristic of a slight stroke' and he used it positively to show that, having regard to the age and history of the patient, what was to be expected was what was in fact happening, 'further trouble leading progressively to deterioration and, unless something else intervened, to a natural death from old age'. The course of the deterioration between 9 October and 13 November offered to his mind no proof that anything unnatural had intervened. By 8 November she was obviously dying. The doses given thereafter were 'being given to stop her getting excited and to keep her peaceful and were not working very effectively'. He 'saw no necessity to link her death with the doses administered'. It was not really a question of explaining the cause of death. 'Old ladies over eighty who have had strokes and arteriosclerosis just die'; a clot on the heart or a coronary thrombosis would be very usual. He got no help from the size of the doses in the last four days. Opiates were unpredictable, especially when tolerance was taken into account. No one could say what would be fatal to a particular patient. Even if she had had all the quantity prescribed, she could have survived. Pressed in cross-examination with various adjectives, he said that survival would have been possible, even likely, but remarkable.

Like Mr Lawrence, Reggie had begun his cross-examination by nipping off a salient. Rebutting the criticism that as soon as she got to Eastbourne Mrs Morrell should have been weaned, the witness had said that weaning would have meant a clear-cut illness lasting about ten days. Reggie made him agree that in the early stages it could have been done without causing acute discomfort. But this was about all that Reggie got out of the cross-examination. While he could match Lawrence in severity, he could not rival him in beguilement. If there are textbooks on how to cross-examine, Reggie had read them. As an advocate he was like a chess player who had learnt the correct openings and whose shortcoming did not begin to show until the middle game.

One of the openings, as practised on Dr Harman, went like this:

> A-G: What were the materials that you considered and on which you based the opinions that you have expressed?
> [*Witness gives a list—nurses' reports and so on.*]
> A-G: And that is all, is it?
> Dr H: I think so.
> A-G: Are you quite sure?
> [*Witness adds a bit more.*]
> A-G: Anything else?
> Dr H: No.

The last answer is incorrect and the player will find himself in difficulties later on. The correct answer is: 'Nothing else that comes to my mind at the moment.' A lawyer is bound to respect this answer since it is the lay equivalent of his own habitual clause: 'And further to all such other happenings, events, things and matters as may from time to time appear, etc. etc.'

Failure to give the correct answer led to the following reproach.

> A-G: Based on the nurses' reports from the Neston Cottage Hospital. Those were the only documents you had before you about that?
> Dr H: No, they were not in fact.
> A-G: What else had you?
> Dr H: I had a proof of a statement from the hospital.
> A-G: I asked you very particularly at the beginning of your evidence on what you based the opinions you expressed in this court, and you made no reference to that.
> Dr H: No, I forgot that.
> A-G: Have you forgotten any other proof of any other kind that you have seen and read that has affected your opinion?
> Dr H: I couldn't say for certain what I have forgotten.
> A-G: Will you think very carefully. Is there anything else?
> Dr H: Not that I recall.

This may impress a jury. I doubt if it impresses a judge. It can disconcert a witness, but Dr Harman did not seem to mind.

He was in the box for Wednesday afternoon and the whole of Thursday 5 April, save for a brief period for the last of the trial's dramatic interludes. When I got back to my room after luncheon it was to be told that counsel desired to make an application before the jury returned. Mr Lawrence rose to say that during the

adjournment he had been handed a copy of a publication purchased in London that morning. The publication, which the
Attorney-General thought it would not be helpful to name, was
the European edition of the well-known American magazine
Newsweek. It had an office in London and a Chief European
Correspondent, Mr Griffiths, but his function was only that of a
reporter. He did not decide what was to go into the European
edition which was compiled in New York. It was printed in
Amsterdam and imported into this country, about 7,500 copies
a week, by an English company and supplied to newsagents.
W. H. Smith, where the copy produced had been bought, sold
about 1,850 copies a week.

In its issue of 1 April 1956 in a column headed 'Britain' and
subheaded 'Doctor on Trial' the following information was
conveyed.

> He employed three servants, and a chauffeur to drive his MG
> or Rolls-Royce on visits to his elderly patients, a remarkable
> number of whom remembered him in their wills when they
> died. Over a period of 20 years, 17 of Dr Adams's grateful
> patients bequeathed to him the sum total of $90,000—and this
> was what started the teacups rattling in Eastbourne. East-
> bourne's frenzied gossip pushed Dr Adams's alleged victims as
> high as 400.

The Attorney-General lost no time after the trial was over in
bringing proceedings for contempt of court in respect of the
publication of matter which, he said, was 'clearly calculated to
interfere with the due administration of the criminal law and to
prejudice the trial of Dr Adams'. He named as defendants Mr
Griffiths, the English importing company and W. H. Smith. He
could not bring the proprietors of *Newsweek* before the court since
they were outside the jurisdiction. The Lord Chief Justice
presided over a court of three judges.

Mr Griffiths was exonerated as having no responsibility for the
contents of the magazine. His statement that he had not supplied
the information himself was accepted; it was not revealed who
had supplied it. None of the defendants argued that the information was not prejudicial.

The British defendants set up the defence of 'innocent dissemination' which the English common law has recognized since
1885 as part of the law of libel. The defence is available to the
distributor of a newspaper containing a libel if he can show that
he was unaware of the libel and had no reason to suspect, from

the character of the newspaper or otherwise, that it would contain libellous matter. W. H. Smith do not handle every newspaper that is offered to them. They have a fine record in this respect. They had distributed *Newsweek* for twenty years without complaint. They argued that there was nothing now to put them on their guard. The court held, however, that innocent dissemination was not available as a defence in proceedings for contempt. Each defendant was fined £50.

The public must have wondered why Mr Lawrence was raising the matter instead of leaving it to the Attorney-General to exact the penalty, especially since he said that the possibility of harm was very slight. Of course, if he had feared that the trial was going against him, he would have canvassed the possibility that some juror might have seen the magazine and he would have then considered the prospects of an application for a new trial before a fresh jury. As things were this would be the last thing he wanted. Even if he did not feel that the trial was going well, he would lose on a new trial all the advantage he had obtained from the surprise disclosure of the books. Anyway he made no application. All he said by way of explanation was that he conceived it his duty to show the offending publication to the trial judge. Eventually it was agreed that I should bring the affair within the ambit of the general warning I had given to the jury and add a bit more for good measure.

Lawrence might have wanted to use *Newsweek* in the court of appeal as an example of the sort of thing from which his client was suffering. Or his object may have been no more than to turn the distributors back by a warning shot across their bows. In this he succeeded. All copies in Britain were immediately withdrawn. Even the American proprietors went so far as to authorize their counsel to say that their only intention was 'accurately and impartially to tell the story of the trial', a statement which did not impress the Lord Chief Justice.

The defence called no further evidence of any importance. At Wednesday midday I had been expecting the trial to go on for another ten days or so. By Thursday evening all was over except the speeches. Dr Harman had done all and more than all that the defence could require of him. Put into a word or two, he had shattered the dogma. Whether he or Douthwaite or Ashby would triumph in a medical debate was not the question. A man is not to be hanged on a debatable point and Dr Harman sounded to me convincing about the unwisdom of dogmatism. Moreover, he had thrust the debate forward from the question whether the dosage was really a crime or only a blunder to the question whether or not it had caused the death, making it sound at least plausible that that it had not.

The inconclusiveness of the medical evidence had to be coupled with the collapse of motive: the acceleration of a paltry legacy was, as Lawrence was to say, as a motive ludicrous. I thought it highly improbable that the jury would convict and almost inevitable that, if they did, the court of appeal would quash the conviction. In a sense it was no longer Dr Adams who was on trial; it was the jury system. A verdict of guilty would be attributed only to the inability of the jury to resist the unprecedented volume of prejudice generated by the pre-trial publicity and increased by the doctor's failure to give an account of himself.

18

Closing Speeches

Mr Lawrence had deprived himself of scope for great oratory. Had he been following Dr Adams, explaining and exploiting, he would have been at his best. But he was speaking for a man who would not speak for himself. The justification for the accused's silence was that there was no case for him to answer. An advocate, who is arguing that there is nothing to be said, has to beware of an over-expenditure of words.

It was the decision of counsel, Lawrence said, in discharge of a burden 'which may at times almost become unbearable', not to put Dr Adams in the box. It was 'the wonderful principle of our criminal law' that the accused could not be made to contribute to the proof of guilt. The jury would appreciate the strain he had been under for the past four or five months, 'in prison, day after day, night after night, awaiting his trial here'. Would the jury want him to endure the ordeal of question after question unless it was absolutely necessary. He would have had no notes of his own to help him cast back his memory over the gulf of six years. But by the mercy of heaven the nurses' notebooks had been preserved and in them the jury, guided by the Harley Street experts, would find the whole case.

Lawrence came fairly speedily to the 'vital fortnight' and made all the obvious points powerfully and in words designed to appeal to a jury. The very strange performance of Dr Douthwaite over the two theories. The 'utterly fantastic hypothesis' of a doctor murdering a 'patient whose life is limited to terms of hours or days or weeks for the sake of getting a bit of silver in a cabinet . . . it is too ludicrous, isn't it?' The nurses' lack of suspicion: 'the eye-witnesses of the murder and they have said in effect with one voice, "We all understood that the policy, the object, was to give her sleep and to keep her from becoming restless"; they know the

difference between that and murder, don't they?' The extent of
the drugging: is a doctor entitled to say to a patient with cancer
and severe pain that he will help with drugs, but obliged to say to
'an old woman in the last days of her life, restless, wakeful,
distressed, miserable through brain trouble . . . if you toss, if you
complain, if you do irrational things, if you exhaust yourself, if
your life is generally wretched, I am not going to help you with
any drugs'. As for the larger amounts prescribed, the doctor
could not know how much would be required to give her the ease
and comfort which it was his duty to give.

'My lord will give you a direction,' Lawrence now said. This
was a reference to what had occurred towards the end of his
submission of no case. He had come to the point when he desired
'to say a word about prescriptions'. I had intervened:

> Perhaps, Mr Lawrence, I may be able to shorten your submis-
> sion on this point by saying this. I have not heard the Attorney-
> General, but at the moment, and until I hear him, I am not
> satisfied that there is enough evidence at this stage to say that
> the quantity prescribed was administered by Dr Adams or
> under his directions. Merely for this purpose . . . you can deal
> with the matter on the basis that the only evidence which
> should go to the jury at this stage of the quantity administered
> is that which emerges from the evidence of the nurses in the
> witness-box.

Having said this, I had expected that one counsel or the other
would ask for a definitive ruling before addressing the jury.
Indeed, I had half expected the Attorney to drop the point;
without what he might have obtained in cross-examination it
added little to the strength of his case. Evidently he was not going
to do that; if he was, he would have intervened at this stage to
relieve the defence.

So the point was still in issue. It is what is called a point of law
and therefore a point for the judge to decide. The layman may fail
to see in it any question of law. If the question whether the
evidence is strong enough to prove guilt beyond reasonable
doubt is a question of fact for the jury, why is it not also a question
of fact whether there is any evidence of guilt at all? And why
on any view is it necessary to make two questions of fact out of
one? Surely the only question is whether or not the accused is
guilty.

When in an earlier chapter I outlined the sort of direction I
should have liked to have given the jury about the Hullett

allegations, I gave incidentally the explanation of the double question. I said there that one of my most important tasks was to make sure that the case for the prosecution had the minimum strength which the professional would think to be necessary for conviction; it was then for the jury to say whether it was strong enough to carry conviction. Logically the first question should be described as a question of fact for the judge and not for the jury rather than as a question of law. The origin of the misdescription is historical. In the working out over the centuries of the division of functions between judge and jury logic and clarity did not play a decisive part. The practical consequences are more important and it is very desirable that the issues for the jury should be simplified. If a judge thinks that there is nothing in the point, a jury should not have to spend time on it.

It would have been open to Lawrence, before he addressed the jury, to ask for a final ruling on whether the case on the prescriptions was going to be left to the jury. I should then have invited the Attorney-General to make his submission. Lawrence chose not to take this course. He had a provisional ruling in his favour and he would know that, if the Crown decided to contest it, he would be given a chance to reply. So he made only a few comments. He had no difficulty in dealing with the first part of the case, i.e. the proposition that what was prescribed must have been injected. But on the second part it became apparent that the burial of Dr Adams's admission was not going to be as easy as it had looked. My thoughts had always taken it for granted that Adams would testify to some explanation of it that the jury would be ready and willing to accept. What was to happen when there was no testimony at all?

What I myself believed to be the truth of the matter—that the admission was a false exculpation—could not without the spoken evidence of Adams be advanced as the explanation. What Lawrence was now suggesting was that Adams was obviously mistaken in a recollection which the notebooks showed to be 'absolutely wrong': they showed that he had not administered nearly all the injections.

There were maybe two flaws in this which I hardly noted at the time, since the mind is carried on the current of the speechmaking and Lawrence, now in the early afternoon of Friday, was coming to an end, to be followed immediately by the Attorney. One was that this was not just a lapse of memory on the doctor's part which would after six years certainly be understandable; it was a positive statement of something which either had happened or was being imagined. Adams was not saying that he did not remember, but that he did remember and that he had given them all.

The other flaw was that the notebooks did not necessarily show the doctor's recollection to be totally wrong. What they showed was that if Adams gave the extra injections the nurses did not know about them.

The transcript for Friday shows that four-fifths of the day was taken up by the speech for the defence. So it must have been about three o'clock when the Attorney began. 'It is not my duty, nor my desire, to seek by any artifice of advocacy to persuade you by my words of the guilt of the accused.' But, if the jury considered the whole of the evidence fairly, they would be compelled to come to the conclusion that 'death was secured by the deliberate acts of the accused'. He began by spending some time on the early history while making it clear that 'the prosecution have never suggested that at that time Dr Adams had formed a design to murder': the intention was 'to make this elderly and rich lady, his patient, well disposed towards him with a view to his benefiting under her will'. He launched, as he had to do if he was to succeed, a severe attack on Dr Harman as a witness. One did not have from him the kind of frankness which one ought to expect. Were not his answers evasive and some 'wholly incredible'? He submitted that he was an unsatisfactory witness. He did not comment on the volte-face of Dr Douthwaite.

The notebooks. 'It was with considerable surprise, was it not, that those books were introduced in the course of this case.' The Attorney did not take up his final position on the books until after the weekend when he submitted that the books, although put in by the defence, proved the case for the prosecution. On the Friday he approached them in what seemed to be a state of muddled ambivalence. Why were they kept, he asked. It appeared that, although they proved the case for the prosecution, the doctor was the only person who had an interest in keeping them: that is, having first taken care to secure that they would not contain any incriminating entries. However, Reggie, who was a great rhetorical inquirer (as indeed we all are, since it is a good way of talking to a jury undidactically), did not inquire by what means the books proved the case for the prosecution without containing any incriminating entries. Nor did he explain how the doctor could have eliminated entries otherwise than by corrupting or bamboozling the nurses. I half expected Mr

Lawrence to object. No suggestion had been put to any of the nurses of any attempt to influence what they wrote.

He did not challenge any entry in the books, the Attorney said, but they did not contain the whole case. There was the difference between the doses recorded and the prescriptions. He invited the jury to conclude that this difference 'was the source from which he took the drugs which he himself administered'. Not all were sent by the chemist to Marden Ash, were they? Here again I expected Mr Lawrence to object. The Crown witnesses were positive that the drugs prescribed were either collected by the chauffeur or delivered direct to Marden Ash. No chemist had been asked whether he had ever made a delivery to the doctor personally.

It had been clear for a long time that the Crown was going to make some capital out of the quantity over-prescribed. I had supposed that it would be worked in as an auxiliary to the case on the books. The Attorney was now making it plain that it would be the other way round; or that at the least the books and the prescriptions would be equal partners. Winding up for the day, he said:

> I do not want you to think that the case for the Crown depends solely on what is contained in the nurses' books. It does not. It depends on a great deal more than that and, in my submission, more weighty evidence than one finds—although it is weighty enough—in the nurses' books, more weighty evidence point-ing, and pointing conclusively, to the guilt of the accused. My submission when the case was opened was based on those prescriptions proved to be made up and supplied. The case for the prosecution after all this inquiry still rests in part but not wholly on those prescriptions.

To this I listened with concealed amazement. What was the point of it? If the quantities recorded and admitted made, as Dr Douthwaite said, death certain, what was the point of attempting a dubious proof of the administration of a larger quantity, just so as to make, again in Douthwaite's words, death even more certain? If Harman had been willing to concede that the addi-tional dosage might tip the scale, there would have been a point to be gained: but he made no concession. There was just a slight advantage on Ashby's evidence. He did put the case on the prescribed dosage as rather stronger than the case on the recorded. On the former, he said, there could not be the faintest doubt; on the latter, while he himself had no doubt, he could accept that some other doctor might have. This would be a small reward to the Attorney for undertaking so heavy a burden of additional proof. Since he concluded his final speech without mentioning it, he cannot, quite rightly, have thought it worth claiming.

Moreover, it looked to me to be impossible to amalgamate the two cases without producing a murderer of incredible fatuity. The Crown's case on the quantities recorded was that they were so large that a doctor as qualified as Adams must have known —not just hoped—that they would kill. Both Douthwaite and Ashby testified to that, the former saying specifically of each dose recorded on or after 6 November that it was intended to kill. The killing was being done most satisfactorily from the murderer's point of view in that it was operating through the nurses without arousing any suspicion. What could be the sense in a plan which would risk discovery by requiring the murderer, merely for the purpose of overkill, to get drugs direct from the chemist and seek opportunities for injections not to be detected by the nurses? The best result to be got would be the advance of death by a few more hours, making Lawrence's 'utterly fantastic hypothesis' more fantastic still.

The adjournment for the weekend came when, as it turned out, Reggie was less than halfway through his speech. But he had said enough to make it clear that he was shifting the emphasis from the books back to the prescriptions. Did he really believe in the point, I wondered. If so, why was he tackling it in this way? He should have been tackling first the point of law which it was for me to decide, whether there was any evidence on which a jury could reasonably conclude that the accused had administered unrecorded injections. I had already said that, unless I was persuaded to the contrary by the Attorney-General, my view was that there was not.

Counsel is not obliged to clear his points of law with the judge. It is quite proper for him to state what he believes to be the law 'subject to my lord's direction'. But he usually does that, as Lawrence had done in his speech, only when he is fairly confident that the direction will be in his favour. If he is going to have to persuade the judge, he is not likely to succeed through the medium of an address to the jury. The judge will want to put questions to him (this sort of submission sometimes comes near to being a dialogue) but will not interrupt an address to the jury to do so. If Reggie was serious, he would have wanted, I thought, to meet and change the contrary disposition of the judge, and he would have been prepared to face the counter-argument from Lawrence which the course he had chosen avoided. This course had obvious advantages if his object was limited to placing under the jury's nose some inhalations from the over-prescriptions.

I suspected that Reggie had not after all disdained the 'artifice of advocacy', to which at the beginning of his address he had referred, and that, being himself but a plain, blunt man, he had chosen the plain, honest artifice of the red herring. Surely, if he had had any confidence in the point, he would have tried for a clean bill of health for it before he addressed the jury.

There was another thing that puzzled me. Why was Lawrence taking no objections? Reggie was exploiting rather shamelessly the advantage of the last word. There was at this time a growing feeling that the defence ought always to have the last word. It was often being conceded by the Crown and it was to be formally conferred on the defence by statute in 1964. Before that, certainly by 1957, any judge would have given defence counsel the oppor-tunity of dealing with a new point. But after the last sentence of his address in which he had perorated that his voice would be heard no more, Lawrence behaved as a man who could do no more. No doubt the strain of the case and of the forceful speech which he had just delivered had taken a lot out of him; he looked fatigued.* But he was not a man who in any circumstances would let pass anything that injured his client. Yet neither was he a man to fall into the error of supposing that in advocacy speech must always be better than silence. In his present situation there was a strong argument for keeping quiet.

In the adversary procedure in a civil case the judge, as I have said, can leave all the initiatives to counsel. I have said also that it is not so in a criminal case. There was not until towards the end of the nineteenth century anything in crime that could be called an adversary procedure. Until then the extent to which the accused was allowed to be represented by counsel was limited and it is difficult to be properly adversarial without counsel on both sides. Even after that, when representation was permitted, the ordinary accused could not afford it. It was the duty of the judge to help

* He never looked very strong. In 1957 he had a large practice and no doubt the acclaim which he earned in the Adams case made it larger. He continued with it, while finding time for public duties, from 1960 to 1962 as Chairman of the Bar Council and from 1962 to 1965 of the National Incomes Commission, until he went on the Bench in 1965. He was a judge for less than two years, dying, greatly lamented, at the comparatively early age of sixty-five. He was a talented amateur musician who got much pleasure from the string quartet.

him with his questioning of the witnesses and to get his defence, if any, and put it to the jury. Now that legal aid has made counsel always available the judge is an overseer rather than a labourer in the field. But the availability of counsel has not destroyed the basic principle. It is still the judicial responsibility to see that every essential point for the defence, whether or not it is taken by counsel, is put to the jury.

Delicate questions may now sometimes arise about the propriety of counsel shuffling on to the judge the more difficult parts of the defence. They did not arise here. Lawrence had formally concluded his part in the trial. He could speak again only with my leave or at my invitation. It would be an invitation, if it came, that he could not in the circumstances refuse. But he was under no obligation to ask for leave. If he still placed his hope of success with the court of appeal rather than with the jury, silence was now his best weapon. If without his assistance I directed the jury to dismiss the case on the prescriptions, he would win the point without talking. If I directed them the other way, he would start in the court of appeal with a strong case on misdirection.

Had he been the sort of advocate who likes always to be up and doing, he had certainly had a grand opportunity for firing off volleys of objections and had a grand opportunity now for demanding to be heard again. But Lawrence never sought an opportunity to display his virtuosity. The lamp that lit his way was his duty to his client. It burnt with exceptional brightness when he felt, as he did here, that his client was being unjustly treated. Like many good people he could sometimes be irritating in the ways that make 'the clever so rude to the good'. Not, of course, that he was unclever, but he put goodness so conspicuously first. Too often he was unable to do or to say anything without first deeming it his duty to do or to say it. But in truth his thoughts were always on his duty to his client and never on the show he was making.

When, for example, Dr Douthwaite advanced his startling theory, Lawrence could, as soon as I had finished my questioning, have bounded into action and asked for leave to cross-examine further. Most counsel would have done it without a thought. Lawrence thought slowly and carefully about everything. The result of his thought on that occasion was, I guess, that it was best to leave the prosecution to stew in the Douthwaite juice. It would not have influenced him in the least that that might make him appear as a man slow in the uptake who had to be prodded into action by the judge.

So here he was serving his client best by silence. It looked as if I might have to prod him once more on the question that was troubling me: was not the admission, although overspread by a pall of implausibility, evidence for the jury to consider?

Now that the defence was complete and the line to be taken by the Crown revealed I could begin to think about the detail of the summing up. I was lucky to get a weekend for its preparation, especially since I would incidentally have to solve the problem of what I should do about the artificial respiration of the case on the prescriptions. I decided to spend the weekend in London. Our flat in Gray's Inn was commodious enough but not free from interruption. So I made the Benchers' Library, which nobody uses at the weekend, my workroom. It is a bookroom rather than a library. The Library of the Inn occupies the whole of one side of South Square. The Benchers' Library is a comparatively small room with shelves on one wall to hold the law reports and on the others bookcases to hold lighter legal literature. Besides a large table on which many papers can be spread, there is a handsome writing table, presented by Mr Justice Hilbery who was for many years the senior Master of the Bench and a prop of the Inn. He had placed on it a large card, sumptuously framed, on which there were inscribed many pious exhortations on judicial behaviour, some of which he must himself have found it quite a struggle to obey. The table stood in front of a window looking north over Gray's Inn Square. A perfect setting.

The pattern of a summing up is always much the same. First, there are the directions on the law. However many times it has been said before, the judge is obliged to repeat that the law puts upon the prosecution the burden of proof beyond reasonable doubt. Then it is usual to go through the facts so that the jury have as the foundation for their verdict an impartial account of the whole story. After that it was my practice to extract the issues which I thought to matter. This has to be carefully done with the warning that it is for the jury to say what matters and what does not; what the judge can do is to give them a blueprint to work on.

The oral evidence consisted of just over 800 pages of transcript. There were in addition all the written exhibits, notably the nurses' notebooks. But they did not add substantially to the bulk since all the relevant passages in them had been put to witnesses and were in the transcript. This was easy for me to work on since I had it all indexed. What I had completed by Sunday evening was the skeleton of the summing up with references attached. The collation of the medical evidence took up most of the time.

I reckoned that Reggie had an hour or so left of his speech and that any new point he made would be marginal. There was nothing in my skeleton about the case on the prescriptions. If I decided to leave it to the jury, I would have Monday evening in which to consider it. What remained of Monday after Reggie had finished and after any further argument I might invite would certainly not be enough for the whole summing up.

The court duly sat on Monday morning and the Attorney duly resumed where he had left off. Having quelled the notion that his case was dependent on the notebooks, he now examined them to show that anyway they proved murder. My concern was to see what modifications, if any, he would make to the case he had opened. I ought to have known that there would be none. For Reggie a point taken was a point to be held for ever and a point to the contrary was best taken no notice of. This was the fate of the reference to the 'utterly fantastic hypothesis'. Likewise the taunt of 'ludicrous' was ignored. Nor did he suggest any unmercenary motive for an eleventh-hour killing. There was no hint of mercy killing; Mrs Morrell remained simply 'this rich old lady whom he made a drug addict'.

Having taken the case on the notebooks down to the death and argued against the theory that it was a natural death, the Attorney, adhering to the pattern in his opening speech and saying that 'the case for the prosecution does not end there', took the jury through the police evidence. He emphasized the doctor's statement that he had himself given all the injections.

> Great stress was laid by the defence on the fact that these events happened some six years before, but there was nothing, was there, to prevent Dr Adams from saying 'Well, really, I do not recollect. It is far too long ago. I have got a large practice with many patients?' . . . Why should he have made these statements to Superintendent Hannam if they were not true? If he did not recollect, what was there to stop him saying 'I cannot remember.'

It was a telling point.

When he had finished I asked him to elaborate on one passage in his address. He had said:

> Dr Adams, we are told, used drugs that he took from his bag.

Did he pay for them himself? The probability is surely that he made out a prescription for the drugs he used himself and either collected those drugs himself or had them delivered to him.

I asked if there was any direct evidence of delivery or collection. Making one of his very rare mistakes, Reggie offered as evidence of delivery to Kent Lodge a deposition by the chemists' van driver. It turned out to relate to 1956 not 1950, and, I suppose, had been intended for use in the Hullett case. So the chemists' evidence that everything was delivered to Marden Ash was left uncontradicted.

For evidence that the doctor was himself collecting drugs the Crown was relying, the Attorney said, on two items. The first was the paraldehyde. Nurse Randall and Sister Bartlett had said that there was none in the house; so the doctor must have brought it himself. The second item related to the note made by Sister Mason-Ellis on 9 November* when she recorded that Dr Adams left a tube each of morphia and heroin 'for future use only'. Mr Lawrence had already cited this to show that the doctor was not always prescribing for immediate use but was building up a reserve. The Attorney cited it to show that the doctor had himself collected the tubes. This left the point incomplete. The doctor could not in this way have filled his bag or any other secret store he might be supposed to have had, since on both occasions the drugs were given to the nurses to administer.

But there remained the point that the accused had himself said that he had injected nearly all that he had prescribed.

* See page 86.

19

The Gordian Knot

Gordius, as every schoolboy (and I dare say only a few others) used to know, was a peasant with an oxcart who had secured the yoke of the oxen to the pole of the cart by a cunning knot. One day, while on the road with his cart, he met with a group of Phrygian notables who had been told by the oracle at Delphi (or maybe directly by Zeus; accounts vary) to stop the first man with an oxcart that they met and make him their king. Thus there was founded the city of Gordium. The grateful monarch erected a temple to Zeus and there the oxcart was preserved. At some later stage a further oracular pronouncement was obtained to the effect that whoever succeeded in untying the knot would become the ruler of all Asia. Alexander the Great, who intended to become ruler of Asia anyway and had no time to waste over knots, eliminated possible competition by drawing his sword and cutting the Gordian knot.

The law tries to tie up human activities into parcels convenient for the administration of justice and in the process sometimes creates Gordian knots. It is the business of the lawyers, resisting the temptation to cut, to patiently untie. But exceptionally the judge in a criminal trial is armed with a sword for occasional use in cutting a knot that binds the accused. No system, even the best, can be sure of so regulating its processes as to eliminate all possibility of unfairness or oppression within the rules. Relief must come from the *ad hoc* decision of the trial judge.

In the Adams case the knot was in the beginning formed—as the tangles in the legal process which lead to injustice so often are—out of the lie told by the accused when he said that he had himself injected all that he had prescribed. I do not doubt, first, that he made this statement; second, that it was untrue. As to the first, I shall later on consider more carefully the value of the police reports of what the accused said; at present it is enough to say that they were not challenged at the trial. As to the second, in the light of the full account of the incident,* which I had but the jury, at least officially, had not, the object of the lie was plain.

It was also plain that Dr Adams, had he given evidence, would not have been so sensible as to belatedly tell the truth, but would have denied that he said anything. This was plain from Lawrence's half-hearted cross-examination of Mr Hannam.

Mr L: Did you say this: 'This is a list of drugs which you prescribed for Mrs Morrell,' or words to that effect?
Supt H: Similar to those, yes.
Mr L: I suggest that at that time Dr Adams was across the room, and he just said quite casually, 'Oh yes'?
Supt H: He was standing right beside me, and I had that list in my hand.
Mr L: You see, I have to put the best of Dr Adams's recollection?
Supt H: Yes, I agree.
Mr L: And that you said something to the effect of a question, 'Were they all given to her?' and that he said, 'I can't remember about that,' or words to that effect?
Supt H: No, sir, that is quite untrue. He was most emphatic about it.
Mr L: And that you persisted in the question and that he still maintained that he could not possibly remember the details and he would not discuss it with you?
Supt H: That is quite untrue, the whole thing. He was most loquacious, and always has been since I have known him.
Mr L: Let me see. This was, on any view of this matter, something that had happened six years before the moment when you were asking him about it?
Supt H: Yes.
Mr L: In his surgery?
Supt H: Yes.
Mr L: What I am suggesting to you is that he said, when you were asking him about it, that he could not possibly remember clearly the details of that case?
Supt H: He did not. He was dogmatic at once.
Mr L: Then I suggest that you did turn to the last page of the document and referred in some way or other to the quantities prescribed, but that Dr Adams still refused to discuss the matter any further with you?

* See pages 102–3.

166

Supt H: Quite untrue, sir.

Mr L: That you said something about drugs or what was left over, and that he did not reply even to that?

Supt H: Yes, he did.

But Dr Adams had not testified. So Lawrence had to address the jury on Hannam's uncontradicted evidence.

When earlier in the week I had cut short Lawrence's submission by saying that provisionally I was not satisfied that there was evidence to go to the jury of any injections beyond those recorded, I was not thinking primarily of Adams's own statement. Apart from that, nothing that the Attorney had as yet said disposed me to alter my view. But as soon as I brought the statement into focus, I had to consider whether it did not by itself constitute a case fit to go to the jury.

On the face of it, it did.

It is not that every admission made by an accused, even if it is a complete admission of guilt, is necessarily fatal. The jury have to be satisfied not only that the admission was made but also that it was true. It is always open to an accused to testify that what he said was untrue and to explain why he lied. Unless the jury is satisfied that it is his testimony on oath that is false, they cannot convict.

But Adams had given no evidence. Lawrence had done his best to make good the deficiency by offering suggestions instead of evidence, but his best was not very good. Nevertheless, whether it was good enough was a question for the jury to answer.

It was not, however, from this angle that I was now considering the point. The Crown was not now resting its case on the admission taken by itself, but on the admission taken in the context of the notebooks. Could the admission and the notebooks be combined?

On any issue which is to be left to a jury the prosecution must present a coherent case. If one piece of their evidence contradicts another, they must state which they adopt and which they reject. In this respect an admission by the accused is no different from any other sort of evidence. The Crown accepted the notebooks and could therefore rely on the admission only insofar as it was consistent with them.

This raised the question of consistency. Another question of equal importance was that of severability. Unless one part of a statement can be severed from another, the party—in this case the Crown—who seeks to make use of it against its maker must take the whole of it, for better or for worse, and the whole of what it takes becomes part of its case. A statement is not severable unless the separation leaves each part with a life and logic of its own. Siamese twins can be severed successfully, but not Solomon's baby.

Severability raises the shorter point and I shall take it first. When Adams was asked specifically about the last prescription of 12½grs. heroin (No. 93), he said: 'Poor soul, she was in terrible agony: it was all used: I used them myself.'* If she was in terrible agony, it would not, as the Attorney had expressly conceded, be murder. So if he *thought*, however mistakenly, that she was in terrible agony, it would not be murder because he would lack a guilty mind.

Is then the Crown allowed to contend that, when the accused said that he used them all, he was admitting the truth, but that when he said she was in terrible agony, he was telling a lie? If he had put it in one sentence instead of two— 'I gave her the whole lot because she was in terrible agony'—could the Crown have split the sentence? I doubted it.

The point of consistency also raised a doubt. The admission was in two parts. There was first a general statement by Adams that he had given nearly all the prescriptions on the list (that is, on Exhibit 4A which covered the whole of the year 1950) and that nothing was left over. The notebooks established that the nurses gave most, if not all, on the list. How could the two statements be reconciled?

Whether or not Adams gave any injections before the murder period began was a peripheral question. The essential question was whether or not after 1 November he gave a murderous injection. In the second part of the admission he stated specifically that he had given all the 75 tablets in No. 93, except for perhaps two. There was nothing in the notebooks which expressly contradicted this. But it would be impossible to give a dose of 12½grs. to a patient, who had never before had more that 1gr. without producing symptoms which would have been recorded in the books. Unless the Crown could point to a corroborative entry, the silence of the books would be inconsistent with the admission.

This is probably about as far as I had got in my musings by the time I took my seat on Monday morning. My weekend task had

* See list on page *x*.

been to lay the ground-plan for the summing up; the musings were for the odd moments when I was not seated at Master Hilbery's writing table. Putting them on paper, as I am doing now, makes them look much more shipshape than they were. Reggie had not on the Friday given any distinct shape to the point he was making about the prescriptions. He had not said, otherwise than by a general implication of guilt, what conclusion he wanted the jury to draw from the difference in quantities between the recorded and the prescribed. It had come towards the end of the day as part of a ramble through the evidence.

> Now, members of the jury, one thing I do ask you to bear in mind is this. Is there not a very significant and important difference between the doses as recorded in the nurses' books and the prescriptions? Is not that rather important? One thing is clear, isn't it, that all the prescriptions given by Dr Adams for Mrs Morrell were made up? The evidence is that they were all supplied by the chemists. They did not all go to Marden Ash, did they? What about the paraldehyde?

A summing up requires greater precision than this. What exactly was it that Reggie thought 'very significant and important'? Neither Dr Douthwaite nor Dr Harman believed, though their disbelief was grounded on opposites, that the difference in quantity mattered at all; even for Dr Ashby the difference was only between 100 per cent certainty and, say, 95 per cent. Yet on the Friday I had thought that there might be a significant point which the Attorney might be intending to introduce on Monday. The point would be, not simply that the accused had increased the dosage; it would not be a matter of quantity at all. It would be that the admission, if it could be successfully combined with the nurses' evidence, showed that the accused, after instructing the nurses to give the patient from time to time all that was necessary to keep her under, had himself given secretly one or more massive additional doses. What except murder, the Crown might ask, could have been his object.

On Friday Reggie had not even hinted at this. He was relying on the point simply as one which in some unspecified way contributed to the proof of guilt. The nearest he got to anything significant on Monday was a passing reference, made a few minutes before he sat down, to the last prescription, No. 93.

> An injection of 12½grs. is not shown in the records of 12 November, but a special injection is. One would not expect,

would one, at that stage, knowing what the policy was then, that a special injection was being given at that time to wake her up?

Neither would one have expected it to be 12½grs. heroin, a dose twelve times as large as any she had had. Whatever it was, it gave her only two hours' sleep, after which she survived for another thirteen hours, mostly awake (at 5.30 pm she drank half a glass of milk and brandy) and sometimes restless and talkative, in spite of 2grs. more of heroin and morphia and 6 or 10cc of paraldehyde. These were the circumstances in which the Crown, having had two experts in the box, had not invited either of them to express an opinion on the character of the special injection given at 11.15 am. It was useless now for the Crown to hint that that injection might have been fatal.

I could not see a clear and complete case to go to the jury on the prescriptions. A judge has, as I have said earlier, a responsibility to see that all proper points for the defence are adequately raised, but he does not help out the prosecution unless he sees a serious danger of a guilty man going free. I did not see that here. Indeed, the danger I saw was of that sort of unfairness within the rules from which the judge should relieve the accused. An admission which I then believed not to be a true and genuine admission was putting him in peril. The Attorney had either ignored or failed to perceive the objections about consistency and severability which I have noted. He had failed to marry the admission and the notebooks. He was not facing up to the difficulty that the nearer to the death he brought the murderous act, the more absurd it became to believe in the motive he was alleging. Yet he had not modified his allegation that the murder was for money.

His speech left with me only a tangle for the sword to cut. So I cut the knot with an Alexandrine sentence. Close to the commencement of my summing up I said:

There are various ways, as you heard from the Attorney-General, of putting the prosecution in this case, and if on any one of them I hold that there is no evidence for your consideration, it is my duty so to direct you. I do therefore direct you as a matter of law that there is no evidence upon which you could properly come to the conclusion that any drugs were administered to Mrs Morrell over and above the injections recorded in the nurses' books.

20

Summing Up and Verdict

The summing up followed the pattern I have indicated, took about three and a half hours to deliver, and was divided as follows:

The Law and General Directions. This took one hour and finished with the midday adjournment on Monday.

The Narrative. Forty minutes.

The Inessentials. Thirty-five minutes.

The Essentials. Sixty-five minutes, divided about the middle by the adjournment on Monday evening.

Finale. Ten minutes.

The Law

First point. Murder is the cutting short of life, whether by years, months or weeks. It does not matter that Mrs Morrell's days were numbered. 'But that does not mean that a doctor who is aiding the sick and the dying has to calculate in minutes or even in hours, and perhaps not in days or weeks, the effect upon a patient's life of the medicines which he administers or else be in peril of a charge of murder. If the first purpose of medicine, the restoration of health, can no longer be achieved, there is still much for a doctor to do, and he is entitled to do all that is proper and necessary to relieve pain and suffering, even if the measures he takes may incidentally shorten life.' This is not because there is a special defence for medical men but because no act is murder which does not cause death. We are not dealing here with the philosophical or technical cause, but with the commonsense cause. The cause of death is the illness or the injury, 'and the proper medical treatment that is administered and that has an incidental effect on determining the exact moment of death is not the cause of death in any sensible use of the term. But . . . no doctor, nor any man, no more in the case of the dying than of the healthy, has the right deliberately to cut the thread of life.' It is not contended by the defence that Dr Adams had any right to make that determination.

Second point. This was my direction in law on the prescriptions.

Third point. This was the exclusion of rumours and what was not evidence. But I thought that in the three weeks they had been sitting the jury had learnt to distinguish 'between what is solid fact, sifted, gone over again and again, and what is gossip and rumour'.

Fourth point. The burden of proof beyond reasonable doubt. This means that where there is a conflict between two versions —of what was said or what happened—the jury must be convinced by the prosecution's version, not just think it more likely. In this case there had been virtually no dispute about the direct evidence. What the jury had mostly to deal with was indirect evidence, matters of inference. Here the application of the rule meant that if on any point made by the prosecution, the defence could advance a reasonably possible inference consistent with innocence, the point failed.

There were two unusual features about the evidence. The first was that so much of it was expert evidence. The jury were not a board of medical assessors which could award marks to each expert. They were in the position of the ordinary person who had to decide, whether for himself or a relative, to have a serious operation and who was getting conflicting advice from the doctors. Such a person would have to follow the doctor that gave him the greater confidence.

The other feature was that the accused had not gone into the witness-box. He had the right not to do so, and to require the prosecution to prove its case without him. It would be wrong in law 'if you were to regard Dr Adams's silence as contributing in any way towards proof of guilt'. So much for the rights of Dr Adams as the accused. But he was also a potential witness for the defence. If they found a gap in the defence—the police evidence, for example, was uncontradicted—they must not strive to fill it.

The Narrative

I ran through the events chronologically down to the death and followed them with a brief reminder of each of the police interviews.

The Inessentials

'Inessential in the sense that they do not really help you to a just determination of the really crucial matters in this case.'

First inessential. The whole course of the illness leading up to the vital period in November. Not a pretty story: lavish use of heroin, angling for a legacy, being taken out of the will and put back again, the cremation form 'which you may think is false'. But there is a big difference between this and murder. Even if they thought the doctor a fraudulent rogue, 'fraud and murder are poles apart'.

Second inessential. Paraldehyde. They need not bother with it. The Crown case was that the doctor had made up his mind to murder by opiates. The most the paraldehyde did was to acceler-ate death by a few hours.

Third inessential. The criticism of the police. Lawrence had developed this along conventional lines. He had criticized the 'contrived meeting' on 1 October 1956 and was apparently shocked to hear that in recording the interview of 24 November the superintendent and his sergeant had made a joint note instead of two separate ones.

Perhaps I may say, for what it is worth, it is my opinion as one who has sat here and heard this criticism made many times—it is not a matter binding upon you—that I have seen nothing at all in the conduct of Superintendent Hannam in this case which appears to me to constitute anything that was unfair or oppressive. But it is for you to decide that and it is your tests that apply.

There is one thing in this case which seems to me to show that the police officers were maintaining in the highest degree the traditions of fairness that we hope govern the conduct of the police: that phrase 'Murder? Can you prove it?' It could have been twisted to sound very nasty, couldn't it? Without altering the words the impression could have been given that what Dr Adams was saying from his attitude, in effect, was: 'Well, murder; you know and I know and we all know that I did it, but you won't be able to prove it.' It could have been given that impression. You heard the evidence that both volun-teered—it was not extracted in cross-examination—which gives it a wholly different meaning. It gives it a meaning which is very much in favour of the defence so far as this one incident goes, and let me remind you of it in case I forget to remind you again. It gives a meaning upon which Mr Lawrence rightly relies, in that it shows that this man, who is said to have committed a calculated murder, who must at this stage in the investigation have known that something was going to happen, answered in such a way as to give the impression to two experienced police officers that murder was the last thing that he thought he was ever going to be charged with.

Fourth inessential. The big discrepancy between the quantity prescribed and the quantity administered. I had ruled that they must consider only what was recorded, but the record included four 'special injections' given on and after 9 November. Could any of these have been murderous? If the quantity over-prescribed was apportioned equally over the four injections, each would have been about four times as large as any previous recorded injection. It must have been followed therefore by some very decisive result. But the first, given at 11.30 am on the 9th, was noted as having had no effect. The second at 2.00 pm on the same day after ten minutes sent the patient to sleep, but twenty minutes later she was wide awake. The third was left by the doctor on the 10th to be given by the nurse when the patient woke; she gave it and recorded nothing unusual. The fourth was given on the 12th and sent the patient to sleep for two hours. The doctors, who were the skilled readers of the notes, disregarded all the special injections.

It was no use saying that, if all the difference was not given, at least some of it could have been. If all was not given, there must have been some channel down which the remainder was disappearing. If there was such a channel, there was nothing to show that it could not have accounted for the whole of the difference. Was there such a channel? The jury should not speculate: 'Supposing you were to think that Dr Adams had been dishonest about drugs . . . how much better would it be that you should unjustly suspect him of that sort of dishonesty than that you should unjustly convict him of murder.'

The Essentials

The Crown had to prove three things:

1. An unnatural death, i.e. not from old age.
2. An act of murder. By that I meant, as I explained, some act capable, if the necessary intent was present, of being murderous. The Crown did not say that the medical treatment was from the beginning murderous; they said that it

became murderous either on 1 November (Douthwaite) or 8 November (Ashby). On one or other of those days they must prove an act by Dr Adams that showed a break in the treatment and pointed to a new design capable of unnaturally accelerating death.

3. Whether or not such an act was murder would depend upon the doctor's state of mind. The Crown had to prove the intent to murder.

The first and second of these issues depended entirely on the medical evidence and the case for the defence did not suffer from the accused's silence on the issues. As a doctor he could have expressed an opinion, but in the circumstances it could not have been of much value.

I discouraged reliance on Dr Douthwaite's new theory. Otherwise, the jury could, as it were, go nap on either Douthwaite or Harman. Or they might prefer the caution of Dr Ashby. To convict on his evidence alone they must be satisfied that it was more than borderline, but they could add it to either Douthwaite or Harman as tilting the balance.

If the jury were not satisfied on both the first and the second issues, that was an end of the case. If they were, they must proceed to the third where they would feel the lack of the accused's evidence. He alone could say what was in his mind; without his evidence they could only draw inferences from his acts.

Dr Douthwaite inferred on medical grounds an intent to kill. He could not see any other explanation of the dosage. He thought that no other doctor could honestly disagree with him. But Dr Harman did and thereby destroyed the point.

Mr Lawrence called the alleged motive 'ludicrous'. A strong word for a strong point. 'It is a point that is required to be answered; I listened carefully to the Attorney-General's speech in closing his case to you to see what the answer was; I did not hear the answer.'

I reminded the jury that explanations given to the police were not the same as if given on oath and subject to cross-examination. They might like to have known what the doctor meant by 'terrible agony' and 'easing the passing'. But they must also take into account the trend of his statements as a whole. He knew that the police were making inquiries: don't hurry, he said, please be thorough, it is in my interests. He gave away a good deal at the interviews. At the last of them he seemed stunned and shocked at the charge of murder.

Finale

Mr Lawrence had not the opportunity to reply to the Crown's comments on the disclosure of the notebooks, so I replied for him. The Crown said that they proved guilt. Did then Adams produce them because he did not appreciate what they proved? But the Crown's case was that Adams must have known that the doses recorded would kill. Did he then produce them because he feared worse, such as the evidence of the prescriptions? But when shown the prescriptions, he at once said that he had given them all.

> Mr Lawrence has submitted to you that the whole case against Dr Adams, from beginning to end, is merely suspicion. It may be so. It may be that, if this inquiry were ever to be completed, Dr Adams might appear as a man misjudged by those who suspected him. Not a man wrongly prosecuted, members of the jury; no one, I think, can say that; no one can say that the Crown was not justified on the material they had at the beginning of this trial in prosecuting Dr Adams. But a man who, if all the facts were known, was guilty of folly, perhaps worse, but who never in his mind came within thought of murder. It might be so. Who can say? Not you, members of the jury, not you. You have not heard the man who knows most about his own mind. You do not sit as a court of inquiry to determine just how and why Mrs Morrell died. You could hardly do that without hearing the doctor who attended her. You sit to answer one limited question. Has the prosecution satisfied you beyond reasonable doubt that Dr Adams murdered Mrs Morrell? On that question he stands upon his rights and does not speak. I have made it quite clear—have I not?—that I am not criticizing that. I do not criticize it at all. I hope that the day will never come when that right is denied to any Englishman. It is not a refuge of technicality, members of the jury. The law on this matter reflects the natural thought of England. So great is, and always has been our horror at the idea that a man might be questioned, forced to speak and perhaps to condemn himself out of his own mouth that we grant to everyone suspected or accused of crime at the beginning, at every stage and until the very end the right to say: 'Ask me no questions. I shall answer none. Prove your case.'
>
> And so this long process that began with arrest and ends with verdict ends too with the question with which it began. Murder, can you prove it?

I dare say, members of the jury, it is the first time that you
have sat in the jury box. It is not the first time that I have sat in
this chair and addressed juries. And not infrequently I have
heard a case presented by the prosecution that seemed to me to
be manifestly a strong one. And sometimes I have felt it my
duty to tell the jury so, reminding them that the case for the
prosecution must be strong if it is to be proved beyond reasonable doubt; and that it rests always with them to say whether it
is strong enough. I do not think, therefore, that I ought to
hesitate to tell you in this case that here the case for the defence
seems to me to be manifestly a strong one and that you must
not find for the Crown until after you have weighed and
rejected all the arguments that have been put before you on
behalf of the defence.

But it is the same question in the end. It is always the same. Is
the case for the Crown strong enough to carry conviction to
your mind? It is your answer. You have to answer it. It is
always with you, the jury. Always with you.

And will you now consider what that answer shall be. You
can take such time as you shall think fit, short or long, over
your deliberations.

It was rightly said to be a summing up for an acquittal in contrast
with the normal summing up which seems to point to a conviction. This is not because the judge is normally unneutral. He has
to put both cases and normally the prosecution's looks the
stronger. Whether it is strong enough is an imponderability best
left to the jury's own thoughts. Exceptionally, in this case the
evidence for the defence looked the stronger. Reggie had staked
too much on the prescriptions, which I had cut out, and he had
shirked a confrontation on motive. If the parties were put on
equal terms, as in a civil case, the defence should win. If the
Crown won, it would be widely interpreted as a win for pre-trial
prejudice.

So I permitted myself in this last passage, which I have quoted,
two departures from neutrality. One was the final heavy
emphasis on the right to silence; if there was prejudice in the air, I
did not want it increased by a dislike of the doctor's refusal to talk.
The other was what was tantamount to a recommendation when
I said that 'the case for the defence seems to me to be manifestly a
strong one'. In theory there seems to be no reason why a jury,
who are amateurs, should not have the benefit of professional
advice, provided that it is made clear to them that they are free to

disregard it. But it should, I think, be exceptional. It is not that there is much danger now of a jury being overawed. But it could tempt them to shirk their responsibility.

The third unusual thing I did was to say that Adams had not been wrongly prosecuted. Although in the early stages the conduct of the prosecution had been reckless, the decision to prosecute was not unjustified. It was hardly my business to say so, but I had a feeling that, if there was an acquittal, Reggie might be in for a bit of trouble.

I had no other case in the list and so was left to occupy myself until the jury returned. Two things could usefully be done. The first was to obtain confirmation of the Attorney's intention to proceed with the second indictment. The ordinary course would be to begin the second trial as soon as the first was over. If the first trial ended in a conviction, I proposed to say that I would not pass sentence until after the second verdict.

When this was settled, my second task would be to read the depositions on the second indictment.

A third and more delicate matter had to be handled some time. Towards the end of the preceding week I had had a telephone call from Rayner. The ostensible object was to ask how the case was going and when I expected to be back at the Strand. Normally this would be dealt with by the judges' clerks whose business it is to ensure that not a moment of judicial time is unoccupied.

I thought it unlikely that Rayner had rung up merely about this. So I was not surprised when he asked me whether I thought there would be an acquittal. I said that I thought there would. I learnt later that this was the general opinion of those who had been following the reports in *The Times*. Rayner then said that he understood that the Attorney was still determined to proceed with the second indictment. In that event, Rayner said, if an application for bail was made to him, he would grant it.

I was extremely surprised. I knew that Rayner was never deterred by lack of precedent, but I had never even heard of bail being granted in a murder case. I doubt if I should have thought of the idea myself. But I now saw no reason why I should not entertain an application. It would be necessary, I thought, to indicate that I was willing to hear an application; otherwise, the defence might not have the temerity to make it.

I invited the Attorney-General, Mr Lawrence and the Clerk of the Court to come to my room. I asked counsel whether they would like the second trial to proceed immediately upon the conclusion of the first or to be postponed until the next day.

Reggie looked glum and said nothing. Lawrence said that he had found the trial a great strain and did not feel that he could face another one at once.

I said that that might mean sending the case over until the next session: had Mr Attorney any objection? He looked glum and said no. I said that if the jury returned a verdict of guilty on the first indictment, Dr Adams would of course be kept in custody; but that, if they acquitted, I would entertain an application for bail. Mr Attorney continued to look glum, as well he might. Either he would have to oppose bail or by implication to concede that Dr Adams was no longer to be regarded as a common murderer.

I then settled down to read the depositions in the Hullett case. I did not need to read much to see how weak they were and to appreciate that an acquittal on the first indictment would make an acquittal on the second virtually certain.

The jury deliberated for forty-six minutes, at the end of which they returned a verdict of Not Guilty.

> *The Clerk:* You find him Not Guilty and that is the verdict of you all?
> *The Foreman:* It is.
> *The Judge:* Mr Attorney, there is another indictment, is there not?
> *A-G:* Yes, my lord. I have most anxiously considered what course the Crown should pursue . . . enter a *nolle prosequi* in relation to that indictment.
> [*A paper is produced. Flourish. Laid on the Table before the Clerk.*]
> *The Judge:* Then, Mr Attorney, all further proceedings on the indictment are stayed and no further action is taken in this court. Accordingly, John Bodkin Adams, you are now discharged.
> [*Exeunt all.*]

The mention of a *nolle prosequi* startled the lawyers present and bewildered the public almost as much as it will now startle and bewilder the reader. Before I say what it means, I shall explain what normally happens when an indictment is abandoned. Counsel cannot just say that he is dropping the case. The public interest is involved and prosecutions cannot just be settled in the way that suits between private persons can. Counsel must obtain the leave of the judge for taking one or other of two courses.

The course that is appropriate when the prosecution is likely to fail is for the accused to plead not guilty and for the prosecution to offer no evidence. Then, since the prosecution has not discharged the burden of proof, the judge directs the jury to return a verdict of Not Guilty. The other quite common situation is when the two or more indictments that the prosecution has filed are really alternatives, that is to say, when a conviction on the first to be tried is followed by a sentence that settles the matter. Sentence of death or of life imprisonment does that; or of any term of imprisonment that would be so long that a consecutive term would be inappropriate. There would then be no point in trying the second indictment unless the first conviction was quashed on appeal. The prosecution can ask the judge to order that the second indictment should remain on the file, marked 'Not to be proceeded with without the leave of the Court'. Such an order would never be made to stifle an acquittal.

So had, let us say, Mr Stevenson been leading for the Crown, the only method of abandonment open to him would have been by the acceptance of an acquittal. But the Attorney-General was not only the leading counsel for the Crown in this case but also a minister of the Crown. All indictments are laid in the name of the Crown; it is the Queen versus the accused. The Queen's consent to bringing the prosecution is assumed. But she can at any time withdraw consent. She does so by her statement made through the appropriate minister, who is the Attorney-General, that she does not wish to prosecute. This is what *nolle prosequi* means. It finishes the case.

A *nolle prosequi* is not designed for use in court. It has to be in writing and it is usually issued out of the Law Officers' Department in response to an application by an interested party. It does not determine guilt or innocence. That is for the courts and is not a question for the Attorney-General. It is used mostly for the protection of the guilty on the rare occasions when it is not in the public interest that justice should be done. A common example of this is when none in a gang of criminals could be successfully prosecuted unless one of them was willing to purchase immunity by turning Queen's Evidence. Another example is when justice could be done only by the sacrifice of lives. Thus the lives of those threatened by a gang of whom only one has been arrested have been purchased by the grant of immunity to the one in custody. The *nolle prosequi* may be used also out of compassion, as in the case of an ailing or elderly person who, whether guilty or innocent, could not face a long trial. In the first and second of these examples the application would be made by the Director of

Public Prosecutions; in the third, it would be made by the solicitor for the accused.

The *nolle prosequi* has not, I think, ever before been used to prevent an accused committed for trial from being acquitted. This one must suppose for reasons of *amour propre* Reggie did not want to have recorded. The ground he gave for its use in this case was the difficulty of securing a fair trial. If he meant by that that the Crown might not get a fair trial, there was something in the point. A second jury would know of the speedy acquittal in the first trial, would suppose that the Crown had brought first to trial the stronger case and would wonder why it was now proceeding with the weaker. But this apparently was not at all what was in the Attorney's mind. His expressed concern was for Dr Adams.

> My learned friend has referred more than once to the difficulty, owing to the reports and rumours that were current, of securing a fair trial for the case that has now terminated. . . . The publicity which has attended this trial would make it even more difficult to secure a fair trial of this further indictment. . . . The length of this trial, the ordeal that Dr Adams has already undergone, the fact that the case for the prosecution on this further indictment . . . depends in part on the evidence of Dr Ashby and very greatly upon the inference, not supported as in Mrs Morrell's case, of any admissions . . . '

It would be complimentary to call this specious. The danger that a second jury would be subject to the prejudice which the prosecution had themselves done so much to create could only be diminished by the knowledge that one jury had already successfully resisted it. Even with an almost unlimited capacity for ignoring what fell outside his beliefs, Reggie could not have supposed that there was any longer the slightest prospect of his getting a verdict. If I had been the judge, the case would not have been allowed to get to the jury.

The use of the *nolle prosequi* to conceal the deficiency of the prosecution was an abuse of process which left an innocent man under the suspicion that there might well have been something in the talk of mass murder after all. It is charitable to suppose that it was a last-minute decision (stimulated perhaps by the probable grant of bail) which the Attorney-General had not fully thought out. If it was what he had had in mind when we were discussing the future of the second indictment, it would have been childish of him to have kept quiet about his intentions.

Anyway, it hardly mattered. Technically Dr Adams was

charged with and never tried for the murder of Mrs Hullett. But for the wide world outside a court of law the fact was that the Attorney-General, defeated on one indictment, had thrown in his hand on the other.

21

Aftermath

It was a curious chance that had brought two of the most self-righteous men in England into silent confrontation for three weeks. During that time each struck a glancing blow at the other's destiny. Dr Adams's life was dented but not ruined. Reggie's ambition was knocked off course but not in the end frustrated. The tribulations of Reggie came first.

The squall blew up within a week of the verdict and is recorded in Hansard.

DR ADAMS (TRIAL)

Mr Wigg asked the Attorney-General whether he will institute an independent inquiry into the preparation, organisation, and conduct of the prosecution's case against Dr Adams, who was recently acquitted at the Old Bailey on a charge of murder, excepting the proceedings in court.

The Attorney-General: No.

A fortnight later on 1 May 1957 Mr Wigg, Labour MP for Dudley, returned to the attack by raising the matter on the adjournment of the House. Criticism of the Attorney-General in the Commons is rare. It must nearly always be personal since he has not really a department to be criticized. His situation is delicate. He is a member of the government and so is answerable to the House. But he is also a minister of justice and as such must be above politics. It is not wrong for him to be questioned in the House about a prosecution. What he does in initiating it and in the course of it is an administrative act over which the courts can exercise only a limited control. It is in a region where the abuse of power could be very oppressive and Parliament is the forum at which overweening or incompetent or just errant ministers can be called to account.

The calling to account of an attorney-general should be outside party politics. It is, however, an unfortunate result of the party system that the duty of seeing that ministers behave properly beckons more imperatively to members of the Opposition than to Government supporters. Unfortunately, too, Reggie was not a warmly popular figure even in his own party and was actively disliked by many of the Opposition.

Mr Wigg, who took the initiative, was of course a Socialist. He was not a lawyer but a tip-and-run raider, always on the look-out for a party point. He had made sure from the start that there would be no calm and impartial review. He had asked the Attorney-General whether he was 'quite unaware that, throughout the length and breadth of the British Isles, the recent case of Dr Adams has evoked discussion in terms which bring discredit upon the law and upon his office'. Sir Lionel Heald, Conservative MP for Chertsey, Reggie's predecessor, was more concerned to know whether his right honourable and learned friend realized 'that there is widespread indignation at the unfair personal attacks that had been made upon him'; he referred to a 'weekly publication which I will not dignify by naming', but which was generally understood to be the *Spectator*.

On the second occasion the Attorney was pressed more quietly and effectively by Sir Lynn Ungoed-Thomas, Labour MP for Leicester, a former Solicitor-General, and Mr Reginald Paget, Labour MP for Northampton and a distinguished QC. No Socialist befriended him and no Conservative criticized him. The discussion went on for two hours, after which Mr Chuter Ede, a former Socialist Home Secretary and a very respected member of the House, rose to ensure that everybody shook hands and made it up. Mr Wigg, he said, had fulfilled, not for the first time, a duty in bringing the matter before the House. The House was under a debt of gratitude to the Attorney-General for the full and frank etc. Mr Melford Stevenson, he added, was the son-in-law of a very old friend of his and would do nothing to prejudice the defence. The ritual cleansing did not include the press 'which was becoming Americanized and must be carefully watched'.

The criticisms had been scattered. An effusion of debaters hinders concentration. Was the prosecution improper? This was answered by what the judge had said. What about the failure of the police to unearth the notebooks and what about their leaks to the press? Nothing doing: the Attorney-General is not responsible for the police. Was the prosecution wise? Reggie denied the rumours, 'maliciously circulated', that the Director of Public Prosecutions had disapproved of it.

The unwisdom of a prosecution, as distinct from its impropriety, is not a matter for parliamentary debate. The debatable point was whether the conduct of the prosecution had been such as to prejudice a fair trial. What Reggie really had to defend was his decision first to admit and then to exclude the two Hullett cases. His shield was that he was winding up the debate and that no one would speak after him.

On Mr Hullett's casè he was not quite candid. He explained the fiasco by saying that 'after the committal proceedings were over, facts came to light which satisfied me that the case did not support the allegation of system'. This contains two implications. The first is that a charge of murder was still viable, but that a 'striking similarity' to the Morrell case could no longer be shown. The second is that it was some unforeseeable development occurring after the Eastbourne proceedings were over that had destroyed the similarity. The truth is that, similar or not, the simplest investigation would have shown that it was not murder.

In the case of Mrs Hullett the Attorney began by endorsing a statement that Melford had made to the magistrates. He had said that the admissibility of the evidence 'could not be the subject of serious debate'. I too endorse it, but only in the letter and in the opposite sense to the spirit in which it was intended. I get not even a glimpse of striking similarity. I can only refer the puzzled inquirer to the textbooks: alternatively, invite him to assume the similarity and to ask why the admissible evidence was not used. Here is the Attorney's answer to that.

> I want to tell the House why it was that I decided, and it was my responsibility, not to call the evidence at the trial on that charge. It is the established practice that evidence of this kind—evidence of system—is excluded if, notwithstanding its admissibility, it is, *in relation to the weight it bears*,* so prejudicial to the accused that its admission would operate to prevent his having a fair trial. It was on that ground, after the committal proceedings had ended, that I decided that the evidence relating to Mrs Hullett should not be called . . .

This statement needs to be elucidated. In the civil law evidence is either relevant or irrelevant and is admitted or excluded accordingly. Relevance is not the same as weight. It may be relevant to prove that the defendant committed a certain act but impossible

* The italics are mine.

to do so without revealing that he had also unpleasant but irrelevant characteristics which might prejudice a jury against him. It may then become material to consider the weight of the evidence, i.e. what it really proves, as against the prejudice which it incidentally creates. In the criminal trial the judge has a discretion (which he exercises as part of his duty to protect the accused from unfairness within the rules) to exclude relevant evidence if he thinks that the harm it would do the accused would be disproportionate to its weight as part of the proof of guilt.

This is the general rule.

It is, however, a special condition governing the admission of evidence of system that it must relate to a crime which is 'strikingly similar' to the crime charged. Proof of such another crime must of its nature be evidence of the greatest possible weight. It may well, as in the Brides in the Bath case, be damning. There is no room left for the idea that it might be of little weight as compared with the prejudice created. It would create prejudice rather than proof only if it were of no similarity. In short, by its requirement that the similarity must be striking, the 'system' rule on admissibility has its own built-in safeguard. Reggie's attempt to split the operation into two parts whereby the evidence is first allowed as being strikingly similar and then banned as preventing a fair trial, is, to adopt the politer of Lawrence's two comments on Dr Douthwaite's new idea, 'not founded upon sound premises'.

In any event, whether it was the general rule that was applicable or the special rule on 'system', all the circumstances were as well known to the Crown at the time when the evidence was noisily introduced and publicized as they were when it was quietly dropped.

The debate was inconclusive but not a waste of time. The House of Commons is a great and manifold institution and is no more to be judged by the reports in Hansard than a car is to be judged by its exhaust. I do not know in what terms the significance of the debate was conveyed to the Prime Minister Harold Macmillan, but they were such as to satisfy him that there was a turbulence in which it would be undesirable to settle Reggie's claim to the succession. He told Rayner that he felt it a difficult time at which to make a new appointment and asked him to stay on for another year. Rayner gladly agreed to do so. The request relieved his anxiety about staying on when the world might think that it was time for him to go. He did not really want to go.

I read an abbreviated account of the debate in the newspapers and disliked it. As it was treated in the press, there was too much in it of The Bloodhound (one of Mr Wigg's nicknames) leading the pack against an unpopular minister when he was down. I must, in June 1957, have written something of this sort to Reggie, for I have a letter from him then in which he thanked me and went on to regret that he failed to satisfy me by his final speech that Dr Adams's admission to Hannam that he had administered the drugs prescribed amounted to a *prima facie* case.

This surprised me. I had not thought it to be a point on which he seriously hoped to get a conviction. I had missed altogether his reference* to it after the verdict in which he had said that the Hullett case lacked the support, as in Mrs Morrell's case, of any admission. He carried the point as usual to Rayner who asked me directly about it; I replied that Reggie could not marry it with his case on the notebooks. When after getting Reggie's letter I read the report of the debate in Hansard, I found that Reggie had in the House, though with all due decorum, complained of my ruling. The defence never challenged, he said, and the judge did not deal with Dr Adams's admission that he had given Mrs Morrell all that was prescribed. This, followed by his letter, showed that, far from the point being a red herring as I had supposed, it was cardinal in Reggie's belief. Thereafter he laid it down in the cellar of his mind where age did not improve it. To his dying day he persisted in the belief that Dr Adams was acquitted by a judicial misdirection.

By the summer of 1958 it was plain that Lord Justice Parker would be the choice of Bench and Bar to succeed Rayner. He was, as has been confirmed by subsequent appointments, of just the appropriate age and status, an appellate judge of around sixty. He was very judicial, very able, and one of the sweetest characters I have known in the law; he never sought a place where he could show to advantage but always one where he could give most service. It was a momentous appointment, breaking cleanly away from the stranglehold of tradition.

Reggie behaved with fitting dignity when as the leader of the Bar he welcomed the new Chief Justice. But he was bitterly disappointed. He could have taken Parker's place in the Court of Appeal, but this was not what he wanted. Yet the future looked bleak. Of all the glittering prizes there once had been for lawyers

* See page 181.

only one was left. This was the office of Lord Chancellor which was now almost entirely political. But this was held by David Kilmuir, not yet sixty. Moreover, the Government was expected to go out at the next general election which could not now be long delayed. It had been in office for eight years and the odds were against it being returned for a third administration.

The election was held in October 1959. Before then, in July, when the sitting Parliament was at its last gasp, there occurred an incident with curious echoes of the past. Reggie undertook the 'prosecution' of another doctor for murder, a doctor who had been 'acquitted' by a Commission* over which I had presided, and found himself able, as he had not been in the Adams case, to 'appeal' from the acquittal. The terms 'prosecution, acquittal and appeal' are here used loosely; the murder, or massacre as it was called at the time, was supposedly contemplated and not enacted. After all, as I have said, history cannot be expected to repeat itself exactly.

The doctor concerned was a Dr Banda, a contemporary of Dr Adams, who practised medicine in Britain from 1937 to 1953, finishing up in North London where his practice was as large as, though perhaps less remunerative than, Dr Adams's at Eastbourne. They never met. If they had and *if* the Attorney-General's suspicions were correct, they would have had much in common to talk about out of the hearing of the British Medical Association. For in Reggie's book they were both experimental massacrists, Adams with a tally of 400 Eastbourne veterans and Banda with the grandiose objective, even though it was entirely unfulfilled, of dispatching the whole of the European population of his native country.

In fact Dr Banda has probably never heard of Dr Adams. From 1953 to 1958 he was in Ghana. In the latter year he returned to Nyasaland, as Malawi then was, to lead the Congress Party in its struggle against federation with Southern Rhodesia. He was arrested on 3 March 1959, the most serious charge against him being complicity in an unsuccessful plot to assassinate the Governor, the Chief Secretary and all the top brass downwards in strict order of precedence, finishing up with the massacre of all Europeans, children to be mutilated, after which, according to the evidence of the police informer, the conspirators 'should retreat into the bush until such time as things had quietened

* Report of the Nyasaland Commission of Inquiry July 1959 under Mr Justice Devlin.

down'. The Commission found that, though violence of a sporadic sort was contemplated, the plot was an emanation of the overheated imagination which seems so easily to infect informers to the Special Branch. Quite why this verdict was displeasing to the Government I do not know; perhaps it was because the Government had proclaimed the plot and the Opposition had pooh-poohed it. Anyway Reggie was put up in the House to demolish the Commission's Report.

Treating the House, as he said, as a court of appeal, Reggie submitted that the acquittal was so far against the weight of the evidence as set out by the Commission itself as to override the Commission's disbelief of the police informers and their acceptance of Dr Banda's denials. The appeal succeeded. It was a remarkable result, even though it would not perhaps have been obtained without the aid of the party whips.

The Prime Minister was very pleased with Reggie. He recorded in his diary on 20 July 1959:

> The Attorney-General opened with a massive speech which greatly pleased our Party. He was given a great ovation when he finished.*

I question, while appreciating the singularity of Reggie's triumph, Mr Macmillan's use of the word 'massive'. The speech, when I read it in Hansard, had struck me as flimsy. Then I remembered that the Prime Minister had listened to it while I had only read it. There is no doubt that Reggie could put things across in a massive way.

Take, for example, his proposition that a Member of Parliament, who had at best read or half-read the Report, was in a better position than the four members of the Commission who had talked to Dr Banda and the informers, to say which of them was telling the truth. The four members, Reggie suggested, one a judge with whom by now the reader is tolerably well acquainted, another a colonial civil servant whose governorship of another African Protectorate had recently ended, a third an Oxford historian who as a brigadier had for four years served Field Marshal Montgomery as his chief of intelligence and was in 1959 Warden of Rhodes House, and the fourth a shrewd Scot, three times Lord Provost of Perth,† were manifestly so overcome by Dr

---

* Macmillan, Harold, *Riding the Storm*, London, Macmillan, 1971.

† The second, third and fourth were respectively Sir Percy Wyn-Harris, Sir Edgar Williams and Sir John Primrose.

Banda's charm as to render themselves unfit to say whether he was telling the truth or not. If Reggie supposed that in contrast the two informers upon whom the Government relied lacked charm, he would have been right. They also lacked credibility: one of them achieved the unusual feat of giving evidence first for the Government, then for the Congress, then for the Government again, changing his story each time.

Or take his criticism of the sentence in the Report in which the Commission distinguished between talk of sporadic beating and killing and the planning of 'coldblooded assassination or massacre'. 'The distinction,' said Reggie 'is too subtle for me.' And he would have said it in a way that made every plain, blunt, honest MP ashamed to disagree.

Massive is certainly the word that describes Reggie, or at least his initial impact. No other practising barrister could have said either of these things without putting his tongue in his cheek. I do not think that Reggie's tongue knew where his cheek was. It was his firm conviction always that what he was saying was right and that deviation from it by a hair's breadth would be wrong. This is what gave to his utterance the massiveness which lasted until a sense of absurdity took its place.

Parliament was dissolved a week or so later and the general election followed in October. I do not think that the Prime Minister would have said that Reggie's speech won the election. It was his own political flair that did that, though both sides overestimated the interest which the electorate would take in Nyasaland. But certainly Reggie had deserved well of his party.

Yet in the new government he was still only the Attorney-General. The next election would be in 1963 or 1964 and would surely remove from the Tories the sweets of office. The Law of Buggins's Turn required that Reggie should have a few months at least on the Woolsack and Kilmuir planned to make way for him some time in 1963.

The event was accelerated by the extraordinary episode that has come to be called the Night of the Long Knives. On 13 July 1962 Mr Macmillan sacked without notice seven senior members of his Cabinet including the Lord Chancellor. It was an unceremonious end for a Chancellor; he himself doubted whether loyalty had ever had to endure so severe a strain; no one could understand why he was so suddenly sent to the scaffold. Some said that Reggie, tired of waiting for his legacy, had got Kilmuir's name included in the list of the proscribed. But there is no evidence for this, not even an admission.

So Reggie held for eighteen months the office of Lord Chancellor and was duly created Viscount Dilhorne of Towcester, the last of the hereditary viscounts until the restoration of 1983.

One duty during his chancellorship that a smaller man might have found difficult he seems to have discharged to perfection. Less than six months after the victory at the general election had made it safe to do so, Dr Banda was released from prison to take, like so many of his peers in the vanishing empire, the first step towards an honoured place in the new commonwealth. The path was by now well trodden down and his march was unimpeded. On 1 February 1963 Nyasaland left the Federation and on 6 July 1964 it became the independent state of Malawi with Dr Banda as its President. The Lord Chancellor, who five years before as Attorney-General had persuaded the Commons that the new President had planned the massacre of all the Europeans in the country, was selected by the British Government to travel out to Malawi to congratulate Dr Banda on his achievement. It was a most suitable embassy. The old empire was going out in the shaking of hands and the letting of bygones be bygones. It was all—just like Dr Banda himself—very British and he must have enjoyed it enormously.

If I have dwelt on this episode in too great detail, it is partly to offer a small revenge to a reader who may have found curious some of the workings of the law which I too blandly take for granted and who may now enjoy without malice my entanglement in a political process which I found incomprehensible. Having got so far, I ought to disclose that the entanglement was not the end of me. It ought to have been. A judge whose incompetence in finding elementary facts has to be corrected by the superior wisdom of Parliament ought to be restricted for ever to activities in which he can do no further harm. Yet, astoundingly, after the election was safely over, the wind of change, as Mr Macmillan had called it, blew for me even more strongly than for Dr Banda. At the end of 1959 I was promoted by Mr Macmillan to the Court of Appeal and eighteen months later, also by him, to the House of Lords. I was there in good time to welcome, as one of his judicial colleagues, the new Lord Chancellor to the Woolsack.

The afterlife of Dr Adams began with nothing so sensational as the Attorney-General's mini-impeachment in the House of Commons. After the verdict he slipped away in the care of the *Daily*

Express who were ready to exchange the customary bounty* for
the revelations of an uneventful life. Then he returned to Eastbourne to await developments.

The drug offences with which Dr Adams had been charged on
27 November 1956, three weeks before the charge of murder, had
been shunted out of the way so as to let the Murder Express
through. They now chugged back on to the main line and,
pausing for a day or two before the Eastbourne magistrates for
committal for trial, reached the Sussex Summer Assizes in the
County Hall at Lewes on 26 July 1957. Mr Justice Pilcher presided,
Melford Stevenson led for the prosecution and Edward Clarke
was for the defence.

I call them the drug offences, but in fact they embraced all the
professional misdemeanours which Superintendent Hannam's
investigation going back over ten years, 'an extremely involved
investigation', he said, 'which covered an enormous field', had
brought to light. Some of them were professionally very serious.
But none of them ranked high in the criminal calendar and, as
compared with the iniquities which Dr Adams was supposed to
have committed during this period, the effect of the vetting was
to give him almost a clean bill of health.

There were three groups of offences in three indictments.
Those in the second indictment were the gravest. Dr Adams was
charged with making a false statement on three cremation forms.
Mrs Morrell's form, which had been closely examined at the
murder trial, was not one of them; the difficulty there was the
doubt that the doctor took anything under the will. One of the
charges concerned Mr Hullett's £500, for which Dr Adams had
himself supplied the essential evidence that he knew what was in
the will. Another was in February 1950 when a Mrs Ware left him
a legacy of £1,000 out of an estate of £8,890. The third was Mrs
Ware's brother-in-law, Mr Downs, who died five years after Mrs
Ware and also left Adams £1,000.

Mr Clarke made skilful use of what might be called the doctor's
dilemma. If he does not answer firmly that he knows of no legacy,
the cremation will be postponed and a post-mortem will be held.
This is distressing for the family. What sort of knowledge ought

* The bounty was £10,000. Some time ago I was told by someone—I cannot
now remember whom, but he sounded knowledgeable—that Dr Adams offered
the money to the Medical Defence Union who declined it. Perhaps this is only a
rumour. If so, it is only right that the doctor should benefit from the nice as well as
suffer from the nasty rumours. Certainly the bank notes with which his fee was
paid were found intact on his death.

to be disclosed? The patient might have said months or years before that he was leaving a little remembrance in the will, but might then have forgotten or changed his mind.

Two of the referees at the Brighton Crematorium, whose duty it was to see that the crematorium forms were in order, gave evidence at the committal proceedings. In answer to Mr Clarke, one of them, who had been examining forms for thirty years, said that he had never known of any doctor who had said in answer that he had a pecuniary interest. The other had had only one case in fifteen years in which the doctor said that he thought he was going to get a benefit. There are thought to be many wealthy invalids who end their days at Eastbourne. Was Dr Adams the only medical beneficiary? The judge was, he said, 'impressed to some extent that it appeared to be almost unheard of for a doctor to admit to any knowledge'.

But the force of these general considerations was greatly diminished by the particular case of Mr Downs. Here, as in the Morrell case, Dr Adams had gone to some pains to make sure of the legacy. As he had done with Mr Sogno, he had alerted the solicitor to the situation and been present himself when the testator gave his instructions; this was only six weeks before the death. Had it not been for the three months which Dr Adams had spent in prison as an innocent man awaiting trial for murder, the judge would probably, he said, have sent him to prison. He fined him £500 for each offence, making £1,500 in all.

The drug offences proper were in the third indictment. They covered the 'foolish behaviour' of Dr Adams on the occasion when the police were searching his house for dangerous drugs. For this he was fined £250. For his failure to keep a register he was fined £500.

The first indictment contained nine counts of forgery which sounds grim. But they were boiled down to four charges* and were treated by the judge as the least serious which Dr Adams had to face. The total of the fines on all four was £150. They are worth describing because they show vividly the sort of person Dr Adams was. Looking at them and looking back at the outpourings deluging the police, (the naïvety, for example, of

> We always want cremations to go off smoothly for the dear relatives. If I said I was getting money under the will, they

---

* They were alleged to be 'representative of a course of conduct', but since the Crown had not given notice with particulars of additional offences, this allegation was ignored.

might get suspicious, and I like cremations and burials to go
smoothly),

one sees how unfitted he was temperamentally for a successful
career as a murderer for money.

The situations in which the forgeries were committed must be
familiar to general practitioners. They are visited in their private
practice by a patient who is on the list of an NHS doctor. The
remedy prescribed is one which might cost the patient outside
the National Health Service several pounds, but which he could
get free or at a greatly reduced price on a form signed by his NHS
doctor. It appears from the evidence in this case that there is
usually little difficulty in getting the appropriate form signed by
the NHS doctor. But it would mean a little extra bother for the
patient and Dr Adams saw no reason why he or she should be
bothered. So when in 1952 a patient who was on the list of a Dr
Emslie needed a vaccine, Dr Adams simplified the matter by
writing out a prescription on the National Health form EC 10 and
signing it with Dr Emslie's name. He himself took the form round
to the hospital. When the signature was queried and the form
shown to Dr Emslie, he was naturally very angry indeed. Dr
Adams apologized and the matter went no further.

Dr Adams reformed himself to the extent that Hannam found
no further case of the same sort until September 1955. Then he
prescribed a pair of elastic stockings for a patient who was on the
list of a Dr Ashforth. This time he conformed with the proprieties
to the extent of signing the form with his own name and adding
'p.p. Dr Ashforth'. But to sign p.p., when you know that you
have no authority so to do, is in the eyes of the law as much a
forgery as if you had imitated the signature. In 1956 Adams did
the same thing for a third patient. When on 1 October 1956
Hannam taxed him with these three cases, Dr Adams agreed that
it was very wrong of him to have signed Dr Emslie's name and
said that he had had God's forgiveness for it: it was to help poor
national health patients and the health people could afford it. But
he does not seem to have grasped the point about p.p. For it was
only a week later that he saw a lady who needed a tonic and some
sleeping pills and once again he signed p.p. The Superintendent
was evidently keeping his investigations up to date, for he added
this case to the other three.

As a result of Dr Adams's misconduct in these four cases the
health service lost £7 9s 6d and Dr Adams was fined £150. The
grand total of his fines was £2,400.

On 4 September 1957 Dr Adams's authority to prescribe under the Dangerous Drugs Act was withdrawn by the Home Office and never restored.

In November 1957 he was as a result of his convictions at Lewes struck off the Register. He had earlier in June resigned from the National Health Service. A person not on the Register is not forbidden to practise medicine; he is forbidden only from holding himself out as qualified. Dr Adams continued to practise in Eastbourne and many of his patients continued to go to him. He still received legacies.

In 1961, after several unsuccessful applications, he was restored to the Register. In 1961, too, he cashed in on the libels. His suit was against the *Daily Mail* who withdrew every allegation and sincerely apologized. It was a settlement in which the other offending newspapers joined and between them all the penitents must have offered a substantial sum.

He kept a sharp look-out for any new offenders and as late as 1969 was still collecting. In that year one of the well-known weeklies made a witty reference to the failure of cash injections to maintain the pound sterling and inquired: 'Can it be that the shade of John Bodkin Adams has moved in and taken charge of the Bank of England?' Two issues later it was unreservedly withdrawing 'some unfortunate and regrettable' statements, while Dr Adams, 'a physician of great skill and integrity', was £500 the richer. Tax free, of course.

The general public did not believe Dr Adams to be a physician of great skill and integrity and quite a large section of it thought of him as a murderer who by the skill and eloquence of his counsel had been saved from the gallows. To defeat in pitched battle the armies of the Crown is not to defeat the guerrillas of rumour. The right to silence can secure an acquittal but cannot restore the reputation that rumour has eroded.

When Reggie died, which happened when he was just seventy-five, surprisingly since he always looked so robust, there were no comets seen. A very generous obituary in *The Times* made some amends for past rudenesses in the popular press, but that was all. When three years later Adams died at the age of eighty-four, the heavens themselves through the media of the air proclaimed at regular intervals the death of a prince. The newspapers were full of it and the 150 friends and patients who attended his funeral at Eastbourne filled the television screen. The *Mail on Sunday*, unimpressed by the sincere apologies of its elderly relative twenty-two years before, rejoiced over several pages in 'the truth that can now be told'. The *Daily Express* affirmed its belief in his innocence. The *Telegraph* gave him an obituary of three columns plus photographs. *The Times* referred to him as 'the classic enigma in the annals of mass killing'.

22

'Impossible to Accuse
a Doctor'

English law does not distinguish between 'Not Guilty' and 'Non-Proven'. 'Not Guilty' does not usually mean that the accused has established his innocence nor that he leaves the court, as the saying is, without a stain on his character; it means no more than that there is doubt about his guilt. This was the sense in which the public read the verdict upon Adams.

There is another sense in which his guilt was non-proven. Dr Adams had been publicly and formally accused of three murders; he had been publicly and informally by statement, hint and innuendo accused of many more, indeed of mass murder. He was tried for only one murder. The process brought with it reminders of trial by battle and trial by ordeal.

For the trial by battle the Crown's selected champion was the Morrell case. The champion was defeated. But the defeat left questions in the air. Was it an unfortunate selection? Was it a stroke of luck peculiar to that case that gave the defence the extraordinary advantage of surprise?

As for the ordeal, the accused declined it. The only way in which he could have challenged his invisible foes was by going into the witness-box and submitting to cross-examination. He could not, of course, have been cross-examined on anything except the Morrell case. The result of the test would have depended not so much upon the content of his answers as upon his demeanour and what he showed of himself to the public. Certainly he had something to explain in the Morrell case and his explanations would have had to have been plausible. If they were and if he had been acquitted, the British public would have acquitted him of all else because he had faced the music. Refusal of the ordeal left him with a verdict of Non-Proven on all that was rumoured or alleged and untried as well as in the trial itself.

A verdict of Non-Proven brings criminal proceedings to an end, but it is no way of ending a story. A story-teller does not have to leave his story unfinished at the point when he realizes that he cannot satisfy his readers beyond a reasonable doubt. It is enough that he should supply them with a plausible ending. Let me try my hand at that. It means speculation, but it will be speculation that accepts the facts as they were proved at the trial and makes no extravagant departures by way of inference from the probabilities.

It means also that the curtain goes down and that when it is raised again twenty-eight years have passed. It means more than that. In the closing passage of my charge to the jury I reminded them that they were not sitting as a court of inquiry to determine how Mrs Morrell died. They sat to answer the limited question whether the evidence left them without a reasonable doubt that she was murdered by Dr Adams. In conformity with that charge they returned what was unquestionably a true verdict, but one which left curiosity unsatisfied.

The jury went back to their ordinary lives and I passed on to the next case. For me almost every case has been a story of which I should have liked to have known more. Usually, as the facts fade from the memory, curiosity dies. In this case it did not. I have not concealed my interest in the character of Reggie as the last of the careerist lawyers to reach the Woolsack. The character of Dr Adams, veiled in court by his silence, likewise intrigued me. And of course, like everybody else, I should quite like to know just what he was up to.

So it is not only the passage of time that has changed the scene. The stage has entirely altered. The narrator is no longer the judge keeping pace with the flow of evidence channelled by the law. I have now unlimited time for the analysis of the exhibits and the transcript and I can look now at anything and everything. Some things I shall see differently.

I find that I have not changed much the impression which by the end of the trial I had formed of Dr Adams. I reject as implausible the portrait of the monster of iniquity which the prosecution painted. It was the portrait of a well-to-do doctor who murdered a dying patient in case she might change her mind about a paltry legacy. Taken as a single instance it was absurd. It had to rely for persuasiveness upon the implication, which might readily have been drawn by any newspaper reader, that it was not a single aberration in a blameless life but part of a regular practice. The rules which exclude evidence of other instances do not apply to speculation; we can now use whatever has been revealed of the material in the police files.

They show that the doctor received many legacies, mostly in small sums, no great fortune. We may presume that they came mainly from fee-paying patients since the National Health patients of 1957 would not have much to leave. The fee-paying patients were capital assets, yielding an annual dividend during life and, if they could be induced to provide a legacy, a tax-free bonus on death. But the bonus was hardly large enough to make an adequate motive for cashing in on the investment before maturity and liquidating the patient.

Mrs Morrell was wealthier and consequently her fees were larger than the average, but in other respects her case was not untypical. I have seen nothing to fault the Attorney-General's selection of it as the strongest (though I should put it as the least weak) on which to prosecute. Certainly the Hullett cases, the runners-up, were decidedly weaker. There has not emerged from the remaining cases any impressive evidence of the unnatural death of a patient who was clinging to life.

This does not mean that Dr Adams was not a murderer, only that he was not a monster. He might have murdered—it must be remembered that euthanasia is murder—either as a mercy-killer or perhaps just to finish off a troublesome patient who was dying anyway and for whom he could do no more. The mercenary mercy-killer fits best the picture of him that I have in my mind. Certainly he had one characteristic which is a good qualification for a killer of that sort, a disposition to think lightly of the law. The cases to which he confessed at Lewes Assizes show a reluctance to be bothered with it. Because he thought of himself as in communication with God (another qualification for a certain sort of killer), he would not have a higher regard for the moral law than for the secular.

Second, he had the quality of compassion which brought him the devotion of his patients. He was assiduous in his care. The evidence shows him to have been an ignorant and incompetent doctor. He could have been a charlatan, but my feeling is that he was not. He believed in his competence as well as in his compassion.

Third, he was a greedy man. His quest for legacies is not otherwise explicable. It may not have been the ordinary greed for money. He was prosperous and for a bachelor had plenty put by. Could it have been that like the gods of old he liked the burnt offerings, the incense, the tributes, the Rolls-Royces, all that showed a proper sense of gratitude?

If this is the sort of man that Dr Adams was, the criminal type to which he belonged would be the abortionist rather than the murderer. As a crime in the calendar at assizes, abortion was in my early years on the Bench quite conspicuous.

Abortion and euthanasia are similar crimes. While the principle is clear, each can have its exemptions. Subject to them, neither crime is within the contemplation of those who respect the moral law which protects the sanctity of life. For those who do not respect it the motive can be compassion or cupidity or a mixture of both. There used to be the amateur abortionist who without thought of reward would help a girl for whom bastardy was a shame or a wife already overburdened. This was the thin end of the crime. At the thick end there were the complete professionals who operated for a large fee to save those who could pay from the inconvenience of child-bearing. In between there was the back street abortionist, who had started out of compassion by helping a distressed neighbour, whose name was given to others in the like distress and who ended by thinking it only fair, having regard to the risk she ran, that she should be paid something. If mercy-killers are likewise divisible into classes, Dr Adams would have been somewhere in the middle class. Reading the transcript again a quarter of a century later did not alter the picture that had remained in my mind.

Reading the transcript brought back also two points that had puzzled me at the time. I have already recorded that I asked Dr Ashby—inconsequently as it must have appeared—whether heroin made death happy. I was thinking of the monks' chant at the close of compline, *noctem quietam et finem perfectum concedat nos, Domine*, the prayer for the quiet night and the perfect end. I was wondering whether heroin could now produce artificially what had been the natural product of monastic discipline. But it was not just idle musing. At the back of it what was puzzling me was the apparent inertia of Dr Adams at the death-bed. Surely the nurses had told him of the spasms which so distressed them. On the last night, if not before, he had seen them for himself. Was it not odd that he thought only of paraldehyde, the soporific with the revolting smell?

Another thing that nagged at me was Reggie's closing speech. It might have been just an obstinate refusal to accept that the notebooks had made obsolete his argument on the prescriptions. But might it not also have been a forward perception that his case on the notebooks had been so weakened by the disastrous evidence from Dr Douthwaite that it had become imperative to try another tack? Nevertheless, I had not been alone in my failure to see what he was getting at. The speech made no impact on the acute and experienced observers who have since written accounts of the trial. Mrs Bedford dismissed it as 'a faithful echo of the opening speech with little added or forgotten'. Mr Hallworth gave it four lines. Mr Hoskins gave it forty lines, saying that 'a great deal of it was repetition of his opening address'.

I read the speech again to see if we had all missed some new and cogent presentation of the case on the prescriptions. But no. There was a surplus: somehow or other Adams had got hold of it: somehow or other he had himself injected it into Mrs Morrell. The whole of it, all 27½grs. or thereabouts, or some of it? Reggie did not say. The whole seemed incredible. But, if only some, what had happened to the rest?

The speech was a splashing in the water; the orator never swam to any point. He used the prescriptions of opiates on 9 November (No. 86 and No. 87)* and of paraldehyde on the 12th (No. 92) to show that the doctor was himself collecting prescriptions direct from the chemist, supposedly for secret use. But the doctor handed No. 86 and No. 87 over to the nurses and used No. 92, which was a safe drug anyway, openly in their presence. If the Attorney had gone on to point to a secret collection for secret use, the obvious candidate would be No. 93. No. 89 was for hyperduric morphia whose injection is recorded. Nos. 88, 90 and 91 were repeats of the prescription on 9 November; these presumably would be sent by the nurses for collection through the usual channels and the doctor would have had no opportunity for interception.

By itself evidence of collection proved nothing. It led to the inference that, if collected, it was intended for use. But that would have to be fortified by some evidence of an occasion on which it might have been used. On this all that Reggie suggested was a 'special injection' or an unrecorded visit; he pointed out that some visits by Dr Harris in September had gone unrecorded. But what he needed was an occasion for a large dose which though it would have failed to kill, would have been followed by symptoms suggestive of its size. The only occasions fulfilling this requirement were reserved, so to speak, for the paraldehyde.

I went back over the evidence about paraldehyde. 4oz was

* See list on p. x.

prescribed (No. 92) on Sunday 12 November. Sister Bartlett made a note about the doctor's visit at 7.30 pm on the Sunday and recorded that paraldehyde 2cc was given without apparent effect. She wrote down also that the doctor said he would visit again at 10.30 pm. Apart from her note, she said, she had no recollection of it being given. When he came back, bringing his own 5cc syringe, Nurse Randall was on duty. He spent some time in the dining-room, filling the big syringe up to about 4cc. He injected it, telling the nurse that it was paraldehyde. Then he refilled the syringe, again up to 4cc, and said that, if the patient was restless, the nurse was to inject again.

The notebook contains no record of another injection. Notwithstanding the omission, Nurse Randall at the trial insisted repeatedly and vehemently and with corroborative detail that she had given it. She resisted the strongest pressure by Mr Lawrence to admit that she had not given it although the admission would have cleared her of the serious fault of failing to note down an injection.

When she was asked about it in chief, she said that she was quite sure that she gave it, though at first she put the time at about 1.00 am. When the entry

12.45 am. Seems a little quieter, appears asleep

was pointed out to her, she said that the injection must have been before the entry. In cross-examination she hardly waited to be challenged.

Mr L: And if this second injection, which is not recorded here, was given by you . . .
Nurse R: It was.
Mr L: Will you allow me to finish my question?
Nurse R: I am sorry.
Mr L: And within an hour of your giving that injection the patient was dead?
Nurse R: She passed away, yes.
Mr L: Miss Randall, it just is not conceivable, is it, that you would have left out of the record that injection if you had in fact given it?
Nurse R: I might have left it out because it was the very last one; we had other things to see to.
. . .
Mr L: And you have no idea seven years later why it is not in the book, have you, if you gave it?

Nurse R: No, I have not.

. . .

Mr L: And if your recollection now is right, there was a serious breach of that duty here that night, was there not?
Nurse R: Yes, sir.
Mr L: Which is quite inexplicable, isn't it?
Nurse R: Yes.

In re-examination she repeated her account of how she had come to give it. It was then that she added: 'Mrs Morrell told me that Dr Adams had promised her he wouldn't let her suffer at the end.'

A-G: If you have any doubt at all as to what happened that night, as to what you did, you will say so. Have you any doubt about that? Did you give her it?
Nurse R: No, I gave it.

When Nurse Randall got back to Eastbourne that evening, she remembered that some hours after Mrs Morrell died, she rang up Dr Adams to give him the news and told him what time she had given the last injection. She told the Eastbourne police that she had now recollected this and later in the trial she was recalled to give this testimony.

There can be no doubt that Nurse Randall firmly believed that she had given the third injection and had surrounded her belief with much circumstantial detail which was either fantastic or true. It cannot have been invented out of any animus against Dr Adams because she resolutely refused to say what the injection was; she just did not know, she said. Mr Lawrence had impressed on us all so firmly the danger of relying on anything that was not in the notebooks that we perhaps too easily disregarded Nurse Randall's explanation of her transgression. She had had a wearing night; the patient had died; she had to clear things up; she just forgot. It would have been much easier for her to say simply that the book was right and that she did not give it.

Looking back now, I think that she did give it.

This brings me back to the puzzle of Dr Adams's uncharacteristic behaviour at the death-bed. Were the three injections of an unpleasant soporific the keeping of his promise that she should not suffer at the end? Why was the heavenly panacea of heroin ousted by a drug about which he knew so little that he began with an ineffective dose of 2cc, the BP standard dose being 5 to 10cc?

An answer is suggested by Mr Lawrence's cross-examination of Dr Douthwaite. He was putting it to the witness that Adams, so far from piling on the heroin was endeavouring to escape from the spiral created by the need to overcome tolerance. Up till the Sunday, the witness agreed, there had been a consistent policy of using the same drugs to meet the same condition, but in increasing quantities. Then, as Lawrence suggested,

> Mr L: . . . the reports on the face of them show that those drugs were no longer capable *at the levels then being administered** of producing the desired results?
> Dr D: Yes.
> Mr L: Then there is a switch to one of the safest of all hypnotics in small quantities?
> Dr D: Yes.

Dr Adams decided upon the switch on a Sunday afternoon when, I dare say, the usual methods of collecting prescriptions were not available. Browne, the chemists, were in the street in which the doctor lived. So in all probability he went himself, as the Crown suggested, to the chemist and fetched the paraldehyde. Ex. 4A shows that at the same time he prescribed and presumably took away No. 93, three phials of heroin of 25 tablets each, totalling 12½grs.

No one at the trial turned the searchlight on No. 93. No one raised the vital question, which was not whether Adams himself collected No. 93 nor even when and how he injected it, but why he prescribed it. He had just decided on the complete switch. If he was thinking of a possible switch back, the nurses had in stock 6½grs. left of what he had prescribed on 9 November; anyway, within an hour or two of his changing his mind he could have got a fresh supply. But he got at the same time as the paraldehyde another 75 tablets for a patient who was likely to die long before the doctor had time to change his mind.

The shock of this illumination sent all the supposed certainties crawling for cover. Had there ever been any paraldehyde at all? What was the evidence for it?

The only evidence was supplied by the doctor himself, that is, by what he told the nurses at the time. No one ever saw a bottle of paraldehyde at Marden Ash. The nurses must by 1956 have forgotten what they had been told; if they had said that they believed it to have been paraldehyde, the Attorney would not in opening have flourished the large syringe with such panache.

What is so curious is that paraldehyde has this unpleasant and unmistakable smell. In the first two injections the nurse might

* My italics.

not have been near enough to the syringe to notice it. But since it is easier to notice and remember a smell than a non-smell, Nurse Randall's inability to say whether the third injection, which she gave herself, was or was not paraldehyde must be significant. Moreover, the injection was in the doctor's syringe and Miss Randall said in evidence that she cleaned it before leaving it for the doctor to collect. Mr Reid, the chemist, was recalled to give evidence of an experiment he had made with a 5cc syringe filled with paraldehyde and left on an instrument tray as Dr Adams would have left it covered with a towel for an hour. At all times there was an unmistakable odour pervading the room. When he cleaned the syringe the smell was even stronger.

Then there is Nurse Randall's uncertainty and anxiety, although she had been left with positive instructions, about giving the third injection. Whatever it was, she was right to give it and, as the Attorney said in opening, it was her duty to obey. But if she had smelt paraldehyde, she would have known it to be a safe soporific and would hardly have worried.

If any of the three injections consisted of heroin, there can be no doubt about the intention to terminate life forthwith.

At opposite extremes there are two possibilities. One is that Adams procured the paraldehyde and talked of it merely to mislead: he never used it, perhaps never brought it to Marden Ash: the talk was a blind to screen massive injections of heroin. At the other extreme there is the possibility that the three phials of heroin were not intended for immediate use. They were acquired either honestly as a reserve for a remote contingency or dishonestly as an addition to the doctor's private hoard.

It is all speculation, of course, but as a speculator I am not attracted by either extreme. It is hardly plausible that Dr Adams took so large a quantity of heroin to put into reserve. He could get from the chemist what he wanted any day he wanted it. If he brought three phials to Marden Ash on Sunday and none of it was used, where could it have got to by Monday morning? Certainly there were in November unexplained losses. Tablets are tiny and, once a phial was opened, keeping track of the contents was not well organized. But this sort of erosion could not account for the disappearance overnight of three unopened phials.

What of the possibility that No. 93 was destined not for Marden Ash but for the doctor's cupboard at Kent Lodge? The doctor's statement that he was not dishonest about drugs does not carry instant conviction. There is evidence that he added left-overs to his illicit stores, as doctor's perks perhaps. But there is a great difference between this and the theft of three phials. Since he could always prescribe at their expense what was wanted for other patients, why should he provide it at the expense of Mrs Morrell's estate? Could he have wanted it for the black market? I do not think so. If he had been involved in that, there would surely have been other transactions between 1950 and 1956. Police inquiries went back a long way and produced no evidence of black market dealings.

The theory at the other extreme—that there was never any paraldehyde at all—is more seductive. But if it is well-founded, I do not think that the object was to conceal a murder. This would signify a higher cunning than I believe Dr Adams to have possessed or at any rate to have been accustomed to exercise. Moreover, if that was the plot, it would be surprising to find that, when questioned six years later, he had in his talk of easing the passing forgotten all about his use of paraldehyde as the easement.

So I do not think that the object of the paraldehyde was to conceal a diabolical murder. But it may have been to conceal mercy-killing or at any rate to stop the nurses from asking awkward questions. It would not, however, be inconsistent with this object that Adams should quite genuinely have decided to try paraldehyde before resorting to the final solution of the lethal dose. The first small injection may well have been paraldehyde and perhaps also the second. The second, if of heroin, would have amounted to 5grs. I doubt if medical opinion would say with confidence what effect what quantity of heroin would have on a woman in Mrs Morrell's condition. (According to Dr Douthwaite all the doses from 7 November onwards were lethal, but they did not kill.) Yet it is difficult to think that 5grs. heroin would have given only an hour's sleep.

The consequences of the third injection were markedly different. An hour after the second injection the entry is 'very restless—no sleep' and an hour later 'restless and talkative and very shaky', the shakiness meaning, Nurse Randall said, convulsions. Then, after the third injection, 'seems a little quieter, appears asleep'; and an hour and a quarter later, 'passed away quietly'. If Dr Ashby was right, there would have been a sense of euphoria at the end. It would have been within the power of Dr Adams to give and I think he gave it.

*

This is, I think, the core of what Adams was saying to the police at the two interviews of 24 and 26 November. At the former he said that she was in terrible agony and that he gave all or nearly all the heroin prescribed. At the latter he said that he had eased the passing; she was dying in any event.

The first interview contained 'the admission'. At the trial I regarded this, as I have said, as an untruthful exculpation. It was an exculpation insofar as Adams's object in saying it at that time was to exculpate himself from what he thought he was suspected of. Some at least of what he was prepared to say for that purpose was certainly untrue. But fundamentally Hannam and he were at cross-purposes. Hannam was thinking about murder and he was thinking about hoarding unregistered drugs. I took 'terrible agony' to be an imaginative effort by the doctor to give verisimilitude to his story that he made a clean sweep of the Morrell drugs. Now I am not at all so sure. Let us look again at the evidence.

For the last days of her life, the Attorney said in opening, Mrs Morrell was comatose. Heroin, he said, while depressing the brain, stimulates the spinal cord and this was the cause of the spasms and convulsions afflicting Mrs Morrell. She had not suffered from them because she was unconscious. 'Terrible agony,' he had commented, 'when the nurses will tell you that she had been comatose for days.' The nurses' evidence of coma had not, as we have seen, emerged unblemished by the note-books nor unaffected by the disclosure of the consumption by an unconscious and rambling woman of a hearty breakfast on 2 November. Nevertheless, the doctors had testified, though with some reservation, that the patient would not suffer from the spasms. 'Not as a rule,' Douthwaite said. 'Very unpleasant,' said Ashby: 'difficult to say whether painful, probably not; but discomfort and an acute, unpleasant sensation.' The nurses' evidence, the Attorney reminded the jury in his closing speech, was that Mrs Morrell did not suffer any severe pain. He went on:

Of course, if she was in terrible agony, no one would complain of the use of drugs in large quantities to kill that pain. That would be the object, wouldn't it, killing the pain, not the object of killing the patient.

But on a murder charge the issue is, not whether Mrs Morrell was in fact in pain but whether the accused honestly believed that she was. 'Terrible agony' sounds like an exaggeration; but the evidence which Adams had from his own observation and from the nurses could have led him to believe that she was suffering. The Crown did not suggest that Adams had the expert knowledge of heroin convulsions which Douthwaite and Ashby had. They had testified that a doctor with Adams's qualifications would know that he was administering enough to kill; they made no similar suggestion about his ability to recognize the painlessness of convulsions. Nurse Randall's distress would not have been so acute if Adams had been assuring her that it was only an unpleasant sensation.

The second interview, 'easing the passing' on 26 November, should also be re-examined. There are three versions of this conversation: the first as recorded in Mr Hannam's notebook and set out in his deposition; the second as modified in the Attorney-General's opening to omit what was clearly inadmissible; the third the version given in evidence, one that was further refined to meet, I suspect, an objection communicated informally by the defence to the Attorney-General which he must have accepted as valid. In this chapter we are not bound by the rules of evidence and I give the conversation in question and answer form.

Dr: You told Mr James there might be other charges. I am very worried. What are they?
Supt: That is not quite accurate. I told him he must not automatically assume the charges preferred were final.
Dr: Well, what else is there?
Supt: Hiding that morphine on Saturday night is a serious offence and I am still inquiring into the deaths of some of your rich patients. I do not think they were all natural.
Dr: Which?
Supt: Mrs Morrell is certainly one.
Dr: Easing the passing *etc.*

The significant word that was laundered out in the trial version is the doctor's 'Which?'. A suggestion to a doctor that some of his patients had died an unnatural death seems to call for an expression of astonishment rather than a request for particulars. Had it come to a ruling, I should have allowed the 'Which?' as admissible evidence to show that the doctor was not, as might have been expected, totally unreceptive of the idea that any of the patients whose death certificates he had signed had died an unnatural death.

In these two conversations on 24 and 26 November Adams was saying that he acted to anticipate death. There are two points of difference between the two. On the 24th he was saying that he did it by a dose of heroin while on the 26th he was not saying how he did it; he might have been referring to paraldehyde. But for the lawyer the critical difference is not whether the end came from heroin or from paraldehyde. It is whether the doctor acted, as he said on the 24th, because the patient was in terrible agony or, as he said on the 26th, because she was dying in any event.

Leaving aside that difference, was Adams telling the truth? I believe that he was. He was telling the truth because it had not occurred to him that there was any reason for lying. He had no thought of murder. He knew quite well that he was vulnerable to drug charges. What on 26 November he wanted to know was whether the Superintendent had come to the end of the professional peccadilloes which he would have to admit. The reference to Mrs Morrell's unnatural death would, I think, have meant no more to him than a suggestion that he had improperly hastened her end. His reply was that he had eased the passing, 'not all that wicked', and that it was impossible to accuse a doctor. Hence the shock and the 'I did not think you could prove murder' when he was charged on 19 December. He did not think of himself as a murderer but as a dispenser of death.

Advocates of euthanasia may say that what I have called the critical difference is of little importance. Its importance to my mind is twofold. First, if Adams did not believe in the agony, why did he invent it? Deceit in this could not be dissociated from the efforts to obtain a legacy which taint the doctor's relations with his patient. Second, we have to consider not what the advocates of euthanasia would like the law to be, but what it is. If he really had an honest belief in easing suffering, Dr Adams was on the right side of the law; if his purpose was simply to finish life, he was not. It is thus that I should have directed the jury, had the issue been raised. A narrow distinction. But in the law, as in all matters of principle, cases can be so close to each other that the gap can be perceived only theoretically. In the criminal law the gap is what is perceptible by a jury. I doubt whether a distinction between terminal suffering and dying in any event would have meant much either to Dr Adams or to a jury asked to convict of murder. Such a jury would not have examined meticulously the grounds for the doctor's belief. They would have acquitted.

This would have been a quiet but satisfying end to the story, bringing it back in a rounded curve to the last interview, the one on which the decision was taken to arrest and charge. The doctor had then by some extraordinary contrariety of nature put his defence into three lines which had proved too terse for the Crown to interpret.

> Easing the passing of a dying person is not all that wicked. She wanted to die. That cannot be murder. It is impossible to accuse a doctor.

However, the trial did not end in that way.

23

The Right to Silence

'Murder?'

A pause.

'Can you prove it was murder?'

The Superintendent replied: 'You are now charged with murdering her.'

'I did not think you could prove murder. She was dying in any event.'

This was at the doctor's residence at 11.50 am on 19 December 1956. Forty minutes later, when he was formally charged at the police station, Adams at last heeded professional advice and said, 'It is better to say nothing.' And in fact he never did say anything more—nothing, that is, for publication—except that when called upon to plead, he said, 'I am not guilty, my lord.' Thereafter he stood upon the accused's right to silence.

Jeremy Bentham, the great theorist and rationalizer, one of those who think that they can put the world to rights with a treatise and who get very angry with those who think otherwise, described the right to silence as 'one of the most pernicious and irrational rules that has ever found its way into the human mind.' 'Innocence,' he declared in an aphorism that his disciples have adopted as their slogan, 'never takes advantage of it; innocence claims the right of speaking as guilt invokes the privilege of silence.' Answers obtained under interrogation were, he said, the best form of evidence.

The slogan gives the English rule a loud whack but does not pierce it. It is off centre in two directions.

First, it does not distinguish between speaking and being interrogated. An English accused has for centuries had the right to speak from the dock. What he is claiming is not that, but the right not to be questioned until after the prosecution has established in his presence that there is a case to answer. Surely that is a right which is as appropriate to innocence as to guilt. Second, innocence and guilt are not usually—at any rate in the characters of those who attract arrest—as separate as black and white. There is a large grey area which is the natural habitat of the Adamses and their sort.

But of course when a man, be his character white or grey, throws caution to the winds, convinced of his innocence, disdaining to shelter behind his privilege, he can do himself a power of good. Judges are prompt to point out to a jury the value to an accused of an instantaneous denial or explanation. Adams, not so much convinced of his innocence as impervious to the idea that he could possibly be accused, teetered volubly on the edge of catastrophe. His lavish admissions of his expectations from 'a very dear patient', of his falsification of cremation forms so that 'things might go smoothly', and of how he injected all or nearly all of the drugs himself, were carefully accumulated by the police. Without them it is hard to see how the prosecution could have got the case against him on its legs. But he had produced the antidote as well as the poison: he had registered his defence. The 'terrible agony', unconvincing if first revealed in cross-examination, had been mentioned as soon as the police queried the quantity prescribed.

This is written on the assumption that Dr Adams made all the statements that the police attributed to him. I have no doubt that in substance he did. I accept, of course, that there were in 1957 some policemen ready to concoct the 'verbals' they wrote into their notebooks. They were the rotten few. No one has ever suggested that chief constables run courses in verbalization. Yet an undetectable verbal requires the elimination of the language to which the police are habituated and the talent of a playwright to replace it with convincing dialogue. 'Poor soul', 'terrible agony', 'easing the passing', 'impossible to accuse a doctor', strike me as authentic Adams.

Nor did Hannam look like one of the rotten few. It is true that he was a believer in the Benthamite doctrine that answers obtained in interrogation are the best form of evidence, that he was himself a wily interrogator and that he hoped in that way to obtain a conviction. Or, as he would have put it, to crack the criminal. But there is a great difference between that and police perjury.

The good citizen may dislike what he perceives in this case of the police methods of cracking the suspect. It is natural that he should. The British favour the idea, which reigns supreme in their courts, that crime should be proved against the suspect by the facts that are against him and not by words out of his own mouth. The British, like everybody else, favour the idea of eating their cake and having it. For historical reasons the trial process is now overloaded in favour of the defence. Proof of guilt on the bare facts has been made so difficult that for many years past it would not have been achieved if it had not been supplemented, often supplanted, by pre-trial statements made to the police. If the prosecution had to rely only on the facts of the case, there would be far too many criminals left at large.

For my part I should like to see reliance upon police interrogation reduced almost to vanishing point. I should be prepared to pay for that by admitting into the trial much that is excluded from it as supposedly unfair to the accused. Let the court of trial and not the police station be the place at which guilt is determined, but let the court be less inhibited about what it listens to. Things are moving that way. On the one side accused are being given better protection against interrogation. On the other side juries are showing that they can safely be trusted with much more information about the accused and about the circumstances of the crime than at present they are allowed to have.

That is for the present and for the future. In 1956 the police were given the task of obtaining proof of murder against a man, manifestly not of the highest rectitude, whom they in company with nearly the whole of the press and, because of the press, with the majority of the public, believed to be a deadly poisoner. There was no hope of a conviction unless they could obtain admissions. The good citizen, who turns up his nose at police methods, should bear in mind that he would be quite overcome by the stench of those employed by the men whom in most cases the police are fighting. The public accepts without complaint what the police have done when they have succeeded in convicting the wicked. Illogically they reserve their criticism for the cases in which the police have unfortunately, but as is bound sometimes to happen, believed to be wicked those who are innocent or only foolish. Whatever the police may believe about an accused, their methods must be clean and fair. This does not mean that they must be without cunning, but it does mean that they must play no dirty tricks.

Of course what is dislikable about Hannam, though it did not enter into the trial, is his flamboyancies and his cultivation of the press, apparently for his own glorification rather than for any assistance which it could give to the investigation. But there is an unbridgeable difference between that and the concoction of 'verbals'. The joint notebook means that this would have needed the collaboration of Sergeant Hewitt. There is no ground for thinking that either Hannam or Hewitt was a dishonest police-man. There is on the contrary every reason to suppose that Adams was a compulsive communicator.

The point at which Adams began his silence was also the begin-ning of an incarceration that lasted for over three months and must have tried even the doctor's phlegm. He had little to reflect on but the hard fact that it had turned out not to be impossible to accuse a doctor and no one to talk to about the case except his solicitor who surely convinced him at last that he stood in grave peril. In due course the solicitor would take his proof, but probably that would not be until after the full disclosure at Eastbourne of the Crown's case. For that he had to wait six weeks.

For days he listened at Eastbourne to the Crown case being acted out before him. I do not think that he lost his belief in his innocence. According to his lights he had done nothing wrong. There was nothing wrong in a doctor getting a legacy, nor in his bestowing in return—would he have thought of it as 'in return'?—a death as happy as heroin could make it. Now he saw the witnesses marshalled against him, the nurses, his own partner, Dr Harris, to speak also of the death of Mrs Hullett whom Adams had kept out of hospital lest her death wish be frustrated, Mr Sogno, the lawyer who had always distrusted him, the policemen who had taken down everything he had said, the Harley Street establishment on solemn parade against him, all these materializing like the images whom the witches conjured up for Macbeth.

'Can you prove it?' Perhaps what shocked him the most was to hear in the police evidence how much he had himself contributed to the proof. All of it had been easy talk, carried away on the breath, by him only half remembered; but by Hannam fixed in words, edited fairly enough no doubt but, as an editor does, putting the emphasis on what he was hoping to hear.

Then, when the process is over, the lawyer comes to take the proof. What a relief it would be to say to him, 'You've heard all the evidence. Tell me, what is the best line of defence? What should I admit and what deny? How much of Hannam's evidence does me any harm? Do you think, if I deny this or that, that I'd be believed?'

But that would not get beyond the hint.

'No, no, all we want, Dr Adams, is just for you to tell us in your own words what you did and said. To the best of your recollection of course. Take your time. Don't hurry.'

There were in 1957 a few rotten lawyers as well as a few rotten policemen. But the Law Society does not run courses in fabricating defences and the Medical Defence Union does not employ rotten lawyers. So Dr Adams would have been on his own. And on his own he would not have had the stamina to stick to the truth simply because it was the truth, nor the perception to see that it was on the whole in his interests to stick to it, nor the ability to distinguish between what was for and what against his case. He denied everything. He had said nothing. Together with the admissions which sustained the prosecution he poured down the drain the vital conversations of 24 and 26 November on which the sincerity of his defence depended. 'Terrible agony', for example. He slammed the door on it. How could he now say at the trial that he did indeed believe that she was in agony, but that it was just by a coincidence that the verbalizing superintendent had put the very words into his mouth?

How do I know this? It is all speculation of course. It would all have been in Adams's proof, the blueprint of his defence. But that document, if it still exists, is under a seal which, so far as I know, has never been broken nor allowed to crumble in the passing of time. It is, however, a document some of whose contents or non-contents may be surmised from what was or was not said in public at the trial. If a witness in the box was narrating any fact which the accused in his turn was or might be going into the box to deny, it was Mr Lawrence's duty in cross-examination of the witness to put the contradiction to him. Likewise, where the accused was going to agree, counsel in cross-examination would want to add to the witness's picture of events the little extra touches which his client's evidence was going to provide. To show, for example, how easily the convulsions might be mistaken for agony.

Instead of this Nurse Randall was vigorously assailed for exaggerating the convulsions; it was put to her also that she could not have given the third injection. On the police evidence I have already recorded the cross-examination of Mr Hannam in which he reacted scornfully to the suggestion that the loquacious doctor had simply held his tongue. This related to the conversation of 24

November. As for 'easing the passing' on the 26th the blunt suggestion was that there had never been any conversation at all on that day. The suggestions were not made forcefully. They sounded as convincing as a formal plea of Not Guilty. A suggestion that the police have fabricated a whole conversation needs to be made by onslaught to have any chance of success. Lawrence was quite capable of mounting an onslaught if he was given the material for it, but evidently he was not.

There is nothing in the cross-examination which offers any clue to what the proof said about No. 93.

I have now gone as far as I can while keeping contact with the known facts, perhaps a little further than I should. No part of Adams's proof is a known fact, but there are parts which can be surmised from the known facts. From now on I must rely entirely on the imagination, restrained to respect what is known and curbed from flying off into the implausible.

So I imagine that defence counsel were from the beginning alive to the acute danger created by No. 93 and that they had not been supplied by the client with any satisfactory explanation of why he prescribed it as well as paraldehyde, let alone what he did with it. They must have been pleased to note from Reggie's opening speech that he had not fully grasped, or at any rate was not enunciating at that stage, the significance of No. 93. Referring to the last injections, he had said only, 'The prosecution cannot tell you what these injections were.' He had not then pointed to No. 93 and asked rhetorically why it was prescribed if not for the 5cc syringe.

When on the next day the defence produced the notebooks, it must have been a relief to see that Reggie was quietly absorbing them and in particular that he was not challenging the use of paraldehyde at the end. Thereafter the thrust of Douthwaite's evidence had been directed to the quantities recorded in the books. If the Crown accepted the books as the battleground, there would be a ding-dong fight between opposing experts on the lethal effect of quantities admittedly injected and no need to account for No. 93. But on the tenth day of the trial the Attorney answered an inquiry from me by saying that he was putting his case first of all on the quantities prescribed. For the defence that was the danger signal.

They had now to ask themselves and answer a crucial question. Had Reggie missed the point or was he keeping it in reserve to ask at the deadliest moment of cross-examination? If the latter,

Adams must not be called. There were several reasons for and against calling him, but this one seems to me conclusive. It may be argued that to keep him out of the box would only postpone disaster since Reggie would then make the point in his closing speech with the implication added that Adams had not dared to face it. That argument would not have succeeded with me if I had been the counsel taking the decision. Unless I was absolutely certain, which I should not have been, that Reggie had got the point, I should have reckoned the danger of his stumbling on it greater in the course of cross-examination than in the course of a speech. In the former there is the possibility that it may be turned up by the plough, a suggestive answer by the witness or an intervention by the judge. Then in cross-examination counsel could drive the point in to a depth that would make its extraction impossible. Made for the first time in a speech which there was no opportunity of answering, the point might not have been accepted as final in the court of appeal.

I am sure that defence counsel took the right course in keeping the accused out of the box and risking the consequences. It was a courageous decision. Insofar as it was a gamble it came off. Reggie had not got the point.

Neither of course had I. It is not part of a judge's duty to look for and expose submerged points—that is a job for counsel—but one likes to keep one's eyes open. But I was doped by the half-truths that the law of evidence fosters. It was quite obvious that the 'certain other offences' with which we were told Dr Adams was being charged had to do with drugs. It was clear that there was no efficient monitoring of the drugs prescribed. I believed that there was a leakage somewhere. But neither side seemed anxious to explore any discrepancies. There were, so to speak, hatched squares on the games board on to which neither side might move its counters. I suspected—wrongly, as I now know—that dealings on the black market might account for the discrepancies. So I drew no conclusions from the possible misuse of No. 93 or any other prescription. My concern was to put the matter to the jury in a way that left them with a thought that Lawrence could not well hold out to them, namely, that a surplus in the prescriptions could possibly be accounted for by a crime other than murder.

For Reggie on the other hand it was an article of faith that the doctor had administered all the drugs that he had prescribed. Had he applied that doctrine specifically to the last injection he would have got somewhere. But he stuck at the barrier of the paraldehyde. He must have had his suspicions about that, especially about the last injection, else he would not have recalled Mr Reid, the chemist, to demonstrate the unlikelihood of its being paraldehyde. But openly he accepted it as such and his final formulation was that 'her death was due to the morphia and heroin and accelerated by paraldehyde'. Perhaps subconsciously he realized that murder by No. 93 was not the sort of murder he wanted. It made nonsense of the legacy motive. Putting an old woman on her deathbed out of life would have been a feeble ending to the tale of the Eastbourne massacre.

Would the Hullett case have produced a stronger ending?

There is ample evidence that Mrs Hullett wished to take her own life. There is no evidence at all that Adams was present while she did so. The suggestion that he was there and in some way administering the drug is not even plausible.

But it is not implausible to suggest that the doctor helped Mrs Hullett to end her life. Did she hoard the dose of 115grs. of barbiturates or was it provided by the doctor? If the latter, what part, if any, did the cheque for £1,000, so speedily cashed, and perhaps the promise of the Rolls-Royce play in the transaction? Can it really be true that the cause of her coma did not occur to him? Was he not concealing it so that her intention, maybe their common intention, should not be frustrated? Did he genuinely want her to recover? Was he really misinformed about the megimide? These questions can be answered by suspicion but not by proof.

For some of these acts, if he was guilty of them, Dr Adams would win from some people sympathy, if not approval. As he would, also, for easing the passing of Mrs Morrell, even if he did not believe her to be in pain. If only his hands had been clean. But if he sold death for money or money's worth, he dishonoured a great profession.

POSTSCRIPT

Early in the book (p.8) I say that the lapse of a quarter of a century since the trial of Dr Adams is 'long enough to allow publication without indecorum'. This view has been generally, but not universally, accepted. I can understand the doubt. A judge on the Bench is a man of silence. Silence and gravity are as much a part of his mien as the wig and robes are of his accoutrement. Certainly he must not write about his cases while he is on the Bench; and when, as is usual, he retires as a septuagenarian, his pen and his memory may both be running dry.

I left the Bench while I was still in my fifties, and for the next six years served as Chairman of the Press Council. This may have had a laxative effect. I came to think, as pressmen do, that in public affairs exposure should be the rule and concealment the exception. The trial is a public performance, but one in which the processes that make it fully understandable are not revealed. Counsel and solicitors are bound to professional secrecy. It occurred to me that, if an occasion arose, a judicial analysis of a trial of sufficient interest to be readable by the public would be useful and unobjectionable.

I adhere to this view. I am confirmed in it by the fact that the objectors have not challenged it directly. The rumbling that it is a matter for his conscience is the worst that I have heard. The plea that what has not been done before should never be done at all has not been put into so many words. Instead of a frontal assault there have been two flank attacks, each mounted against what is proclaimed as an objectionable feature of an otherwise uncriticized whole. One is by the *Daily Express*; the other by the top-most of the top judiciary. I feel sure that they were not concerted.

The *Express* was concerned for the reputation of Dr Adams. The jury had acquitted him, but the judge in his book, so the *Express* said, 'tampered with the verdict'. It was hinted that 'fat publishers' cheques' (though loosely written, this is not, I am sure, intended to be offensive to my publishers; it is the obesity of the cheques that the writer had in mind) were the inducement to 'a squalid exercise in legal revisionism'. This is the product of careless or selective reading. Nowhere in the book do I question the verdict at the trial: quite the contrary. Writing (p.153) of the period before the verdict was given, I say that if, improbably, the jury convicted, the verdict would be quashed on appeal. On p.198 I speak of the verdict, after it has been given, as 'unquestionably a true verdict'. On mercy-killing, an issue not raised at the trial, I say on p.209 that, if it had been, the jury would have acquitted.

The attack by the high judiciary was more sedately delivered. The charge of damaging beyond repair 'the reputation of the impartiality (sic) of the judicial bench', with which the *Daily Express* had concluded its denunciation, was reduced to one of uncharitable or deplorable conduct in attacking the Attorney-General; the reputation threatened was not that of the judicial bench but only, and in an unspecified way, my own.

The high judiciary made two sorties, both, as is proper for a flank attack, at unexpected places. The first was by Sir Robin Dunn, formerly a Lord Justice of Appeal, in a letter to the *Field*; the second was in a letter written jointly by the Law Lords Scarman and Bridge to *The Times Literary Supplement*.

Sir Robin describes the book as 'an attack upon the character and ability of the Attorney-General at the trial'. This is (among other things) substantially what it was. Sir Robin offers no defence; he writes 'only in an attempt to redress the balance'. This he does by reference to Lord Dilhorne's speeches a decade later as a Lord of Appeal: 'widely acclaimed', 'robust approach ... clarity and certainty'. This is a sensible letter, making the legitimate point that, whether or not he was a failure at the trial, Dilhorne was considered a successful Lord of Appeal. I have no quarrel with Sir Robin's prophecy that 'many of Lord Dilhorne's judgments will be remembered when the more obscure pronouncements of some who regard themselves as his intellectual superiors are forgotten'. If he meant to include me, I have started the process myself by forgetting most of mine: they were not addressed to posterity.

The Scarman–Bridge letter was written in response to an extremely provocative review of the book. In it the reviewer referred to my 'profound contempt for an obtuse mediocrity as the theme of the book'. Scarman and Bridge found this description of the book to be regrettably true. Thus they were presented with a double target – the reviewer, who called Lord Dilhorne an obtuse mediocrity and myself, who allegedly had a profound contempt for him.

As to the first, the Scarman–Bridge letter follows Sir Robin with much the same phrasing – 'notable contribution to the law', 'robust common sense', 'exceptional clarity', 'speeches a pleasure to read and throw light on every subject they touch' (an echo here of Johnson's *nullum quod tetigit* epitaph for Goldsmith; he touched nothing that he did not adorn) 'an outstanding appellate judge'. Like Sir Robin, the Scarman–Bridge letter says nothing about the trial or about my criticism of the Attorney-General's part in it. What it complains of is an attack which was (a) posthumous, (b) upon a former judicial colleague, (c) made with contempt. I discuss each of these in turn.

Undoubtedly the publication was posthumous – by the decent margin of five years. But posthumous is a word frequently used, as here, not so much to mark the time as to imply a reproach. This makes it much the same as saying that you should criticize a man to his face and not behind his back. These are worthy injunctions although, if strictly complied with, they would cause a lot of unpleasantness. Anyway, in the present case compliance was impracticable. It would as a rule be wrong to attack a judge in office about his conduct of a case as counsel because his office would hamper him in answering back. Unhappily Lord Dilhorne died only a few weeks after he left office.

That is one answer. The other, perhaps more down to earth, is that Dr Adams outlived Lord Dilhorne. This book is uncomplimentary about Dilhorne, but it is also, and necessarily, defamatory of Adams. Lord Dilhorne's book, if he had written one, would have been even more defamatory. No publisher would have touched either of them while Dr Adams was alive.

The 'former judicial colleague' is another pebble of the same sort. All Lords of Appeal in Ordinary are formally colleagues of the Lord Chancellor, but he rarely sits on judicial business and I never sat with Lord Chancellor Dilhorne. After we had retired, we were both on what may be called a supplementary list and in this way came to sit together in perhaps half a dozen cases during the rest of the 1960s. Such was the extent of our judicial colloguing. It did not begin until the period covered by the book was over and the book has nothing at all to do with it.

Lords Scarman and Bridge must, I feel, be using the word 'colleague' less precisely. The sentiment they are invoking is more tenuous. They are saying that Dilhorne and I were men of a kind and that birds of a feather should flock together; or, to vary the animal and the adage, that dog should not eat dog. This sentiment is the natural product of association, and I am not mocking it. But it precludes impartiality. So there was no place for it in what I was doing. A judge, when writing an account of one of his trials must write of it as impartially as he has conducted it; else the account is of no value.

The charge of displaying contempt is quite a different matter. I find it hardly believable. I can understand an act being called contemptible, though I myself would be frightened of the adjective, fearing the thought of 'there but for the grace of God'. But to have contempt for a person is to despise him or her as a human being. It is destructive of 'the love and charity to your neighbours' which the Book of Common Prayer enjoins. The emotion, if it gets into the mind of a judge, poisons the springs of justice. I have not in this book, and never anywhere else, expressed contempt for Lord Dilhorne. I have never felt it. I wish that Lords Scarman and Bridge had done me the honour of putting their judgment into their own words instead of concurring with a reviewer with whom at every other point they disagree. I wish that they had signified the passages which they condemn.

Dilhorne was a man who took himself much more seriously than I can take either myself or him. There is irreverence in the book and there are teasing passages. There are comments, sometimes appreciative, but mostly critical. There is a lack of admiration. None of this is contempt. Dilhorne's defects, chiefly narrow-mindedness and obstinacy, were not those which excite contempt. Think of General de Gaulle who almost turned them into virtues; no one dreamt of despising him.

So much for the specifics in the Scarman–Bridge letter. In general the letter is wholly irrelevant. It is no defence of a man's performance as an advocate to say that a decade later he was an excellent judge. But it turns the mind to one of the themes of this book which I take the opportunity of pursuing to the end. For this book is something more than the story of a criminal trial: it is also part of the story of how the politicians' grasp of the highest offices in the judiciary was prised loose. What the Scarman–Bridge letter says about Dilhorne completes the tale.

The rewarding of political service with lucrative office began in the times when the king's servants, then mostly clerics and the educated élite of the country, were given all the best bishoprics. They were succeeded by the lawyers who demanded all the best judicial offices. They nearly always got them, though the only one to which they established a prescriptive right was the office of Chief Justice of the Common Pleas. But they were strong and usually successful candidates for many other places. When, in

1836, the claims of Sir John Campbell, admittedly a grasping Attorney-General, were rejected, he was dissuaded from resigning ('by way of protest', as he put it, 'on behalf of the privileges and honour of the Bar')* only by the grant of a peerage to his wife. He was a persistent man who later became Lord Chief Justice and then Lord Chancellor. I have already (p.92) recounted the similar achievements of his successors.

In 1897 there arose an interesting problem; the manner of its solution illustrated the grip of the system.** The Prime Minister was the great Lord Salisbury; the Lord Chancellor was Lord Halsbury; the Attorney-General was Sir Richard Webster and the Solicitor-General Sir Edward Clarke. There was a vacancy at the Rolls which Sir Richard did not then want. (He took it with a peerage in 1900, but only on his way to the Chief Justiceship.) Failing the Attorney, was the Prime Minister bound 'on party grounds' to offer the Rolls to the Solicitor despite the Chancellor's 'unfavourable judgement as to Clarke's judicial capacities'?

It would be no solution, the Prime Minister pointed out, to press Webster to go to the Rolls because, if he did, Clarke must become Attorney and that would be worse than sending him to the Rolls, 'even without taking into account that it would give him a claim, which could not be passed over to higher possible vacancies'.

One solution was 'to throw Clarke over altogether', but the Prime Minister would not do that. 'It is', he wrote, 'at variance with the unwritten law of our party system and there is no clearer statute in that unwritten law that party claims should always weigh very heavily in the disposal of the highest legal appointments.' He had asked 'Arthur Balfour and other advisers specially competent in the matter with the same result'. 'After all,' he wrote consolingly, 'there have been in our recollection men who have sat in high places of the law with a very slender garment of legal knowledge to keep them warm.' He cited three names which, to spare the blushes of their descendants, I do not repeat.

So the place was offered to Clarke and he solved the problem by declining it. It was in these circumstances that the Prime Minister was driven to fill the vacancy with the great judge who later became Lord Lindley.

When in 1927 Manningham-Buller was called to the Bar the

* J. B. Atlay, *The Victorian Chancellors*, Vol.2.p.158, Smith Elder, 1908.
** I am indebted to Professor R. F. V. Heuston, *Lives of the Lord Chancellors, 1885–1940* pp.52–4, Clarendon Press, 1964.

four top places in the hierarchy were all held by past politicians. The Lord Chancellor, the Lord Chief Justice and the Master of the Rolls were all former Attorneys-General. The fourth place, the Presidency of what is now the Family Division, was held by Lord Merrivale. He resigned political office in 1918 and in the next year travelled via the Court of Appeal to the Presidency. Members of Parliament who had not been law officers could hope, when their party was in power, for smaller rewards. One or two might make the High Court and the lower courts were sprinkled with the less vociferous. So it was not unnatural for an ambitious young man in the 1930s to see political activity as the best way to the top.

A system which was theoretically indefensible did not work badly if not pushed to extremes. The House of Commons is a legislating body and needs in its membership good lawyers and accomplished debaters. There were many – prominent among them Kilmuir, the Lord Chancellor in 1958 when the Chief Justiceship fell vacant – who considered that it was vital to have lawyer-politicians in the House and that the system was the only way of making sure of good recruits. The politician-lawyer, that is, the man who was a politician first and a lawyer second, was a rare specimen. Most lawyers went into the House with their practices established, with an eye no doubt on the Bench as well as the Bar, but also with the desire to take part in great affairs and to serve constituents as well as clients. Experience gained in the House was not wasted in the law and such men might make excellent judges.

But it was a lottery with tickets issued only to those whose party was in power. The ticket, as Kilmuir is reputed to have put it, was for a place in a procession which might put the holder beside an empty chair when the music stopped.

Jacob served seven years for Rachel and it was after seven years that the music stopped for Manningham-Buller. If he had had only a fraction of the qualities with which the Scarman–Bridge letter credits him and no defects that outweighed them, it is inconceivable that he would not have been given the place which tradition had reserved for him. Mr Macmillan, the Prime Minister, was not one who thought ill of patronage and tradition and Kilmuir was his chief adviser. Four years later, the Solicitor-General, now Lord Simon of Glaisdale, a man of all the qualities and no defects, was duly appointed to the Presidency of what is now the Family Division. His was the last appointment under the old system.

But the decision in Dilhorne's case is rightly regarded as the turning-point. It killed the tradition that political service established a claim for a place in the judiciary. Yet the revolution would not be complete until a prime minister had appointed to judicial office a politician from the other side. When the final step was taken, the whim of the gods made Lord Dilhorne the first to be raised. He, whose attempt eleven years before to force an entry into the old tenements had been repulsed, was the first to take possession of the new; the revolution which he had involuntarily begun in 1958, he willingly completed in 1969. Five years after he had ceased to be the Tory Lord Chancellor, a socialist Prime Minister offered him a place as a Lord of Appeal in Ordinary and he gratefully accepted it.

So his career falls into two parts, divided by his brief Chancellorship. Lords Scarman and Bridge ignore the first part, with which alone this book is concerned, and I am ignorant of the second. I know nothing at first hand of his career as a judge except that on the few occasions I sat with him he seemed to me to preside neatly. I confess that I find the very high claims which his friends make for him rather startling, particularly the *nullum quod tetigit*. But if Lord Scarman, himself universally regarded as a judge of great distinction, rates him an outstanding appellate judge, he must at least have been well worth his judicial place in the House of Lords. The Rachel, for whom he served seven years and more, turned out to be the skill he acquired as a law officer in the science of statutory construction which, then as now, formed so large a part of a Law Lord's work. But anyway the evidence is clear. Just as his rejection in 1958 must be taken as proof of his unfitness to be Chief Justice, so his vindication in 1969 is the warranty for his appointment as one of the Law Lords: in the five years before it was made he had often presided over them and so had been tested and found fit.

There is no incongruity in this. Dilhorne's virtues and vices never changed, but in different lights they looked different. His handicap was that he went through life blinkered. He wished to see only what was in front of him. In the Adams case he could see only the guilt of Adams and, I believe, never deviated from his profound conviction that he was prosecuting a mass murderer. For an advocate or for a trial judge or for the Chief Justice who presides over trial judges, blinkers would be disastrous. But in the very highest court, a case that is being argued for the third or fourth time is already mapped in detail and the choice of route is very limited. If the choice is right, blinkers may even be an advantage. They keep out doubts and distractions and make the brevity, for which Dilhorne is rightly praised, easier to achieve. I do not dispute his abilities; I mention them whenever they appear at the trial. But there it was that his faults, particularly his utter inflexibility, dominated. I am still a little shocked that an Attorney-General should persist in a prosecution in which he had to leave unanswered the charge that it had become ludicrous; and by the pettiness of the refusal to give Dr Adams his acquittal on the second indictment. But all this flowed from his incapacity to look at more than one side of a coin.

In this book I am handling an episode, not writing a biography. A biographer will find a place for much that is irrelevant to my story. There is the pleasant side of his character at which I just glance (p.40). There is his family life. There will be the recollections of those who worked with him as a law officer; they will be varied, but many with something happy to say. Since the book was published, I have had letters from several who knew him, not resentful of what I wrote but affording glimpses of the other side. I get the impression that he was an acquired taste rather than an instant source of joy and that was how I found him.

But much depends on the period and the setting. I depicted him as I saw him in public life, a man of average abilities not then equal to his high ambition, a hungry man fighting for what he thought to be his rightful place at the banquet. The Scarman–Bridge letter is a portrait of the man more than a decade later in the contentment of age, a Samson Agonistes, 'with all his trophies hung and acts enrolled ... and calm of mind, all passion spent'. There is no reason why both should not be true: Samson was not without blemish in his active days.

If the Scarman–Bridge letter had been content to emphasize that the picture I painted was not the whole picture of the man, I should have been glad to agree with the obvious. But its loud deplorings and threats of a lowered reputation are worth no more than the lamentations of viewers at an exhibition who, if a portrait has not the likeness with which they are familiar, condemn the painter.

Mojacar,
March 1986

REFERENCES AND NOTES
Mainly for Lawyers

In criminal proceedings there are no pleadings of this sort. The defendant makes only the general plea of Guilty or Not Guilty. If he pleads not guilty, the prosecution must as a matter of procedure prove by evidence all the facts necessary to establish guilt.* 'A prisoner can consent to nothing'; *R v Bertrand* (1867) L.R. 1 P.C. 520

---

* This was the law in 1957. The Criminal Justice Act 1967 s. 10 now allows formal admissions under certain conditions

The evidence may, however, include proof of what may be called informal admissions of fact made by the accused. These are statements by the accused, made perhaps in the course of a police interrogation or perhaps casually in conversation with a third party. They are not conclusive; they can be withdrawn, explained or denied; see *Heane v Rogers* (1829) B & C 577 at 586. They must be taken in their context. If made upon one hypothesis (e.g. that Mrs Morrell was in agony), they are not binding upon any other; *Powell v M'Glynn* (1902) 2 I.R. 154. They must be consistent with the other evidence tendered by the prosecution as proof of guilt.

141 **Sybille Bedford has described** *The Best We Can Do*, Collins (1958) (hereinafter cited as Bedford) p. 184

161 **so rude to the good** *Oxford Dictionary of Quotations*, 3rd edn (1979) p. 576 (23)

173 **apparently shocked . . . a joint note** As a general rule what a court of law wants is the independent recollection of the individual witness. It does not want a number of observers to get together and agree among themselves upon a common version. This is a very sound rule, but it cannot be made universal. I have already suggested a modification for witnesses who, like the nurses in this case, are asked to recreate their recollections after a long interval; see p. 80. The rule is not applicable at all to witnesses who are not independent observers but, as police officers do, work together as a team. Nevertheless, for many years the similarity of notes made by a pair of police officers was a favoured topic for cross-examination. Differences suggested that one or other of the officers must have been at fault; resemblances suggested that they had put their heads together.

Superintendent Hannam devised an alternative method which came to light in Mr Lawrence's cross-examination of Sergeant Hewitt.

Q. When you were giving your evidence . . . you were refreshing your memory all the time from your notebook?
A. Not my notebook, sir.
Q. What?
A. Not my notebook, sir. I have adopted Superintendent Hannam's notebook. I did not write any notes of that conversation at all.
Q. Am I really hearing what you are saying?
A. Yes, sir, you are.
. . .

Q. And is this really right, that all the time you were giving your evidence Superintendent Hannam's notes were open in front of you in that witness-box?
A. I was reading them, sir.

Q. Well, that accounts for, then, that what you said, as I followed it, from Superintendent Hannam's evidence, was word for word the same?
A. I would hope it would be, sir.
Q. Well, otherwise you were misreading?
A. Yes, sir.
. . .

Q. Well now, let me see if I can try to understand this. When did you first see that notebook?
A. Twelve midnight, sir, on the occasion of our first visit to Dr Adams, which was on 24 November.
. . .

Q. By which time Hannam was already compiling his notebook?
A. No, sir.
Q. Well, then, it was my fault for not making the question precise enough. When did you first see the record in Hannam's notebook which you have been reading this morning?
A. I watched him write it, sir. I was with him the whole time.
Judge. Did you take any part in the preparation of the notes which are written down by Mr Hannam in his notebook?
A. Yes, sir, on his directions it was done that way, and he said that if I disagreed with him I was to tell him.

In fact, though evidently it came as a surprise to Mr Lawrence whom the sergeant was, perhaps a little playfully, leading up the garden path, the officers were adopting a course already sanctioned by the Court of Criminal Appeal, against whom rather than against the Superintendent criticism after the trial should have been directed. In *R v Bass* (1953) 37 Cr. App. R. 51 at 59 the court said:

This court has observed that police officers nearly always deny that they have collaborated in the making of notes and we cannot help wondering why they are the only class of society who do not collaborate in such a matter. It seems to us that nothing could be more natural or proper when two persons have been present at an interview with a third person than that they should afterwards make sure that they have a correct version of what was said. Collaboration would appear to be a better explanation of almost identical notes than the possession of a superhuman memory.

181 *nolle prosequi* . . . **an abuse of process.** But not an abuse which in 1957 the courts could have corrected. In *R v Allen* (1862) 1 B. & S. 850 it was argued unsuccessfully that the entry of the *nolle prosequi* was

irregular because the Attorney-General had failed to give the prosecutor and the accused a chance to put forward their own views. Cockburn C. J. said at 855: 'Suppose it possible that there could be an abuse of his power by the Attorney-General, or injustice in the exercise of it, the remedy is by holding him responsible for his acts before the great tribunal of this country, the High Court of Parliament.' In *R v Comptroller-General of Patents* (1899) 1 Q. B. 905 Smith L. J. said at 914 that the Attorney-General's power was not subject to any control.

The *nolle prosequi* is an emanation of the royal prerogative; see B. S. Markesinis, *The Royal Prerogative Revisited* (1973) C.L.J. 287. The dicta cited above are now outmoded by the development of the doctrine of judicial review. The decision of the House of Lords, given as I am writing this on 22 November 1984 in *Re the Council of Civil Service Unions*, makes it clear that immunity from legal process must in the words of Lord Roskill 'depend upon the subject matter of the prerogative power which is exercised'. When the Attorney-General enters *nolle prosequi* for reasons of state, his act would not, I think, be subject to judicial review; in any other case I believe that the courts would now be ready to inquire whether or not there was a misuse of power.

185 **the textbooks** The principle was first laid down in *R v Makins* (1894) A.C. 57. If any student wants to examine the authorities just as they stood at the time, he should go to the late Mr Justice Pritchard's *The Common Calendar* (1958) pp. 141 to 168. This book, written by a first-class judge, whose judicial life (but fortunately not his happiness and friendliness) was cut short by ill health, was in proof when the Adams case was being tried and the author offered the section on 'system' for my use if I needed it.

190 **he himself doubted** Earl of Kilmuir, *Political Adventure*, Weidenfeld & Nicolson (1964) pp. 323–4.

192 **intact on his death** Hoskins p. 216

199 **received many legacies** There is a list in Hoskins p. 13

201 **a faithful echo** Bedford p. 213; *four lines*, Hallworth, p. 162; *forty lines*, Hoskins p. 179

211 **adopted as their slogan** Criminal Law Revision Committee, Eleventh Report, June 1972, para. 31.

ACKNOWLEDGMENTS

My first acknowledgment is to Geo. Walpole & Co, Official Shorthand Writers to the Central Criminal Court, and in particular to Mr Frederick Lovett their senior partner who was one of the team engaged in the Adams case, for permission to copy such extracts as I wanted from their transcript of the evidence. In the course of oral questioning there are bound to be repetitions and elaborations which the stenographer may not omit but which in a narrative it would be tedious to print; apart from them the extracts quoted in the book are as in the transcript. I am grateful too to the Honourable Mrs Maurice for permission to print in full the letter to me of 1 March 1957 from Lord Chief Justice Goddard.

I have exchanged thoughts about the trial with Sir Theobald Mathew who was at the time Director of Public Prosecutions and with Mr Geoffrey Lawrence QC and Mr (as he then was) Edward Clarke, the counsel for the defence. The book owes a little to them but not too much since our conversation was inevitably confined by their duty to their clients. It owes something too to Sybille Bedford's vivid and contemporary account of the trial, *The Best We Can Do*, which has taken its place among the classics of court reporting; also to the two recent books which put from the journalist's angle the case for the prosecution and the defence; Mr Hoskins' book, *Two Men Were Acquitted*, is especially useful for his account in Chapter 12 of the proceedings at Eastbourne; and I am especially indebted to him and his publishers, Secker & Warburg, for providing me before publication with a proof.

I am grateful to Venetia Pollock for advice on the arrangement of the chapters and for helping to bridge the gap between the legal and the lay minds; to Jill Black for seeing the book through the press; and to my wife for the index.

ADDENDUM

I want to add a footnote to the passage at p.23 where I say that, a doctor who obtains a supply of dangerous drugs for use in his practice must keep a register showing how they are acquired *and how disposed of*. The words in italics were not part of the law in 1950 nor did they become law until after, and no doubt as a result of, the Adams trial. Until then, a doctor could build up a reserve of dangerous drugs out of 'leftovers' and the like which the law did not require him to enter in his register. The Attorney-General's theory means that Dr Adams, instead of forming and using a secret reserve for the murder of Mrs Morrell, had drugs delivered to himself from the quantities he had openly prescribed for her. This makes him out to be a very foolish murderer. I am indebted for this correction to Dr Barkworth, who was Dr Adams's partner from 1948 to 1957.

INDEX